WOODEN PONIES

A THRILLER

GEORDIE GILMAN

This is a work of fiction. Names, characters, places, and incidents are products of the author's imagination or are used fictitiously and are not to be construed as real. Any resemblance to actual events, locations, organizations, or persons, living or dead, is entirely coincidental.

World Castle Publishing, LLC
Pensacola, Florida

Copyright © Geordie Gilman 2023

Hardcover ISBN: 9798394388330

Paperback ISBN: 9781960076724

eBook ISBN: 9781960076731

First Edition World Castle Publishing, LLC, June 5, 2023

http://www.worldcastlepublishing.com

Licensing Notes

Cover: Karen Fuller

Editor: Karen Fuller

PROLOGUE

Groveville Country Club
Saturday Morning
May 14, 2016

The entrance to the property was not altered in any noticeable way. Only a drainage ditch was added on both sides to help limit the winter's melting snow from running onto the graveled roadway leading to the core of the property. The trees and thick underbrush remained unchanged, giving the property a natural appearance. The end of the half-mile road, however, was drastically altered to build an eighteen-hole golf course and country club. The transformation was nearing its completion. Only the clubhouse needed to be completed.

Stanton Crosby stood proudly on a grassy knoll that gradually sloped down toward a small oval-shaped pond, about an acre in size. He watched the thin veil of fog hovering over the pond dissipate as the morning sun ate away at the smoky mist. At the pond's edge, he clearly saw the glowing florescent-orange baseball cap the heavyset excavator wore as he sat at the controls of a large front-end loader. The man was scooping out buckets full of heavy sludge to make the pond more elongated than oval.

Beyond the pond, up the far side where the glaring sun rose above the tall evergreens and shorter hardwoods, Stanton saw the immense green fairway flow like a river down toward the changing pond. He visualized a foursome cresting the slope on the eighteenth fairway, two to a cart, bearing down toward the plush eighteenth green on the other side of the pond.

Looking beyond the eighteenth green, farther up on the back slope, stood the wooden framework of the elaborate clubhouse taking shape. Inside the framed building, purposely positioned in the center to overlook the eighteenth green, Stanton noticed the framing for the dining hall's four doublewide picture windows overlooking the fairways. Upstairs, directly above the dining hall, he pictured his office. A much different office than the one he worked in now. This office would be peaceful with a scenic view, not hectic with emergencies.

Stanton's passion, besides healing the sick, was golfing and owning a piece of paradise. He hoped his son had a similar interest, but so far, in his son's brief existence on earth, he showed no interest in either. The time will come, he supposed, and someday his son will inherit his dream.

"I know it doesn't look like much now, Simon, but you have to imagine what the clubhouse will look like when it's completed to appreciate it," Stanton Crosby told his son as he pointed toward the wooden skeleton structure. He then let his soft, unlabored hand drop atop his son's recently cut blond hair, rubbing the coarse hairs like he was soothing away pain. "We're going to have a long veranda, stretching along the whole length of the clubhouse, where club members can sit outside and have lunch or just sip on a couple of cocktails while watching the golfers finishing up on the last hole," Stanton excitedly said as he lifted his hand across the horizon to emphasize the length.

"And see, over there," he said, pointing further up the slope, "tennis courts. And next to the courts, we're building an Olympic size pool next year, with maybe a diving board, I haven't decided yet. What do you say to that, Simon? I know you like swimming."

* * *

Simon Crosby did like to swim, and the idea of swimming in a much larger pool than the one in their own backyard would seem exciting if he were paying attention to his father's elaborate details of what the future of the country club would look like. At the moment, however, he was no longer looking where his father was pointing or even listening. He was more interested in the activity down by the pond than trying to imagine what the clubhouse and the added features, like the swimming pool, would look like after its completion. What did he care about a gigantic white building with older folks sitting around sipping on cocktails? He was only seven and more interested in fishing in the pond. His father told him the pond was full of large trout, as large as two feet long, which was slightly exaggerated. There were trout in the pond, but the largest of the fish were closer to one foot in length.

"What's going on down by the pond, Dad?" Simon inquisitively asked his father. The sunlight was beginning to bounce off the water, making it harder to see what they were doing down at the pond. Simon could see several men running over to the front-end loader, where the big scoop dumped a bucket full of sludge, adding to the pile.

* * *

Stanton Crosby was also perplexed at seeing all the sudden commotion down by the pond. Something did not look right to him. From his distance, he could hear loud shouts but could not determine what they were shouting about. The conspicuous activity made him feel slightly nervous. So far, nothing had gone wrong with the project, and he hoped it would continue progressing smoothly.

"I'm not sure, but it looks like they found something interesting down there. Let's take a walk down and see what all the excitement is about."

As Stanton and his son walked down the grassy slope toward the pond, the man running the front-end loader jumped down and began waving to get Stanton's attention, which caused Stanton and his son to hasten their pace.

"Doctor Cosby! Hey, Doctor Crosby, you've got to see this," Bruce Doiron shouted, waving his fluorescent-orange cap high about his balding head to get Stanton's attention.

"What is it, Bruce?" Stanton asked, not realizing he was holding his breath in anticipation.

"I'm not sure exactly," Bruce answered, as he held up a muddied, whitish-bronzed object for Stanton to see, which was almost a foot long and slightly a little less than a half-inch in diameter. "It looks like some kind of a bone, maybe from an animal, I suspect." He continued venturing an uneducated guess, and then after unconsciously scratching the bald spot on the top of his head to think about it, he added. "But I'm not so sure."

Being a surgeon, Stanton Crosby knew what Bruce Doiron was holding in a hand large enough to palm a basketball, and it did not come from any animal. It was a human femur bone, the large bone between the hipbone and knee.

"Let me see that," Stanton demanded as he grabbed the bone from the excavator, a man who knew a lot about what lay below the earth's surface and nothing about the human anatomy.

As Stanton was wiping off the mud and twisting the smooth bone around for a better examination, making sure it was what he presumed it to be, one of the hired workers noticed another partially exposed object sticking out of the same pile of sludge where they found the femur bone. Not wanting to pick it up himself, the worker nudged Bruce to look at his find.

"Hey, Doc, there's another one over here," Bruce said as he pulled the bone from the pile to show the Doctor.

Stanton walked over to where he stood and, after looking around, noticed other bones of varied sizes mixed in a pile. He curiously pulled one of the bones from the sludge pile and held it in both hands between his fingers and thumbs like he was holding a barbequed spare rib. The thin bone was shaped like a ruler, only shorter and slightly warped.

"Rib bone, and it's definitely human, I'm afraid. Looking at the size of this and the one you're holding, I'm sad to say they had to have come from a child, a very young child," Stanton despondently said, looking down at Simon, who was leaning against him, holding tight onto his father's leg.

Bruce dropped the bone he was holding on the ground when hearing it was from a human being. There was something about touching a human bone that repelled people, and Bruce Doiron was one of those. Worms and crawling insects he could tolerate, but he drew the line on touching human remains.

"How do you suppose they ended up in the pond?" One worker asked, but the only response was the assorted mumblings from his co-workers. Each had their own theory, with basically all the theories adding up to the same vicious conclusion.

Stanton paused, thinking about what reason anyone would have to deposit human remains in, or even near, a pond. It surely was not a gravesite, being too close to water. The only explanation he could logically conceive was what the others were thinking, the body was dumped there. How long the body had been there, he had no clue, and he could not recall hearing of any child reported missing in the twelve years he lived in the area.

As Stanton began to pull out more of the bones from the pile of sludge, he suddenly became aware there were too many of the same type to have come from only one body. It was a sad realization, but he now knew all the bones were those of young children.

"You think I dug up a gravesite, Doc?" Bruce wondered as he pulled on his bushy beard.

Stanton looked up the hill at the builders hammering away on his future and then glanced at the pond. The pond looked serene, with the light morning breeze rattling the thin leaves of the poplar trees surrounding the backside of the pond. The pond itself was covered with green lily pads, with beautiful white and pink flowers sprouting from them. Below, he thought he spotted a fish swim by – a long, plump one.

"More like a murder site. These bodies were dumped here."

PART ONE

CHAPTER ONE

Saturday Morning
May 12, 1989

Kyle Bryant could not have conjured up a more perfect day for the outdoor activity he planned for his best friend, Amanda. If it rained or was just spitefully cold, he knew he would have to postpone the event until a better day because he was sure Amanda would change her mind about going with him, as girls her age were too delicate to subject themselves to unfavorable conditions. Fortunately for him, the morning turned out pleasantly warm and sunny, with only a few high cumulus clouds to enhance the bold blue sky.

Kyle was anxious to start the day. He hardly slept a wink the night before, thinking about fishing with Amanda. So, he quickly finished his breakfast of cornflakes and orange juice and rushed out the backdoor without saying goodbye to his mother, who, by the sounds of her giggles, he knew was having an amusing conversation with a friend on the telephone and would not notice his departure even if he had acknowledged he was leaving. Normally, Kyle would eavesdrop on his mother's phone conversations, trying to figure out whom she was talking to, but today he had no time for snooping. He had something else on his young mind.

On his way out the door, Kyle grabbed the two fishing poles he purposely left leaning against the back porch railing and the small plastic container of night crawlers he had gathered from the lawn in the backyard the night before. He then walked around to the front of the house and carefully placed the items on the lawn next to his red bicycle, and hastily sprinted across the street toward Amanda's house. On the narrow side door, he lightly knocked once and quickly entered the house before anyone inside could answer.

Inside, he found Amanda's mother, Janelle Prescott, quietly sitting at the kitchen table, sipping a cup of lukewarm coffee and reading the morning newspaper.

"Kyle, I see you're up early this morning. Amanda hasn't even come downstairs yet. So, you kids have something planned today I'm not aware of?" She asked with a knowing smile, having already given Amanda her approval, though she still had reservations about allowing Amanda to run off to an unknown fishing pond.

Kyle took a couple of anxious breaths while looking around the kitchen for Amanda. There was only one thing on his mind, and he had not heard Mrs. Prescott tell him Amanda hadn't come down from upstairs. He expected to see her sitting at the table in her usual chair opposite her mother's, but her chair was vacant.

"Why don't you take a seat while you're waiting. Amanda will be down in a couple of minutes. I only just call her down."

"It's her birthday. I thought she'd be up early today."

"Yes, it is. My sweet little girl is turning thirteen today. My, how time flies by. It seems like only yesterday I was cradling her in my arms."

* * *

Mrs. Prescott focused her stare off toward the living room, remembering sitting in the rocking chair, gently rocking her baby daughter in her arms. She was adorable, with soft golden curly hair and chubby pink cheeks. Now, in what seemed too brief of a time, her daughter had changed. Her soft golden curls turned to a light-brown color, which she wore long and flipped at the ends, and her once chubby pink cheeks, thinned, matched her gangly body. She tried to picture an older Amanda, how she might look like a young adult woman, but she couldn't. She could only picture Amanda with the face she wore last night when she said goodnight and skipped up the stairs to her bedroom.

Mrs. Prescott glanced at Kyle squirming in the chair across from her. Even though they were about the same age, he looked much younger than her daughter, too young to be hanging out together, but she knew girls matured faster than boys; therefore, she accepted their friendship. "And don't you have a birthday coming up soon?"

Kyle briefly smiled at the mention of his upcoming birthday, then slightly nodded his head. "Yup, in five days. Amanda is five days older than me. Then we'll both be teenagers."

When Amanda appeared in the doorway, Mrs. Prescott stared for a moment at her young daughter, thinking how quickly she had grown up. Standing there, smiling as bright as the morning sun, she seemed only two heads shy of reaching the curved archway. It was hard for her to believe her daughter was now a teenager. The thought of someday she would be gone from the house, out on her own, entered her mind for a split second. She felt her heart jump a beat.

"Hi, Mom," Amanda said, then pulled her chair out from under the table and joined them.

"Hey, my birthday girl. Happy birthday," Mrs. Prescott managed to say without showing her true emotion creeping inside her.

"Thanks, Mom. Hi, Kyle."

"Happy birthday Amanda. Ready to go?" Kyle said, rising from the table.

"Sit back down, young man. Amanda has to have breakfast first. She may be a teenager, but she's still a growing girl and needs her protein like everyone else," Mrs. Prescott informed Kyle.

Kyle shrugged, then reluctantly sat back down and watched Amanda eat her cereal, willing her to eat faster.

After she finished and before Kyle and Amanda walked

out the kitchen door Mrs. Prescott had a stern warning for Kyle.

"Now, you listen to me, young man. I want you to watch out for Amanda and make sure she's home by noon, in time for lunch. Not one second later," she told him, wagging her pointed finger inches from his complex expression. She then went to the window and watched Amanda and Kyle jump on their bicycles and pedal up the road, then waited until her daughter's red shirt faded in the haze of the morning's sunlight.

She told herself not to worry. Amanda would be home before she knew it, and the two of them would spend the rest of the day together. She then busied herself with meaningless overdone household chores to make the time go by faster. Across the street, she could easily see the Bryant home and wondered if Kyle's mother had the same worries about her son being away from the house on his own as she did about her daughter. Kyle's mother, however, never knew about the planned fishing trip, and if she did, she would have put her foot down hard. There was no way she would have let him anywhere near the pond he was heading for.

* * *

For over a week, Kyle wrestled with himself, trying to come up with the perfect birthday present for Amanda. He saved some money from his allowances, enough to buy a descent present for Amanda, but he was planning to spend the money on himself to purchase a new fishing pole he had his eye on down at the local hardware store. It was while dreaming about the new pole he suddenly got the idea for a birthday present for Amanda. He knew Amanda had never been fishing before, or she would have mentioned it to him when he told her about his fishing expertise. He was also sure she'd be thrilled about going to 'His' secret trout pond, which she was when she told Kyle she'd be happy to go fishing on her birthday, wondering what it would be like to catch a fish using a squiggly worm for bait.

Although Kyle's secret fishing hole had plenty of fish, the location was not very desirable. In fact, it was probably in the least desirable location in the county. Kyle only learned about the fishing hole a year earlier when he overheard his older brother, Jimmy, tell a friend about a pond in the woods behind the old farmhouse on Osborne Road. He heard Jimmy mention the pond was full of large trout because no one ever fished it in fear of being anywhere near the old, haunted farmhouse and the farmer who disappeared after murdering his family by chopping their heads off with an axe. Kyle heard the gruesome story himself, where anyone caught trespassing on the property would have his or her head chopped off by the deranged farmer. The most gruesome death Kyle thought imaginable.

Even though Kyle was a little skeptic about the farmhouse being haunted, he still believed the farmer was hiding somewhere inside the farmhouse. But he also believed if he stayed a good distance away from the farmhouse, he would be safe from the clutches of the farmer. So, after hearing about the pond, Kyle bravely ventured out to the Osborne property on the very first sunny day after school let out for the summer vacation, which was three anxious days later after the late-spring rains subsided. Kyle rode his bicycle down the long-graveled road leading to the Osborne farm in search of the elusive pond. After searching for most of the afternoon with no luck and feeling disappointed and very hungry, Kyle decided to forget the whole idea and headed toward home. But to his surprise, when he least expected his luck to change, he noticed a path partially covered over by tall grass and shrub brush angling off into the tall pines.

After leaving his bicycle on the dirt road, not thinking about the possibility of someone coming along to steal it, Kyle walked the length of the path, pushing away low tree branches and hopping over mud puddles left from the recent rains, until he came upon a pond. The pond was picturesque, with white and pink flowers sprouting from green lily pads floating on the top of the dark water.

Was this the pond he overheard Jimmy talking about? Kyle wondered. After all, it was rather small, smaller than any pond he had fished before. It was so small he felt he could almost throw a rock to the other side, but the pond looked deep, so he imagined it was also deep enough for fish to swim in and figured it must be the pond he had heard about.

The next day Kyle rode his bicycle back to the pond, lugging his fishing pole and container of worms with him. When he settled himself along the bank near a large fallen log, he proceeded to ready his fishing pole by baiting his hook with a slimy night crawler. After securing the worm, he carefully cast the line into the murky water so as not to get the line tangled in the tree branches hanging low over the edges of the pond and watched the squirming worm disappear into the dark abyss. He then anxiously sat on the log and waited for the fish to take the bait. Within minutes, his line tightened, and his pole bent in a steep arc. After a couple of minutes of playing with the fish, reeling and pulling on the pole carefully upward and sideways so as not to lose him, Kyle landed his first fish of the day – a good size trout with a frowning mouth and sad-looking eyes.

He tried his best to gently yank the hook out of the fish's mouth without hurting it too much, but his small fingers failed him, and he accidentally ripped the lower jaw completely off. Kyle felt sorry for the fish, as he often did whenever he held the innocent creatures in his hand seeing their sad droopy eyes staring back at him, but he felt more sympathy for this fish when he closely began to examine the bloody jaw hanging from the hook and wondered if the fish was in any pain. Nevertheless, he figured the fish was meant to be caught and eaten, or they would not have invented fishing poles, so with that in mind, he tossed the fish in the plastic bag he brought from home and did not give the matter another thought.

On his way home, after catching several more fish, Kyle decided to keep the pond a secret and lie to his mother about where he caught his bounty, but when he got home and was confronted with where he caught the fish, he gave in. He told his mother the truth. She was furious with him for going up there without telling her and was even more furious he went by himself. He had not been back to the pond since. Not until today when he brought his next-door neighbor and best friend Amanda with him.

CHAPTER TWO

Saturday Morning
May 12, 1989

The road to the Osborne farm was approximately two miles from Kyle and Amanda's neighborhood. After crossing the narrow wooden bridge, spanning Miller's creek, they turned left onto the Old County Road and then pedaled their red bicycles up the steep hill. From there, they rode a short distance and then took a sharp right onto the graveled Osborne Road. The rain-rutted road was about half-mile in to reach the fishing pond for which they were heading. The road also led them past a century-old family cemetery.

The previous two times Kyle ventured down the road, he rode right past the cemetery with only a slight glance in that direction. The creepy-looking cemetery seemed eerie to him, being alone and knowing there were bodies buried beneath the stones, skeletons by now. He also felt a chill each time he rode his bicycle past the cemetery and suspected it was because the area was shaded by tall, thick pines. To make his experience seem worse, he also imagined the old farmer, who was suspected of murdering his family, was lurking somewhere nearby. Maybe even hiding behind one of the gravestones, and if he were, most likely one of the taller ones where the shadows grew long.

When Amanda spied the cemetery, she steered her bicycle to stop before yelling for Kyle to stop as well. It was something she just could not pass up without at least taking a look.

"Hey Kyle, look at this. It's an old cemetery. Let's go check it out."

Kyle skidded his bicycle to a stop and looked back over his shoulder. "No, that's a cemetery. I don't want to go in there. Let's get going. The pond is just up the road a way."

"I know it's a cemetery. I just said it. What, are you too scared to go in a cemetery? Are you afraid of the dead? Scaredy-cat."

"No, I'm not scared, and don't call me a scaredy-cat."

"So, then, why don't you want to check it out? Nobody's going to attack you. They only come out at night." Amanda laughed and then set her bicycle down on the road along with the fishing pole she had been awkwardly holding in one hand. She then walked up a stone path toward the cemetery.

"Are you coming?" she asked, looking back at Kyle.

Kyle hesitated and nervously looked up the road, focusing on an area opposite the farmhouse. He could visualize the pond, which lay hidden in woods down a narrow path not far beyond the old farmhouse. The pond looked the same as when he last saw it, pristine and full of fish. He could almost smell the stagnant musty water, a satisfying smell for boys of his age savored. He then turned and noticed Amanda leaning with her hand against the wooden gate, swinging it back and forth teasingly. She had a smug look, and Kyle knew he had to follow her into the cemetery, or he would be labeled a coward for the rest of his life.

"I'm coming," he reluctantly mumbled, dropping his bicycle and fishing pole down next to hers, and then, with a slow, deliberate walk, he made his way to where Amanda was anxiously waiting.

Amanda swung the gate open for him to pass through first, but Kyle hesitated. "You go first. I'll follow."

"What a wimp you are," she said, amusingly shaking her head. "I just want to see the gravestones, that's all. Take a quick look around, and then we can leave. I've never seen gravestones this old before, and I think it will be interesting."

"I'm not a wimp. I just wanted to get to the pond ... best fishing is now."

"What, fish only feast in the morning?"

"Well, that's what I heard anyway, and that's when I catch the most fish."

Once inside the boundaries of the fenced-in cemetery, Amanda knelt on both knees, sitting comfortably on her haunches next to the nearest gravestone, taking in the brief history of the person who was laid to rest beneath her. She rubbed her index finger over the engraved dates and the name of the person buried there, reading them out loud.

"It says here the person was born on June 12, 1844, and died on January 4, 1888. My gosh, she was only in her forties when she died. Her name was Vivian Osborne, wife of John Osborne. I guess they didn't live very long back in the old days."

"They probably didn't have good food to eat back then. They didn't have a MacDonald's," Kyle honestly answered.

"No kidding, you're a genius. You know that Kyle, a real genius."

"Well, what I meant was, it must take a lot of energy out of you to have to do all the work cooking every day. I know my mother gets angry sometimes when she has to cook at home."

Amanda looked up at her younger friend, who was hovering over her, not wanting to get close to the dead.

"That's true, having to grow their own food and all other chores, but I think the reason they died younger back then was because they didn't have the luxury of all the medicines we have today. Hey, look at this guy," she said, looking at the next gravestone over. "This must be Vivian's husband. John David Osborne. Oh yes, says right here, husband of Vivian Osborne. He was born in 1836 and died in 1868. He was only thirty-two, says he was a civil war veteran."

"Amanda, can we go now?" Kyle anxiously asked.

"Wait a minute, I want to look at those gravestones over there," Amanda said, pointing toward the back of the cemetery. "They look newer than these. I want to check out the dates when they died."

Amanda walked over to the back of the cemetery and looked down at the six gravestones, which were spread out evenly in a row. The gravestones were much shorter than the others and had a dark gray color to them, whereas the others were a washed whitish gray with dark streaks of dirt where the stones cracked.

"Another Osborne. Must be a whole family of Osbornes here. This woman was Ellie Osborne, born May 4, in 1944, and died January 12, 1967. Let's see, that would make her twenty-three. No, wait, twenty-two... gosh, she was only twenty-two when she died, and not that long ago. I wonder what she died of."

"Probably got killed in that haunted farmhouse over there," Kyle said, pointing through the sparse woods at an old, dilapidated farmhouse. The paint on the farmhouse had peeled and washed away from all the neglected years of sitting under bright summer suns and harsh winter weather. All that remained now of the exterior were warped, brittle clapboards and broken windows. From his view, standing in the cemetery, the farmhouse looked like a warning, even in daylight.

Amanda had never seen the old Osborne farmhouse before and had only heard stories about the place of how the farmer brutally murdered his whole family and then mysteriously disappeared, never to be seen again. It was the same story Kyle had heard and the same story almost everyone else, who also lived in the small town of Groveville, had heard.

"I guess that's the old Osborne farmhouse?" she asked, knowing it had to be.

"Yup, that's it. Pretty weird looking, ain't it," Kyle said with familiarity, having seen the place twice before.

A wisp of wind blew through the trees, eerily fluttering the green golden-tipped leaves on the slender poplar trees that sprouted sporadically throughout the woods. Feeling the light breeze against her face, Amanda turned her back to the farmhouse, avoiding what one could conceive of as a warning.

"Not so bad. The farmhouse just needs to be fixed up a bit."

She then inquisitively walked past the other five gravestones taking in the names and the dates engraved in the stones. She realized, by the dates on the stones, the people buried six feet beneath the grassy surface were all young, very young, and it gave her an awful feeling in her stomach. She roughly calculated the dates on three of the stones, figuring their ages to be between three and five years of age, and then suddenly realized they had all died on the same day, January 12, 1967.

"Kyle, this is weird. They all died on the same day. Look at these three gravestones, January 12, 1967. And over here, these two also have the same date," Amanda excitingly said, pointing at the last two gravestones.

Kyle looked at the gravestones, studying the dates with shifting eyes as he suddenly remembered the story about the Osborne farmhouse where the family living there was gruesomely murdered back in the 1960s.

"Gee, they must be the ones that were all killed in the farmhouse. I didn't know they were buried here. This is spooky. Let's get out of here."

"What a wuss you are. They're all dead. They ain't going to hurt you."

"I know. I just want to get out of here. Let's go fishing."

"Okay, scaredy-cat, let's go find this great fishing hole you've been so anxious to show me.

* * *

Back on their bicycles, slowly pedaling toward their destination, which lay peacefully in the quiet woods across from the farmhouse, Amanda could not take her eyes off the old place. She was intrigued at the sight of it but also felt sad for the farmhouse. To her, the house looked like it was dying, and there was no one to take care of it. She could clearly see the broken windows in the sunlight glistening – broken panes of glass sticking out of their wooden frames, which looked like the breath of life was escaping from within. The aged clapboards, she noticed, were pulling away from the building, curled like witches' fingers, and all around the building, tall stringy bushes grew like hair growing on a dead body's scalp. The building leaned, and she felt one big gust of wind could blow the place to the ground.

Amanda noticed the barn connected to the farmhouse was in the same sad rundown condition as the main house or in worse shape. She also noticed the door to the barn was wide open, and to Amanda, it was too inviting to pass up a look inside. Without saying anything to Kyle, she rode past where he had stopped and steered her bicycle onto the grassed-over driveway.

"Come on, Kyle, let's check this out," she yelled back.

Kyle twisted around and saw Amanda pedaling up the driveway toward the barn, and seeing the open door, he realized she was heading straight for it. "Are you crazy? The old farmer might be in there. He'll chop our heads off."

"It will only take a minute, come on. I want to peek inside."

"No, your mother said I was responsible for you. I don't want to get into trouble."

Amanda stopped her bicycle, placing one foot on the ground with the other foot on the pedal, ready to resume her quest, and looked over her shoulder at Kyle. He was standing at the edge of the road, near a stand of tall grass, with his small-sized bicycle wedged between his legs holding his fishing pole in one hand and his other hand on his hip, demonstrating his newly acquired authority.

Seeing his determination, Amanda reluctantly turned her bicycle around and slowly started back down the driveway. "Okay, Kyle, let's go fishing. I wouldn't want you to get in trouble with my mother. She might hang you with your fishing line if you disobeyed her."

CHAPTER THREE

Saturday Morning
May 12, 1989

When Candi Bryant finally hung up the phone in the living room, gently replacing the receiver in the cradle with a satisfied smile, she strolled into the kitchen expecting to see Kyle still planted at the kitchen table eating his breakfast, but all she found was his empty cereal bowl and juice glass. Candi then walked out to the back porch and peeked out through the screen door to see if he was there. She figured he was probably tossing a baseball off the garage roof playing catch by himself, or just idling bored on the old tire swing the boys strung up in the large oak tree several years ago like he had yesterday when the light drizzle dampened the ground but not enough to keep him indoors. But that was yesterday. Today there was no sign of her youngest son.

The only thing Candi noticed in the backyard, besides the lounge chair on the brick patio she was planning on relaxing in later for the purpose of tanning, was his red bicycle was gone. Remembering he sometimes left his bicycle in the front yard, against her weak protest, Candi went back to the living room and looked out the front window and noticed his bicycle was not there either. She then looked across the street toward Prescott's house, hoping to spot it there, but she only saw Janelle Prescott's silver Vega sitting in the driveway. Kyle's bicycle was not there either.

Candi was not worried Kyle was nowhere to be seen. She was only disappointed she had not talked to him before he left to find out his plans for the day. She did not think she had been on the phone for very long, but she realized she must have been. She had been chatting with her hairstylist, and the conversation went on much longer than necessary to make an appointment for that morning. Candi mentioned she wanted a trim and patchwork the dark roots, for she was planning to go out on the town with her girlfriends, which was really a cover-up for deceiving her husband. She was planning on going out alone and hopefully running into the same guy she had met the last time she told her husband she was going out with the 'Girls.' With that said, her hairstylist had to know which tavern they were going to. Maybe she would run into her as she was expecting to go out with her new boyfriend and show him off. Candi had to know all about him, and when her hairstylist finally finished describing how wonderful her new boyfriend was, Kyle was long gone and already pedaling his bicycle toward the Osborne farm road.

Now, the house was quiet with her eldest son, Jimmy, off on a weekend camping trip, having left the previous day and would be gone until late Sunday afternoon. Her husband, Fred, was also gone. He left early that morning to get an early start. Being a salesman on the road meant long days, and for Fred Bryant, Saturday was his longest and most profitable, so Candi didn't expect him home until before dark.

And now, with Kyle gone, for who knew how long, she had the house to herself, just like during the school year when the boys were in school, and Fred was off making money. Candi spent the first few hours picking up the house and freshened herself up with a lukewarm shower, then dressed in a pair of tight-fitting jeans and an attractive low-cut short-sleeve pullover, her favorite, the one with a colorful floral design weaved across the chest. Bringing the flowers to full bloom.

After checking her face in the rearview mirror, a second time, she then drove to Denton and spent the next two hours in the beauty shop, having her hair trimmed and touching up the roots with her usual platinum-blonde dye. While her hair was drying, she had Kristen, her favorite hairstylist, apply red nail polish to her long fake nails. Candi enjoyed her time in the parlor. It gave her a chance to hear all the gossip and also time to add her own, which amounted more to bragging than gossiping.

"Anything exciting planned for today before sneaking off with the girls tonight?" Kristen asked while applying a coat of nail polish to one of Candi's fingers.

"I'm not sneaking off, Fred knows. But no, I don't really have anything to do today. With the boys gone, I'll have the whole day to myself, so I guess I'll just lie around on the patio and catch up on some reading."

"That sounds boring."

"Maybe for someone like you, being young and unattached, lying in the backyard sounds boring. But if you were married with kids like I am, just an afternoon of relaxation is like heaven."

"You can't be that much older than I am, and you look great for your age."

"Okay, Kristen, let's not talk about ages. So, you have a new boyfriend. What happened to your last boyfriend, the one I saw you arguing with the last time I was in here?"

"Oh, you mean Malcolm. No, I haven't seen him in a long time, at least a couple of months."

"Has it been that long since I've last been in here?"

"Yeah, I'm thinking it was at least a couple of months ago," Kristen answered, thinking it was early spring, a time when most people had hopes of finding new love when she dumped Malcolm.

"He seemed like a nice guy. What happened?" Candi said, trying to picture Malcolm standing dejectedly outside the beauty parlor. She remembered smiling at Kristen as she walked by the two arguing, giving her a triumphant boost of encouragement and remembered the sad, grim expression on the young man's face, but his full face she could not conjure up.

"Malcolm was just the wrong guy for me. He never had any money, and he spent all day long with his loser buddies down at the pool hall. And another thing, he had no ambition at all. He didn't have any interest in pursuing a better life. Bottom line, he was a total loser, just like the losers he hung around with. Besides that, he was kind of weird."

"Weird, like how?"

"Oh, I don't know. It's hard to explain. I guess maybe it was the things he said that spooked me. Things like when he was in juvy."

"Juvy?"

"Yeah, the Juvenal Detention center over in Hancock. Anyway, he said some weird stuff that I didn't like. But anyway, he's out of my life now. I have a new man in my life, Justin. I can't wait till you meet him. Maybe we'll run into each other tonight."

"Maybe."

On her drive home, Candi thought about the lounge chair, picturing herself cozying up in the chair with the new Stephen King novel she purchased the previous day at the quaint little bookstore in Groveville. With a thick layer of suntan lotion splashed evenly over her winter-white body, she would relax in the backyard and wait till Kyle came home hungry, which, with the nice day, she suspected wouldn't be until mid-afternoon at the earliest. When he did finally find his way home, he would be mighty hungry and eat half the contents in the refrigerator.

But the image Candi had of herself bathing in the hot sunlight dissolved in a flash when she pulled into her driveway. In the rearview mirror, when she attempted another look at her updated hairstyle, she spied Janelle Prescott storming across the street toward her house. Janelle was moving so fast that Candi had not even had the opportunity to open her door to greet the woman when she noticed her neighbor standing next to the vehicle with her arms folded under her small breast.

The angry look on Janelle's face gave Candi pause, and she wondered what possible reason there could be for her alarming expression. Her only thought was something had happened to Kyle since he most likely was with Janelle's daughter, Amanda. But she quickly dismissed that notion when she determined Janelle's expression was more frustrating in nature than a concerning one. Now she was thinking Kyle had only done something to irritate Janelle, and she was here to complain about his impolite manner, which she'd take up with Kyle after Janelle left to tend to her own household, which she knew only consisted of two.

Before hearing Janelle's complaint, or whatever it was she brought across the street with her, Candi politely invited Janelle into the house for a glass of lemonade. The invite was meant as a neighborly gesture, but her intent was to settle the woman down. After all, Kyle was still a child, not a grown adult. One couldn't expect him, or any child, to behave all the time.

She only knew Janelle through their brief conversations during the several years living across the street from each other and the few snippets from Janelle's daughter, Amanda, when she came over to the house to hang out with Kyle. But those times were few as Kyle spent most of the time at Amanda's house than with her at his own house. What she knew of Janelle was that her husband died a few years ago, and she had to raise her daughter as a single parent, and Candi felt she was doing a great job raising her.

Janelle quickly refused the offer of lemonade, saying her concerns about Amanda's whereabouts were more urgent than wasting time sitting around sipping lemonade and demanded to know where Kyle had taken her daughter fishing. Candi had no idea Kyle had gone off fishing and shrugged a questioning look.

"What's that look for? You don't know where your son has run off to?" Janelle rudely asked.

Still baffled as to why Janelle seemed agitated at her son and not at her own daughter, Candi's only response was to support her son.

"No. He's old enough to go off on his own. I do like to know where he's going, but I also trust his judgment," Candi said defiantly, thinking the woman she hardly knew was now showing her true colors as it showed in her heated face.

"He said he was taking Amanda to some 'secret' fishing pond for her birthday and promised he'd bring her home before noon. It's now well past one, and they haven't come back yet."

"Oh, he did, huh? Well, I wouldn't worry too much about them. Kyle's pretty good about keeping his word. I suspect they'll be home soon." Candi smiled, trying to calm her neighbor down a bit with words of encouragement. She suspected Kyle most likely took Amanda down to the creek on the Old County Road and probably were already on their way home, but just before she was about to turn and walk away, leaving Janelle where she angrily stood near her vehicle like an old schoolmarm lurking over the desk of an unruly child, the word 'secret' finally sunk in.

Could Kyle have gone back to that pond in the woods near the Osborne farm when he swore he'd never go back? She could not believe he would, not after she scolded and threatened to ground him for life if he ever did again. No, her neighbor must have heard wrong. *But why would she say secret?* Surely there was nothing secret about the creek, but there was about the pond located somewhere on the Osborne property. *But did she tell Kyle he couldn't go back there 'alone' and he felt if he went with someone, like Amanda, it would be all right?*

"Well, my Amanda is pretty good at keeping her word too. She always obeys her mother," Janelle retorted with a huff and pulled her arms tighter to emphasize her hold on Amanda.

* * *

Janelle had been very vigilant with Amanda since she was an only parent. Her husband, David, died in a single-car accident three years earlier when he failed to negotiate a curve on the very dangerous Old Cobb Road, a back road that led to the town of Denton. He also would have failed to negotiate a sobriety test if one had been administered.

Janelle and her husband were quarrelling that dreadful night, and he stormed out of the house, saying he would be back later. Hopefully, by then, she would have calmed down. The argument was about David's infidelity. Janelle had finally confronted him about her suspicions that he was having an affair. For weeks, and even longer if she thought about the glow of excitement frozen on his face one Saturday morning when pouring rain cancelled a scheduled golf outing (one he had waited all year long for) but failed to dampen his spirits, Janelle had suspicions her husband was having an affair because he was starting to come home later and later at night from work. And to put an exclamation point on her fears, their sex life was non-existent, and she could not remember the last time he kissed her with any amount of affection. When they were first married, Janelle was a cute young woman attending nursing school, but after a few years of marriage and one lovely child, her cute young features were not cute anymore to satisfy David's shallow desires and were replaced by a younger 'cute' female coworker in David's office. Janelle had been restlessly sleeping when the heavy knocking on her door and the flashing blue lights from the sheriff's patrol car awakened her with the shocking news that David was never coming home again and would be resting peacefully six feet beneath the plush, green lawn in Pine View Cemetery.

Candi Bryant, on the other hand, had a husband who worshipped her and would never consider or even dream of infidelity. She was the one who was not faithful in their marriage but stayed with Fred because he was a good provider for her and the two boys. She felt her life was as good as it gets for a married woman with children and not having to work. It was what some 'daydreaming' wives called 'The best of both worlds,' and she was living it.

The two women were neighbors but lived contrasting lives and had contrasting ideals on raising their children. Both assured themselves their ways were the proper way.

* * *

"I'm sure she does. From what I have seen, she's very obedient," Candi honestly agreed but also knew what the woman standing in front of her was trying to convey about her lack of control over Kyle.

"Yes, she is. So, you can see that something must have happened to them, and we need to go find them immediately. Are you sure your son didn't mention anything to you about going fishing?"

"No, he didn't, but if what you said about going to a secret pond is true, I'm pretty sure it must be that pond he found out on the Osborne property. I strictly told him to never go back there again."

"I guess Kyle's not too trustworthy after all. It looks like he disobeyed both of us." Janelle felt like adding more, asking Candi what kind of boy she was raising, but decided to hold her temper until Amanda was safe at home, and then she would consider whether grounding Amanda from seeing Kyle for a while for not keeping his promise or tell her neighbor to keep her ill-mannered son on his side of the street.

CHAPTER FOUR

Saturday Early Afternoon
May 12, 1989

After being persuaded they needed to look for their children immediately, which seemed more like intimidation than persuasion, Candi halfheartedly crawled into Janelle's silver Vega and then buckled herself in, preparing for an unpleasant ride. With her plans of relaxing in a lounge chair out on her patio now disappointedly placed on the back burner or having to wait until another sunny day, she now found herself being carted around in an uncomfortable compact vehicle driven by an unstable woman whom she had no desire to even have a brief conversation with. To make that point clear from the get-go, she sat in silence, staring out the passenger window at the fast-moving scenery. It was not until they drove beyond the entrance to Osborne farm that Candi finally spoke, saying you just passed the road.

Janelle, who was driving at a faster rate of speed than posted, braked to a stop in the middle of the road. She then looked over her shoulder to where Candi was pointing and noticed the narrow entrance on Candi's side and felt like blaming her for not pointing it out sooner but held her tongue.

After turning around in the middle of Old County Road, an awkward four-point turn, Janelle continued her aggressive speed down the dusty Osborne Road, driving past the cemetery and farmhouse they had not noticed. Candi could see the thick hardwoods at the end of the road close in on them and wondered if Janelle was planning on using her brakes to stop the car before the trees made the vehicle more compact than it already was.

When the vehicle suddenly stopped, Candi unbuckled her seatbelt and hastily hopped out before Janelle had a chance to put the transmission gear into the park position.

While she waited for her neighbor to join her, Candi glanced around, seeing the farmhouse for the first time. It was more hideous than she had expected from the descriptions she had been told by both her sons, whom she had since told them never to set foot on the Osborne property again.

'It's just a rundown farm with overgrown fields, that's all.' The boys told their mother. But seeing the farm in person, she now realized it was in much worse shape than just rundown. She felt if the farmhouse were a human being, it would be like a decrepit old man lying on his deathbed, and his diseased condition would rub off on anyone who touched his rotting flesh. The first disease that came to her mind was leprosy. The most grotesque disease she could imagine.

With her right hand, Candi gently brushed the few strands of blond hair away from her forehead, then used the same hand to shield the harsh rays of sunlight from her eyes. She had not expected to see her young, veteran explorer son suddenly come running out from behind the dilapidated building or even appear off in the distance field she was now scanning, and she wasn't too concerned either, for she knew her son and knew he'd eventually turn up at home, as he always did, with some wild story about his adventures. She would listen to his words with a forced scorned expression, not hearing the words true meaning at first, being happy just to see his small wholesome stature pacing the kitchen floor in his attempt to act out his excitement. When he finished telling his adventure and his excitement abated, Candi would decide then if a stern warning was warranted or let it slide as just another day in a boy's life.

In past summers, when Kyle was old enough to spend most of the daylight hours outdoors by himself, her warnings about his wanderings had almost become a weekly sermon. But he always came home, so those motherly lectures soon became nothing more than a shake of her head and a nod toward the sink to wash up for supper. At the table, Kyle would anxiously tell his father about his exciting day. Candi would pretend to be listening, but since she had already heard the story at least twice, her mind would be on something else, mostly what she'd be wearing if she was planning on going out with her (phantom) girlfriends to meet a new face or an interesting face she had met the previous night out and had since been dreaming about in her restless sleep.

Not seeing any sign of the children, Candi turned her attention to the inside of the car and could see Janelle silently staring out the windshield.

* * *

Janelle had remained in her car for a moment, trying to relax her hostility toward Kyle and why she agreed to let Amanda go with him. This was not how she had planned the day to work out for Amanda's birthday. It was supposed to be just the two of them, happily spending the day together doing what Amanda wanted to do. Then Kyle showed up with his idiotic plan to take Amanda fishing. She did not care very much for Kyle at the moment, and as she watched Candi standing outside looking toward the farmhouse, her dyed hair glistening gold in the early afternoon sunlight, she wasn't caring much for her either. It was not so much that she disliked the woman. Personally, she hardly even knew her. What she knew of her was from Kyle, his ill-mannered upbringing, and the woman's looks, which, by her appearance, she spent more time applying her makeup and having her hair dyed than she did raising her boys. Although Janelle thought the dyed hair looked good on Candi, and even attractive, though she was not aroused herself – she had no desires for a woman or even another man for that matter, not after having endured a marriage with an unfaithful husband, thinking all men were the same.

When Janelle finally exited her vehicle, the first thing she noticed was the shocking condition of the Osborne farmhouse, and, like Candi Bryant seeing it for the first time, she made a mental note to never come again. Even if the place were burning to the ground, she would not dare to be a spectator.

"Do you see them anywhere?" she asked Candi, hoping she had already spotted the children and was just standing there waiting for them.

"No, I don't see any sign of them anywhere," Candi said and glanced across the open field to double-check that she had not missed seeing them.

"Amanda, Amanda!" Janelle hollered, and then, in bated breath, waited to hear her daughter's voice, but there was no answer to her shouts.

Simultaneously they both began shouting out for their respected child and waited impatiently for the sight of them, or to at least hear their distant, tiny voices calling out. After a while, Janelle started to become emotionally distraught at the possibility her child may be missing and began to cry. Tears dripped from her light-blue eyes and rolled down her narrow face. She did nothing to wipe them away, for they went unnoticed but not to the woman standing next to her.

Candi gave it her best effort to console the woman by wrapping an arm around her frail shoulders, but Janelle did not want any sympathy, not from her anyway, and pulled away, saying she was going to the sheriff's office to report Amanda missing. There was nothing Candi could do about her decision, and since she had no idea where the secret pond could possibly be located, she got back in the car. They turned the vehicle around in the Osborne driveway, not noticing the barn door was partially open, and at the same high rate of speed Janelle had driven to get there, drove past the cemetery and straight to the sheriff's office.

CHAPTER FIVE

Saturday Afternoon
May 12, 1989

Every road has a name, but some roads, like the old roads around Groveville that weave through farmlands and acres of dense forest leading to other towns, have two names, their official name and the name folks around town call them, always adding 'Old' to their name. Old County Road is one of those roads. Same as Old Cobb Road, named after the farmer Cobb who lived there many years ago, halfway down Cobb Road just past the new cul-de-sac built on the land he uses to plow with an old mule named 'Sally the Mule.'

When Janelle decided to drive to the town of Denton, instead of calling the sheriff's office from the convenience of her home phone, she took the quickest route to get there, which just so happened to go by way of the Old Cobb Road, the same road she swore she would never drive on again. The only other road would have led her through downtown Groveville and have cost her at least an extra five minutes, that is, if the town's only light was still set to blinking yellow and not set to the tricolors of red, yellow, and green.

Janelle knew a phone call would have been much quicker than having to drive the ten minutes to the sheriff's office in downtown Denton, but Janelle was too upset to make the call, so she drove her vehicle instead, with Candi chatting the whole time about some guy she had met in a bar over in Hancock.

Candi had not meant to sound like she was bragging; she only wanted to calm the emotional woman so she could concentrate on her driving and not the possibility that her daughter was in danger. Candi was beginning to worry also, but she was more aggravated at Kyle for not telling her where he was going. If he had, she would be home enjoying the afternoon in her backyard, not sitting in the passenger seat next to her unpleasant neighbor.

Janelle, however, had only one thing on her mind, and that was Amanda, and she had not been listening to a single word Candi had been saying about her out-of-marriage love life. This was the first time the two women had spent more than a minute together, and Janelle was sure it would be the last time. She was even entertaining the idea of forbidding Amanda from hanging around Kyle, even if her daughter protested, and steering her to make friends with girls her own age who lived nearby.

* * *

The sheriff's office was located in the center of town in a two-story brick building directly across the street from the town's administrative office. When the protruding sign above the door came into sight, the words 'Madison County Sheriff Office' brought assurance Amanda would soon be home, and life would be back to normal in the Prescott household.

Seeing a parking spot in front of the office, not caring it was marked as a handicapped spot, Janelle quickly steered her silver Chevy Vega into the open space, parking at an odd angle. Candi was still talking about the man from Hancock when Janelle opened her door and jumped out.

"Are you coming in with me or not?" Janelle snapped and then slammed the door shut.

Inside, Janelle noticed an older woman with graying hair pulled back in a tight bun sitting behind a desk punching the keys on a Smith-Corona typewriter. The nameplate on the desk only suggested the woman was employed there, not her true function being the firewall between the citizens of Madison County and the authorities who pursued peace and justice for all. Other than the woman, the office seemed deserted.

"Is the Sheriff in?" Janelle hastily asked in a tone sounding more like a demand than a question.

Mrs. Helen Pinkham, the woman behind the desk, looked up and removed her eyeglasses, setting them down on the desk. "May I help you with something?" she asked just as Candi walked in through the door.

"Yes, you can. I need to see the Sheriff immediately."

"What's this all about... is she with you?" Mrs. Pinkham nodded toward Candi Bryant.

Without turning around to look at Candi, Janelle leaned up to the desk and placed both her hands firmly on top. "Look, my little girl has disappeared, she's lost, and I need to see the Sheriff right now to help find her. Can you tell me if he's here?"

Mrs. Pinkham could see the urgency in Janelle's face but knew, from her long years of service being the front person, most expressions were over-exaggerated and motioned them to a bench along the wall.

"You can take a seat over there while I go see if he's available," Mrs. Pinkham told the two women, wanting to speak to the Sheriff in person instead of having to speak over the phone and having the two women listen in.

"This is extremely important. It can't wait. Where's his office?" Janelle demanded.

"It's just down the hall, but you're not allowed to go down there. I'll only be a second. You can wait here."

Before Mrs. Pinkham could even move two steps from behind her desk, Janelle disappeared down the hall toward the office, with Candi moving at a slower pace behind her.

CHAPTER SIX

Saturday Afternoon
May 12, 1989

Roger Lefebvre had been the sheriff of Madison County for the past twenty-two years after being elected in a closely heated race with the long-time incumbent at the age of thirty-six. Since then, he has always won in a landslide, with some elections going unopposed. He was the kind of sheriff every county strived for – a large posing man with great determination to do the best job he could, but most of all considerate toward the citizens he protected. Even though there were several highly publicized unsolved cases during his years in service, the public still admired his dedication. Most of these unsolved cases involved the Osborne farmhouse, the worst one being the first, and unfortunately, in his first year of office.

It was in his first term as sheriff when the historic winter snowstorm hit back in 1967 that he had his first encounter with the Osborne farm, and then again seventeen years later when a female real estate agent was found hanging from a beam inside the barn, so he was well acquainted with the horrors of the place. In fact, he was so acquainted with the Osborne farm that even twenty-two years later, after the first incident, he shuddered whenever anyone even mentioned the Osborne place because the images of the dead were as vivid today as they were when he first saw their bloodied corpses.

But it had been five years since the last horrible incident and five years of not having heard mention of the Osborne farm. Until now, when the two distraught mothers came rushing into his office hysterically shouting their two young children had gone missing up to the old Osborne farm Roger Lefebvre's horrors came back to light.

Before they entered his office, Roger was contently relaxed with his heavy frame leaning against the back of his comfortable, black-leathered chair and his feet resting up on his old oak desk, which he had rescued from the one-room schoolhouse the town demolished about fifteen years earlier. His meaty hands were resting easily behind his head as he thought about his retirement, a retirement that was only a few months away. He had just been saying to himself how quiet it had been around town, and his job had been rather easy the last few years with only minor incidents to deal with. But the recent tranquility abruptly changed when the two mothers came into his office unannounced, bringing with them a flood of unwanted horrible memories of the Osborne farm.

* * *

The office was of normal size, about the size of an average bedroom, nothing impressive. When Janelle opened the office door and walked in without knocking, she immediately spotted the Sheriff sitting behind his large oak desk with his arms relaxing behind his head. His reaction was spontaneous as he quickly straightened up to a professional position. Before he could utter a response to the woman's intrusion, Janelle nervously attempted to explain her dire urgency.

"Sheriff, I need your help immediately, my Amanda didn't come home, and she was up by that awful place, you know, that dreadful place in Groveville where those murders occurred? You need to go up there right away. She's up there alone and probably scared out of her mind," Janelle shouted from just inside the doorway.

The only words Roger comprehended from Janelle's ramblings were Groveville and murders, but those two words were enough to bring him back to reality. His thoughts of tranquility and retirement vanished with those two words.

"Sheriff, my son is also up there with her daughter. Both our children are missing," Candi added, standing slightly behind Janelle.

Behind the unfamiliar women, the Sheriff could see Helen trying to push her wide body between the two mothers. "I'm awfully sorry, Sheriff, but I couldn't stop them from barging in on you. If you want, I can take their report out front?"

"No, that's okay, Helen. I'll take care of it from here," the Sheriff answered, waving her off with his hand.

Roger took a moment to study the two women, wondering if he had seen them before. The blond, he was almost positive he saw around town, but the other, the one with the shoulder-length dark hair and eyes that seemed too large for her thin-shaped face, which narrowed at the jawline to her chin, he wasn't so sure. When trying to determine their age, at first glance, he would have assumed the blond to be about ten years younger than her acquaintance, partly because of the discrepancy in their selected attire, but Roger knew one's outward appearance could be deceiving and suspected them to be about the same age, early to mid-thirties.

"Sheriff. Please!" Janelle pleaded, moving another step inside the office.

"Ladies, you're going to need to calm down. Now please come in and take a seat over there," he said, pointing to a couple of uncomfortable plastic chairs against the wall. "Are you talking about the Osborne place up in Groveville?"

"Yes, that's the place. That dreadful place should have been destroyed a long time ago," Janelle said, looking at the chairs but declining to sit and instead stood in front of the Sheriff's cluttered desk and leaned over, placing her hands down on the only visible space between two uneven stacks of manila folders. Her neck was long and narrow, and she wore a silver chain with a Saint Christopher medallion that dangled loosely over her blouse.

"Well, Mrs."

"Prescott, Janelle Prescott."

"Well, Mrs. Prescott, I agree with you on that point. The place is definitely an eyesore. But first, I'll need to know how old they are. This is important in deciding how urgent the situation is."

"Twelve, they're twelve years old," Janelle answered, not remembering that today was Amanda's birthday, and she was now a teenager.

"Okay, good, at least they're not youngsters."

"What do you mean, they are youngsters!" Janelle protested.

"I'm sorry, you misunderstood me. I meant they're not too young, and they're old enough to make sound judgments. I'm sure your kids are fine, and they probably decided to go play someplace else. You know how kids are at that age these days, they say they're going one place, and without telling anyone, they decide to go someplace else."

"Not my Amanda," added Janelle, "she always does what she's told, and I told her and that Bryant kid to make sure she's home by noon, and here it is, almost three o'clock in the afternoon. Something happened to them up there, and you have to go find them now before it's too late."

Candi just gave Janelle a harsh look that said *don't worry after this is all over with 'that Bryant kid' won't be going over to your house anymore.*

"Now, hold on a second, ladies. I know you're both worried about your children, but you're going to have to remain calm. I'd be worried too if my child failed to come home on time, but it's only two o'clock," Roger added, looking at the wall clock behind the women.

"What difference does that make? She should have been home long ago," Janelle retorted.

"I'll tell you what," Roger calmly said, and then after a short pause, added, "I'll have my deputy take a ride over to Groveville and take a look around the Osborne place. In the meantime, why don't you ladies give Mrs. Pinkham your names and addresses and the description of your children? I'm sure everything will work out fine."

"That will not do!" Janelle argued. "We've already been up there, Sheriff, and there was no sign of them anywhere. There's no place else they could have gone, or we would have seen them somewhere on the road. I'm telling you they're up there and most likely lost in those damn woods, so you'd better be sending more than just one deputy up there. If it were your child missing up at that horrible place, you'd have more than just one deputy there looking around. You'd have a whole search party scouring every inch of the damn place."

Roger looked at the distraught mother remembering his own child, a young girl who died years ago at the tender age of ten from leukemia. The woman was right. If it were his child, his daughter, up there, he would have every available body searching every inch of the place.

Not wanting to end his career of protecting the citizens of Madison County by not being more cautious, the Sheriff grabbed the radio mike and radioed his deputy, who was out on patrol. "Wayne, this is Roger. We have an emergency that just came up, and I'll need you back in the office ASAP. I'll fill you in when you get here."

CHAPTER SEVEN

Heaven's Institute
May 2011

The first time I saw Groveville was from the 'Overlook,' a scenic spot for tourists and the like to view the millions of trees that stretched all the way to Canada. In the autumn, when the leaves turn color, the parking area is full of tourists clamoring to see the magnificent foliage. The day Luke drove us up there was early summer, before tourist season, and we were the only ones enjoying the view, just Luke, Peter and myself sitting on the hood of Luke's Dodge Charger.

I recently moved to town a few days before to stay with Peter, who was still living at home with his parents. He wanted to show me a good place to bring a date and have a few beers, but he didn't own a vehicle, so he called his friend, Luke Townsend, to pick us up in his vehicle. It was the first time I had met Luke. We became instant friends, maybe because we were alike, both living for fun at the expense of others.

From my view, looking down at the valley below, Denton looked like a small model town with fake buildings and a main street made out of light-brown string that ran through town and disappeared into the foliage of trees, only to reappear again for short stretches at a time. As I followed the road up farther on the right, I noticed a small section of buildings, which Luke pointed out as the town of Groveville. I could make out the rooftops of some buildings, but the road I was following was no longer visible. Out beyond Groveville was a large barren area I was told used to be the town's dump, a burning dump where they burned everything except garbage. The garbage was picked up once a week in small buckets that were placed at the end of driveways and then hauled off to a pig farm.

Luke pointed out one of the larger pig farms. I could see the top of the farmhouse and two large barns, and a fenced-in area for the pigs. He also pointed out cutouts of farmland. One of those was the Osborne farm. It was not hard to recognize. You could see the L-shaped building, farmhouse and attached barn. Behind the main building were smaller buildings, which were hard to identify as they had collapsed in on themselves, almost level to the ground. The property's layout seemed to tilt a bit, higher toward the north, near the edge of the woods. The land also looked uncultivated, overgrown from years of neglect.

From my observation, the valley looked peaceful, a nice quiet place to raise a family, and mighty boring being a teenager. But after I asked about the Osborne farmhouse, which Luke and Peter were more than obliged to fill me in on what had taken place there, I quickly changed my mind about small towns being boring, figuring looks were deceiving. The mystery surrounding the farmhouse seemed quite intriguing, and I wanted to see it. I wanted to go right then, but Peter was against the idea saying there was nothing there except an old rundown farmhouse. Luke did not want to go either. He thought it would be more fun to drive down to the public beach at the lake and check out the babes. So that's what we did.

I was seventeen then, and I can only suppose the valley looks different now. I suppose it's grown considerably over the past twenty-two years with more buildings and less forestland. But at night, in my nightmares, I see the old valley, the old Groveville and worst of all, I see the old Osborne farmhouse with all its horrors. I see the shadowy cemetery and decaying farmhouse with rotting dead corpses hanging inside the barn. I wake up screaming in sweat, believing I'm still there, only to realize I'm not. I sit up in my bed in the dark, not wanting to go back to sleep. I can't see the others in the room with me, but by the sounds of their breathing, some snoring, I know they hadn't been awakened by my screams, which probably were only in my head and had not escaped from my arid mouth.

I remember on a clear day, you can see a great distance from the 'Overlook,' other hills and tall mountains on the horizon, a blue sky that stretched as far as I could see. I knew there were other valleys on the other side of the hills with other towns, but I couldn't see them from the 'Overlook.' Same as I knew my unseen future was out there beyond those hills. I wish I had seen what lay ahead for me, my dismal future. If I had known what was to become of me and what my future would be, my life would have been drastically different, but I was too wrapped up in enjoying my lazy lifestyle to notice I was heading in the wrong direction. Back then, I was a young man on the verge of doing nothing great or even merely worthwhile with my life. Unbeknownst to me, I was traveling on a dead-end road I thought would go on forever. I should have read the signs – *Stop. You're going in the wrong direction – Turn around before it's too late – Your future is in jeopardy – This road only leads to trouble.*

But I didn't read the signs. I blindly ran down the road laughing at my freedom and any advice shoved in my face. It was my life, and I was going to live it as I pleased, without reservation.

Now, I wish I had read the signs and listened to the more experienced. If I had, I wouldn't have ended up in this miserable place with that foul-smelling barber breathing his bad breath down my neck once a month while he cut my hair. It's cut short, no more curls and the rich color that shined like gold in the sunlight is now as colorless as my life – a life with no deviations, one long straight road leading nowhere.

The only two things I look forward to now, and they aren't very pleasant, to say the least, are the incredible tasteless meals they serve with unconvincing smiles and those horrible nightmares I told you about and probably will be mentioning them from here on out until I do something about it, which won't happen unless I get out of this miserable place. When I do get out, those nightmares will be long gone from my mind.

I'm sure you can't understand why I don't like this place, not yet anyway, so let me tell you. First of all, I've been confined in here for almost twenty-two years, half my lifetime, and all I do all day, besides the boring required daily sessions that are supposed to help cure the mind but only confuse it more, is stare out this filmy window and gaze at my past life. Oh, they let me outside once in a while, on nice days, and let me tell you, those nice days are far and few. When I do get out to breathe in the fresh country air and soak up the warm sunshine, it's only for an hour or so, and there is always someone standing near me to make sure I don't hurt myself, so they say, but I know it's because they're worried, I might wander off. And you know, they're right. I'm just waiting for the perfect time, the time when they think they have me under control, and then, I'll walk right out of here, right down that long driveway past that black ironed-gated wall and keep on going, far away from this miserable place. But until then, I'm stuck here to think and stare out the window like I'm some kind of lunatic.

I keep thinking about how I got into this situation, and I'm still a little fuzzy about it. They, the people who run this place, tell me one thing, but my mind says another, and I'm almost certain I know what really happened back in the spring of 1989 because I was there, and they weren't. I was twenty-three years old and unemployed with no desire to find a job because I was having too much of a good time hanging around the pool hall, playing pool, and drinking beers with my friends. I know it probably sounds like a good time to some people, young people, that is, and it was fun, but I knew deep down something awful was about to happen. And it did.

* * *

For you to understand my predicament, how I arrived in this hellhole, I have to go back to that day in the pool hall. It was six years after I arrived in Denton, six years after I had first glimpsed the old Osborne farmhouse from the 'Overlook.' I remember the day clearly, even though it was over twenty years ago. On that day, the day it all started, I was in town with my buddies when Deputy Wayne Leon James casually strolled into the Denton Pool Hall looking for help, but he sure took his time asking for it. He was either being polite, which I didn't believe was the case, and waiting for the pool game to be over, or he didn't feel the urgency.

Deputy James had this odd way about himself, especially odd being a deputy, where nothing ever seemed urgent to him. Not even if someone's house was on fire. And that afternoon at the pool hall was no different. I was playing a game of eight ball against one of the best pool players in town, Al 'The Pal' Deluca, and beating the crap out of him. But with Deputy James staring down the back of my neck, my game went in the crapper. Not that he made me nervous, but it was more that my surroundings had changed, causing me to lose my concentration.

After I slapped the buck in Deluca's hand, I looked over at the tall, slender man in the droopy tan uniform and shiny tin badge and gave him a forced grin. I wanted him to know he didn't intimidate me, which he did somewhat, more the badge than the man behind it.

"What do we owe the honor of your presence, Deputy Wayne Leon James?" I smartly asked, accenting his middle name.

He waited a moment until I got the full authority stare, a stare I believe all law enforcement officers are required to practice. "How would you boys like to do your town a good deed?"

His inquiry sounded a little suspicious to me, and I looked around at my friends' faces to see which one of them had broken the law. Being an occasional lawbreaker myself, I was quite familiar with peacekeeper's tactics, and I was almost a hundred percent positive Deputy James was only being sarcastic, and the good deed he was asking from us was to confess to whatever crime one of us had committed. Besides, what possible reason could there be for him to believe lowlifes like 'us' could honestly do the town a good deed?

Deluca looked the guiltiest, but that wasn't saying much because he always looked guilty – he was born looking guilty. He had a gangster's face, round and cheeky with lazy eyelids. One had to look extremely hard to see the color of his eyes, and I often wondered how he could see through those slits and still play pool as good as he did. It was almost as though he was playing blindfolded. And Deluca always seemed to have money but never had a job, at least one that I knew of. *So where was the money coming from?*

So, Deluca was my top candidate that Deputy James was inquiring about. The other two characters hanging out at the pool hall with me were Peter Finch and Luke Townsend, who happened to be my two best friends. Al Deluca was a friend but more of an acquaintance than a friend, not someone I often hung out with.

Peter, short in stature and goofy looking with a big nose and ears on a narrow face, looked the least incriminating. His mouth was gaped open, wide enough to fit the cue ball plus the eight ball inside. I could see his mind was slowly trying to process the question put before us. If he were guilty of something, I would have known about it long before the authorities. He couldn't keep anything secret from me. Like the time Peter and Luke went for a joyride in a stolen vehicle. Luke told Peter if he ever told anybody, even me, he'd brain him. Peter told me the very next morning, but I never told Luke. Maybe that's why Peter tells me everything, because he trusted me.

Luke 'The Cuke' was as cool as a cucumber. If he had done anything, I couldn't tell by the look on his relaxed face. Luke just leaned back against the wide railing, running alongside the wall, calmly lit a cigarette, then gave me a quick smirk as he let the smoke escape from his nostrils.

"What's up?" I asked, too curious to wait for Deputy James to enlighten us.

"We have a situation up at the old Osborne place, and the Sheriff is looking for volunteers. He asked me to check the pool hall for volunteers. From what I gather, it looks like slim pickings around here, so I guess you guys will have to do," he said, glancing around the nearly empty pool hall. The only other person he could see besides the owner standing behind the bar was old man Norman, a regular customer nearing the age of eighty and looking like he might not reach it.

Just hearing the name Osborne made my skin crawl, and I wondered if my expression looked like Peter's, his chin was almost touching his upper, bony chest. I knew he had heard the horrible stories about the Osborne farm, as did most folks who grew up in the area, because he was the person who had told me. A lot of people died in that house, all gruesome deaths.

"What kind of situation would the Sheriff need volunteers for, hunting for ghosts?" Luke laughed.

"No, Smart Ass, not this time. We've got a couple of runaway kids, and they were last seen heading up the road that way."

"Why would anybody want to go up there if they were running away? I sure the hell wouldn't," I said, shaking my head at the absurdity of the idea, but unbeknownst to me at the time, that was exactly what I would do later, and it would be the worst decision I would ever make.

The story Deputy James gave us as to why the kids had gone up to the old Osborne farm wasn't totally accurate, and as we found out from him later, it wasn't even close to being accurate. He informed us the kids had run away from home, but the real reason why the two lost souls had gone up there was to go fishing in a pond somewhere near the Osborne property. They hadn't run away at all; they were supposedly lost in the woods near the Osborne farm.

"What's in it for us? We getting paid?" Luke asked, exhaling a puff of smoke and then placing the cigarette back in his mouth, letting it hang there as though it was a magic trick.

Deputy James rolled his eyes in Luke's direction and placed his hands around his thin waist. "I said...." he paused to make sure Luke was paying attention, "we're looking for volunteers. You know what volunteers do, don't you, Mister Townsend?"

"No, I don't. Why don't you enlighten me."

"They don't get paid. If you had gone to school, you would have known what the word means. Or maybe you've been smoking too much pot to remember?"

"Well, in that case, if there's no money in it for me, you can count me out. I don't do anything for nothing."

Deputy James looked over at Deluca, who was standing with a cue stick in one hand and the cue ball in the other, rolling it around in his hand. "What about you, Deluca? You in? You want to do something worthwhile for once in your life instead of wasting it in a smoky pool hall?"

Deluca continued to roll the cue ball around in his hand while contemplating the question, then set the ball on the table, spinning it like a top. "You can count me out as well. I'd rather play pool than play hide-and-seek. Mal, you lost the last game. You going to rack them?"

I grabbed the ball rack from the hook under the table and began placing the pool balls in the rack.

"How about you, son? You in, or are you going to waste your life with your loser friends?"

Without looking up, I knew the deputy was referring to me and not Peter Finch because I didn't believe he knew my name, and he definitely knew Peter's name; they were related. Peter's mother's sister was Deputy James's mother. Aunt Gloria, Peter referred to her as whenever the subject of their relationship was brought up.

I placed the last of the pool balls in the ball rack and lined it up on the small round black mark on the table, and then carefully pulled the ball rack free, keeping the balls in a tight triangle.

"Fire away!" I said to Deluca, then replaced the ball rack back on the hook. Deluca lined the cue ball up on the other end of the table and smacked it as hard as he could with his cue stick. The sound cracked the silence.

"Come on, Finch, let's go. I guess your loser friends don't want to help us find those lost kids." Deputy James nodded toward the door.

Peter guzzled the remainder of his beer and set the bottle down on the railing, and then stood to follow the deputy out the door.

"Hey," I shouted toward the deputy. "I thought you said the kids ran away from home. You didn't say they were lost."

"Did I say they were runaways?" Deputy James said with a frown. "They went fishing at some pond up at the Osborne property. They didn't come home when they were expected, and their mothers are pretty worried. So, we need all the help we can to search the area."

"Well, that makes a total difference. The situation seems to have changed," I said, thinking it may be interesting after all.

"Mal, you playing? It's your turn." Deluca nodded at the array of balls spread out across the green felt table.

I could see there were a lot more striped pool balls than solid ones, so I easily figured out I had the striped balls. I took my time surveying the table for my best play.

"So, are you changing your mind? You coming with us?" Deputy James impatiently asked.

"Yeah, Mal, I don't want to go up there by myself," Peter pleaded for me to go with them.

"I might," I answered. I was intrigued by the idea of searching for the lost kids, but I didn't want to go anywhere near the farmhouse itself. I figured we'd help search around the pond and see if they pulled anything out of the murky water. Maybe see a gross dead kid. As for going near the farmhouse, they could do that themselves.

"What about the game? You quit, you lose, and you owe me a buck," Deluca said with a hint of irritation.

I glanced over at Deluca, he was trying to stare me down with squinting eyes, but I wasn't intimidated by the look. I wasn't intimidated by anyone, but at the same time, I didn't want to lose another buck to him. A buck was too important to me, especially when I only had a couple of those greenbacks in my wallet.

"Let me clean this table off first. It shouldn't take too long, and I can meet you up there," I said, then proceeded to hit the cue ball into a blue striped ball but missed the shot.

"How are you going to do that? You don't have a car?" Peter smartly asked.

I tapped the cue stick on the edge of the pool table and glanced over at Luke.

"I can get Luke to give me a ride up there in his. What do you say, Luke? This sounds like it could be exciting – maybe we can see them fish a couple of dead kids out of the pond."

I could see Luke was intrigued by the expression on his face. Who wouldn't want to see a couple of dead kids?

"Yeah, Wayne, we'll meet you up there. I'll catch a ride with them," Peter said and sat back down on the same stool he was previously sitting on and folded his arms across his chest in defiance.

"You guy's better show up, or I'll pull you in for that house break last weekend out on Sawyer Road," Deputy James said and then walked out the door. Through the window, I watched him angle across the street toward the sheriff's office, avoiding the crosswalk.

The Sheriff was standing with one foot on the top step of the office and the other foot on the step below, talking to a couple of women I had never seen before. One woman, the one with dark hair and wearing boring librarian attire, looked edgy and was shaking her head at the Sheriff while he talked. The other woman, a blond in a pair of tight jeans that looked like they were ironed on, seemed calm and was smiling at the deputy as he walked across the street toward them. I figured they were the mothers of the lost kids. I never knew my mother, or even my father, as I was raised in an orphanage, so I couldn't feel their plight.

"Hey Luke, ever seen them before?" I asked about the women thinking he may have known them. He knew a lot more people in town than I did, having lived here his whole life.

Luke sauntered up beside me and looked out the window, focusing on the odd group diagonally across the street. I could see he was studying the women, and from the angle of his face, I could see he was concentrating mostly on the sexy blond.

"Can't say if I have. The blond is sure something. Looks like she has the hots for Wayne, though. Look at her staring him up and down. Must be the uniform she likes. It sure can't be the pencil wearing it."

"You know, I almost think I've seen her someplace now that I think about it. It's the hair I recognize. She looks like the woman who came out of the Denton Beauty parlor over there, the Saturday Kristen broke up with me." I nodded up the street. "I remember she smiled at me when she walked by. It was one of those sarcastic smiles like she was liking the idea of Kristen breaking up with me. I felt like spitting on her. But maybe it wasn't her."

"So Mal, speaking of Kristen, you never told me if you ever did her."

"What do you think?" I smartly answered.

"I think you didn't. That's what I think, old buddy boy," Luke said as he walked away.

I felt like telling him I don't kiss and tell, but I let it drop. He just would have kept hounding me until I told him a lie.

When I looked away from the window, I saw Deluca standing there, holding out his hand. I glanced at the pool table and noticed there were only striped balls left on the table. I opened my wallet and pulled out a dollar bill. I had two bills left.

"Well, that leaves me with just enough money for one more beer, and if we're going up to the Osborne place, I think I'll need another beer," I said and handed Deluca the dollar bill.

CHAPTER EIGHT

Saturday Afternoon
May 12, 1989

Sheriff Roger Lefebvre removed the sweat-ringed cap from his head and then proceeded to wipe the beads of sweat off his wide forehead with a red bandana he pulled from his back pocket. He glanced up at the bright yellow orb beaming down on him and groaned, thinking it was too hot for this time of year. It felt more like July than May. He then stared into the waiting faces of his hastily assembled search team, thinking it was going to be awfully miserable out in the woods looking for the two missing children, but he had no choice in the matter at hand, it was part of his job, and he gladly accepted his responsibility.

Even though he was disappointed with the meager turnout of volunteers, his only regret was having the two mothers tagging along. Looking at them, standing apart from the others, he could see they did not look the type to be going traipsing through the woods, and they surely weren't dressed for it.

Mrs. Prescott was wearing a moderately styled light-gray skirt hemmed just below the knees along with a plain white blouse, which seemed to be made out of a thin material and would rip apart when coming into contact with any size branch. The shoes she wore were the type made for walking on a polished floor and light as a feather for comfort, not heavy-duty for searching in the rough terrain they were about to enter.

Although Mrs. Bryant seemed better dressed to tackle the unknown elements of the woods, wearing jeans and a light body-hugging pullover, her shoes were flat-soled and made of canvas, not the kind of footwear to be wearing hiking through the woods. She also seemed the type to complain when the going got tough, and someone vital to the search would have to bring her back.

Roger tried to dissuade the mothers from joining in on the search, telling them to go home and wait. They vehemently refused. Mrs. Prescott was definite, saying 'over my dead body.' To not cause any more tension than there already was, he raised his hands in defeat. He figured after seeing the terrain they'd have to hike, they'd change their minds anyway and wait out on the road or under the shade of a tree near the parked vehicles.

Besides the Sheriff and the two mothers, the search party included three of the Sheriff's four deputies. His only other deputy on duty, Fredrick Dairy, remained back in Denton, supposedly to take care of any emergencies that arose, but due to the slow afternoon, ended up bothering Helen Pinkham, the secretary\ dispatcher, with his knowledge of apprehending fugitives and the like, which she knew he had learned from reading crime novels and not from personal experience. The only other member of the search party was Henry Wade, the eighty-year-old owner of the two sad-looking bloodhounds that were hooked to the end of a double leash. The three recruited volunteers from the pool hall never showed up, and, with the lateness of the day, the Sheriff decided he was not going to stand around waiting for them.

Before he divided the search team into two groups and got the search started, the Sheriff casually strolled over to the front of the Osborne farmhouse, where Henry Wade was kneeling on the cool-shaded grass next to his relaxed hounds. Roger had known Henry for years, having used his services previously when conducting similar searches but seeing him now, his aged worn body, Roger wanted to make sure he was fit enough for the challenge ahead of them.

As Roger approached, Henry politely rose and gave the Sheriff a welcoming smile. The few remaining teeth left in his mouth were stained from chewing tobacco and chipped from the constant grinding as he restlessly slept at night. His restless sleeps had nothing to do with any turmoil in his life, though he had his share of having to endure his aging years without the companionship of his wife, whom he lost to cancer several years earlier. It was his constant twisting and turning from the nagging aches and pains most elderly people had to live with that caused his restless sleeps.

"It's good to see you, Henry. It's been a while since the last time we needed your services," Roger said as he held out his hand.

"Well, howdy, Sheriff. Hot enough for ya?" Henry said, taking hold of Roger's sweaty hand.

"You got that right. It is a rather hot one, very unusual for this time of year. Feels more like July than May. What about them? Think it's too hot for them?" Roger asked, looking down at the droopy hounds.

"Hell no, my babies will outlast the best of us."

"What about you? It's going to be rough going out there."

"I've never felt better," Henry eagerly told the Sheriff, which was a lie. The past few months, Henry was starting to feel his age and spent most of the day lying on his couch, watching game shows on cable. He knew he'd be sore and figured every bone and muscle in his body would be aching in the morning. Knowing the potential pains he faced, Henry still was not about to pass up what may be his last opportunity to do what he considered was his right. Besides, there was no one else who could do the job.

After Roger was satisfied Henry and his bloodhounds were fit to go, he gathered the search team in front of the deteriorating farmhouse, who impatiently listened as he shouted out his instructions, which basically said to stay together in their assigned group. No one was to wander off on their own under no circumstances. The Sheriff then divided the searchers into two groups. That way, they could simultaneously search the woods on both sides of the road for the elusive path that supposedly led to the pond where the children had gone fishing. They were to regroup back in front of the farmhouse in one hour's time if Amanda and Kyle were not found by then.

Two of the deputies and Henry Wade, along with the two bloodhounds, set out to search the woods directly behind the farmhouse, a decision that was made by the two anxious hounds. Henry had rubbed a red shirt Amanda had worn the previous day in the hounds' long snouts to give them a good scent of what they were sniffing for. Their first reaction had them twisting in circles, wrapping the leash around the dog handlers' legs. After Henry straightened the leash, the hounds began to sniff at the ground around them, walking slowly in opposite directions until Henry yanked on the leash, jerking their heads back. One of the hounds, Baby Blue – the younger and least seasoned of the two, began to howl in the direction of the woods behind the farmhouse and dug his front paws into the graveled road pulling the leash taut. The other hound, Rose, quickly joined in, and within seconds they were off and running, pulling Henry along with them.

"What are you two waiting for? Go follow them," The Sheriff waved at his deputies, then shouted at their backs. "Don't forget to fire off a warning shot if you find something."

Deputy James stood looking confident with his thumbs stuffed inside his gun belt, trying to impress the women. "Roger, how are we going to handle this? You want to spread out along the road and walk in the woods in a parallel line?"

Roger shook his head at his deputy of five years. "No, Wayne, we're sticking together. I don't want anyone else getting lost. Remember, we're looking for some kind of path that may lead to a pond. When we find one, we'll walk together, in single file."

Roger glanced at the farmhouse and watched his two deputies disappear around the back, hoping they would find the missing children before he had to hike in a mosquito and tick-infested woods. He then looked up the narrow Osborne Road to where it abruptly ended, keeping his eyes focused along the edge of the woods, trying to spot an opening. There was none that he could see, only low thick pines surrounding a dense forest of their taller cousins. Behind him, he could see the length of the road they had driven to where he now stood was lined with trees, some as old as the town of Groveville, he supposed, and smaller ones, saplings from the much taller trees. In some places along the road, he saw tall waist-high grass.

"Let's take a walk back down that way, toward the cemetery. Maybe we'll find a break in the tall grass that could be the path we're looking for," The Sheriff stated, thinking it was a better place to start than the dense forest at the end of the Osborne Road.

"Sounds good to me, Roger," his obedient deputy agreed.

* * *

Swinging her arms nervously back and forth, Janelle Prescott struggled to keep pace alongside the two men as they briskly walked, with long strides, toward an area of tall grass. It had been nearly four hours since she started worrying about Amanda, and her mind was beginning to frazzle. She had already lost her husband, and she could not bear the thought of losing her only child.

Kyle's mother, Candi, shook her head and reluctantly followed. She was hoping they already knew where the pond was. If her eldest son were home instead of away at a friend's camp, she would have brought him along to show the way. Up in front, she noticed the trio had stopped near a patch of tall grass, and the Sheriff was pointing toward the woods. She put her discontent behind her and hurried to catch up.

* * *

"I don't know, Wayne, this looks more like a deer trail than a path, and I highly doubt the pond the kids went to is in there," Roger said, pointing at a narrow space in the middle of the tall grass that angled off toward what seemed to be dense woods.

"You want me to go check it out anyway?" Wayne asked his boss.

"No, it will only be a waste of time. Let's go back up that

way. We'll walk up to the end of the road."

Just past where they were originally standing, beyond the parked vehicles, Roger spotted what he was looking for.

"This is definitely a path. Not sure if it leads to anything, but it could," Roger said.

"Great, I'll check it out."

"No, I'll go in with you. Let me go first, and you can follow me."

"What about them?" Wayne noticeably nodded in the women's direction but went unnoticed by the women who were staring blankly into the dense woods where the path led.

Roger removed his tan cap and brushed back his thin graying hair with his sweaty palm, pausing to determine if he should leave the mothers behind. It would be too much of a shock, he thought, if they came upon an ugly sight.

"You ladies will have to stay here, and I don't want either of you following us. If we find the pond, Wayne will fire off a shot, and you can tell the others when they come back which way we went."

"Like hell, I'm staying here, that's my little girl, Amanda, in there, and she'll need me," Janelle protested.

Candi Bryant reluctantly nodded her agreement, wanting to go with them, but she was not going to argue with the Sheriff. She knew he was more experienced with finding missing persons than either her or her distraught neighbor, so she was willing to let the Sheriff do his job without complaint. All she wanted was to get Kyle home safely. She was worried herself, but Kyle had pulled this kind of stunt before and had always made it home safe, so she kept positive thoughts.

"Look, I don't want you going in there, plain and simple," Roger said, pointing a stern finger toward where the path led. "Both of you are going to stay right here. It probably doesn't lead to the pond anyhow, but if it does, I promise I'll come back myself and tell you. Hopefully, with your children in tow."

"Why can't I go with you? She can stay here and wait for the others. You don't need both of us to stay here," Janelle argued to no avail.

"Mrs. Prescott, I know you're worried and anxious to see Amanda, but you'd be better served to stay here and keep Mrs. Bryant company. Now I let you come along against my better judgment, and if I hear any more argument about this, I'll lock you up in my cruiser. It's going to be damn hot and buggy in there. Now stay right here and wait till we return."

* * *

Janelle Prescott dejectedly stared at the Sheriff as he turned and led his deputy down the path through the knee-high grass and disappeared into the woods. Suddenly, she was unsure what to do next. Part of her wanted to follow, and she almost did, but her more sensible part won out, and she began to impatiently pace up and down the road with her eyes peeled toward the ground, avoiding any eye contact with Candi Bryant.

Candi also wanted to avoid eye contact with Janelle as much as possible and remained fixated on the area where the Sheriff and the deputy had disappeared. She could only hear the snapping of dry twigs and then no sounds at all. She weakly smiled as she pictured the two men reappearing with Kyle and Amanda, trudging behind them. When they did reappear, she would try to remain calm, not frighten her young son in front of strangers. Her displeasure and discipline would come later, at home. As for Amanda's mother, Candi had no idea how she would react when her child appeared. She hoped she would only be relieved, satisfied her daughter was safe.

CHAPTER NINE

Saturday Afternoon
May 12, 1989

While quietly walking through a dense area of tall pine trees, carefully checking the unfamiliar surroundings for clues of the missing children, Roger and Wayne could smell the fresh scent of pine and feel the cool dampness on their exposed skin. It was a welcoming relief from the humidity. However, only a brief break as the path they were on soon led to an open area of low bush berries and patches of higher bushes. From there, the trail continued for a short stretch and eventually led to a steep, slippery mud-covered slope, which caused the men to be extra careful in keeping their balance. At the bottom of the hill, they plowed their way through a ticket of waist-high scrub brush and a scattering of thin poplar trees. Finally, they came upon a body of water, a small pond no more than an acre in size.

The pond was surprisingly picturesque and serene, no comparison to the rough terrain they traversed through on getting there. The only sounds they heard were from a pair of chirping blue jays and the light breeze rattling the thin leaves of the poplar trees surrounding the pond. The pond itself was covered with bright, colorful lily pads and green leaves with white and pink flowers floating on the top of the still water. On the far side from where they stood, they saw a wide layer of wind-blown greenish-yellow pollen, which had fallen from a large pine tree that leaned its heavy weight over the pond.

On their right side, they noticed a fallen tree, naked of bark, partially submerged under the water. A good spot to fish from, Roger thought, but he also wondered if it was worth the hike through the rough terrain lugging fishing tackle. If he were a kid again, maybe he would not have batted an eye and endured the hike with triumph, but then again, these kids had bicycles to deal with, and it was not an easy task maneuvering down a slippery narrow path.

"What do you think, Wayne?" Roger asked, rubbing his chin, adding to the difficulties it took to reach the pond.

"I don't know, Roger. I don't see any sign of them kids anywhere," Wayne surmised as he surveyed the area around the pond. He, too, was skeptical.

"I think you're absolutely right. If they were here, their bikes would be right here. There's no place else to put them," Roger said, adding to the skepticism that they were on the wrong trail and at the wrong pond.

"Except maybe in the pond," Wayne said as he slapped at a mosquito. "Damn buggers."

Roger leaned over the edge of the pond. The bottom was sandy on the edges and gradually sloped into a muddy darkness. "No tire marks. The only way the bikes could have made their way into the pond would have been to throw them in." He turned and looked back at the path for any sign the kids even rode their bikes and, remembering the rough hike down the slippery slope and the thick scrub brush, quickly concluded it would have been impossible. "It looks like a dead end to me. There's no way they rode their bikes down here. It's hard enough to hike it in with fishing poles, let alone trying to navigate your bike down that narrow, slippery path and through that waist-high crap we plowed through."

"Yeah, that's true. We sure this is the pond they went to?"

"No, I'm not sure. It's doubtful this is the pond, but I'm not going to be trudging through these damn woods, searching every inch of it, looking for fishing holes. There are probably several ponds in the area. If we don't find them today, I'll send up a plane tomorrow morning to search the area. Hope we find them before then. Hope we find them before nightfall."

"Well, what do you want to do now?"

"We can't do much more out here. Let's head back and see what Henry's dogs turned up. Hopefully, they have good news. That Prescott woman is driving me nuts."

* * *

When Roger and Wayne emerged from the woods, they spotted the other group slowly ambling their way toward where the anxious mothers stood. The worn-out bloodhounds drooped alongside their owner, followed by the weary-looking deputies. Roger sighed at the sight of his out-of-shaped troops and vowed to get them into an exercise program. Riding around in patrol cars all day eating junk food sure took a toll on one's physique, something he was well aware of, having spent too many long hours himself riding around and then going home to a full delicious meal and an evening on the couch.

Janelle became very agitated at not seeing her child with the Sheriff and started to panic as she moved toward them. With each agonizing step, she increased her speed, hoarsely yelling to the Sheriff questions her mind refused to believe.

"Didn't you find her? Didn't you find my Amanda?"

Roger sadly shook his head, but his demonstrated answer did not stop Janelle from running toward them as they made their way through the knee-high grass. Roger had to put both his hands up to stop her from running into him.

"I'm sorry, Mrs. Prescott, but we didn't find them in there, and there's no sign that they had even been there. They must have gone someplace else."

"Did you find the pond?"

"We found a pond, but it's highly doubtful that was the pond they went to. Before you get hysterical, let's find out what the other team found."

"Are you sure you could have missed them? You didn't look for very long?"

"Yes, ma'am, I'm sure they aren't in there. There weren't any bikes in there, and I didn't notice any tire tracks either. Like I said, they must have gone someplace else. Now please, let's go back up there." Roger nodded up the road. Even though he could sympathize with Mrs. Prescott's concerns, he was getting extremely frustrated with her interference.

Gently moving Janelle Prescott aside with a light touch of his hand, the Sheriff made his way past her and hopped up the ditch to the road. He was hot and tired and had no patience for the woman.

Wayne laid a soft hand on Janelle's trembling shoulder and led her toward the others. "We'll find them, ma'am. You can be sure of that. They couldn't have just disappeared into thin air. Who knows, maybe they're already home. The Sheriff has someone periodically checking your house for the kids, and he'll let us know if they're there."

The words were meant to encourage her, but Janette was not buying it. She knew Amanda wasn't home and was somewhere near and in serious trouble. She felt it in her trembling stomach, a mother's intuition.

The other group did not have any luck either, even though there was a high moment when the hounds got excited over a rabbit and yanked the leash loose, and Henry Wade off his feet and ran off in a mad dash to catch the frightened animal. Henry laid a few choice words at his prize hounds and threatened to put them out in the pasture if they ever did anything foolish like that again. The bloodhounds rolled their sad eyes at their owner and then laid their heads low to the ground.

After hearing the team's depressing report, Roger took a deep sigh of regret and glanced up at the farmhouse, thinking he'd now have to search the decrepit place. It was the last place on earth he wanted to set foot in. He wished the town of Groveville would burn the whole miserable place to the ground once and for all and burn the horrible memories away with it, but he had no voice in the matter. It was up to the town. From what Evie Cross, the owner of Cross Realty, had told him, the town of Groveville was attempting to sell the place. But that was five years ago when she told him, and the Osborne farmhouse still hadn't sold and was looking even more deteriorated now, ready to collapse at any moment.

Roger really could not fathom why two youngsters would want to go snooping around in the old creepy place, but then again, kids had no fear their parents would protect them from all the evils of the world. He looked over at the distraught mothers and knew he could not call off the search without searching the farmhouse. Mrs. Prescott would scratch his eyeballs out. He then moved his stare beyond the farmhouse and noticed the attached barn and that the barn door was partially slid open. It just may well be Amanda and Kyle got bored with fishing and, on their way home, noticed the barn door was open. Seeing the open door as an invitation, they could have decided to explore the barn out of curiosity and were so intrigued with the place that they were still exploring it. Or, more likely, had fallen asleep up in the hayloft. From what he remembered (which was almost every detail except the insignificant ones), there was plenty of hay in the loft for a comfortable nap.

"Let's take a walk up there," Roger said, nodding toward the barn.

"The barn?" Wayne questioned with a hint of displeasure.

"Yeah, the barn. The kids might have noticed the barn door open and took it as an invitation. You know how kids are."

"Not really," Wayne said more to himself but loud enough for Roger to hear.

"I know you don't have any kids, but it wasn't too long ago you were one, too, and I'll bet you were mighty inquisitive."

Wayne nodded his agreement with the Sheriff, but in truth, he could not remember what he was like as a child at the age of twelve. He remembered his childhood, his friends and the games they played together, but how his young mind functioned, he had no remembrance. He only knew those days seemed a long time ago. Even at twenty-five, being twelve to him was a lifetime ago.

From where they stood on the outside, the barn looked even more dilapidated than the farmhouse itself, leaning as though the next violent storm that came along would blow the barn to the ground. Being blown away would have been fine with everyone, especially the Sheriff and his deputy, because they had their own nightmares about the place.

Roger cautiously walked up the wooden ramp with his hand instinctively gripped to his sidearm and his senses in full alert. Before entering, he stopped and peered inside but could not see anything beyond a few feet. The interior was dark, with only a few thin rays of sunlight streaming in through where some of the barn boards had fallen off. He stood quiet for a moment longer and listened to hear if there were any noises coming from within. Hearing nothing, he slowly entered the barn, loudly sliding the door open wide to let more light inside. Doing this, and his looming presence, spooked most of the smaller variety of birds out through small openings in the decaying barn. The barn owls had been spooked earlier in the day but would return by nightfall when the dust of intruders settled.

* * *

Not wanting to enter the barn first, Wayne remained a few steps behind Roger. The last time he entered the barn alone, he was confronted with the most horrifying sight he had ever seen, and the image was still with him when he followed Roger through the open door. He was not surprised to see the interior of the barn had not changed much in the five years since he last stepped foot into the creepy building, which was his first and only time. Even the large spider webs that were weaved across the eves and sturdy beams looked the same to him, and he imagined the spiders that had spun the webs were large and ugly and maybe even deadly if bitten by. Wayne hated spiders almost as much as he hated standing in the eerie barn.

As Wayne stood there, he felt a chilly draft of air wash over his face, the same chilly sensation he had felt before when he stood on the creaking wood floorboards looking up at the nude woman hanging from the sturdy beam that held the loft in place.

Her eyes bugged out of her swollen blue face, and a thin line of dried blood had trickled down from her open mouth where flies flew in and out. Her right breast had been gruesomely hacked off, and the blood from the wound, which had since dried to a deep crimson, had flowed down her leg and onto the floor below. Wayne knew there was no body hanging from the beam today, but he could imagine the hanging corpse in his mind and slowly reached up above his head with his shaking hand to make sure she was not there and then dropped the hand aimlessly by his side. On the floor beneath the beam, he noticed the faded bloodstain had soaked into the wood. He imagined the stain would always be there as a reminder of what had happened five years ago, almost to the day.

* * *

Roger Lefebvre glanced over at his deputy and noticed the odd expression on his face, like he was uncomfortable and not wanting to be standing anywhere near the awful place. His deputy stood erect, very still, with his hands drooping long by his side, his mouth gaped open, and his eyes rolled from side to side, taking in the entire barn as though he was making sure nothing evil was lurking within.

Roger could not blame him one bit for being nervous; he did not like being in there himself. The two times he had been in the barn, he had seen a corpse hanging from the beam, the second time was when he followed his deputy in through the barn door and saw the woman they had been searching for, and by the odor, she probably had been hanging for at least a day when they found her. It was a gruesome sight, to say the least. Deputy James was in his first week on the job and had never seen a dead person, never even seen one at a funeral parlor, and to see one hanging and stinking from the heat and humidity was too much for him to handle. Roger found Wayne bent at the waist, puking his egg and sausage sandwich he had eaten for breakfast earlier that morning at the Denton diner. The smell of the puke and ripe corpse almost caused Roger to puke himself, but he managed to hold his breakfast down and escorted his rookie deputy outside the barn for a breather.

* * *

The woman they found hanging in the barn that day, five years ago, had been reported missing the previous night by her husband. She had not been missing for a full twenty-four hours, so, going by the regulations book on reported missing persons, Deputy Wayne Leon James took the report and placed it on the Sheriff's desk for the next day's to-do list.

When the Sheriff arrived at the office the next morning, his first priority, besides pouring himself a freshly brewed cup of Helen's famous coffee, was to go over all the reports left on his desk from the night before to determine which ones would be the most important, prioritize the day's agenda. When he read the report on the missing woman, he immediately called the husband, Geoff Gorman, hoping it was only a husband-and-wife thing and his wife, Whitney, had since returned home, and he could cross the report off his to-do list. Roger was not too familiar with the young couple, knowing only from reading the report they had recently moved to town and the wife was working at the Cross Realty office. He had no idea what line of work the husband was in or even if he held a job, being new to the area.

Geoff Gorman told the Sheriff that after getting no help from the Sheriff's office and his calls to the realty office had gone unanswered, as with the call to Evie Cross's home, who had gone to bed early with a headache and turning the phone off, he drove around town, and the surrounding towns, all night in a desperate search for his missing wife. He said he even stopped and checked all the nightspots he knew of, thinking Whitney may have had to meet a potential client and forgot to mention it to him.

When he was asked if there was any kind of trouble between them, Geoff Gorman told the Sheriff everything was fine, no spats of any kind. Not since his wife complained about his lack of enthusiasm in painting the interior of their new home, which he had since accomplished. He also told the Sheriff, Whitney would never 'ever' consider cheating on him, and him likewise. She was plain missing, and he was certain his beautiful young wife had been kidnapped.

Knowing this was now a top priority, Roger sent his rookie deputy out to take a formal statement from Geoff Gorman and ask for a recent photo of his wife. While his deputy was doing that uncomfortable task, Roger drove up Main Street and parked his cruiser next to a handicapped parking space in front of the Cross Realty office and casually walked inside as though he were a customer. Inside, he found an older woman with dyed light-brown hair and too much eye mascara sitting at a desk in front of a stack of manila folders, a pile like the folders on his own desk, only not as unorganized. Roger knew the woman as Evie Cross, the widowed owner of Cross Realty.

The only lead Roger could ascertain from Evie Cross about the missing woman turned out to be the only lead he needed. Evie told Roger Whitney Gorman was going to drive over to the old Osborne farm on her way home to take some photographs of the property so they could place them in an advertisement. The town of Groveville finally decided to put the place up for sale, and the Cross Realty office was the closest real estate office to Groveville.

Roger did not go into much detail as to why he was inquiring about Evie's young assistant realtor. Only she was of some interest and thanked Evie for her cooperation, then moved toward the front door.

"Oh, Sheriff," Evie thought at the last minute, "if this has anything to do with why you are inquiring about Whitney, she should have been here an hour ago. I was just about to call her at home to see why she's running late. You know it's not like her to be late. In fact, she's usually early. She's a very reliable employee, and I'd hate to lose her if she's done anything wrong."

Roger paused as he held his hand on the door handle and looked over at the worried woman. He did not want to start any rumors if he could help it. "I'm sure there is nothing to be alarmed about. I was just heading over to her house now. I'll see what's keeping her."

Back outside, standing on the top step in front of the realty office, Roger looked up and down Main Street, trying to decide if he should handle this himself, drive out to the Osborne farm, or have his deputy meet him out there. The sky above was gray, looking ominous, like it would rain again like it had the night before. Seeing the threatening sky, Roger suddenly felt a strong urge to rush out to the Osborne property. If Mrs. Gorman had indeed gone there and had not been seen or heard from all night, it only spelled one thing, and it was not going to be a pretty outcome.

Roger knew the Gorman house was in a cul-de-sac on the edge of town, not far from Groveville, and Deputy James was probably finishing up with Geoff Gorman's statement and could be at the Osborne farm a lot faster than he could make it. But he was not too keen on sending his rookie deputy of one week out there alone. Nevertheless, he radioed Wayne and told him to take a drive out to the Osborne farm and have a look around the place, and most importantly, to wait for him before going inside, even if the missing woman's vehicle was there.

After giving Wayne brief directions to the Osborne Road, which he had already known being a lifelong resident, Roger hung up the mike. He then peeled off down Main Street and headed toward Groveville and the farmhouse he swore he'd never step foot in again for as long as he lived if he could help it.

While Roger drove along the graveled Osborne Road toward the farmhouse, his thoughts were back in the winter of 1967, the first time he had been to the Osborne farm. As he drove, he could visualize the tracks in the snow that were left by the town's plow truck and the backend of the green '54 Ford pickup truck the plow driver had to veer around off in a ditch. He then thought of the Osborne children, how frightened they appeared, staring out the first-floor windows at him as he and his deputy trudged up the snow-covered driveway, but that was a long time ago. Today there was no snow on the ground, only small puddles left from the previous night's rains.

When Roger pulled up behind his deputy's cruiser, he spotted a red Ford Mustang parked up near the barn and his young deputy, Wayne Leon James, waving at him. Roger hopped out of his cruiser and nodded to Wayne as he placed his hat on his head and adjusted his gun belt. He was not sure what to expect, but all indications pointed to no good. Roger was just about to tell Wayne to hold on till he got there, but before he could, he saw his rookie deputy disappear inside the barn.

CHAPTER TEN

Saturday Afternoon
May 12, 1989

"You okay, Wayne? You look a little bit queasy," Roger Lefebvre asked his deputy even though he knew the answer; his deputy was fine, just a little aftertaste of bile that took five years to surface. He figured Wayne was only reminiscing about the awful sight he witnessed as a rookie. He also knew the five years Wayne served in law enforcement had toughened his demeanor to the point where he could say *he'd seen worse*. Roger himself felt a little uneasiness standing there, and who wouldn't after witnessing gruesome evil.

Wayne glanced over at Roger and weakly nodded his head. He knew his boss was thinking about him tossing his breakfast at the sight of a hanging corpse and the nauseating smell that accompanied the horror. "I think it's something I'll probably never forget, and I hope I never see anything like that again. But if I do, I know I'll handle it better."

"I'm with you on that," Roger answered as he scrutinized the interior of the barn, seeing the same familiar ugly sight. There was nothing unexpected, and nothing he hoped to find like the kids, or at least their bicycles lying in the middle of the floor.

Roger stood with his hands on his hips and glanced up at the loft. From his view, the loft looked unused, except for the stored seasonal items like the empty wooden apple crates stacked high in three even rows on the far side and the several broken bales of hay spilled haphazardly on the other side.

"Wayne, you're younger than I am, climb up that ladder over there and check out the loft. See if they're sleeping in the hay. I'll look around down here," Roger said, pointing toward the wooden ladder built into the wall underneath the loft.

"Roger that," Wayne responded with a hint of sarcasm.

Roger shook his head. He had heard that expression one too many times when he gave his deputies an order, but at the same time, he knew his men respected him when it was said.

With a bit of apprehension, Phil Hardy, Roger's seasoned deputy but on a part-time status, slowly walked into the gloom of the barn and glanced around at the interior as though he had never actually seen the inside of a barn before. But he had seen the interiors of barns before, plenty, including the one he now stood in. He also had the unpleasant experience of touring the inside of the farmhouse itself, but even though he had been throughout the whole house previously, he still had a foreboding feeling about the place. To him, it did not matter how many times he entered the Osborne barn, he'd still feel jittery, and maybe even more so each time he did, so he chose to stand close to the open door and hesitated a moment before asking Roger what to do next.

The Sheriff's other deputy, Ben Alden, came in a few steps behind Phil with a different feeling about entering the barn. Ben had heard the gut-wrenching stories of what had taken place there, especially all the horrors of the last incident involving the real estate agent, hearing it firsthand from Wayne. After hearing Wayne's account, Ben assumed one day he would have his own encounter with a gruesome death and felt when he did, he'd handle it professionally.

"Charming place. Absolutely charming," Ben smartly remarked at his introduction to the dismal barn.

Phil Hardy shook his head at the facetious comment, thinking if Ben had seen the horrors he witnessed, his expression would not have looked so smug. So, he ignored the comment and looked toward his boss, who was picking through some dusty old, neglected farm equipment like he was examining their value for possible purchase.

"Want us to continue searching outside, or do you need us in here to help you and Wayne out?" Deputy Phil Hardy asked. He had been Roger's longest-serving deputy and a deputy before Roger was elected sheriff twenty-two years earlier and was now semi-retired, working part-time out of boredom. He had no hobbies, and his wife did most of the chores around the house, leaving Phil to spend his time watching cable TV and drinking beer. When Roger asked Phil about working part-time, he jumped at the offer, but, unbeknownst to him, it was his wife who had whispered the idea in the Sheriff's ear. She knew her husband's lack of exercise would send him to an early grave if he did not get his butt off the couch and do something worthwhile.

Roger set the gadget he was holding down on the workbench and dusted off his hands, briskly rubbing his palms together. "Might as well have Henry bring the dogs in here and have a sniff while they're here," Roger answered.

Henry Wade was standing out in the driveway with his two bloodhounds tugging to follow, but he held tight on their leash, not wanting to come any closer. He knew his days were nearing an end, but when the time came, he wanted to be buried in the ground, not under a collapsed barn. When he saw Phil Hardy walking back out of the barn, staring in his direction, his aging heart strained to pump harder.

"Need us?" Henry halfheartedly asked, hoping Phil was going to say no and the Sheriff no longer needed their services. He could go home and relax in the shade of his porch, sipping a cold beer, but that's not what Phil answered to his inquiry.

"Yeah, Roger needs you. I guess he figured since you're here, might as well put your dogs to work."

"Sure thing, my boys seem mighty excited as it is."

* * *

Hearing the conversation about the use of the dogs, Janelle Prescott and Candi Bryant anxiously followed Henry and his two hounds up the ramp and stood cautiously, peering in through the open barn door. They were worried when the Sheriff called for the use of the hounds, which most likely meant their little ones hadn't been found.

At first glance inside, the two women couldn't imagine anyone would want to set foot in such a filthy place, let alone a child, and definitely not their child. The barn was deep in length, too deep and too dark to see the back section of the barn. What they could view from the entrance was what one would have expected to see in a barn. One side of the barn was sectioned off for the purpose of storing unused farm equipment, items that needed to be repaired when time allowed, but time had long passed for most of the broken equipment to even consider repairing. There was also a long wooden bench near the pile of useless junk where the Sheriff was standing. The bench was littered with small objects and plastic containers. Behind the bench was a pegboard with a few rusty tools hanging on nails. Not much else could be seen from the doorway, so they stepped further inside, keeping a little distance between them and the Sheriff so he wouldn't order them back outside.

Through the cracks between the barn boards, thin rays of light exposed billions of dust particles floating aimlessly in all directions. Through the dust, on the other side of the barn, they could see a row of stalls, a dozen on each side with a narrow corridor between them leading toward the back. There were overturned buckets on the floor next to the stalls. The floor itself was covered with sawdust and hay, and other debris not recognizable; feces dropped from invading rodents.

After getting an eye full, Janelle glared at Candi with a look that said it was her son's fault for bringing Amanda to this despicable place. Candi turned away, not wanting to get into a shouting match with her neighbor and looked out toward the road where she could see a plume of dust rising up from the graveled road caused by a fast-moving vehicle, nearing the Osborne family cemetery.

* * *

From the loft, Wayne followed the same vehicle and watched it pull up behind Henry's ancient green truck. When both doors opened, he watched two young men step out of the vehicle and lean their thin frames against it. He then squinted his eyes to make out who they were. Not a second had slipped by when he realized the occupants.

"Hey, Roger, I think the boys from the pool hall have finally arrived. Their vehicle just pulled up at the end of the driveway."

Roger walked to the barn door and saw the two hooligans leaning up against a red Dodge Charger, smoking cigarettes and looking as enthusiastic as a pair of city workers on a coffee break. He then noticed a third occupant casually crawling out from the back seat, looking as enthused as his two comrades.

Seeing the three young men his deputy recruited from the pool hall, knowing what type of guys they were, Roger thought it was only fitting to complete the odd composition of the search team. He had the two distraught mothers whose attire was more fitting for a walk in the park than a hike in the woods, and an old man with one foot in the grave along with his two worthless dogs, dogs who probably couldn't sniff out their own food if the bowls weren't placed directly in front of them. Now the three lowlifes wanting to join the circus. What a search team.

"That's who you recruited. Some bunch they are. I think I may have locked the lot of them up before. Ben, go out there and make sure they don't come in here." Roger nodded to his newest recruit, who was only hired five months earlier when Deputy Phil Hardy retired. "Maybe we can still use them later to search the woods if we don't find anything in here."

Being young and fearless, so he thought, even though his only encounter with fear was asking his future wife out on their first date, Ben was eager to help search the barn and even the farmhouse if need be. However, he did as he was ordered and reluctantly exited the barn, brushing passed Phil Hardy, who was still hanging near the entrance.

Just after Ben Alden exited the barn, the hounds picked up on an interesting scent. After sniffing the dusty floor near the entrance of the barn for Amanda's scent, the two hounds yanked hard on the leash and pulled their master to the side of the barn where the cow stalls were located. Behind one of the cow stalls, the hounds began howling like crazy.

"I think Rose and Baby Blue found something, Sheriff. There's a couple of bikes lying over here, and one of them looks pretty darn new," Henry surmised.

On the floor behind the stall, the two bicycles, both red in color, were leaning tangled against one another. There were also two fishing poles and a container of worms on the floor next to the bicycles. To Henry, the odd way the bicycles were left indicated they most likely had been tossed there, and he told the Sheriff his thoughts. When Roger saw them, he quickly agreed with him.

Hearing Henry's mention of the bicycles, Janelle and Candi came rushing over toward the cow stall. Roger quickly intercepted the mothers, wrapping his beefy arms around their waists. He did not want the mothers contaminating the area if there was a crime scene to secure. Not that he suspected one of them would harm their child, but just in case one or both had a hidden dark side, he wanted to make sure they did not trample over any evidence they may have left behind. If he had to decide which one of the two mothers might be capable of possessing an evil trait, his vote would have been on Janelle Prescott.

"Ladies, I can't let you in here. You're going to have to wait outside," he told them, then glanced over to where Phil was standing just inside the door. "Phil, I need you over here to take Mrs. Prescott and Mrs. Bryant outside. I can't have anyone messing up a crime scene if we have one here."

"Like hell, I'm leaving. That's my little girl in there," Janelle Prescott shouted as she struggled to break free of the Sheriff's strong grip.

"Ma'am, we're not sure the kids are even in here. I just want to make sure we don't contaminate any of the evidence if we find something. Now go with Deputy Hardy, and let us do our job," Roger explained as Deputy Hardy gently grabbed the women by their arms to lead them outside.

On the way out, Janelle spun her head around to look back in the direction of the cow stall. "Amanda, are you in there? It's me, Mommy."

"We'll find them, ladies; don't you worry about that," Deputy Hardy said, trying to encourage them as he led them outside.

"You'd better find them, or I'll sue your ass," Janelle Prescott threatened the deputy and then snarled at Candi Bryant. "And I'll sue your ass too."

Candi gave Janelle a quizzical look, wondering if her neighbor was a crazy lunatic. She was worried herself about their children's safety, but she still had a hold of her senses, where it looked like Janelle totally lost all control of hers.

"I think we should be thinking about finding our children and not lawsuits at the moment," Candi advised Janelle.

"What do you think I've been doing? It's your son's fault my Amanda is lost, and if anything has happened to her, I'll kill you and your whole family," Janelle shouted loud enough for everyone to hear, and then reached out with her raging claws and started shaking Candi's neck. Candi attempted to tear the crazy woman's hands away by grabbing her wrist but with not much success. She then kicked Janelle in the shin with the toe of her canvas shoe, which only caused Janelle to hold on tighter.

The three young men at the end of the driveway came running up to see the catfight, it was the most excitement they had witnessed in some time, and they didn't want to miss any of the action.

Deputy Alden jumped into the fracas to help Deputy Hardy separate the two women, who were struggling to get a hold of them, not wanting to hurt one of them. Ben Alder was much larger than Phil and wrapped both arms around Mrs. Prescott's small waist but still had a hard time yanking her off.

As she was being pulled away, Janelle was still reaching out toward Candi in a fit of rage. Candi rubbed her neck to check for damages. The first thing she thought of was suing the bitch.

Hearing the commotion, Roger came rushing out of the

barn and was surprised to see so much rage coming from such a petite woman whom he thought was as frail as his own mother, who was pushing eighty. He shook his head when the shouting died down and ordered Deputy Hardy to drive Mrs. Bryant home and to then drive back out to the Osborne farm. He then ordered Deputy Alden to escort the deranged woman home and make sure she stayed there, even if it meant he would have to stay there himself for the rest of the day.

CHAPTER ELEVEN

Saturday Late Afternoon
May 12, 1989

From his view high in the hayloft, Deputy Wayne Leon James watched the bizarre commotion outside the barn. He was baffled seeing the two women kicking and clawing at each other's throats. Wayne knew the mothers were extremely upset and wanted desperately to find their missing children, but even with all that had happened to them in such a short time, they still seemed to have had their wits about them, and now it was hard for him to believe they turned into raging lunatics. He wanted to climb down from the loft and go out and jump in the fracas, but there were plenty of others already breaking the fight up, so he just sat there on the edge of the loft and watched until the two women were placed in separate cruisers and driven off down the Osborne Road, in a cloud of dust.

"What the hell was that all about?" Wayne asked his boss, Roger Lefebvre, when the Sheriff walked back inside the barn with a disgusted look on his face.

Roger glanced up at his deputy, noticing him sitting on the edge of the hayloft with his feet dangling over the side. "Just a little upset, I guess, and I don't blame them much. We look like a bunch of idiots just standing around when their kids are missing. Let's get this place searched and find those kids. I'd like to find them before it gets dark. This is one scary place at night."

"Roger that," Wayne answered and jumped to his feet, knowing Roger was referring to him sitting on the job when he should have been making sure the loft wasn't hiding any clues to the whereabouts of the missing children.

Henry Wade and his two bloodhounds had also watched the two women going at each other from the inside of the barn, and now, with the Sheriff barking orders, Henry had the hounds back sniffing the ground floor of the barn. The barn smelled of wet hay and decay, which made it difficult for the hounds to pick up the missing children's scent, but when they neared a narrow side door, they got extremely excited and started to howl and scratch with their front paws to open the wooden door.

"Got something here, Sheriff!" Henry shouted.

"Great, wait for me before you open the door."

"Not a problem here. I wasn't intending on doing anything foolish. I've heard too many unpleasant stories about this place, and I rather not put me or my babies here in jeopardy. It's bad enough just being inside this creepy old barn. I can almost hear the beams starting to give way."

Roger walked over to the door and cautiously wiggled it slightly open, hearing the old hinges creak. After a moment, he pushed it wide. The room was dark except for a faint light at the far end. Having been there before, Roger knew the light was coming from the kitchen.

"Wayne, I need you to come down from the loft. We're going to have to search the main house. Henry, why don't you take the dogs outside and wait for my deputies to come back. When they do, tell them to come in through this way and to bring their flashlights in case we need them."

"Okay, Sheriff, but didn't you tell Ben to stay with that crazy woman?"

Roger paused, recalling his orders. "Oh yeah, that's right, Mrs. Prescott. Well, anyway, tell Phil when he comes back to bring his flashlight."

"Will do. And thanks for not asking me to join you guys. I sure as hell don't want any part of going in there," Henry said, and then turned to lead his hounds outside, yanking the leash taut, indicating their duties were over, and they'd soon get their deserved reward, which would most likely be the remains of the ham bone Henry had cooked, almost to the marrow. He made one big meal a week and worked on it until there was nothing left for human consumption.

"Hey Henry, don't go too far. We still might need to use the dogs," Roger called out to him before he walked out the door, thinking Henry might skip out after Phil came back from dropping Mrs. Bryant off at her house.

Reluctantly Henry nodded his head and started to lead his dogs out the door but then quickly spun around. "Roger, the three guys from the pool hall are still out here. You still going to need them?"

Roger let out a deep sigh and looked out the filmy side window. He could see the three young recruits kicking at clumps of grass and dirt in the driveway, looking bored and wanting to be somewhere else, like he did. He then glanced at his wristwatch, noting the time, calculating they had about two hours remaining of sunlight. By the time he and his deputy finished searching the house, there wouldn't be enough time to conduct another search of the woods again. There were acres of dense forest surrounding the Osborne farm, and searching in the dark would be futile.

"No, send them home. That is if they have a home."

Henry nodded and wished he was leaving with them, he was tired and thirsty for a cold beer, and his bloodhounds were tired and thirsty and probably hungry, too, having not been fed since early morning.

"I guess we're going in there by ourselves," Wayne reluctantly said, nodding toward the dark entrance, which sounded more like a question than an assumption.

Roger pulled out a stubbed black penlight from his gun belt and pushed the door wide. The door led into a dark narrow hallway with floor-to-ceiling cupboards on both sides, which Roger remembered to be the pantry. He was well aware most farmhouses had a room to store can goods and the preserves the farmers had tediously jarred for the long winter months, having lived on a farm himself when he was growing up.

Roger opened one of the cupboard doors and flicked his dim penlight on the items that were neatly stacked on the various shelves. Most of the items were dusty old can goods containing vegetables and beans. On the top shelf, he noticed mason jars filled with some unidentifiable food and hoped that was exactly what they contained. From his last experience searching the Osborne farm, it wouldn't surprise him if the jars contained something not meant for human consumption – he still had the image of the Osborne children's faces imprinted in his memory, and it wasn't a very pleasant sight, by no means.

"I wonder how old these things are?" Wayne curiously asked, hefting a can of beans.

"Have to be at least... well, let's see, before 67' anyway. So that would make them at least twenty-two years old."

"That's not too old. My grandmother has cans of food older than these."

"She does?" Roger asked, wondering why.

"Yeah, she bought a truckload back after WWII was over just in case there was another world war with food rationings. Before my time, so I don't know what it was like to go without."

"Not before my time. I was a growing teenager during that war, and what I wanted most during those years was food."

"I can see you got your share of it," Wayne joked at his overweight boss. Roger was once considered on the slender side, but being sheriff meant most of his time was spent behind the wheel of his cruiser or sitting at his desk doing paperwork. Lately, it had been the latter, with very little time outside in the field.

Roger knew he was a little overweight, gaining a few pounds each year, but he didn't figure it was that noticeable and didn't take the ribbing too kindly. He glanced over his shoulder and flashed the penlight in his deputy's face, and watched the smile wash away. "Nothing here of any interest. Let's keep going, wise guy."

The pantry led them into a dusty cobwebbed kitchen that was dimly lit. The only light coming into the room was through the two partially boarded windows on the driveway side of the house. There was also the small window over the sink with limited lighting, which looked out over the back hundred acres of cow pastures, now a breeding ground for spiny poplar trees. Beyond was a dense forest of pines and hardwoods.

Through the window, Roger could see darkening clouds moving over the horizon of trees at the edge of the fields, indicating a storm was approaching. It didn't look good, and he wondered why he hadn't been informed about the weather.

On the countertop, he noticed layers of dust mixed in with small pellet size feces dried to a weightless power. In the sink was a decomposed body of one of the culprits that disposed of the waste. The carcass looked repelling.

"Looks like the rodents hadn't only invaded the barn, they found their way inside the house, too," Roger said aloud but more to himself.

"What's that?"

"Rodents. The counter is littered with their shit, and one of them found his final resting place. Right here in the sink," Roger answered, then started opening cabinet doors above and below the countertop.

Wayne was occupied with the items he found on the long wooden table in the center of the room. There were only a few items, but they held his interest, an overturned coffee cup on a matching saucer and a small glass sugar bow. The sugar in the bowl was long gone having been digested by ants years ago, and several of the culprit's skeletons remained in the bottom of the bowl.

Wayne picked up the bowl and shook the black bodies, swirling them around, then placed the bowl back on the table with disgust. "My mother always said, 'too many sweets can kill you.'"

"What's that?"

"These ants in the bowl here must have eaten too much

sugar and died right in the bowl."

Roger ignored his deputy's pointless observation and looked around the rest of the kitchen in remembrance. It hadn't changed a bit in the twenty-two years since he last stood in the kitchen. On one side of the kitchen was an old Queen Atlantic iron stove. A tin coffee pot sat on one of the front burners, and a black cast-iron frying pan behind it. More dust and dried feces occupied the remaining surface.

Next to the stove was a neatly stacked pile of bone-dry split wood, which was used to burn in the stove for the purpose of heating the burners for cooking and heating the kitchen in the cold winter months. Leaning up against the woodpile, Roger noticed an axe, the kind with a sharp double-edged head. A perfect tool for splitting wood, but Roger wondered what it was doing in the kitchen. There was no one he knew would split wood inside the house. It was always done outside, with more room to swing the axe.

The head of the axe looked rusty, and Roger suspected it wasn't rust but something more sinister. A closer look, however, proved him wrong as it was indeed only rust. No cause for alarm, he thought, but it still gave him the creeps to think what it might have been used for.

"What's that antique thing over there? Some kind of chest?" Wayne asked, pointing toward a wooden cabinet. It stood four feet high and was pushed up against the wall next to an open entranceway leading to the front section of the house.

Roger snickered, knowing what the unusual wooden chest was. "Believe it or not, that is an icebox. It's an old fashion refrigerator. An ice truck would come around about once a week and put a large square chuck of ice on one side to keep the food chilled. We had one of those when I was a kid. The ice was kept in straw in the iceman's truck. We'd find pieces of ice on a hot summer day and brush off the straw and suck on the ice. Much like today's ice cones but without the colored syrup."

"Wild, you ready are old."

"Thanks, pal. Your day's coming faster than you realize."

"So why did they have this old thing taking up space when there's a refrigerator over there?" Wayne asked, nodding toward a fifties-style refrigerator on the other side of the room.

"I don't know, maybe for show, maybe for storing things. Take a look inside."

Wayne grabbed one of the brass handles and pulled the door open, noticing that side of the icebox was empty. He opened the other side, also empty.

"Ha, nothing, it's empty."

"What did you expect to find, the kids in there? Come on, let's check that room out in there," Roger said, nodding toward the open doorway.

After leading his deputy through the doorway and down a narrow hallway into the next room, Roger found himself quietly standing in the middle of the ill-lit living room, familiarizing himself with his surroundings. The room was sparsely furnished with only three pieces of furniture, which were placed in an unarranged pattern clumped together on one side of the room, leaving a wide-open space on the other side. The furniture was considerately covered with white linen bed sheets that had yellowed over the years.

Seeing the covered furniture, Roger inquisitively wondered who had bothered to cover them. He was sure it wasn't one of his men or any of the other investigators loaned out by the State Police Department. He supposed trespassers had entered the house over the years the place had been vacant, but what would be the purpose of covering the furniture. It was a mystery he supposed he'd never figure out unless whoever had fessed up to the deed.

From the shape of the larger piece of furniture, he could tell it was a couch. He remembered the couch was rather shabby looking, a light gray color made with some type of rough cloth and spotted with stains. It was pushed up close to the far wall but not so close a child couldn't hide behind it. The other two pieces of furniture, he figured, were a recliner and a rocking chair, but he wasn't quite sure. It had been quite a few years since he had set foot inside the room.

Curiously, Roger walked over to the rocking chair and tossed off the bed sheet, giving the chair a gentle push. Even without any weight on it, the old wood runners eerily creaked against the hardwood floor, sending a chill through his veins. He then turned his attention toward the three partially boarded windows on the driveway side, remembering the Osborne children's faces peering out at him and his deputy back when they trudged up the snowy driveway twenty-two years ago. Seeing the children from the outside, their faces seemed to have a strange inauspicious look, like their expressions were frozen on their sad faces. It was a gruesome sight. A sight that still haunted his dreams.

Wayne had no recollection of the room himself, having never previously been inside, and nonchalantly walked around the spacious living room with his hands on his hips, looking for any sign indicating the missing youngsters may have been in there. He stared at the fireplace for a moment and then, not expecting to see anything but wanting to be efficient, decided to look up inside. He knelt in front of the fireplace and pulled the iron handle toward him, opening the flue. Clumps of black soot and rotten dead creatures that had unfortunately fallen down the chimney dropped to the brick fireplace floor stirring the ashy dust in his face.

"Nope, nothing of importance up here," Wayne said, more to himself than to the Sheriff, who was still transfixed with staring at the images in the windows that were not there.

After brushing the soot from his face, Wayne squeezed his way around the narrow space behind the covered couch. On the floor, partially hidden under the couch, he found a three-foot-long wooden pole. The pole was round, like a wooden dowel, about an inch in diameter, with a red ribbon knotted around the end. "What's this stick supposed to be, I wonder?" Wayne asked the Sheriff, but the Sheriff was deep in thought in another time.

Getting no reply, Wayne walked over toward the Sheriff and, using the stick as an extension, lightly tapped the end on his shoulder. Roger quickly came out of his trance and turned to face his deputy. The moment he saw the pole, and dangling red ribbon, his eyes widened, and his body tightened from remembrance.

"Where did you find that?"

"Over there, behind the couch," Wayne said, pointing with the pole.

"I wonder how we missed that one?" Roger rhetorically asked.

"What do you mean?"

"Oh, nothing. I guess I didn't do a thorough investigation. That's what I meant." Roger Lefebvre was remembering the day after they found the mutilated bodies, and since he was the sheriff at the time, meant he was in charge of the investigation. If evidence went unnoticed, he was to blame. There hadn't been a homicide in his county in years, and nobody really had any idea how to investigate one properly. But since they knew who had committed the crime, he felt there really wasn't any need for a thorough search, so they quickly went through the farmhouse and then, without delay, boarded up the place.

"You talking about Zeke Osborne, Sheriff?"

"Never did find the creep. I wished we had then we could have closure. But even though he was never found, I'm one hundred percent sure he's dead somewhere out there in those woods. No one could have survived out in the woods that winter. It was the worst one we ever had," Roger said, shaking his head.

The room began to change in contrast as the shafts of light streaming in through the narrow spaces between the boarded windows suddenly disappeared as the approaching storm clouds arrived, blocking out the setting sunlight. A strong wind accompanied the storm, rattling the loose clapboards and aging windows, along with the nerves of the Sheriff and his deputy.

"There you guys are! I was hoping to find you up here and not down in the basement. It's spooky enough walking around alone up here," Deputy Phil Hardy had suddenly appeared out of nowhere, startling Roger and Wayne. With the outside wind knocking on the farmhouse and Phil Hardy's light stature, standing just under five-six and weighing under one hundred and fifty pounds, masked the sounds of his entrance.

"For Christ's sake, Phil, you scared the shit out of me," Wayne huffed.

"Sorry, Wayne, I didn't mean to. Hey, what's that stick for, battling ghost?"

"Not actually. I found it out behind the couch over there," he said, handing it to Phil for inspection.

Phil grunted his disinterest and handed it back without giving it a second look. To him, it was just a useless stick.

"Okay, I think we better continue searching the rest of the house before it gets too dark," Roger said, and then looked toward the front hallway, which he knew led to the second floor and the crawl space above that was considered an attic. "We'll need to search the whole upstairs and also down in the basement. I'm thinking we should probably split up so we can do a thorough search before it gets too dark."

Not wanting to be chosen to search the basement alone, Phil held a large flashlight up and flicked it on, shining a wide beam of light in his boss's direction. "Roger, I brought my Maglite with me, so maybe we don't have to split up."

"Good! Did Henry Wade tell you to bring it?"

"Nope, just thought it was needed. Henry just said you guys were in the house and then hopped in his truck and drove off."

Roger shook his head at Henry leaving, but it hadn't bothered him much, figuring the hounds were not needed. Let them rest up for a fresh start tomorrow if nothing breaks today.

"Roger has a flashlight, too," Wayne jokingly added. He was starting to feel somewhat relaxed knowing there were two experienced veterans at his side, but he didn't realize his two superiors were a little on edge standing in the old farmhouse that moaned with age and still smelled of death – although the smell was only their imagination. It was a smell that would always be associated with the room they were standing in.

"All right, we'll stick together," Roger said, sidestepping

his deputy's sarcastic remark. "What a bunch of pusses I've got working for me."

"Roger, if you want, you can give me your flashlight, and I'll go search upstairs. You guys can check out the basement. You'll probably need the large flashlight for that," Wayne reluctantly volunteered, not wanting to be labeled as such. For as long as he could remember, he wanted to work in law enforcement, hoping to eventually become sheriff.

"You going to search the attic too, Wayne? You never know what could be hiding up there. Who knows, maybe old Zeke's hiding up there?" Roger joked.

"I wasn't thinking about an attic. I didn't know this place had one. But sure, I'll check it out if there is one."

"They all do, but if I remember correctly, this one is rather small, like a crawl space, and you can't go walking around up there. Come on, follow me. We'll all start with the second floor. We can each take a room. From what I remember, there can't be more than three or four rooms up there anyhow. It shouldn't take long to do a thorough search."

Roger led the way to the front parlor and up the creaking stairway to a dark second floor, with Phil taking up the rear. The only light coming in was the dismal light being reflected from a small oval window in an alcove on the front side of the house. With the storm clouds now blocking the sun, the small ineffective window didn't give an adequate amount of light to see worth anything.

Before reaching the landing, Roger took out his penlight, but before turning it on, he quickly placed it back in its holding place on his gun belt and asked Phil Hardy to hand him his Maglite. Phil reached around Wayne with the flashlight and handed it to his boss with satisfaction.

"Here you go, Roger. Just replaced the batteries last week, should work fine."

Roger flashed the stream of light down the long narrow hallway. Along both walls, he could see several doors, all closed. He then remembered all the doors had been left open when he had last been on the second floor, and he hadn't remembered closing them when he left. *Maybe one of his deputies at the time had politely closed them. Not sure why he would have done it as it wasn't necessary... maybe out of respect for the dead. Or, most likely, someone had been inside since.* He thought.

Not giving the matter another thought that maybe someone had been in the farmhouse, Roger moved to the nearest door on his right and wiggled the round brass doorknob, gently pushing the door open to the master bedroom. It wasn't a large bedroom, as master bedrooms went, but large enough for the sparse furnishings it held. The two windows overlooking the driveway and the one looking out front had not been boarded over like they were on the first floor, so there was no immediate need for the use of the flashlight.

Roger handed the Maglite back to Phil without saying thanks. No need for pleasantries when on the job. Those could come later when the job was done.

From what he could see, framed wide in the doorway, the bedroom had minimal furnishings, much like the living room below them, only wanting for needed necessities, accommodating their living conditions. On the far left, Roger noticed a queen size bed neatly made with a handmade quilt covering the bed and two feathered pillows. On the right side of the room were two five-drawer oak bureaus, side-by-side. The only other piece of furniture in the room was an uncomfortable-looking wooden chair positioned between the bed and one of the windows. Probably used for reading, Roger thought.

As Roger took a couple of steps inside the threshold, allowing his deputies to enter behind him, he noticed a large green footlocker positioned directly behind the door that he hadn't remembered seeing before. *Had it been that long ago, and he had forgotten about the footlocker, or was it the first signs of Alzheimer's disease?*

While Roger stood over the footlocker, somewhat puzzled, Wayne walked over to one of the bureaus and picked up a framed black and white photo of a grim-faced young woman standing next to an equally enthusiastic stout older man. It was the only photo he had ever seen of the Osborne couple, and he wondered why such a young, somewhat pretty woman would want to be with an old farmer like Zeke. Surely, she could have done much better. Maybe she knew, and that was why she attempted to leave him, he thought.

Phil stood behind Roger and watched him study the footlocker. He had also been in the room during the investigation. "I don't recall seeing that," Phil said.

"Neither do I," Roger answered, then knelt next to the footlocker, his knees creaking like the floorboards beneath him as he opened the lid.

Roger was confident he wouldn't find the two missing children hiding in the footlocker. He was opening it out of curiosity. Inside, he found the heads of several toy wooden ponies. He picked up one of the toy heads and stared at it for a moment, wondering why they, he, hadn't noticed them before, or even the footlocker itself.

The footlocker had to have been here right along because the items inside had belonged to the Osborne children, he surmised. Then he remembered they hadn't found the missing pony heads, only the wooden poles the pony heads should have been mounted on. Someone had to have returned to the farmhouse, and there was only one person that came to mind. Zeke Osborne.

But that was ludicrous. Unless he somehow survived, snuck off before the storm ended, and found another place to live, maybe far away in another State.

"What've you got there, Roger?" Wayne asked, setting the photo back down.

Roger glanced over at this deputy and then looked back at the toy pony head he was holding, turning it slowly in his hands. "It's one of those toy pony heads, you know, those wooden ponies the kids hop around on."

"Oh yeah, no stick, though. Must have broken off," Wayne said, and then bent at the knees to retrieve one of the heads from inside the footlocker. He looked at it inquisitively, rubbing his finger over the piece of wood under the neck, feeling the rough edges. "Or, more likely, someone sawed it off. I wonder why?" He added, shaking his head.

"Yeah, I wonder?" Roger said with a slightly disturbed grin knowing the bastard who had done it.

"Wayne, finish searching this room. Phil, you come with me. Let's check the other rooms," Roger said, coming to a stand, and then led Phil out into the hallway. He now was not only looking for the missing kids but also other evidence Zeke Osborne was still alive and roaming the farmhouse. If this were true, he'd be the top candidate in the Whitney Gorman murder case. As of now, they had no one.

CHAPTER TWELVE

Saturday Before Sunset
May 12, 1989

Roger Lefebvre had his deputy, Phil Hardy, search the room further down the hall, and he chose the room directly across from where they stood. Besides looking to find any evidence that the missing children were hiding in there, he told Phil to look for anything unusual, anything that didn't belong there or anything that he hadn't remembered seeing during their last investigation.

When Roger entered the room, he was searching. He found four twin-size beds, two on each side of the large bedroom and four small bureaus stacked against the back wall with a closed closet door between. The beds looked professionally made up with their top sheets and sun-bleached tan blankets folded at the corners and the pillows fluffed. There were four boys in the Osborne family, and this was their bedroom. Their beds had been left turned down, ready for a good night's sleep, but Roger knew the beds had not been slept in for over twenty-two years, causing him to have a moment of sadness, knowing they would probably never be slept in again.

Roger continued his search, looking under each bed and inside the closet, a small narrow space with shirts and pants on hangers and other clothing neatly placed on the shelf above, slippers and other items on the floor. There was nothing out of the ordinary and nothing to indicate the missing children they were looking for, or anyone else, had been there.

Once he was satisfied, there was nothing noteworthy about the room. He walked back out into the hallway, closing the bedroom door with a loud thud. He then pushed the door back open again, leaving the room fully exposed. His two deputies were standing down the hall in front of the last door, inquisitively staring at their boss's odd actions.

"Nothing?" Wayne asked.

Roger shook his head as he walked toward them. As he did, Phil swung the door to the last room open and poked his head inside. "The bathroom. I don't see much in here, just the usual toilet and tub. There's also a washbasin but no cabinets beneath to search, only a couple of shelves with usual toiletries."

"What was in the other room?" Roger asked Phil, hoping for another clue about Zeke having been here.

Phil knew what his boss was asking him but could only give him a description of the room's contents, nothing of interest.

"Just another bedroom… two small beds, a bureau, and a few dolls, small closet. No kids and nothing unusual. They ain't up here, and I don't believe they ever were, and neither has anybody else been up here lately that I can gather."

"I don't know. Something seems strange to me. Maybe it's just my imagination. You said there were two beds in there?" Roger asked Phil.

"Yeah, two small beds, side-by-side."

"Must have been the girl's bedroom," Roger thought out loud. "But why two beds? The Osborne's only had the one daughter."

"Now that I think about it, I'm pretty sure one was a baby crib. I noticed the side railings were pushed down," Phil added.

"Oh yeah, that's right," Roger said, remembering, "they had that small kid. Must have shared the room with his sister. I guess I knew that but forgot."

"How many children were in the family?" Wayne asked. He had once known, hearing the stories, but had forgotten.

"Let's see, there was the one girl and five boys. She was

the oldest, I believe, and the youngest was the kid we found in the basement."

"Dead or alive?" Wayne asked.

"Yeah, we found him alive. Scared little shit, shivering to the bone. Probably been down there a day or two, at least, maybe three. It snowed for almost three days straight. No heat and below freezing outside, close to it inside."

"Where to now, Roger?" Phil asked, wanting to get the hell out of the creepy house and get some needed fresh air. Even if it were raining outside, he'd still prefer it to the atmosphere inside the house, the musty odor of death.

"We still have to search up there," Roger said, pointing at a small trapdoor in the ceiling.

"That's the attic?" Wayne asked his boss, knowing it had to be."

"That would be it, my friend, or more like a crawl space than an attic. You can't even walk around up there."

"Why even bother? The kids couldn't have climbed up there without a ladder?" Wayne said, wondering.

Roger also knew the kids couldn't have climbed up there on their own, but he was thinking of a more obvious one. He was thinking of the worst scenario, one that involved Zeke Osborne. "Wayne, wasn't there a chair in the bedroom back there?"

Wayne thought for a second, picturing the room. "Yeah, I believe there was. I'll go fetch it."

When he returned, Wayne placed the chair beneath the ceiling door and stepped up. He then wiggled the door and slid it open. Dust fluttered down his face. "Shit!" he muttered as he turned his head and brushed his hand over his face to clear away the dust particles. He then slowly stuck his head through the square opening and peered inside. It was too dark to see anything.

"Phil, can you hand me your Maglite?" Wayne said, holding his hand out.

Phil flicked the flashlight on and placed it in Wayne's outstretched hand. "Here you go, Rookie," he said, knowing full well Wayne was no longer a rookie, but rookies did the grunt work, and since he was the least experienced of the three, it was his rightful duty.

Wayne struggled to wiggle his arm up through the small opening, squeezing it past his shoulder. He then flashed the stream of light straight ahead toward the back wall. The roof pitched from the peak and gradually slanted toward the eves where spider webs clustered. He could almost feel the black buggers crawling over his skin. The floor of the attic was lined with two-by-fours spaced about six inches apart. Wayne sprayed the light around the attic and saw more spider webs, nothing else, not even a box or any of the other usual things found stored in attics.

"Not a thing up here, Roger, that I can see."

"You sure? You took a good look? Could be something behind you."

"Yup," Wayne said, poking his head out of the opening. "Nothing but spiders. Want to take a look?"

"Well, if nothing's up there, slide the door closed and jump on down. Put the chair back where you found it," Roger's tone of voice sounded angry and disappointed that nothing was found in the attic, but he was rather glad the children weren't up there. The reason for his disappointment was there was nothing of Zeke Osborne to prove of his reincarnated existence. But they still had one more place to search.

The entrance leading to the basement was a narrow door in the kitchen next to the Queen Atlantic stove. The stairway was also narrow and angled to the right, forcing one to duck as not to hit their head on the low, angling ceiling. The floor was made of dirt and muddied where the spring rains seeped in through the stone foundation. Heavy rains would flood the basement a good foot or more, so any stored items were placed on wood pallets or layers of brick. The back section of the basement was a foot higher with a six-inch plank at the base of the doorway and remained dry. This was where Zeke Osborne stored most of his unused household items.

Roger shined Phil's Maglite on the floor to watch his step.

He could see all sizes of footprints in the dirt floor, footprints from all the traffic that had been in and out of the basement. Even his own footprints, from the day he had ventured down there when the boy was found, the boy who was a young man by now, were still in the dirt. Roger hadn't seen the boy since he had been placed in an orphanage twenty-two years ago and had no idea what he had been up to since or even if he was still alive.

The trio milled around the main section, with Roger holding the Maglite he had swapped with Phil for his penlight. Phil did the best he could with the small penlight, shining the thin beam of light from side to side, all the while thinking how much more efficient his Maglite was compared to the dinky thing he was holding. Even though the Maglite was his, purchased with his own money, he was satisfied, having given it to the man in charge. Roger had a good eye for detail and wouldn't be content until every inch of the basement was searched.

The basement was long, the same length and width as the farmhouse, and separated into two rooms, the main room with the higher ceiling, which they were now standing in, and the room at the far end. The main room was cluttered with an assortment of household items and farm equipment parts piled on wooden benches like Roger had seen in the barn. There were also other objects tossed about the chaotic room that Roger could not make out what they were used for. In the corner, on top of a wooden workbench, were rusty piles of broken pieces of metal, and above the bench, they noticed an assortment of tools hanging by hooks on a plywood pegboard, same as in the barn, like the farmer had two workshops to choose from.

On the other side of the room stood an old black potbelly woodstove with a black five-inch pipe poking out of the back, which was awkwardly fitted into a brick chimney chute. Next to the stove was a stack of split wood, like in the kitchen, dried enough to burn like paper.

After searching the main room, finding nothing of significance, Roger flashed the beam of light toward the far end and angled the light through a doorway. He knew what lay beyond – at least, it was there the last time he had been down in the basement.

Slowly he led his deputies through the narrow doorway, stepping over a six-inch high board between the door framing. The floor in the room was at least a foot higher than the main room, causing Roger, and his deputies, to hunch their backs when they entered.

Roger shined the flashlight in the far corner and saw what he was looking for. It was a five-foot-high oblong wooden chest, which looked like a coffin standing on end. The only thing that differentiated it from a coffin was the latch with a bolt lock for keeping things hidden. It was definitely handmade, pine, Roger suspected.

Roger reached for the handle on the side of the chest and attempted to yank it open. The door was bolted shut.

"What the hell?" The Sheriff wondered aloud. "I'm sure we busted the lock. It should open."

Looking around with his flashlight, Roger noticed an iron rod leaning against the wall. It was the same tool he had used the last time he pried the latch open. He handed the flashlight to Wayne and then grabbed the iron rod and pried the latch open again. This time, because the pinewood had aged dramatically in the unfavorably damp conditions, it shattered into splinters.

Wayne flooded the chest with the spray of light, and all they could see was a crumpled-up blue blanket. Roger held his breath and quickly grabbed the blanket as though he expected to find someone or something hidden beneath it, but there was nothing to see.

For a moment, Roger thought he was reliving the day he found the Osborne boy hidden underneath the blue blanket. The fourteen-month-old boy huddled on the floor of the cabinet, sucking on his thumb. His dirty, teary-eyed face had long since dried, and the dark eyes had a look of shock. When Roger picked the frightened boy up in his arms, he noticed his one-piece pajamas were covered with dried blood and soiled by urine and brown, moist crap stains. He could also see large bloody hand imprints on the pajamas, as though someone with bloody hands had purposely picked the boy up and placed him in the chest.

"Is this where the Osborne kid was found, Roger?" Wayne asked.

"Yeah… right in there, curled up in that blanket and scared shitless."

"Whatever happened to him after that?"

"Not sure. He was placed in some orphanage over in Hancock. Never heard anything after that. Not even sure if the kid is still alive. He'd be about twenty-three or twenty-four if he were."

The two deputies stared at the Sheriff, wondering what to do next. It was well-passed daylight, and with the storm overhead sending sheets of rain across the countryside, an outside search would be futile. Plus, it had been a long day, and they were worn out, tired and ready to go home for the night.

"I guess that's it for today, boys. You guys go on home and get some rest," Roger said, as though reading their minds. "I'll take a ride over to the families and let them know we'll resume the search in the morning. Maybe have Doc Gallagher come along with me to give Mrs. Prescott a sedative, more for me than her."

CHAPTER THIRTEEN

Heaven's Institute
May 2011

I vividly remember propping my pillow on the windowsill on warm summer nights, watching car's headlights crest the distant hill, thinking (or wishing) they were airplanes in the dark night sky, wanting to be in that airplane taking me to some faraway place where candy grew on trees and fountains were filled with soda. Those are some of the sweet things I was never allowed to enjoy being raised by unaffectionate parents, who weren't my real parents, only substitute spouses thinking their unhappy marriage would benefit by adopting something they couldn't create themselves.

Hilary and John, as I referred to them if anyone cared to ask, are most likely gone now, having taken their last ride in the dark night sky to some faraway place. Just like Amanda Prescott and Kyle Bryant, who took a ride on their bicycles one sunny spring morning and ended by flying off to their own faraway place. I truly believe some night, my airplane will lift me off into the great unknown, but for now, I'm stuck here in this miserable place, sitting alone, staring out the window into the dark night, into the dark past when those two young children disappeared.

The agonizing search for Amanda Prescott and Kyle Bryant had gone on for a good solid week with just about everyone from Groveville and Denton volunteering, at least a day or two, to help in the search effort. But after finding no signs of their whereabouts, except the bicycles and fishing rods they found in the barn on day one, the search was sadly called off. Just before dusk on the following Saturday evening, eight days after the youngsters went missing, Sheriff Roger Lefebvre gathered everyone in front of the old farmhouse and, with a failed attempt to wipe his embarrassed expression off with his red bandana, regrettably told everyone to go home. The search was over.

I'm sure the Sheriff felt terrible about calling the search off and not finding the children, as did everyone else, except maybe the grieving parents, who wanted the search to go on until they were found. The parent's only concern was finding their child. The Sheriff had to face the facts. Already too many resources had been exhausted on the relentless search, and there were other issues to deal with, ones mounting on his desk and requiring immediate attention. From what I heard, he had tears in his eyes when he spoke and had a hard time looking into the parents' faces, especially Mrs. Prescott, who had to be restrained from ripping his teary eyes out.

They searched every square inch of woods surrounding the Osborne farm and beyond, along with the several murky ponds in the area, with no luck, including sending a scuba diver into the very pond Candi Bryant's eldest son, Jimmy, had told them was the pond Kyle must have been planning on fishing, the same pond Roger and his deputy hiked to on the day they went missing. The only significant item the diver found in the pond was a skull, a mucky human skull the authorities assumed belonged to the late Mrs. Osborne. Ellie Osborne's head had never been located after they found her nude body swinging by her feet from a beam in the barn back in January of 1967. The same sturdy beam Whitney Gorman was found hanging from seventeen years later.

As I quietly sit here in the gloom of this dreary room, I often wonder what could have possibly happened to Amanda and Kyle and why their bodies had never been found. It was inconceivable to me, and I suspect, as with many other people living in surrounding areas of Groveville, that those poor young souls could have simply vanished into thin air. One theory I came up with, if I think back, I believe it was Deputy Wayne Leon James who put the idea in my head, was that animals had dragged their bodies off and devoured all their remains – bones included. It was gruesome to consider such a horrible fate – their small tender bodies ripped apart, arms and legs torn from their torsos by hungry wild creatures, birds pecking out their eyeballs and flying off with stringy intestines to feed their young, springtime when the nests were full of clucking chicks. If Candi Bryant and Janelle Prescott had heard the same horrible theory as I had, I could only imagine how they must have felt. But I never did find out if Amanda and Kyle's mothers heard that theory or were told a more humane version. And I never saw the mothers again after that day out at the Osborne farm, the day their little loved ones had gone missing.

I heard from a reliable source, the guy I still owed a buck to and will never be paid, that Candi Bryant, Kyle's mother, moved in with a man she met at a tavern in the town of Hancock. From what Deluca told me, the man was a barber and part-time bartender, hence meeting him at a tavern. He was also several years younger than Mrs. Bryant. From what I remember about her, she was a hot ticket, so I can't really blame the guy, whoever he was, for shacking up with an older woman.

Deluca also had information on the whereabouts of Amanda's mother, Janelle Prescott. He told me a friend of his got a job working at a retirement home, and he was there the day they wheeled Mrs. Prescott in through the front door. Wheeled her right up to her room in a wheelchair, and he never saw her again. Locked her up in her room and probably tossed the key away, he had told Deluca, laughing. Deluca's friend wasn't sure why she was sent there, and he didn't get a chance to find out because he was soon let go for smoking pot on the premises.

What disappointed me most about the whole episode was that I wasn't physically involved in the search. Oh, I showed up on the first day but never ventured further than the driveway.

When Deputy James came into the pool hall that afternoon to ask us if we wanted to do a good deed for the town, I had at first said no, wanting to play pool instead and win my money back from Al Deluca. I also had been to Groveville earlier that same day, borrowing Luke's Dodge Charger to run an errand. So, I wasn't anxious about going back so soon, not after having driven out to the farmhouse. My reason for driving out there was to smoke a joint away from the prying eyes of the authorities. I knew I'd be alone – cops stayed away. But after Deputy James told us the good deed was helping to search for a couple of missing kids, I changed my mind and decided to help. The only thing, however, was I had first wanted to win my money back from Deluca and stuck around the pool hall a little bit too long, missing out on the search.

If I had put a little more effort into getting out to the Osborne farm when they first began the search, I might have been lucky enough to have found them, but unfortunately, I stayed at the pool hall and lost the two dollars and still owed him a buck. When I did eventually arrive at the Osborne farm, it was too late to help. The search was over for the day. That damn Deluca was a lot better pool player than I had given him credit for. If I had gone when Deputy James had first asked, I would have had the two bucks still neatly tucked away in my front pant pocket, which, back in 1989, was enough to buy a six-pack of Old Milwaukee, the inexpensive beer we referred to as 'Old Swill.'

When Sheriff Lefebvre reorganized the search team the following morning, my friends and I were not included. My thoughts were that when they went around town asking for volunteers, we probably were still snoozing away in our respected beds, mine in the basement of Peter Finch's parents' house, seeing I didn't have any place of my own to call home. Peter had his own room, the same bedroom he always had, having lived in the same house his whole life. Luke Townsend also lived with his parents and talked of moving out soon on his own or with me if I wanted, but since neither of us had a job, the prospect of us getting our own place was far in the future.

Later that same day, I ran into Deputy James driving through town, and he informed me they had no luck in finding the missing youngsters. I inquired why he hadn't asked us to help like he had the previous day and if he needed us the following morning. He offered no reply, only shook his head, and then just drove off in his cruiser toward the sheriff's office, and I moseyed over to the pool hall and met up with my buddies. It was another wasted day in my life.

If I'm remembering correctly, and I'm almost positive I am, it was about three months later, after the Sheriff called off the search, that the subject about the missing children and the Osborne farmhouse came up again. It was a late afternoon in August, and I was out behind the Denton pool hall, leaning relaxed against the smelly green dumpster smoking a joint with Luke and Peter. It was a habit we always did to keep our minds in a funky frame of mind. Peter happened to nonchalantly mention the time we went up to the Osborne farm looking for the missing kids, laughing as he rambled on about the mothers tearing at each other's throats. That was when Luke came up with the bright idea to break into the Osborne farmhouse. He said he had never been inside the farmhouse and wondered if there was anything worthwhile we could steal. Being stoned and having nothing else planned for the night, I also thought it was a good idea. Actually, at the time, I thought it was a fantastic idea.

In hindsight, it was maybe the worse decision I had ever made. I had made some bad decisions in my lifetime, but this one ended it and also ended my friends' lives too. But still, I can't really put all the blame solely on myself. It was a bad decision all three of us made.

After we agreed to take a ride up there, the next thing I knew, I found myself riding in the backseat of Luke's 1974 Dodge Charger, heading back to that creepy Osborne farmhouse. If I close my eyes now, I can picture the cloud of dust and bits of gravel the tires on the red Charger made as the powerful vehicle tore up the curvy, graveled Osborne Road. Luke was flying at a good clip, driving like he was racing on a road course with the best racecar drivers in the world. Rounding every corner and flying over the quick inclines made the ride feel like I was on a roller coaster and especially so being as stoned as I was. On one sharp curve, where the woods suddenly ended and the fields began, we caught the setting sun splashing laser-like rays of sunlight into the windshield. The bright light was so fierce I thought I was going to go blind if I looked at it for too long.

With surprising expertise, especially from someone who's stoned on pot, Luke corrected his steering by yanking the wheel hard to the right saving the Charger from sliding off the left side of the road and into a tree or one of the many boulders that laid partially exposed on the edges of the woods. I suspected Luke was feeling quite nervous at first but, after having accomplished his dramatic feat, most likely felt exuberant when the vehicle came to a skidding stop, idling alongside the old Osborne family cemetery.

After my excitement abated, I unintentionally glanced toward the cemetery and noticed the gravestones were casting long eerie shadows, which seemed to grow in length as though they were alive, a trick of the setting sun. That was eerily odd itself, the growing shadows, but when I glanced beyond the shadows, I noticed something else that spooked the hell out of me.

Looking through an old crumbling wooden fence, which I suspected was once sturdy and painted white to enclose the purity of their soles, and up beyond a knoll of golden-brown grass was the old, abandoned farmhouse we came to pilfer. The glaring sunlight that had pierced the windshield of Luke's Charger had now found its way through the leafless branches of the large hardwood trees that leaned menacingly around the farmhouse and caused fiery-orange reflections to bounce off the broken windowpanes on the front side of the house. To me, this spectacular sight gave the farmhouse its true identity, a monstrous power that looked like it rose from a place called Hell.

The only times I had seen the farmhouse were during the daytime, and even though it took on an ominous presence in the light of day, seeing it at sunset, the farmhouse was finally living up to its infamous appearance. When I stood at the end of the driveway, staring at the farmhouse the afternoon the two children went missing, I thought at the time the farmhouse looked sad and very lonely with a great deal of pain to endure or give. I wasn't quite sure which – I know I was feeling its pain. It was a pain like being alone in the world and locked away until it was time for you to go to the grave, buried without a casket, to be feasted upon by worms and crawling insects.

But, seeing it again, I then realized this monstrous farmhouse could not be compared to a decrepit human being. It was much too evil and soulless to be considered as such, and I was beginning to have second thoughts about going inside. And I wasn't the only one. I could tell my friend, Peter, was having the same weird feelings I was.

"You still want to go in there? It looks damn creepy to me," Peter asserted as he stared wide-eyed at the farmhouse.

"Yeah, Candy Ass, I didn't come all the fucking way out here for nothing." Luke pushed a friendly hand against Peter's shoulder.

"I'm not afraid, I was only thinking it's going to get dark soon, and we won't be able to see anything in there," Peter lamely explained.

"We have at least a half hour before it gets too dark. The sun hasn't even set yet."

"Yeah, I can see that," Peter said, staring out the windshield at the setting sun.

Luke reached inside his front shirt pocket and dug out his pack of cigarettes, then shock out another joint, smoothing it straight. After lighting the joint and taking a hard drag, he leaned over the front seat and passed it to me, holding the smoke deep inside his lungs for maximum effect.

"What about you, Mal," Luke asked, still holding his breath, and then before finishing his question, let the smoke drift out of his open mouth.

When the last of the smoke drifted away, he coughed once,

then looked me square in the eye. "You still want to go in, or are you going to be a Candy Ass, too, and back out?"

I hesitated before answering and took a hard hit myself. Knowing Luke's demeanor, especially when he was stoned, thinking himself superior to his friends, I wanted to answer him without getting him upset when I said 'no.' I could see in his eyes he was telling me not to chicken out, but that's what I wanted to do. I didn't want to go any farther. I wanted to leave. I wanted Luke to turn the vehicle around, get the hell out of there and go back to the pool hall. But I was intimidated by his glaring stare and mumbled, 'Yeah… I'm in.' Or something weak, like that.

Now that I think about it, sitting up here on the second floor of this miserable place I've been in for most of my adult life, I really wasn't scared at all. I believe I was more excited than scared. It was Peter Finch who was scared. I could see it in his eyes – he was frightened to death. Peter liked to play everything safe, and the only reason he got himself in trouble was that he let everyone bully him into doing illegal things. I think he felt if he didn't, we wouldn't let him hang around, which wasn't the case. It was just his pathetic way of thinking.

Before pulling the car up to the farmhouse, Luke stopped a few yards away from the driveway to get a better view of the place. He wanted to see what he was up against. The best way to get in. The front and side doors were partially boarded, but the barn door had been left open.

I remained quiet in the back seat staring at the farmhouse through a thin veil of smoke and the bug-spotted windshield. To myself, I was constantly changing my mind about going inside. I kept talking myself into it and out of it in split seconds. That's how fast my mind was working. I told myself it wasn't that bad. Except for the glow of the setting sun, a glow that shimmered over the tin roof and around the edges of the sagging building, the farmhouse seemed to be at rest, waiting for its final phase of existence, waiting for Mother Nature or human intervention to throw the final blow. Behind the neglected house, I noticed the tall leafless trees that seemed to be holding the farmhouse up with their long bony branches that crawled over the slanted, rust-covered, tin roof.

Then I thought about being inside the place when it got dark. It was not a place to go snooping around in the dark, and knowing dusk was about to fall upon us, darkness would arrive soon. I decided right then and there that I wasn't going in. Even if they still planned on going in themselves, I was going to remain behind, sitting in the comfort of the backseat.

"We'll go in through the barn." Luke nodded toward the open barn door with authority as though he was in charge. He then drove up the driveway and shut the motor off.

I shook my head. The guy didn't have a scared bone in his body, or so he seemed as his actions dictated. But you never really know about those types of guys, the guys that show no fear until they are face to face with the reality of danger. I was soon to find out what type he was.

"How do you know we can get in through the house that way?" Peter lamely asked, with a bit of uncertainty of wanting to go inside.

"Lefebvre and that pencil-neck deputy of his went in that way... remember? Besides, I don't see any other way in unless you want to bust the damn door down," he said, pointing at the side door that was boarded with wooden planks, which could have easily been pried off with a little effort.

"Oh yeah, I forgot about that. I was more interested in watching those old ladies going at it," Peter answered, thinking about Mrs. Prescott and Mrs. Bryant clawing at each other. That was something hard to forget. He had seen girl fights in high school, but two mothers going at it was the highlight of all fights he had witnessed firsthand.

Luke opened the driver's door and slid his tall, lanky body out. He stood with his hands firmly on his hips and stared at the barn. "This is going to be fun. Look at this place... wide open and waiting for us. There must be something worth taking, souvenirs from the Osborne massacre. Maybe find the bloody axe he used to chop their heads off."

I cringed at the thought of the axe. Who, in their right mind, would want such a keepsake? Besides, the axe Zeke Osborne used to chop his family up with most likely would have been taken as evidence. Just sitting there thinking about the horror the crazy man caused made me shiver.

I glanced up at Luke, seeing the smile on his face. It looked like an evil, sinister smile, probably a similar smile to the one the farmer wore when he chased down his family, chopping their heads off one by one. I looked beyond the smiling Luke, up on the second floor where I imagined the bedrooms to be, and imagined the kids hiding under their beds, thinking they'd be safe. Then, in the upstairs window I was looking at, I saw movement, like someone moving away from the window, not wanting to be seen, maybe watching us.

Seeing this gave me an instant chill, a vision of the farmer watching us, waiting for us to enter his domain. But then I thought that maybe I had imagined it, and what I thought I had seen was only a shadow of the sun setting behind the trees, a trick of the setting sun winking its goodnight, passing the baton to its counterpart.

"Come on, let's go, you guys. We don't have that much time before it gets too dark," Luke said, poking his head in through the window.

Peter did as he was ordered and slowly exited the vehicle. I could tell he was eyeing the place suspiciously as his head remained fixated on one spot – the open barn door. To me, the opening seemed to lead into a dark cave or a black hole where anyone entering would never escape.

When Peter finally pushed his small frame out of the car, he graciously left the passenger door open, expecting me to follow. He must have thought I had made up my mind and was going in with them. I, however, was still debating with myself on whether or not I was going to follow and bided my time in making my decision. I was content to stay where I was, sitting in the back seat and vegetating until they came back, which I figured wouldn't be very long considering the limited amount of daylight left before darkness swallowed it. Then something crawling inside my head was telling me I was going in even if I decided not to, knowing Luke's persuading powers. By the time I finally made up my mind, Luke and Peter were already halfway up the ramp leading into the barn.

Not hearing me behind them, Peter stopped and turned around to see what was keeping me. "Coming?"

"Yeah, I'm right behind you," I obligingly yelled, and then reluctantly urged myself out of the backseat and slowly followed. In hindsight, I wish I had remained behind. I wish I had a better glimpse of the shadow I had seen in the upstairs window.

CHAPTER FOURTEEN

Heaven's Institute
May 2011

By the time I reached the barn, my friends had already disappeared inside, not wanting to wait, figuring I was just behind them. I can see myself slowly walking up the wooden ramp and peeking inside, seeing only darkness and feeling the musty dampness of death hanging just inside the doorway. Even twenty years later, I can still smell the odor of death waiting to cling onto anyone who entered.

When I walked through the door, I found myself standing alone in the dark. It felt strange standing there, feeling the clinging dampness, feeling my skin tingle with goosebumps caused by a draft of cool air brushing across my bare arms. The air inside the barn was a complete contrast from the warm August humidity on the outside, and I wondered why the contrasting difference. It should have been hot and dusty, trapped from the heat of the day. That alone should have been a forewarning.

I paused a moment to get my bearings straight, to see which way my friends had gone, but it was dark inside the barn, coming in from the lighter outside. The only light illuminating the inside of the barn was the diminishing daylight coming in through the open barn door and the faint light filtering through a filmy two-pane window on the same side of the barn, which was hardly noticeable because of the bushes growing high on the outside. The limited amount of light made it impossible for me to even see the far wall to determine the barn's depth or even if my two friends were standing somewhere nearby. I stood still and held my breath, trying to hear their sounds, but all I heard was my own heartbeat pounding in my chest.

Once my eyes adjusted to the darkness, I looked around for my friends, but I couldn't see them or any movement at all. The barn felt deserted and eerie. I wondered if I should just walk back outside and wait for them to finish their inquisitive quest and join me out by the car. I didn't believe they'd be in there for too long because of the lack of light, and I knew they didn't have a flashlight.

Just as I started to walk out the barn door, I heard a noise coming from somewhere inside the farmhouse. The noise startled me. It was loud and sharp, like a frying pan hitting a solid object. The boys were horsing around, causing havoc – boys having fun.

Cautiously, I walked toward where I thought the noise had come from and found a narrow door partially open. Creaking the door open wide, I stepped through. The room I walked into was even darker than the barn, and I could hardly see anything, not even my hand in front of me, causing me to use both my hands to feel around like a blind person in an unfamiliar house, grabbing at air.

In the back of the narrow room, I noticed a thin band of light coming from another room. Eighteen short tantalizing steps later, I cautiously pushed the door open to a dimly lit kitchen. The only adequate light in the kitchen was the sunlight coming in through the narrow window above the sink, facing west where I could see the sun sinking below the tree line. Daylight was disappearing fast, and so was my courage. This wasn't a place to be exploring without a flashlight, but there I was, standing alone, feeling vulnerable to the unknown. A feeling you can only describe being there in person.

As I looked around, familiarizing myself with my surroundings, the most intriguing characteristic I noticed about the kitchen was the enormous spider web hanging from the cabinet by the sink. The diminishing sunlight was still strong enough to cause the web to sparkle like hundreds of tiny translucent spiders moving about the web. At first, it caused me to twinge, but the moment I realized they weren't spiders, and only reflections of light, I had to laugh at my weird imagination. But at the same time, I knew there could be hundreds or even thousands of spiders crawling, hidden throughout the house. Like most people, I hated spiders. I had rather the house be infested with rats. That's how much I despised spiders.

On the kitchen table, I noticed a coffee cup resting on a matching saucer with the remains of coffee still in the cup and a stirring spoon lying next to it. I lifted the cup and stuck my finger inside, feeling the cool liquid. I hadn't imagined the coffee to be warm, that would have been impossible, but I wondered why the coffee hadn't evaporated. The only explanation I could consider was that someone had been in the house recently and made the coffee. Maybe the shadow I saw in the upstairs window was not my imagination after all.

There was also a sugar bowl on the table next to the cup. When I picked the bowl up, I could see ants crawling inside, enjoying the sweet tasting sugar. It reminded me of the story I heard about Zeke Osborne, who lived in the farmhouse twenty-two years before. How he sat at that very table drinking a cup of coffee and contemplating going after his wife, who had left him and their six children only days before. That was the story I heard anyway. Of course, there was no way of telling if the story was true or not because there were no witnesses to confirm its accuracy.

As I continued to look around the kitchen, I noticed a coffeepot on the stove, conveniently sitting on the front burner. I lifted the coffeepot and shook the contents, hearing the liquid splash around. Standing there, holding the coffeepot, and seeing the coffee cup on the table, I was beginning to realize there was indeed someone else inside the house.

Thinking of this as a possibility, I started to feel nauseous and more nervous than I already was, standing in rapidly decreasing light, alone in the dreadful kitchen, even though I suddenly didn't feel I was alone. It felt like eyes were watching me, red-veined eyes hidden inside the walls. Then I imagined the eyes were above me, suspended from the ceiling, dangling on thin bloody fibrous tissues. It was a chilling feeling and was made worse when I felt a cold breeze blow across me like someone had opened a large freezer door but just as quickly shut, as the cold breeze hadn't lasted long. Like a ghost had moved through my body, a warning for me to leave.

I shook off the weird feeling of being watched as only my imagination and began to wonder where Luke and Peter had gone. If what I had suspected was true, that we weren't alone in the farmhouse, they too could be in trouble. Without realizing what I was doing, maybe more out of instinct than anything else, I grabbed an axe leaning against a stack of split wood next to the stove and started to walk toward the front of the house, assuring myself my friends had gone in there.

Before I did, however, I spotted an old icebox. I was curious as to what was inside and reached for the handle to pull it open. As I was just about to yank it open, I heard voices coming from a room down the hallway.

"Is that you guys?" I shouted loud enough for anyone in the next room to hear me, but I didn't get a response. If the noise I heard was coming from my friends, they should have heard me and answered, but they didn't. I was starting to get anxious thinking of the other possibility that whoever made the coffee had also made the noise I heard. I was about to turn and run out of the farmhouse, but my conscience of leaving my friends behind was greater than my fear, so I stayed.

There was also another possibility where my so-called friends were playing a game of hide-and-seek, and I was the seeker, trying to scare the shit out of me. It was Luke, I was sure, making Peter go along with his childish game of scaring the last guy in, which, unfortunately, was me. That was probably the most logical explanation.

Play all they want...I love head games. I assured myself

and slowly walked through the archway, brushing away nasty, clinging webs from my face. At the end of the narrow hallway, I found the door leading to another room was left ajar, and I could hear whispering voices coming from within. The voices were too low for me to recognize, but I was sure they had to be my friends' voices.

Before pushing the door open and walking into whatever game they planned to scare me with, I shook a cigarette out of the pack and grabbed for my book of matches, lighting the cigarette with a jerky inhale. I then took two more long drags off the cigarette and slowly pushed the door wide. The cool, musty room was almost in complete darkness. Night had finally fallen. It smelled and felt like the walk-in cooler at the Denton Butcher shop where they stored fresh meats. The owner of the shop, old man Harvey, let me go in there one hot afternoon to see how cool it was, but the smell of the dead cows hanging on hooks is what I'll always remember about the place. The smell caused me to gasp, and I almost puked on the man's sawdust floor.

I hit the cigarette hard and could see the red ash glow just enough to see a few objects blocking my way.

"Okay, I know you guys are in here. Come on out."

I paused a moment to wait them out. As I stood still, the room felt like it was getting cooler. I could feel the meat cooler door open again, and I shuttered with the image.

"You're not scaring me," I lied.

I pulled my matchbook out and lit another match, half expecting to see dead cows hanging on meat hooks or, worse, bloody dead people with their gross tongues hanging from open toothless mouths. But before I got a good look at my surroundings, the match went out. I quickly lit another one and saw ghostly sheets draped over a couple pieces of furniture. One piece, the larger of the two, I figured, was definitely a couch. Another piece, I believed by its shape, was a chair. As I moved the lit match around to get a view of the whole room, my eyes caught a glimpse of a rocking chair that was not covered by a sheet.

From where I stood, the chair seemed to be rocking on

its own. Seeing this somewhat startled me because I didn't see anyone near the chair.

"Okay, you guys, that was funny. Not sure how you managed it, but it had to have been something simple. You guys are not very creative."

It was dead quiet in the dark room, and I attempted to prick my ears for sounds, but there weren't any sounds to be heard. I couldn't even hear my friends breathing, or even my own breathing, for that matter. I walked over to the rocking chair expecting to find one of them hiding behind it or some sort of a string tied to it, but no one was behind it, and there was nothing tied to the chair to make it rock.

"Okay, where are you guys? Hiding behind the couch?" I assumed.

I lit another match and began to move toward the couch when suddenly, just like in the kitchen, I felt a cold breeze blow across my neck, cold fingers of death attempting to grip my neck, strangling me. But the grasp was too light, and the cold fingers floated by. I also felt slight waves of movement all around me. Then, in the corner of my eye, I caught a glimpse of what the rest of my eye didn't want to see. The rocking chair was rocking again and at a good clip.

As I slowly backed away, with my eyes circling the room and the axe held tight in my hand, the rocking chair slowed to a stop. I walked back over to the rocking chair to study it again, trying to figure out what caused it to rock. I knew it had to be at the hands of my friends, but for the life of me, I couldn't figure out how they were doing it.

"Come on, you guys. You can come out now. You had your little joke, and I have to say it was a good one... the jokes on me."

After my match fizzled out and fell harmlessly to the floor, I just stood in the darkness, trying to detect any kind of movement or sounds from my friends. It was spooky standing there in the darkness, but I knew they had to be hiding somewhere in the room. After a moment of not seeing or hearing anything, I lit another match and slowly walked around the room.

I looked inside the fireplace and behind the door I had purposely left open for a quick exit and saw nobody, nothing at all. I then peeked behind the couch just as the match burned out and thought I saw something. When I lit another match, whoever was there was gone.

Did I miss them when my match went out, and the cold breeze I felt was my friends moving past me and out of the room? Must have been! I thought, scratching my head.

I lit another match. You can see so much more when a match first gets lit. That's when I saw the piece of paper sitting on the rocking chair that I swore was not there before. The paper was old and brittle, looking like it would crumble when I picked it up. The ink also looked old and faded, but I was still able to read it using one match, which was a good thing since I only had two left in the book.

Somewhere along my path toward wickedness, I left the slimy trail of a snake. As my mind traveled through all those emotions that leave you vulnerable – anger, fear, loneliness, rage, and the most troubling one of all, revenge, the Devil took over. The Devil is in all of us, hiding in wait, and when your mind starts to corrode with those emotions, evil comes out of hiding and takes over your mind and your body. You are no longer the person you were, and there is nothing you can do about it. You have become the Devil, and fire is the only way to destroy me.

I had no idea what it meant, but when I noticed it was signed with the name 'Zeke Osborne,' the farmer who lived there twenty-two years ago and most likely died somewhere on the property, even though his body was never found, I suddenly knew what it meant and that he must have realized the terrible thing he had done to his wife and children were not in his control – the Devil had done the deadly deed, so he said, and the Devil was still in the farmhouse. Was that what I saw in the upstairs window?

Along with the spent match, I dropped the note to the floor, not wanting to touch it any longer, and wiped my hand on my pant leg. I then lit another match, and as soon as it fired up, I was suddenly startled when the floorboards behind me began to creak, like someone was sneaking up on me. I quickly turned around, swinging the match at eye level, to see who it was, but as I did, the match blew out. I then quickly fumbled to light another match, my last one, and beyond the bright glow of the light, at the edge of darkness where I presumed dropped straight to Hell, I saw something unimaginable moving slowly toward me.

What I saw seemed unreal, and I almost couldn't believe my eyes. What I saw looked like two toy wooden ponies. Wooden sticks with the head of a pony stuck on top. The kind of toy children played with. The heads were moving slowly toward me, bobbing up and down. Then, just as suddenly as they had appeared, they stopped moving, but only for a moment. They were so close I could see the hideous smile on their fake faces, two large buckteeth protruding from their mouths. I could hear laughter all around me, getting louder and louder. I thought I was going mad and wondered if the weed we smoked before coming inside the farmhouse was perhaps laced with a more powerful drug, causing hallucinations.

I was just about to turn and run out of the room, but before I had time to react, to make my move and run, the two ponies reared up again, almost touching the ceiling with their heads. When the pony heads came back down from the ceiling, I leaned back with the axe, and with both hands holding tight, I swung at the frightening heads as hard as I could, knocking one of the heads clean off and watching it disappear into the darkness.

The laughter continued. Or at least I thought it was laughter. It could have been screams that I mistook for laughter. Or it could have been both laughter and screams mixed together because I had never heard sounds as hideous as those.

I still held the axe in my hand, so I lifted it with both hands and swung wildly in the darkness like a madman in a fit of rage. I felt the axe hit something solid and stuck. I yanked the handle hard, pulling it free and swung again and again until I felt a sharp pain running down the side of my abdomen and another pain go right through my heart. The pain was almost unbearable, and I dropped the axe where I stood and clutched my chest to ease the pain. In the dark, I saw shadows on the floor crawling toward me and heard their haunting moans. The sounds, of what I thought, were coming from the living dead. I hysterically screamed and ran as fast as I could from the room.

CHAPTER FIFTEEN

Heaven's Institute
May 2011

There are events that happen in your lifetime you'll remember for the rest of your life, good or bad, every single little detail. Other insignificant things you forget by the next day. The details of what happened that night, which was more than twenty years ago, I will always remember, every stinking little detail. I relive the night over and over again, in my daily thoughts and in my dreams at night. I can still feel how frightened I was, the horror of what I witnessed. I can even vividly picture myself running out through the barn and down the driveway, fleeing for my life. I was so frightened out of my mind I didn't even remember if I saw Luke's car or not or if they had left without me. For all I knew, they were as frightened as I was and bolted, leaving me behind, thinking I was dead. But I knew that wasn't so. I knew they were still inside the farmhouse.

Thinking back, I probably should have stayed to help my friends out, but I had to get out of there, so I just kept on running. I only stopped running when I stumbled into a deep washed-out rut and found myself lying on the road next to the old cemetery. I could barely see the outline of the gravestones because the sun had already set into darkness. But when I glanced back toward the farmhouse to see if anyone was chasing after me, there was still a slight glow around the house, causing it to resemble a setting for a horror movie.

Needless to say, I quickly pulled myself up and started running again, and I didn't stop until I reached the end of the Osborne Road. Once there, I just stood bent at the waist, feeling nauseous and panting for air, wondering what had just happened.

At the time, I wasn't even sure if what I witnessed in the Osborne farmhouse really happened or if the whole episode was just my imagination. It was just too preposterous to believe what I had just witnessed really happened, but it couldn't have been my imagination because it felt so real. Everything that happened in that farmhouse was real, and I suddenly realized I was lucky to have escaped with my life, knowing if I hadn't picked up the axe, I would have died in that horrible place.

But according to Sheriff, it was the axe that had done me in. It was the axe that put me where I've been for the last twenty-two years. Here in this miserable place, they call Heaven's Institution. I call it...well, let's just say I don't call it Heaven. Anyway, if I had to do it all over again, besides not going there in the first place, I still would have picked up the axe. I'd still have swung it at what I had thought at the time were pony heads attacking me. And even though I was confused then and now know it was something else, someone else, not the pony heads at all but someone more sinister, I'd still swing the axe.

Yes, back then, in August of 1989, my mind was confused as to what had happened and, most importantly, what I was going to do next. I remember pacing back and forth on the pavement in the middle of the country road, trying to make reason, trying to calm down and get my senses straight. I couldn't feel the air around me or hear any noises other than my heavy breathing. It was like a dream, a nightmare, and I was hoping to wake up at any moment – wake up to a new day.

In hindsight, I know I probably should have stayed or at least gone back to look for Luke and Peter, but for some reason, I thought it was too late, and they were already dead. Whatever attacked me most likely had also attacked them. But if they weren't dead, and my assumptions were wrong, the best thing I could do for them was to get help.

I instinctively looked behind me, down the long pitch-black Osborne Road, hoping to see headlights from Luke's car or at least hear the tires crunching over the graveled road. There was nothing to see or hear. Only darkness and silence filled the weird night.

I stood quiet for a long while. I'm not sure how long I stood staring at the black night for time escaped me, but I imagine it seemed longer than it actually was, maybe a good ten or fifteen minutes. When I came out of my semi-trance, I glanced in both directions, contemplating which was the best direction to go for help. I needed to find a house or place of business, store or gas station, but I couldn't think straight. I couldn't get my mind to concentrate on my whereabouts. It was almost as though I had never been on that road before, a stranger in an unknown place. Then, almost suddenly, as if I were jolted awake, the familiarity of where I stood came back to me.

To my right, I saw only darkness. There were no streetlights to mark the country road, no moon in the clear moonless sky, just total darkness – a long stretch of darkness. I knew the town of Hancock was at the end of that darkness, but Hancock was at least ten miles away with nothing in between but farmhouses, distantly set apart from one another that I could recollect from the few times I had driven there.

Off in the distance, beyond an open field, I saw a faint light flickering against a black background like a faraway star. I figured the light I was seeing was a house light but hesitated in deciding whether or not to go knocking on their door for help. What country folks would open their door to a total stranger after dark in the middle of nowhere to use their telephone, especially a stranger who looked as deranged as I must have looked?

I passed on the idea of knocking on someone's door and having a shotgun pointed at my midsection and tried to remember what was down the road, the way we had come. Picturing the drive, I remembered seeing a variety store a mile or so away. Without hesitation, I quickly began to run in that direction, running as fast as I could and picking up speed when the road turned downhill. At the bottom of the hill, I ran out of energy and started to walk, clutching my sides.

While I was crossing the narrow Miller's Creek Bridge, I heard the whining noise of a compact vehicle coming toward me from behind. When the vehicle closed in on me, near where I was standing on the bridge, I noticed it was a dark colored Volkswagen Beatle, maybe dark-green or blue. I wasn't sure. Thinking the driver may not have noticed I was standing there, I moved closer to the guardrail so as not to get run over. With the day I was having, it would be just my bad luck to get run over.

As the vehicle passed, I tried to flag the driver's attention, but when he saw me, he gave the small Beatle the gas and motored off, disappearing around the next curve. I stood there on the bridge, disappointed he hadn't stopped and listened until the whining motor dissolved into the night. Maybe another vehicle would come by, I thought, but there would be no other vehicle to come to my rescue. The road was as desolate as my hope of having a happy ending.

As I continued to walk along the lonely road toward what I hoped to be an open store, my fears began to slowly dissolve into the quiet night like the whining motor had, and when I noticed a faint, yellowish light rising above the distant trees, knowing it had to be emitting from the variety store, I felt my fears had almost completely vanished. It was like slowly waking up from a terrible dream, and the light from the morning sun was bringing a new day. Whatever the dream was would dissolve and be forever forgotten.

By the time I rounded the last bend and finally seeing the brightly lit Groveville General Store sign, I had almost forgotten what my purpose for going there was. Along the way, I had been thinking of all sorts of things to keep me from going insane. I thought about waking that morning, seeing the sunshine spilling in through the bedroom window in the basement of Peter's parents' house, thinking it was going to be a wonderful day. I thought about Luke picking both Peter and I up, then driving around smoking weed, talking about what we were going to do.

Then, when the sight of the Volkswagen Beatle parked out front of the store with its motor still running, smoke puffing out of the narrow exhaust pipe, my thoughts of the morning vanished.

The car was green, like the color of lawn in spring, not yet summer when the grass turns yellowish-brown. I was sure it was the same vehicle that passed me on the bridge, the same vehicle that had not bothered to stop and motored off into the night.

Seeing the WV with the motor running, I suddenly had a great urge to steal it. Not in spite of the driver for not picking me up, but to drive away from all this and put the matter behind me, but I couldn't, for my loyalty to my friends was stronger than my selfish needs. I ran away from a lot of things in my lifetime because it was easier than taking responsibility for my actions. Even though I knew none of the night's events were any of my doings, I still felt I had the responsibility to act in accordance with what was right, and, at that moment, before walking into the store, I decided I was going to be a changed person.

Before entering the store, I rubbed my eyes and ran my fingers through my hair. It was a vain attempt to smooth away what I assumed was a frightened look, not wanting to appear like a lunatic. I then wiggled my shoulders to loosen up any muscle tension and walked into the store, trying to act like a regular customer.

When I entered the store, ringing the tinny sounding bell above the door, I noticed there were only two customers inside. One was a male with shoulder length dark hair and a red pimply complexion, which I assumed was the person behind the wheel of the Volkswagen. The other person was a pretty blonde female sporting a red bandana banded tightly around her head, two inches wide. She was short in stature, maybe five-two at best. She was also young looking, still in her teenage years.

The only other person in the store was an old, frail-looking man about ten years passed retirement age. His thinning gray hair was brushed straight back in a sad attempt to cover his baldness. The man also had small suspicious shifting gray eyes, most likely acquired from years of dealing with underage customers attempting to purchase alcohol. He stood defiantly behind the counter, reciting his position on the laws governing the sale of alcohol to minors.

"No ID, no beer. Plain and simple," the storekeeper told the male customer. He then placed his thin arms over the case of beer on the counter in front of him, pulling it close to his midsection. The webbed lines around his gray eyes, and the deep streaks down his pale cheeks and corners of his mouth, should have told the young man in front of the counter the store clerk meant business, but he persisted in his quest to purchase beer.

"I do have an ID, but I left it at home on my kitchen table. I meant to bring it, but you know how it is?"

"No, I don't know how it is. If you want to buy beer in this store, then you'll have to go home and get your ID. Then I'll be glad to sell you all the beer you want." The storekeeper waved the back of his hand in the young man's face like he was waving at a pesky mosquito.

The young man seemed unfazed by the rejection and continued to smile, trying to be friendly. "Look, all we want is that one case of beer. How about I give you an extra five bucks for your trouble?"

The storekeeper glanced in my direction, eyeing me as I slowly walked toward the counter. He then motioned to the young man with the palm of his hand to pause their conversation, which I took as meant for me, so I stopped dead in my tracks, a slight distance away.

"Yes, what is it?" the storekeeper skeptically asked me.

The odd expression he gave me looked like he thought I was going to rob the cash register or I was an uninvited customer invading his precious store. He surely didn't look like he was welcoming my business.

I looked over at the two teenagers who were quizzically staring at me with glossy, red-veined eyes, the all too familiar stoned eyes. I recalled seeing my own blurry eyes in the mirror after smoking a few joints with the boys, and I suppose after what

I had just been through, my eyes may have had a more telling look, and that's what the storekeeper saw in me.

"Well, what do you want?" the storekeeper repeated.

I mumbled I needed to use the telephone. I thought I was relaxed, but I must have been more traumatized than I realized.

"What was that young man?" he asked, frowning. The lines on his forehead seemed comical.

"Could I use your telephone?" I asked again, this time a little louder.

The storekeeper paused and looked at me for a moment. I figured he was wondering if I was going to be a paying customer and he'd let me use his telephone or if I only wanted to use his telephone free of charge.

"The phone is for emergency use only. What's your purpose?"

"This is an emergency," I told to the old man. "I think something terrible has happened to my friends."

Mentioning my friends suddenly flooded my mind with the horrifying events that occurred only minutes before, back at the Osborne farmhouse, and I started to get hysterical all over again. In a flash, my fears came rushing back to me like it was happening all over again. I could see the smiling bucktooth pony heads above me, coming down from the ceiling. My head was spinning. The inside of the store was spinning. I was spinning out of control and began hyperventilating. I placed my hands over my head and held tight. I held it so tight my face felt like it was ready to explode like a balloon.

"Son, you, all right? You're not going to die in here, are you?" The storekeeper asked, wondering if I had AIDS or some other terminal illness.

I started to shake my head that it wasn't me that needed help, but I must have needed help because I suddenly became extremely dizzy and collapsed to the floor in a heap. I could see myself going down, slowly falling to the floor in slow motion. As I lay there, I could see a pair of red sneakers plodding toward me. It was odd watching the sneakers clomp along the floor and then stop in front of my face.

The red sneakers belonged to the pretty blond with the red bandana. She bent and knelt beside me, placing a soft hand on my trembling shoulder. Her voice was soft with compassion. "Are you alright? You have blood splattered all over you. Your face is covered with blood, and your shirt is soaked in it. Were you in a car accident or something?"

I hadn't realized I was covered with blood. I thought it was perspiration from running away.

"Here," she said, taking off her red bandana and rubbing it gently over my face in an attempt to clean off the blood.

I looked up into her face and could see her concerned expression. Her large brown eyes were outlined in heavy black eyeliner, and her cheeks rosy colored with rouge matching her lipstick. She looked so sweet, so kind, and I just wanted to kiss her right there in front of her boyfriend, or whoever he was, who was hunched over us.

"Is he going to die?" He asked her, sounding hopeful.

"I don't think this is his blood. I don't see any cuts. What happened?" She asked me again.

"They're back there at the Osborne farm, and I think they're dead," I managed to spit out and then fell into total darkness.

CHAPTER SIXTEEN

Zeke Osborne
January 12, 1967

On an ugly and extremely cold day in the early afternoon of January 12, 1967, Zeke Osborne quietly sat at his kitchen table sipping on a cup of lukewarm coffee while staring vacuously out his farmhouse window. Outside the window, five of his six young children were playing in the yard, but Zeke didn't seem to notice them or even the blackening sky approaching the treetops bordering the western edge of the farm's fifty-five acres of plowed-over corn and alfalfa fields. He had something else occupying his mind that afternoon, his young wife Ellie, who had been gone for three days now, having left a note saying she wouldn't be coming back. Zeke was contemplating going into town to bring her home. Home to take care of their six children, the oldest being only five years old and the youngest a mere fourteen months old.

Zeke hadn't said much to his children as to why their mother suddenly disappeared without saying a word, it was not their concern, and they – the oldest ones who were old enough to realize something was wrong – knew not to ask. The youngest two, the two-year-old and the fourteen-month-old, however, cried often for their mother's warm comfort and got no sympathy from their father for their loss. The only thing Zeke did for his children after Ellie left was to feed them with food that tasted bland, mostly beans and cabbage. Some of the children sulked when the food was placed before them but sat up straight and began to eat when their distraught father lightly tapped the top of their heads with the palm of his hand and said 'eat' in a harsh tone.

After lunch, no breakfast was served. Zeke rushed the children outside into the cold winter weather, leaving the youngest to cry alone in his crib in an upstairs bedroom and return to the barn where he axed away on firewood or just plain hammered on anything solid to get his frustrations out. The physical activity, however, never worked, as he remained frustrated at his wayward wife throughout the day and into the night.

Even his children felt his frustrations and suffered drastically by being sent off to bed for the night right after an early supper. There would be no game playing in the living room by a warm fire and no bedtime stories to put them to sleep. They'd be kept awake listening to their father as he sat alone in the unlit living room shouting out cuss words not fit for the youngster's innocent ears. Zeke would stay awake in his discomfort until the sun rose and the children stirred.

For three days, this went on, the same ugly routine, until Zeke could not take the thought of his wife leaving him any longer. So, while sitting at the table on January 12, 1967, Zeke mentally sketched out his plan to retrieve his wife, which basically was to just go into town, find where his wife was staying, and drag her back to the farm by her neck if necessary. No wife of his was going to saddle him with a bunch of whining brats when he had farm chores to attend to.

* * *

It was a brutally cold overcast afternoon the day Ellie Osborne left her family and farm life behind, but not nearly as bad as it was going to get. Three days later, the day Zeke decided he could no longer endure living on the farm without her, large ominous snow clouds began to appear over the Osborne farm, which, unbeknownst to him, was the beginning of the biggest snowstorm to ever hit Northern New England. The snowstorm would last for two solid days and not stop until the town of Groveville was blanketed with three feet of heavy wet snow.

Ellie left a note on the kitchen table saying she was tired of not having any money for store bought food or even enough money to buy the children winter coats, ones not handed down several times over until there was no material left to stitch the holes. So, she was going into town to find a paying job and not to come looking for her.

What Ellie wrote in the note was true, she was tired of not having enough money for the necessities in life, especially for the children, but in all actuality, she was leaving her hateful husband for another man, a nice handsome man she met in the nearby town of Denton the week before while looking for a job as a waitress. But little did she know at the time, the nice man Ellie thought she was running to was just some sleazy character trying to pick up an easy prey who was naive enough to believe his colorful lies. Ellie fit the profile perfectly.

Ellie was the easy target Tim Simpson was looking for. She was desperate, having had enough of the farm life Zeke carved out for her and their six children. She was sick and tired of his griping about money problems because the crops were poor last year and the year before that, and every year she could remember living on the farm with Zeke. She was also tired of Zeke's raging fits every time she mentioned getting a job in town to help with their money problems. *'Who is going to watch the children and take care of their needs when you are off on some meaningless low paying job, even if you are smart enough to get one? Which you aren't! Surely, it's not me!'* He'd yell in her face, standing inches away. *'I have work to do. Your job is here…not there.'*

Ever since she left her father's farm at the age of sixteen to marry Zeke Osborne, Ellie dreamed of having friends to hang out with on Saturday nights, or any time of day for that matter. But that never happened. Zeke seemed to be just like her wicked father, do the chores and then do me. With Zeke, it was a newborn every year or less. Ellie bore and raised five boys and a girl in just over five years of marriage, and at twenty-two – even though she was still an attractive woman – she was looking a good thirty-two. She was starting to turn into what her mother had turned into, and she didn't want to settle on a life she hadn't dreamt about.

The first time Ellie met Tim Simpson was just a week earlier, the day she applied for a job at a roadhouse tavern called the Barn Tavern located at the edge of town in Denton. Ellie quickly accepted the waitress job the owner, Mary Orleans, offered, thinking she could always change her mind and remain at the farm with Zeke and their six young children if the situation at home changed dramatically in her favor. But after her introduction and persuasive conversation with the handsome bartender, Tim Simpson, who lightly held her hand in his and then softly kissed it, Ellie knew she was going to leave the farm for good, even if it meant not seeing her six young children again. That's how disgusted she was living with her hateful husband, Zeke Osborne, and how instantly attracted she felt to the man she had just met.

"Ellie, it will be a pleasure working with you," Tim Simpson complimented, giving back her hand.

"Well, thank you for the compliment," Ellie smiled. She was excited at the thought of having a job and finally meeting new people.

"Do you live here in town, Ellie?"

Ellie paused a moment before answering his inquiry. She didn't want to mention her difficulty with her life on the farm with Zeke, the man she detested who happened to be her husband, and also that she had six young children at home, which she was going to have to leave behind when her job started the following week.

"Presently, I'm staying in Groveville, but hopefully, I'll be moving here, to Denton, next week when I start work."

"That's a good idea, closer to work. Where are you moving to, Ellie?" Tim wanted to say her name often so as not to forget. Sometimes he had problems remembering names, mixing previous girlfriend's names with current ones, although he had no current girlfriend at the time.

"I don't have a place in mind at the present time. I'll have to look around for a room at a boardinghouse or rent a small apartment."

Tim immediately saw an opportunity and grasped at it with a sly smile. "Well, Ellie, if you're single, I have the apartment above here," he said, pointing at the ceiling to emphasize the closeness and make sure she understood the apartment was directly above the tavern. "If you want, you could always stay on my couch until you find a place. I'll promise to be a gentleman, Ellie, unless, of course, you're the promiscuous type."

Ellie hesitated at the offer before committing. She hadn't expected to get a job and a place to stay as easily as she had. When she came to town in search of a job, she didn't know what to expect, but she surely hadn't expected it to be this simple. The Barn Tavern was only the second place she attempted to apply for a job, having no luck landing a job at a grocery store.

"That's very considerate of you, Tim. If I don't find a place, I'll definitely take you up on the offer. Of course, that's if it's still available next week."

"I'll hold it open just for you, Ellie. I would be delighted to have someone as beautiful as you stay with me." Tim winked at the timid young woman, then opened his hands to her like he was holding an empty gift, and that's exactly what it was, empty. He was offering her a key to his apartment, but not to his heart, and he was taking hers.

Ellie thanked Tim for his kind offer in letting her stay at his apartment and then sweetly walked out the door, turned back and smiled at him before she closed the door behind her. She then drove back to the farm to relieve her eldest son from his duty of watching his younger brothers and sister and preparing supper for Zeke and their six young children.

Ellie was extremely proud of herself. She made the trip to Denton and accomplished what she set out to do without

Zeke being any the wiser, telling him she was going to visit her mother, who was ailing from a bad cold. Which was true, but the stop was an in-and-out visit lasting no longer than ten minutes. Still, she had to hold her breath for the whole next week, hoping he wouldn't catch onto her scheming plan. Ellie had feared she might unknowingly slip up somehow by talking in her sleep or something unintentional like that, and if she did, she was sure Zeke would beat her to near death. He had threatened her before when she mentioned leaving him, and by the raging expression on his round sweaty face, she knew the man she had never loved was serious.

So, on January 9, 1967, while Zeke was in the barn doing his winter chores, Ellie left the note on the kitchen table and told the children to stay in the house until their father came in because she was going into town to start a new life. The children probably thought that meant she'd be back later in the afternoon in time to get supper ready. After kissing them goodbye, Ellie put on her old gray winter coat and walked out the door for the last time, carrying a lone suitcase containing two pairs of plain-colored slacks, a couple of blouses and the multi-colored sweater she had finished knitting just before the cold weather arrived. The only other items she packed were a few unfashionable undergarments and several pairs of white ankle socks, plus her best dress, leaving her only other dress, the one she wore the day she got married, hanging in the closet. The one pair of shoes she owned were the ones she wore that day. There was nothing else she owned she cared to take with her.

Ellie then drove the family's old model Chevy wagon through the quaint little town of Groveville and headed straight toward Denton, ten miles away from her miserable life on the farm. Ellie quickly settled into her new life, moving into the apartment above the tavern with Tim Simpson and, with Tim's help, learning the ropes of her waitress job.

Tim was patient in teaching Ellie her responsibilities of being a waitress and even other things about the bar business that were nonessential to her work. Having worked at the Barn

Tavern for over seven years and in another tavern in another town for several years prior, Tim considered himself an expert on the subject and wanted Ellie to know he was not just a handsome man but also intelligent. Those, however, were the only things he told her about himself, except his brief fling with Mary Orleans, which he figured he'd might as well mention because Ellie would eventually find out from one of her co-workers or from Mary herself. Other things, like his womanizing and gambling debts and overindulging drinking binges, were never mentioned. He wanted to start a clean slate with her, and to do that meant not mentioning his past, which was not flattering, to say the least, and the least she knew of him, the better things would go his way.

But Tim hadn't known anything of Ellie's past either, and if he did, he may have known Ellie could have cared less about his prior womanizing or even his addictions to gambling and alcohol. Being infatuated with Tim, Ellie would have ignored his faults, thinking of them as an experience of life, something all men of his type explored, not one-dimensional men like Zeke.

Ellie only saw Tim's outward appearance and his persuasive comments. Like most women who were first introduced to Tim, Ellie considered him to be quite handsome, with neatly combed light brown hair cut above the ears and trimmed straight across the back of his neck and whose warm smile and blue eyes melted her heart. In reality, his outward appearance was a far contrast from his true self. Tim was a self-centered thirty-five-year-old who thought of himself as the town stud, having conquered half the available women who entered the Barn Tavern but had since worn-out his allure.

When Ellie came into the Barn Tavern the day she applied for the job, Tim immediately put the moves on her because he thought she was the last girl in town he hadn't gone out with. The fact was none of the other women were interested in being added to his reputation list. Most of the women on the list were either picked up at last call in an inebriated state of mind, having been given an extra measure of alcohol in their drinks, or caught on stressful times, the latter type Tim enjoyed the most and Ellie fit the profile perfectly.

Just like the other women he conquered, Ellie couldn't see through his outer skin and quickly felt at home in his cozy studio apartment. On the first day, Tim told her to make herself feel at home and rearrange anything to accomplish the feeling, including the furniture, if she liked. She touched nothing, liking the way things were.

The apartment was small, with one large open room. The kitchen was sectioned off to one side and separated from the living room and combined bedroom by a three-stool countertop, which was a small replica of the bar in the tavern. The bathroom was not much larger than a walk-in closet, just large enough for a shower stall, toilet and small washbasin with a mirrored cabinet above, and located behind a multicolored curtain in the hallway. Basically, the apartment was just the right size for one person or a young couple who were madly in love with one another.

The first couple of nights they stayed together were exciting for both Tim and Ellie. It was mainly because of the sex but also the newness of their love affair, a love affair that was a first for Ellie and one of many for Tim Simpson. The way Ellie felt about Tim was as though she had never been in love with anyone until she met him. She wanted to cling to him every second of the day, hold onto every word he uttered – the way his mouth moved as the soft words flowed through her ears and rang deep in her throbbing heart. She also wanted to memorize all his mannerisms so she could see him alive in her dreams and fantasize about their future life together. When Tim wasn't around for her to study him, Ellie's mind was constantly thinking about him. She thought about how much better looking he was than her husband, Zeke, and when she compared the lovemaking, she'd get a sick feeling thinking of the sex with the man she married out of contempt for her father.

Zeke Osborne would force his obese, farm-smelling body on top of her small frame and make grunting noises until he got off, which seemed to take longer and longer each time they had sex. To make the nightly jaunts feel even more grotesque than they were, Zeke seldom took a bath after his full day of tending to the farm animals and the other sweaty physical farm chores he performed, and the strong reeking odor from his sweaty body would linger on her until she immersed herself in the tub, scrubbing the smell away.

Tim, on the other hand, was the polar opposite of Zeke in their appearance and mannerisms and also in their affection toward women. Although Tim was a bit on the wild side, acting tough behind the bar and carelessly walking around Denton like he owned the town didn't matter. When it came to pleasing women, he'd display his passionate side, treating them like queens to get what he wanted, and he did even more so with the timid Ellie.

In their lovemaking, including foreplay which Ellie had never experienced, Tim showed Ellie different ways to perform the act, which drove her mad with more climaxes than she had in her entire sexual years. This was becoming a lifestyle she had never dreamed possible and a lifestyle she never wanted to end.

Ellie's shift at the Barn Tavern began at four o'clock in the afternoon when the after-work crowd began piling in and lasted until closing, which was close to two in the morning after the bar closed and cleanup finished. Tim's day ran from eleven in the morning until seven at night on weekdays, but his hours were much longer on weekends, staying until closing.

When Ellie's shift finished, she'd walk up the flight of stairs in the back of the building and gently awaken Tim with love and affection. In the morning, after being cuddled around him all night, Ellie wanted more of Tim's love before he left for his shift, which he gladly reciprocated. But Tim's affection for Ellie was rapidly deteriorating.

After three days of being in love, Tim was starting to feel a little claustrophobic and was having second thoughts about the arrangement with Ellie. On their last morning together, which was exactly three days after Ellie had driven away from Zeke and their children, Tim told her he was too tired for sex and hurriedly got out of bed to take a shower. After a meek breakfast of toast and coffee, Tim brushed a soft kiss across Ellie's cheek and rushed off to work arriving twenty minutes ahead of schedule, a first for him. Tim was going to tell Ellie later that night after her shift was over, and after a last round of sex, if he felt the urge, she'd have to find another place to stay. The apartment just wasn't large enough for two people.

* * *

Just after dark, on January 12, 1967, the snow began to fall on Southern Maine. By eleven o'clock that night, four inches had already fallen over the Osborne farm. Zeke Osborne was sitting on a rocking chair in the living room, staring out the window at the wet snowflakes as they plastered the window. He had no idea when the snow started and no idea how much snow had already fallen, for there was something else on his fragile mind. His mind was preoccupied with going after Ellie, and he didn't care how much snow had fallen or even how much snow was expected to fall. All he cared about was going after his wife and bringing her home to take care of him and 'Her' six children.

Zeke heard of Ellie's whereabouts from a neighbor he happened upon in Groveville that morning when he took an off chance and drove his old Ford truck to town to see if maybe Ellie happened to be staying there. The neighbor, Josh Miller, had gone to the Barn Tavern in Denton the previous night for a couple of beers and was surprised to see Zeke's wife, Ellie, waitressing. At first, he hadn't recognized Ellie, but when she came up to the bar, where Josh was sipping his beer, and started talking to the bartender, Josh immediately recognized her soft unmistakable voice.

One thing Josh Miller failed to mention, in fear of the grumpy man taking his frustrations out on him, was it seemed to him Ellie was rather friendly with the bartender in a flirtatious way. Josh was about to say hello to Ellie but thought otherwise when he caught a glimpse of the two touching hands. It may have been only a gesture of compassion, he thought at first, but when he heard part of their conversation about spending some time together after she got out of work that night, he realized it was a lot more than just a little compassion amongst co-workers. Before Ellie recognized him, Josh paid his tab and slid out the door.

Zeke thought about driving into Denton that very morning and dragging his wife home where she belonged, but not wanting to rush into anything without first planning and doing something he might regret later, he decided to drive back to the farm and think things through, which he did over a pot of lukewarm coffee.

After he finished drinking his second cup of lukewarm coffee, setting the empty cup in a saucer on the table, Zeke went outside and unconsciously grabbed the dull handsaw he had placed on the porch railing the day before with the intention of sharpening it on a whetstone inside the barn. He then headed straight for the barn, walking past the five children playing out in the driveway as though they didn't exist.

In the barn, Zeke stood quietly looking around, trying to come up with a plan on how to bring his wife home without causing a stir and keeping her from ever leaving the farm again. His mind was not functioning normally, and every plan he came up with was either too complicated or just didn't make sense. After standing in the same spot for about twenty minutes, Zeke looked down at the handsaw he was holding and wondered why he was holding it. After a long pause, he remembered he had planned to sharpen it the day before. He then walked over to the workbench and picked up the whetstone, and methodically began the slow process of sharpening each tooth on the saw blade.

From the workbench, Zeke could see his wife's children playing out on the driveway, hopping around on wooden ponies playing Cowboys and Indians, he supposed, but wasn't sure. His childhood had been much different being an only child with no siblings to play with, although life on a working farm wasn't much dissimilar, the only difference being Zeke did all the chores when he was growing up on this same farm where the children playing out on his driveway shared the chores, cleaning inside the house mostly, being too young for farm chores.

When Zeke finished honing the blade, he laid the handsaw down on the workbench and performed the same sharpening on both sides of a two-headed axe that was conveniently in his reach on the workbench. He then went outside and gathered the children to go inside for supper and early to bed. The children were hungry and eager to eat and hoped for a meal other than beans and cabbage, but their hopes vanished when supper was placed before them. After cleaning the food off their plates, none asked for seconds. The children were rushed off to bed, brushing their teeth and kneeling before their beds for nightly prayers. The prayers that night was for the return of their mother. Even Zeke looked toward the dark stormy sky and silently prayed for her return.

* * *

At about the same time, Zeke Osborne was honing away on the saw blade and axe while mentally sketching out his plan on how to retrieve his wife, Tim Simpson was trying to think of a gentle way of telling Ellie she had to move out of his apartment in the morning and needed to find her own place to live. Living together in his small studio apartment was just too confining for his lifestyle. The first two days were exciting for Tim, but the arrangement grew old very fast. Since he was accustomed to having his space for so many years, the thrill of sharing his precious space with a woman, even with the likes of an attractive young woman like Ellie, dissolved rapidly. Claustrophobia had started to creep in around him so fast that Tim felt he would explode if Ellie stayed one more night.

Tim had finished his shift at the Barn Tavern early on the night of January 12, 1967, even though it was a weekend night when he usually worked the bar until closing, but due to the lack of business because of the violent nor'easter blowing outside, Tim told Ellie they were closing at nine, per phone call from the owner, Mary Orleans. When nine o'clock came, Tim told the few remaining customers it was the last call, and by nine-thirty, he locked the front door and told Ellie he'd see her upstairs after she finished cleaning up the place.

About an hour later, after hurrying to finish with clearing and wiping down the tables and vacuuming the rug, Ellie locked the back door to the Barn Tavern and walked up the snow-covered stairs to the apartment. Ellie didn't need to use the key Tim gave her because Tim left the door unlocked like he usually did when he was in the apartment.

While Ellie was cleaning the downstairs tavern, Tim was trying to decide if he should tell her as soon as she came up or wait until morning that she would have to find another place to live. Ellie helped make his tough decision easier when she walked through the door. Her hair was snow-covered white, and her cheeks flushed red from the hurried cleaning and the cold howling wind. Seeing her then, seeing her innocent beauty, made the decision a lot easier than he had anticipated.

Tim was sitting on the couch watching the Friday Night fights on television and sipping a beer when Ellie walked in through the door.

"You look like a snow queen," Tim complimented, raising the beer can in a gesture of a toast.

Ellie brushed the snow off her head with her hand and then removed her worn gray winter coat, shaking the coat clear of snow before placing it on a hook by the door. She then removed her boots and sweetly walked over to Tim, sitting as close to him as possible without being considered connected.

"I missed you," Ellie said and kissed his warm moist mouth. She could taste the beer and thought to have one herself like she did every night after her shift was over. Ellie had never tasted a beer before, and at the urging of Tim on their first night together, Ellie tried it and was instantly won over, more so for the buzz than the taste. The taste, Tim told her, would come with time.

"It hasn't even been an hour," Tim said, pulling away.

"An hour seems forever being away from you, my handsome sweetie."

"It feels good to be missed. Hey, why don't you go get yourself a beer out of the fridge and get me one while you're at it?"

"Me, you're the bartender. You should be waiting on me," Ellie said, getting up and walking toward the kitchen.

"I only wait on people who give me tips."

"Oh, I'll give you a tip later when we're in bed," Ellie retorted with an affectionate smile as she grabbed two beers from the refrigerator.

"Why wait till then? How about right now?" Tim said, spreading his arms wide as an invitation to swallow him up, and Ellie did just that.

After Tim and Ellie enjoyed themselves on the couch and the eleven o'clock news was over, they moved their passionate lovemaking over to the bed, a mere ten paces from the couch. Tim wanted to make their last night together a memorable one for Ellie, one fantastic lovemaking night. Ellie would remember him forever as the best lover she ever had. In the morning, when they awoke, and after he showered to clean the night away, he'd gently explain to her that she'd have to find a place of her own.

There was always the YWCA over in Hancock where she could get a room if she couldn't find a place closer to her job, he thought to ease his conscience for suddenly changing his mind about her staying with him, kicking her out like she was a piece of trash. He knew she'd take the news hard, but she had to have known this day was coming. Maybe not as soon as it had, but eventually, the day would have come. Tim also told himself Ellie shouldn't place all the blame directly on him. After all, when he suggested she could stay at his place, he only said till she found a place of her own. How was he to know it would take her longer than three days to find a place?

After they finally wore themselves out from their passionate lovemaking, Tim rolled over on his side and closed his eyes to sleep. While his sleep crept in, he thought about the three days he shared with Ellie had been just the right amount of time to spend with someone before people started considering them as a couple, but he didn't get rid of her soon enough. The night brought more than just a violent snowstorm to his door.

* * *

Just about the time Tim rolled over on his side to sleep, Zeke Osborne found himself mindlessly plowing his truck slowly along the snow-covered roads on his way to the town of Denton. When he called and asked Mary Orleans if she had a woman by the name of Ellie Osborne working at her establishment, informing her with the false information that he was a longtime friend of Ellie's, Mary kindly said 'yes.' Unaware the man she was talking to was going insane, she also inappropriately mentioned Ellie was staying in the upstairs apartment till she found her own place.

Zeke left the farmhouse just after one o'clock in the morning to make the treacherous drive to Denton. By then, the storm had already hit with fierce winds and about eight inches of heavy wet blinding snow. Zeke's old green '54 Ford pickup was equipped with chains, wrapped around all four tires for extra traction to help navigate the difficult country roads during the tough Maine winter season, but even with the chains, Zeke quickly found out how unsafe the driving was and almost skidded off his own road into a tree.

A drive that usually takes about fifteen minutes to get to the town of Denton took Zeke over an hour. There were severe whiteouts, which made seeing the road almost impossible. Several times Zeke had to stop his truck in the middle of the road to make sure he was still driving on it. After putting the truck in the neutral position and applying the parking brakes, making sure it didn't roll on its own, he stepped out onto the snowy roadway to survey his surroundings, trying to gauge the direction of the road. He couldn't make out the contour of the ditches running alongside the road because the snow was too deep and it was also too dark, and that was what was worrying him. If he did drive off the road and into a ditch, he'd be stuck there until someone came along and pulled him out, and with the worsening storm, he doubted very much someone would come along. He could, however, see the tree line on both sides of the road for a short distance, roughly twenty yards at most, and then nothing but white falling snow against a dark backdrop.

So, every half-mile or so, Zeke would stop in the road and check his bearings. One hour later, after he left his 'wife's' children asleep back at the farmhouse at the end of Osborne Road, Zeke Osborne finally arrived at the Barn Tavern and parked his old green '54 Ford pickup truck in the snow-covered parking lot next to his own old model Chevy station wagon.

It was just after two o'clock Saturday morning when Zeke stepped out of his truck and peered through the falling snowflakes up at the apartment on the second floor of the Barn Tavern. The apartment was dark, no lights on from what he could tell, and he suspected his wife would be sound asleep alone in a warm, comfortable bed. He would go inside and force her to dress and leave with him to go back to the farm where she belonged to take care of him and 'her' six children that he had fathered.

Tim and Ellie finished making love for the last time around midnight, which wore them out, and they fell into a deep sleep. Ellie went to sleep dreaming of waking up with Tim in the morning and making love to him again like they had the first two mornings together. They skipped having sex on the third morning for reasons unknown to her. She thought, at the time, it may have been that Tim was running late opening the Barn Tavern and put no more thought into it.

Tim fell asleep thinking he'd be sleeping alone the next night or with a totally different woman, one he hadn't met yet. Little did he know the next person to step into his bedroom had no expectations of sharing his bed.

As they slept soundlessly in the semi-darkness – the only light illuminating the studio apartment was from a night light plugged into an outlet next to the kitchen sink – Zeke Osborne walked in through the unlocked door. Zeke was carrying his sharpened two-headed axe, which he planned to use if the door was locked.

With one vicious swoop, he cleanly separated Tim's head from his nude body when the stud sat up in a dream-like state, wondering whose cold hand had touched his face. The blood splattered everywhere, on the wall above the bed, on the white bed sheets and pillowcases, and on the oval multicolored rug on the floor next to the bed, but mostly the crimson blood covered Ellie's frightened face. She had been cuddled up warm against the man she loved when Zeke swung the fatal blow that awoken her. Ellie had no idea what was happening, thinking it was a nightmare.

After Zeke unemotionally watched Tim's head roll along the floor and come to rest against the couch, he grabbed his hysterical wife by the neck and dragged her nude from the bed and down the snow-covered stairs. He then roughly shoved her into the passenger side of his old green '54 Ford pickup truck and walked around to the other side, and calmly hopped in, driving his frightened wife home for the final step in completing his simple plan.

* * *

The snowstorm lasted for forty-eight hours, two entire days, dumping a total of three feet of heavy wet snow on the once-frozen, bare ground. It took another two days to clear the roads adequately enough to allow the traffic to flow once again. Ellie and Tim weren't even missed for those four days. Mary Orleans hadn't planned on re-opening the Barn Tavern until after the roads were properly cleared and the power restored, so if she wondered about the two of them at all, she may have thought they were holed up together in Tim's apartment waiting out the storm and enjoying what she once had herself.

The first clue something was wrong was when the Barn Tavern reopened on Tuesday morning, January 16, 1967, and Tim Simpson failed to show up for work. Mary Orleans called Tim repeatedly that morning to open the Barn Tavern, but when his phone went unanswered, she opened the tavern herself.

While she was turning on the grills for the anticipated hungry lunch crowd, Mary sent one of her other employees up the un-shoveled stairs to check on her bartender. When no one answered her repeated knocks on the door, and after seeing Tim's rusty old clunker in the parking lot next to Ellie's station wagon, the employee, Jennifer White, went back down the stairs to inform her boss.

Mary located her spare key to the apartment in a desk drawer in her office and attempted to use it to unlock the door, which she was not surprised to find unlocked, as he was accustomed to leaving it unlocked when he was inside. Once she pushed the door open, she was instantly hit by a horrendous skunky odor and wondered if a skunk had found its way into the apartment. Being considerate of other's personal property, Mary stomped her snowy feet on the rug inside the entryway and softly called out to Tim. When he didn't answer, she cautiously walked into the apartment, looking for any signs of an intruding skunk. It wasn't long before she realized the odor wasn't emitting from a skunk but coming from something much more shocking.

Mary Orleans locked her eyes on the bed and could see the bed sheets and pillowcases were covered in blood and what looked like a headless body lying on top. It took Mary a few seconds to understand what she was actually seeing. When she did, she clasped her hands on the top of her head and let out a dry horrible scream that was loud enough for Jennifer White to hear from downstairs in the Barn Tavern, even with the radio on a high volume.

Mary turned and ran out the door, stumbling down the snow-covered stairs in her quick descent. She immediately placed a call to the sheriff's office from the bar phone.

Sheriff Roger Lefebvre, along with his deputy, Phil Hardy, arrived ten minutes after the phone call. Roger had his deputy stand outside in the snow and cold at the foot of the stairs leading to the second-floor apartment while he went inside the Barn Tavern to have a brief conversation with Mary Orleans. He wanted to tell her not to tell anyone about what she had seen in Tim's apartment. He didn't want any rumors spreading around town before he could find out what had happened.

After getting Mary's chilling description of what she had seen and her assurance of silence, Roger Lefebvre led his deputy up the back stairs, stepping in the freshly made footprints. When they reached the top landing, both lawmen had their guns drawn in case the person, or persons, who had done the hideous crime was still inside – that is, if there was a crime. For all Roger knew, the whole thing could have been just some kind of sick prank, one he had no time for, considering all the other important issues he had on his plate relating to the storm's aftermath.

The door to Tim's apartment had been unintentionally left wide open when Mary Orleans hysterically ran out to call the sheriff's office, and it didn't take long for the blowing snow to fill the entryway, but the door being open didn't alleviate the odor any. As soon as Roger walked in, he knew he was going to find a deceased body, and most likely, the perpetrators had long fled the rank-smelling apartment.

The horrific scene was just as Mary Orleans described to Roger down in the Barn Tavern. Roger had never seen a headless corpse before, but when he spotted Tim Simpson's nude, headless body lying on the bed, he knew it was no prank. It was further confirmed when Deputy Hardy pointed out that Tim's head rolled up against the couch, a mere ten paces away.

Back downstairs in the Barn Tavern, Sheriff Roger Lefebvre politely questioned Mary Orleans as to what she thought had happened, who had a grudge against Simpson and wanted him dead. Mary had ideas, plenty of ex-girlfriends, but none she could think of who wanted him dead, at least not figuratively, and none who could have done that!

"Who was this woman staying with him?" Roger asked.

"Her name is Ellie Osborne. She started working here last Tuesday afternoon at four o'clock," Mary answered, wanting to be precise.

"And you said that's her vehicle parked out next to the deceased's vehicle?"

"He has a name, and you know him well, Sheriff," Mary said, indicating she knew that Sheriff Roger Lefebvre was a regular customer of the Barn Tavern as well as most of the deputies that worked for him.

Roger nodded his head in acknowledgement. "Yes, I knew him all too well. He was a good person to chat with. But I'm trying to be official here and find out who killed him, so please bear with me. Okay, Mary?"

Roger looked back down at the notes he had quickly scribbled in his notepad, trying to see where he'd left off. "Let's see, the Osborne woman's vehicle is still in the parking lot next to Tim's."

"That is correct."

"And you don't know anything else about the woman?"

"Only what I have already told you is that she's from Groveville. Other than that, I was only trying to help her out. She looked so sweet and innocent that I thought she'd be a perfect fit for the Barn. You don't suppose she had anything to do with Tim's murder, do you, Sheriff?"

"At this time, no. But from what you have been telling me, I think she may be in danger herself. She didn't happen to mention anything about being married or having a jealous boyfriend?"

"Nope, from what I gathered, she was a single woman. What are you going to do now, Sheriff?"

"Go to Groveville and find Tim Simpson's killer. And hopefully, find this Ellie Osborne alive," Roger said, then turned to leave. As he reached for the door, Mary remembered the phone conversation she had had the day of the snowstorm.

"Oh, wait a second, Sheriff, I just remembered something else. Some guy called asking about Ellie last week and said he was an old friend of hers and wanted to know where she was staying. I told him she was staying in the upstairs apartment and offered to give him her phone number, but he said it wasn't necessary, saying he wanted to surprise her. You don't think that guy could have had something to do with it?"

Roger paused and glanced up at the ceiling toward the apartment above. "Maybe, it's just possible. Thanks for your help. If you can think of anything else about the phone call, let me know. Call my office."

After calling in a backup deputy to wait for the coroner, who had to drive in from Hancock, Sheriff Roger Lefebvre and Deputy Phil Hardy drove to Groveville and quickly found out who Ellie Osborne was and where the family lived, which was only a couple of miles away. The woman at the store where they had obtained the information looked puzzled, wondering what the authorities would want from the likes of Ellie Osborne. Ellie hardly ever came to town, and when she did, she had her brood with her – six shy, good-natured children who gazed at the candy counter with watering eyes but hardly ever tasted the sweets.

"We're just checking up on her, that's all," the Sheriff informed the woman, and then thanked her for her cooperation and walked out the door.

It looked to them like they would have a quick answer to the whereabouts of Ellie Osborne, but when they reached the Osborne Road, Roger had to radio into the Denton town garage to get a plow truck out there as soon as possible.

After waiting for nearly twenty minutes for the plow truck to arrive from Denton and another thirty minutes for Norman Phillips, the town's longtime snowplow driver, to plow a single lane up the middle of the half-mile long road, Roger impatiently drove the cruiser a little too fast up the curvy road and almost skidded into a green '54 Ford pickup truck that was off in a ditch alongside a small family cemetery. Roger had his deputy check out the vehicle to make sure no one was inside, and after the deputy confirmed the truck was unoccupied, Roger continued to drive up toward the farmhouse.

From a distance, the farmhouse and surrounding landscape looked like a picture postcard to them. The farmhouse and attached barn, along with the surrounding fields, were covered in new snow as white as cotton and not a person or creature moving about.

The odd thing about the view, however picturesque, was it looked like no one was living there. The two chimneys sprouting from the roof of the house had no smoke coming from them. On a day as cold as this day, there should have been a cloud of smoke spilling out from them. It also didn't look like any shoveling had been done. The driveway alongside the house wasn't plowed either, although this may have been expected since the half-mile long road to the farm had not been plowed.

Roger parked the cruiser in the road at the end of the long driveway and looked up at the mound of snow the plow created when the driver plowed the road and then looked down at his foot-high boots. The snow was clearly higher than the roof of his cruiser, and he could only imagine the depth of the unplowed driveway on the other side. He had just been elected Sheriff of Madison County in the November election, and he was beginning to wish he had lost the election.

"Maybe you should have told Norman to plow the driveway while he was at it?" Phil Hardy jokingly asked.

"Remind me to have a talk with Norman when we get back to Denton."

"You could radio in to have him come back out here."

"Norman's probably halfway back to Denton by now, and knowing him, he'd take his time getting back here in spite because I beat his drinking buddy out of a job," Roger harrumphed.

Roger and Phil climbed out of the cruiser and reluctantly scaled to the top of the mount of snow at the foot of the driveway and then stood there for a moment to scan the farmhouse for any signs of life. There were no tracks leading to or from the house that they could see from their high perch. The farmhouse itself seemed to be uninhabited, almost as though the house had been left abandoned and the owners had flown south for the winter.

They climbed down the backside, sinking up to their crotches, and began the slow walk up the driveway through the waist-deep snow. As they got a closer look at the farmhouse, they noticed the Osborne children were staring out at them through the first-story windows. Ice carvings covered most of the windows, so they couldn't see the children's faces very clearly, but good enough to know they were the young Osborne children, the woman at the store in Groveville said belonged to Ellie Osborne.

The pair of lawmen trudged slowly through the snow and worked their way up the side porch, and then knocked on the door. No one answered. Roger then knocked harder, pounding the side of his gloved fist, and as he did, Phil peered in through the iced-covered kitchen window to see if anyone was coming to answer the door.

"See anyone, Phil?" Roger asked.

"Nope, I can't see much of anything through these windows. They're all iced up. Must have gotten cold in there for these windows to ice up like this."

"Can you see any movement at all?"

Phil placed his hands around his face to block the sun's glare for a better view. "Not really. I can barely make out anything through this window."

"What about those kids we saw in the other windows? Surely, they must have heard us knocking?" Roger said aloud, but more to himself.

"I'll take a walk back there and get one of those kids to let us in," Phil answered and then walked along the porch. He disappeared down the side steps and trudged through the snow to where they had seen the Osborne children staring out the windows.

As Phil Hardy slowly made his way toward the windows, he could see the youngster's faces were still there, staring back at him. As he neared, he smiled and waved to them, but the children didn't wave back or even show any indication they were aware of his presence, as their faces never changed expression. To Phil, they looked stone-faced, frozen like the ice cravings on the windows. When he reached the first window, Phil lightly tapped his finger on the ice-covered pane, but still, there was no reaction from the face he was looking at. The face just stared back at him with what the deputy would later describe as dead, lifeless eyes. He then stuck his face right up to the window and couldn't believe what he saw.

While his deputy was trying to get the Osborne children's attention, Roger jingled the door handle to see if the door was locked and wasn't surprised to find it opened, as most country people never locked their doors. Roger announced himself as he entered the cold farmhouse, but there was no reply.

The moment Roger walked in through the door, he felt

something was wrong, the house was too quiet, and the air in the kitchen felt colder than the temperature outside, which was below freezing even with the sun shining. It was as though no one was living there, but he knew better than to believe that he had seen for himself the Osborne children's tiny faces peering out through the windows. As he stood in the cold kitchen, rubbing his gloved hands to get the blood flowing, he noticed the stack of firewood piled next to the stove and wondered why they hadn't started a fire to warm the place. On the stove, he noticed a coffeepot and an axe lying next to it. Roger walked over to look at the axe noticing it had dried blood on both sides of the two-headed axe and on the handle.

"Sheriff?" Phil yelled as he entered the house, startling Roger. "You're not going to believe what I saw!"

Sheriff Roger Lefebvre thought of himself as a skeptic, but after seeing Tim Simpson's headless corpse and now the bloody axe, Roger was ready to believe anything, even ghosts, at this point.

"What is it, Phil?"

"I'm not sure exactly, I couldn't see through the windows very clearly with all that ice covering them, and they could have only been doll heads, but I don't think they were. If those were the Osborne kids, they looked pretty dead to me."

Roger looked down at the axe he was holding and then glanced over toward the doorway that led into the next room where the Osborne children supposedly were.

"I thought there was something wrong. Stay behind me, Phil," Roger said, setting down the axe and drawing his gun from his holster. Phil pulled his own gun out and followed Roger at a slow, determined pace toward the doorway.

Leading with his gun, Roger poked his head into the living room and looked around the room. Nothing was moving, not even his heartbeat. He then felt a cold chill, even colder than he already was, go right through him. Later he would say it felt like the cold breath of death ran right through him, and he was on his way out to see his maker.

Phil entered the room behind Roger and slowly turned his gaze toward the windows. What he believed he had seen from the outside, he now determined they were only doll heads stuck on wooden poles. From the window outside, he thought they were the frozen faces of the Osborne children, but from the backside, looking at them now, they looked like doll heads. One of the heads had long blond hair, and the other four had short light-brown hair.

"I guess they're only doll heads," Phil said, almost sounding disappointed.

Roger wasn't so sure; he was still thinking about Tim Simpson and the bloody axe he found in the kitchen. He walked over to the windows and turned one of the doll heads around. The eyes were lifeless, and the frightened mouth had a trickle of blood frozen to the chin. They were all the same, all five of them. Their severed heads had been stuck on the wooden poles that used to be the children's toy wooden ponies. The same wooden ponies they were playing with when Ellie Osborne left for good, or so she thought.

Back outside, Roger immediately went out to the cruiser, crawling over the high snowbank, and radioed into the office to get the State Police and an ambulance out to the Osborne farm.

"And, Helen, see if you can get a hold of Henry Wade to bring his bloodhounds out here. We're going to need them as well, I'm afraid. Oh," Roger paused, looking up the snow-filled driveway, "tell Norman we'll need him to come back out here ASAP to plow this damn driveway. Tell him I want him out here before the troopers get here. You got all that, Helen, I hope," Roger told Helen, who had only just been hired a couple of months previously.

Before long, the Osborne farm had more vehicles parked in front of the farmhouse than had even driven down the half-mile long Osborne Road. Four State Police vehicles were pulled up behind the Sheriff's cruiser, having arrived before the plow truck, and a Hancock ambulance along with the coroner's long black station wagon were parked in the plowed driveway.

The initial search of the farmhouse turned up nothing other than the children's heads and the bloody axe. The lawmen were now lingering around out in the driveway watching the two men from the ambulance crew carry out the children's heads, packed in black plastic bags, for the coroner, who was shaking his head as he exited the farmhouse.

The coroner walked over to where the Sheriff was standing and looked into his grim face. "Roger, I've been a coroner for over twenty-five years, and I have to say this is the worst case I've ever seen in my entire professional career. I've worked in big cities where murder is committed at least once a week, and nothing has even come close to this horrible crime. I think I'm going to retire after this one."

"You're too young to retire, but I don't blame you one bit, Mitch. This is the beginning of my career as sheriff, and if it's going to be like this, I think it's going to be a short one," Roger sympathized, patting the slender-built doctor on his narrow shoulder.

"I sure hope not. Look, Roger, I'm going to take the remains back to the lab in my vehicle so Mike and James can stay here with the ambulance for when you find the rest of the bodies," Doctor Mitchell Diehl said, nodding toward the two men placing the plastic bags in the back of the coroner's station wagon.

"I wonder what's keeping Henry with the dogs?" Roger said, looking down the road to see if he could spot Henry Wade's green truck.

"I'm sure he'll be along soon. Have someone call me when you find the bodies."

"Will do, Mitch," Roger answered, sounding a little frustrated. "But to tell you the truth, I hope we don't. How could anyone do something that hideous?"

Mitch nodded his head in agreement with how evil someone had to be to dismember a child's body and wondered if the children were alive when the person did it. He was also thinking about the autopsies he'd have to perform.

"Suppose Zeke Osborne was the one?" Mitch asked.

"Most likely, but we won't find out until we locate the parents. It doesn't look good for the mother."

Henry Wade arrived just as the coroner was pulling out of the driveway and waited for him to leave, then drove his truck up the driveway where the coroner had been parked. It then took Henry a moment to coax his lazy bloodhounds out of the warm truck.

"Old Lady Blue just getting too old, going to have to retire her soon, I reckon," Henry said to the group of lawmen as he pulled on the old dog's leash. "Rose, here, is right active, but she don't like working alone, so's I brung um both."

Roger looked down at the two dogs standing next to their owner with their heads hung close to the ground. "Fine with me, Henry. Let's start in the living room and see if they can pick up a scent. I found an old coat in there, which I believe belongs to one of the kids. Maybe the dogs can get a good scent and lead us to their bodies."

"We're looking for youngster's bodies?" Henry asked, not knowing what he had been called in for.

"That's right, Henry, we're looking for children's bodies, all five of them. And we're also looking for the culprit, or culprits, responsible."

Since Roger was in charge of the investigation, he glanced around at the available bodies standing around him to see which ones he would need to help with the search. He had Henry Wade to control the bloodhounds and thought he'd only need one or two others to help out, so he selected two of the troopers, the ones he knew best and had worked with before. He told the other two troopers and his deputy, Phil Hardy, to wait outside and ward off any curious intruders in case word had gotten around town about the horrific tragedy. The two ambulance crew members sat in the ambulance, keeping warm.

Once inside the farmhouse, the bloodhounds quickly picked up a scent from the coat Roger found on the floor near a rocking chair in the living room. The bloodhounds circled the entire living room, and after a quick tour of the hallway in the front of the house, they made a quick U-turn back to the kitchen and scratched at a door leading to the basement.

"I wonder where this leads to?" Henry Wade asked to no one in particular as he reached to open the door.

"The basement. I've already been down there before you arrived. Nothing of importance, and it's dark, no lights, the electricity hasn't been restored, so let me go first. And watch your step," Roger informed him.

"Not a problem, be my guest," Henry said, pulling at his bloodhound's leash to move them out of the way for the Sheriff to pass by.

With the snow piled higher than the small basement windows, the basement was almost in total darkness. Roger turned his flashlight on and directed the beam of light down the narrow stairwell and carefully descended the stairs with the two troopers, along with Henry Wade and his bloodhounds, close behind.

Roger sprayed the narrow beam of light around the basement, taking in the cluttered room he had previously seen.

"Henry, take the lead. I'll direct the light ahead of you."

"Why me?" Henry complained.

"You have the dogs."

The bloodhounds continued where they left off, sniffing at the frozen ground for a scent and immediately picked one up, pulling their master along with them into the darkness. Roger quickly shined the light toward the back of the basement and saw Henry disappear through the doorway.

The other section of the basement was much lower, and the men had to crouch once they crossed the threshold. Roger shined the light on the bloodhounds that were anxiously jumping up and down in front of a five-foot-high oblong wooden cabinet in the back of the room. It looked like a casket standing on end. The cabinet door was held closed by a padlock, and Roger wondered what could possibly be hidden in the locked cabinet that agitated the dogs. His first thought was the children's bodies were stuffed inside, but he decided the cabinet was too small for all five, maybe large enough for two but not all five.

Roger shined the light around the room, looking for something to use as a pry bar and saw a narrow iron pole leaning up against the wall. It was just the kind of tool he needed to pry the door open.

"Stand back while I pry this thing open," Roger anxiously told them.

"What do you think is inside?" One of the troopers asked, thinking the same horrible thought.

"Don't know what we'll find, but whatever it is can't be too good," Roger answered.

Roger placed the narrow pry bar behind the door hinge and slowly pried the door open. Inside, he found only a light-blue blanket crumpled on the floor of the cabinet. It was under the blanket where they found the fourteen-month-old boy. They previously thought there were only five children, not six.

The little boy was curled up in a tight ball, sucking on his thumb. His face was muddied with dirty dry tears and splatters of blood, and his eyes were scared with fright.

After finding the youngest Osborne child alive, they continued the search through the rest of the house and then moved on to the barn, where they found Ellie Osborne's nude, headless body swinging from a beam by her feet. They never did find her husband, Zeke Osborne, the father of her six children.

"What about the other bodies, the Osborne kids? Think we'll ever find them, Roger?" Deputy Phil Hardy asked his boss.

Roger paused for a moment and tried to picture the children's headless bodies being found by some innocent person out for a nature walk. At first, wondering what they had come across and the horror on their faces when they realized what they had found.

"Don't know. Zeke Osborne could have taken the bodies deep into the woods sometime during the snowstorm, and his tracks were covered over. If he did, I hope to hell he perished out there, and it was a slow, agonizing death. The monster deserved it," Sheriff Roger Lefebvre, the rookie sheriff, said and then added. "Who knows, some hunter will probably find his remains someday."

CHAPTER SEVENTEEN

Saturday Evening
August 11, 1989

Beyond the beam of headlights that bounced over the uneven country road, Deputy Wayne Leon James could see the light rising above the trees as he gave the gas pedal a little more foot. It was a dim yellowish light and could have come from any open establishment, but from driving these country roads for the past five years at night, Wayne knew there was only one place the light could have been coming from, and that was the Groveville General Store on the old County Road, two miles from Groveville's most infamous landmark, the so-called haunted Osborne farmhouse.

The only information Wayne was told by Helen was that there was a hysterical young man curled up on the floor of the Groveville General Store, shouting something about the Osborne farm and that they were all dead. Helen also mentioned the storekeeper seemed concerned about the young man's health but, nevertheless, wanted him removed immediately from his store because he was scaring all the customers away.

Since Wayne was the nearest to the location, he got the emergency call and slowly turned his cruiser around. He then curiously headed toward Groveville doing the speed limit, wondering what he was going to encounter. At first, Wayne figured it was probably only some drug-induced teenager hallucinating about the old Osborne murder stories, about the farmhouse being haunted by the crazy farmer caring a bloody axe, so Wayne felt it didn't warrant flipping on the emergency lights. Now, as he neared Groveville, a mere ten-minute drive from the sheriff's office in Denton, where he had been having an uneventful shift cruising the downtown area, he started wondering about other possibilities.

The most logical one, he figured, was maybe the young man was having some kind of a seizure and needed medical attention. Wayne was somewhat familiar with epileptic seizures, having dealt with them in the past where the person having a convulsion attack would blackout for a few minutes and then slowly regain consciousness.

Another possibility being maybe the young man had actually been out to the Osborne place since it was in proximity to the store, and maybe, just maybe, the young man happened across the missing bodies of Kyle Bryant and Amanda Prescott. Thinking this a possibility, although a remote one since the area had been thoroughly searched, Wayne flipped on the emergency lights and stepped on the gas pedal.

Wayne pulled his cruiser to a stop next to a green Volkswagen Beatle, thinking the owner of the compact vehicle was most likely the person causing the disturbance since there were no other vehicles in the parking lot. After getting out and adjusting his gun belt to a comfortable position, higher on his slim hips, Wayne entered the store fully alert for the unexpected. Once inside, Wayne looked around the store, familiarizing himself with his surroundings by taking in the entire space with one quick glance. He expected to see some kind of commotion, but instead, the store had a different atmosphere, as though it was closed for the evening and nobody was there. Wayne immediately knew this was not the case once he noticed there were two people inside.

The person on his left, leaning against a long glass top ice cream freezer, seemed nervous but not hysterically out of control, so he ruled him out as the person of interest. The only other person he saw was an aged, thin-faced man behind the counter who was pointing his bony finger toward a tall rack of potato chips.

"Over here, Sheriff, on the floor," The storekeeper said, and then came around from the other side of the counter to lead the way.

Wayne walked past the young man leaning on the freezer, keeping an eye on him as he did to make sure there was no funny business going on. He could see his glossy, red-veined eyes and nervousness of being watched. It was an all too familiar sight in teenagers, the deputy had come to realize with his years patrolling at night, as being stoned from smoking pot.

"Not a sheriff yet," he told the storekeeper and smirked at the man's combed-over hair, trying to cover the balding areas.

On the floor in the potato chip aisle, Wayne found a young woman kneeling on her haunches next to a man with his head resting on her hand. She was also gently rubbing a red bandana across his face and forehead. A caring attempt to soothe whatever pain was ailing him, Wayne thought.

"What's wrong with him, Miss?" the deputy asked the young woman, thinking she had all the answers since she was evidently with him. "Did he have an epileptic seizure or something?"

"I don't have the remotest idea what's wrong with him."

"Why's he laying on the floor? Looks like he's been in some kind of a fight. Did you have anything to do with it?" Wayne asked the guy leaning against the ice cream freezer, who paused a moment to register the question and then just shook his head no.

"Okay, I got an emergency call that some guy's throwing a fit in the store. Now, when I get here, no one seems to know anything. So, let's start from the beginning. How about you tell me what's going on, young lady," Wayne said, turning his attention back to the woman who was still tending to Malcolm.

"I don't know. All I know is this guy came in here freaking out saying something about the Osborne farm and that his friends are dead," She sympathetically said, looking at the bloodied man next to her.

Wayne looked confused, then asked. "What's going on here? Aren't you with him?"

"No," she firmly answered, finally looking up at the deputy, "I don't even know this guy. Like I said, he just came in here, all covered with blood. I was just trying to help calm him down until you got here. All I know is the guy was freaking out when he came in here and then collapsed on the floor."

The young woman gently set Malcolm's head on the floor and then stood up. "He's all yours now. Come on, Mole, let's go before he arrests us for murder or something," she said, grabbing her boyfriend, Alfred Molino, by the arm to lead him out of the store.

"What about the beer, Kerri? We can't leave without getting the beer. There's not another store around here for miles," Mole anxiously said, not thinking about the deputy standing next to him.

"Shhhh, let's go," Kerri whispered.

"Wait, no one's leaving yet. I may need you for questioning," Wayne said, and then knelt beside the young man on the floor. Even though the man's eyes were closed and his face covered with splotches of dried blood, Wayne instantly knew who the person was. He was very familiar with the young man, having seen him almost daily, roaming the streets of Denton with his pals, looking for something to do, which basically ended up getting into trouble.

Malcolm Ridge was the last person Wayne had expected to be the person Helen had described to him over the radio. *The young man is hysterical and curled up on the floor, screaming about dead people out at the Osborne place.* She told him through the police radio's speaker. From her description, he expected to see some freaked-out teenager like the one leaning against the ice cream freezer, not the coolheaded Malcolm Ridge, who didn't have a care in the world. Now here he was, lying in a fetal position on the floor of the Groveville General Store with blood covering his face and on his ragged clothing.

"Ridge, what the hell happened to you?" Wayne asked, trying to lift him into a sitting position.

Malcolm Ridge awkwardly tried to sit up, using his hands for support, and looked dazedly up at the deputy. When he recognized him as a person of authority, seeing the uniform and the badge on his chest, Malcolm suddenly became hysterical and started to push the deputy away from him, shouting. "Sheriff, you need to go up to the Osborne farm right away. They're in trouble. You need to go, now."

"Ridge, Ridge, calm down. I'm not the Sheriff. I'm the deputy," Wayne said, grabbing Malcolm's arms to settle him down. "Who's in trouble, and what the hell happened?"

Malcolm blinked his eyes a couple of times to clear his vision. After Wayne relaxed his grip, Malcolm then pulled his arms free and rubbed his eyes with his bloodied hands. Slowly, he began to recognize the man in front of him as the deputy he had been acquainted with in Denton but couldn't remember his name.

"Hey buddy, you alright? Do you need me to radio in for an ambulance?" Wayne asked with a sense of concern.

"He's been like that since I called you, in and out of consciousness," the storekeeper informed the deputy.

Wayne looked up at the storekeeper and then down at Malcolm Ridge. He looked bad physically, in need of medical attention, and emotionally frightened. There was only one thing to do for him, and that was to get him help.

"I'm going out to my vehicle and radio in for an ambulance. Keep an eye on him," Wayne said with authority to no one in particular.

"Wait…." Malcolm said, reaching out, "you need to send someone out to the Osborne farm. Luke and Peter are in trouble and maybe hurt really bad, or possibly even dead."

"That's what he's been saying all along," Kerri confirmed. She then looked at the balled-up bandana in her hand and slipped it into her back pocket for a remembrance, in case there really were dead people involved in the weird night's events. Kerri and her boyfriend, Mole, were looking for something exciting to do besides smoking pot, which was easier to obtain than buying beer. This was beyond her expectations of an exciting night, and it had only just begun.

Wayne looked back at Malcolm. He was concerned that what he was saying to him had some truth behind it, and seeing the young man's bloodied condition knew it had to be true, and something terrible happened out at the Osborne farm.

"Peter Finch? He's out at the Osborne farm."

Malcolm nodded.

"You serious? What happened?"

"Yes, there was this guy in the farmhouse who attacked me. I had an axe in my hand, and I swung it at him. I was lucky to get out of there alive."

"What about Peter, is he still out there?"

"I think so, Peter and Luke. I think it was them I saw lying on the floor in the living room, but I'm not sure. Everything happened so fast. It was just a blur. The crazy guy was huge and ugly. He came at me with something in his hand like a big stick with a horse head on the end of it."

"I think this guy's crazy if you ask me?" the storekeeper said, nodding in Malcolm's direction. "A stick with a horse head. More like horse shit to me."

"Okay, I want everyone to stay right here. I'm going outside to radio this into the Sheriff," Wayne said, then added on his way out the door. "I'll only be a minute."

* * *

Deputy Wayne Leon James leaned inside his cruiser and grabbed the microphone to radio into the sheriff's office, hoping the Sheriff would still be there or at least listening on his car radio, but he wasn't. He then told Helen to call Roger on the phone ASAP and to have him radio back…it was urgent if he asked.

"Sure, Wayne, but what do you want me to tell the Sheriff? I just can't tell him it's urgent. I don't think he's going to like being disturbed, it's his wife's birthday, and he said he was planning on drinking Champagne to celebrate. Over."

"Hope he isn't too drunk; I think we may have a problem up at the Osborne farmhouse. I have that Malcolm Ridge kid out here. He is pretty shaken up and covered in blood from head to toe. He told me he was up to the old farmhouse with Peter Finch and that other friend of theirs, Luke what's-his-name, and that some deranged man with some kind of weapon attacked them. And by the looks of the Ridge kid, I have to believe him. Over."

"Isn't Peter Finch related to you? Over."

"You are correct. He's my aunt Gloria's kid. Over."

"I'm calling Roger now. Over."

"Thanks, Helen, I'll be waiting by the radio. Over." Wayne clicked off, then anxiously sat in the passenger seat with the door open and waited for the Sheriff to radio him back.

It wasn't long before the radio crackled to life with Sheriff Roger Lefebvre's husky voice, briefly startling Wayne.

"Wayne, it's Roger. You there? Over."

"Yeah, Roger, I'm here. I'm at the Groveville General Store, and it looks like we have a situation up at the Osborne place again. I'm going to need to head out there to take a look. Over."

"Not so fast, Wayne. Why don't you tell me what's going on first? Over."

Wayne gave his boss a general overview of the situation at the store – Malcolm Ridge's mental condition and his bloodied clothing, and what he said about the crazy man who attacked him and his friends up at the Osborne farm.

"This is what I want you to do, Wayne," Roger calmly told him after pausing a moment to give the matter a thought. "First, I want you to get the names and addresses of the witnesses in the store. Then I want you to drive the Ridge kid to the emergency ward at the hospital in Hancock and have a doctor examine him to see if he has any physical issues.

"Since Fred Dairy is out of town on vacation, I'll have to call Phil Hardy and see if he's available to take a ride over to the Osborne farm with me. If Phil's not available, I'll get Ben Alden to drive over. I can't believe he's too far away, covering the Dixfield area tonight, if I remember. I'll let you know what we find. Over."

"I'm right down the street from the Osborne place. I can get there a lot faster. Over."

"No, I think you'd better get that Ridge kid to the hospital first. You can come out after. Over."

"I can radio in for Helen to get an ambulance out here to take the Ridge kid to the hospital. Over."

"Look, Wayne, I understand Peter Finch is your cousin, and you're concerned, but Phil and I will handle it. I'd rather have you take the Ridge kid to the hospital. I'll see you when you get out to the Osborne place. Over."

"Roger that. Over," Wayne dejectedly ended and then clicked off the mike.

* * *

"That damn Osborne place. The place should be burned to the ground," Roger Lefebvre angrily said aloud after clicking off the mike. Roger then called his part-time deputy, Phil Hardy, telling him to be ready in ten minutes. He then grabbed his gun belt and kissed his wife goodnight, leaving her frowning at the kitchen table in front of a half-empty bottle of Champagne and a thick slice of birthday cake, sitting partially eaten on her best china plate. His wife wasn't too upset. He was going out to work on her birthday. She was used to it. It had happened before, and she suspected it would happen again. She was upset because he was going back to the Osborne farm, and she knew he'd start having nightmares again, waking up in the middle of the night screaming in sweat.

* * *

"Okay, listen up. I need to take all your names in case we need to contact you at a later time," Wayne announced when he returned to the store. "I'll start with you. What's your name, young lady, and where do you live?"

"Kerri, Kerri Barr. That's Barr with two r's."

"And your address?"

"69 Cherry Street, over in Hancock."

"You serious?" Wayne asked, stopping his note taking and quizzically glanced over at Kerri Barr.

"Don't look at me like that!" Kerri huffed.

Wayne shook her retort off and continued to write her information in his notepad and then turned to the person next to her. "And you, what's your name and address?"

"Alfred Molino, 110 Deer Valley, Hancock. Anything else you need, officer?" Mole answered, saying his address like it meant something special. Wayne had no idea the Deer Valley section was where the well-to-do resided in Hancock, and even if he did, it wouldn't have made a difference to him; he treated all the teenagers the same.

"Yeah, your age."

Mole paused, thinking his response, then told the truth. "Nineteen."

"Thought so," Wayne mumbled, then turned his attention toward the storekeeper. "And you?"

"I'm the owner. I'm not going anywhere. You'll know where to find me if need be. I live in an apartment out back."

Deputy James looked hard at the stubborn old man and decided to just note the owner of the store in his notepad. No sense in writing more than he had to.

"Just make sure you don't sell them any beer tonight. I'd hate to see you lose your liquor license," Wayne informed the store owner.

Alfred Molino frowned. "Can we go now, officer?"

"Yes, you can go but don't drive too fast and stay out of trouble. I've got enough problems to handle tonight. I don't need any more."

Wayne then helped Malcolm out to his cruiser, placing him prone in the back seat, and then drove him to the hospital over in Hancock, passing a parked green Volkswagen Beatle on the straightaway in front of the Osborne Road.

CHAPTER EIGHTEEN

Saturday Evening
August 11, 1989

Sheriff Roger Lefebvre stood outside his cruiser, looking at the dark, moonless night sky. Even though he lived on the outskirts of Denton, he was close enough to be in the halo of the town's lights so he could only see the brightest of the night stars, but he knew the sky would look a lot different out at the Osborne farm, and so would the farmhouse. Seeing the house in daylight was spooky enough. At night it would be worse.

If what Wayne had described about the condition of Malcolm Ridge, covered in blood, he knew something awful had to have occurred out there. Wayne was too good of a deputy to not know if a prank was being pulled on him.

He now wondered if the job was going to be too big for just him and the sixty-year-old Phil Hardy, who was now being mainly used for backup purposes. Ben Alden would be a better deputy to handle a more physical situation, being younger, but he was still a rookie and inexperienced in law enforcement, and he could make a costly mistake. The rookie reminded Roger of when the gangly Deputy Wayne James first started out, fearless and eager to please until he was hit by a crisis. It took years of experience before you could be considered a first-rate deputy, and Ben Alden hadn't even been on the force for a year.

Roger now wished he had let Wayne go to the farmhouse

instead of having him take Malcolm Ridge to the hospital, but at the time, he was more concerned with Wayne's reaction, being related to the possible victim. Sometimes family can get in the way of your thought process and cause damaging consequences, ones that may be irreversible to correct.

Roger opened the rear door of his cruiser and tossed his gun belt on the backseat. He only liked to wear his gun when it was needed, and even though he speculated tonight would be one of those occasions, he'd wait until that moment came. Once settled in the driver's seat, he slammed the door shut and radioed his rookie deputy to meet them out at the Osborne farm, along with some details about what they were facing. Ben told his boss he should arrive in fifteen or twenty minutes when asked what his ETA was.

After hearing his estimate, Roger figured he'd arrive ahead of his deputy, so there was no sense mentioning to stay put if he arrived first. In hindsight, Roger wished he had because he had to wait longer than expected for Phil Hardy to get ready. When he did arrive at the Osborne farm, Ben was already there, leaning, with his arms folded across his chest, against the side of his cruiser parked at the end of the driveway.

"About time you guys got here," Ben joked as his boss and Phil Hardy exited the Sheriff's cruiser.

After retrieving his gun belt from the back seat, Roger buckled the belt around his thick waist and discontentedly walked toward his young deputy. He was feeling moody for having to leave his wife alone on her birthday, but what made him feel even more agitated was having to deal with the Osborne farm once again. Each time he drove up the graveled road toward what he considered the Devil's house, he hoped it would be the last time, but here he was again, standing before the old, dilapidated farmhouse, and this time, in the dark of the night.

"How long have you been waiting, Ben?" Roger annoyingly asked, side-stepping his rookie deputy's sarcastic remark. He was standing less than three feet away from Ben and could barely make out his facial features to see if he was still grinning because the moonless night made it difficult to see beyond the length of one's arm.

"I actually just got here a couple of minutes before you guys."

"Well, I'm glad you waited before going inside. Notice anything unusual, or hear any noises coming from inside the farmhouse?"

"I haven't heard anything except crickets and the rattling leaves, nothing inside the house. No lights of any kind either. But didn't you tell me there should be a vehicle up here, a red Dodge Charger?" Ben asked.

Roger looked around in the dark and strained his eyes to see the outline of a small compact vehicle parked up the driveway and what looked like another vehicle in front of the compact.

"Yes, that's what I was told. Why, what's up there?" Roger asked, nodding up the driveway toward what he assumed were two vehicles.

"There are two vehicles, one's a dark colored VW bug, and the other, I believe, is the Charger. I took a quick peek at them and then walked back down here when I saw your headlights coming down the road," Ben explained.

"Let's check it out," Roger said as he walked up the driveway but stumbled to the ground before reaching them. He was staring at the dark forms and not concentrating on where he was walking and stumbled into a washed-out rut. He felt somewhat embarrassed at his ungraceful fall, skinning the palms of his hands on the rough graveled driveway, but was more agitated than embarrassed, grumbling his feelings when asked if he was all right. He could have blamed his unsteady balance on the two glasses of Champagne he had with his wife, but he didn't want his deputies to think he couldn't handle the small amount of alcohol.

When he reached the vehicles, he opened the driver's door to the Volkswagen. The interior light was dim, barely illuminating the inside. He quickly detected the strong odor of marijuana. In the ashtray, he saw the remnant of a rolled joint. He picked the stubbed joint up with his thumb and index finger, taking a sniff, and then tossed it to the ground.

"You ever smoke that stuff, Ben?" Roger asked, not expecting an honest answer. Roger had a feeling every young adult tried smoking pot at least once, and even though he had never smoked pot himself, he felt it was a natural thing to experience one time.

"Me, never. You know, I had to pass a drug test to get hired."

"Yeah, right. I forgot," Roger said, turning toward the farmhouse.

The house, being totally dark, seemed really spooky to Roger. It was the most despicable place he had ever seen. To make it feel even spookier, the wind had picked up. A warm front was moving through the area, causing the bare, finger-like branches from the trees that grew tall and gnarly around the house to scrape across the tin roof. The sounds were haunting, like creatures with long sharp claws crawling toward them.

"I'm not liking having to go back in there, Roger, but it doesn't look like we have a choice," Phil Hardy grimly said.

"I'm ready. I've got my flashlight here," Ben eagerly said, pulling his Maglite out for proof, but it was almost impossible to see the foot-long black object in the dark.

"If you had been inside that evil house before, Ben, you wouldn't be so enthusiastic about going in," Phil said, remembering the horror he had seen when he found the Osborne children's heads mounted on wooden poles years ago.

"I've been here before. Remember back in May when we were looking for the missing kids? Besides, I don't believe in stuff like that."

"Like what?"

"Like haunted houses."

"Suit yourself. Be my guest," Phil motioned his hand toward the open barn door.

"Okay, hold on a second. Before we do anything, I'd like to cover the facts we have at this time. According to what the Ridge kid said, and the fact he was covered in blood, there may be a crazy man inside wielding an axe. Ridge also mentioned his two friends were attacked by this person, and they could be dead. I also noticed a woman's purse sitting on the passenger seat inside the VW," Roger told his deputies, and then as he looked back up at the farmhouse, he added. "I'm not sure what that all means, but we may have more people involved than I first suspected."

"Want me to take a look to see if there's an ID in the purse, Roger?" Ben Alden keenly asked, thinking it may be important.

"No, not yet," he told Ben, then after a short pause to think how they were going to play this out, he looked over at Phil. "Phil, I want you to go up by the barn and flash your light inside. Take caution and be ready for anything, but don't get too eager and pull the trigger. It could be only some teenagers in there. Houses that are labeled as haunted have a way of attracting adolescents."

"You want me to go inside the barn or just stand by the door?" Phil asked, not sure what his boss had asked of him.

"Just stand inside and look around. I don't want you to go any further. It's just to see if anyone is hiding in there or attempts to sneak out of the house that way," Roger said, giving his deputy a more defined explanation, and then added, "And, when Wayne shows up, give me a shout."

"Roger that," Phil Hardy confirmed, then disappeared up the driveway. He wasn't seen again until he flicked on his Maglite, aiming it toward the open barn door.

"Ben, you're with me. We'll go in through the side door up there on the porch. There are only a couple of old rotten boards holding it in place. I'm pretty sure we can easily pry them off with no trouble."

"Great," Ben smiled, liking the idea of action.

Roger walked back to his cruiser and grabbed a pry bar from the trunk and his 'own' Maglite. He ordered everyone in his department a new Maglite after his last visit to the Osborne farmhouse when only Phil Hardy had one, which Phil purchased with his own money.

When he returned from his vehicle, Roger led his young

deputy up the porch steps and shined his light through a partially exposed kitchen window. The first-floor windows and doors in the farmhouse had all been boarded up after the first incident twenty-two years earlier, but over the years, some of the inexpensive pine planks had dried to rot and fell on the porch.

"Can't see much of anything inside from out here. Ben, hold this light and shine it at the door while I pry the boards off."

Roger handed his flashlight to Ben and proceeded to pry off the old wooden planks, which came away easily without making much noise.

"See, hardly made a sound," Roger said and took his flashlight back from Ben. "But take your gun out just in case that Ridge kid's story has some truth to it, and they did hear us breaking in. I don't want any of my men dying in this place. There's already been too much death here."

Ben Alden was excited. He had his gun out previously when he was backing up Wayne on a traffic stop of a suspected drug dealer, who turned out to be the dealer's younger brother, but this was the first time he needed his gun entering a building. To make it more exciting, an insane killer could be hiding inside.

"I'm right behind you, Roger."

Roger cautiously twisted the doorknob and then pushed open the door with his left hand, the hand holding his Maglite, and held his .357 magnum in his other hand. Slowly he aimed the beam of light around the dark kitchen. It looked the same as he remembered, a lone table with seven chairs around it and dusty with cobwebs. Ben filed in behind him, shining his light in the same areas. Together, they made their way silently across the kitchen floor and through an open doorway that Roger knew led to the living room, the room Wayne had said the crazy man with the axe had attacked the Ridge kid and his two friends.

"Just beyond here," Roger whispered.

When he first inched his way into the living room, Roger hit the far wall with a beam of light and then aimed it left toward the three windows where the Osborne children blindly stared out on that cold, snow-covered day twenty-two years ago. After a brief stop in remembrance, Roger continued to shine the light around the room, hitting the floor in front of him with the beam of light at about the same time Ben had. On the floor, not five feet away from them, they saw the grotesque bodies of Luke Townsend and Peter Finch lying in a giant pool of blood.

It was a sight Ben had not expected to see, at least not then. He expected to see gruesome dead bodies sometime in his career as a law enforcer when he first entered law enforcement, but not at this early stage. When he did, he knew he'd be able to handle the situation, that's what he told Sheriff Roger Lefebvre during his interview eight months ago, but now, seeing the real thing, Ben gasped at the horrible sight, backing up against the doorframe covering his mouth as not to puke.

Roger also had not expected to see anything like what he was looking at, but he wasn't as grossed out as his young rookie was because he had seen it all before and seen worse. Although these bodies were hacked to death, they were at least somewhat intact, not headless or bodiless like the previous ones he had encountered, so the sight was less traumatizing to him than it was for his deputy.

Roger circled the floor with his Maglite to make sure they were the only two bodies in the room and then turned to his deputy, motioning him back toward the kitchen.

In the kitchen, Roger flashed a light on Ben's face, seeing his grim expression. "Ben, you don't look so good. Why don't you go out for some fresh air and tell Phil to come in here. Then I want you to get on the radio to the office and tell Helen to send out a couple of troopers that are in the area to guard the entrance to the road and send out an ambulance. Also, have her call the coroner. Have Helen tell the coroner, we have two bodies out here, and bring all the gear he'll need, including lighting and a camera. And Ben, Wayne should be arriving soon. You can fill him in when he gets here."

Ben was feeling nauseous, and as soon as he got the instructions from his boss, he rushed out the kitchen door and stumbled toward the porch railing. He then leaned over the railing and wrenched his guts out. Phil Hardy was standing in the driveway next to the two teenagers he had found hiding in the barn. He immediately knew Ben had seen something repugnant by his actions.

Phil found Alfred 'Mole' Molino and Kerri Barr in the barn, giggling behind one of the cow stalls. They panicked and ran into the barn when they spotted Ben Alden's cruiser driving up the Osborne Road. They were stoned and didn't want the deputy to find them, but they had absentmindedly forgotten about their vehicle parked in the driveway. When they were found, Kerri innocently told Deputy Hardy they only wanted to peek inside the windows. They become curious about the farmhouse when Malcolm Ridge had told them about the crazy man attacking his friends. They hadn't believed a word, thinking he was on some kind of drug trip, and the blood he was covered in was some kind of a gag because they didn't notice any cuts on him, but even if there wasn't anything going on out there, they wanted to come anyway to see the infamous farmhouse.

Mole told the deputy they weren't really trespassing because they didn't go inside the house. Phil Hardy told him they technically were trespassing as soon as they drove past the NO TRESPASSING sign posted at the end of the Osborne Road, where they couldn't have missed it, and he could summons them a ticket, but before he did, he'd wait to see what the Sheriff had to first say about the matter. He also told them they had found a marijuana cigarette in the ashtray, so be prepared for further citations.

"Ben, you okay? What did you guys find in there?" Phil asked.

Ben Alden wiped his mouth and chin with the sleeve of his uniform and then slowly descended the steps and awkwardly stumbled toward Phil and the two teenagers. "I've never seen anything like it. There's blood everywhere."

"Where's Roger?"

"Inside, he wants you to go in. Phil, you don't want to look in there."

"What is it? Don't keep me in suspense."

"I'm not sure, but I think it's those two guys we were looking for. They're all chopped up."

"Gross," Kerri said as she placed her hand over her mouth.

Her boyfriend, Mole, only laughed. His drug-induced mind couldn't comprehend the reality of what was happening.

After Phil disappeared inside the farmhouse, Ben led the two trespassers down the driveway and then placed them in the backseat of his cruiser, telling them they'd have to wait until the Sheriff had time to talk with them. After he contacted Helen and gave her the instructions from Roger, Ben stood outside leaning on his cruiser and waited for the troops to arrive.

CHAPTER NINETEEN

Saturday Evening
August 11, 1989

Deputy Wayne Leon James was the first to arrive, having anxiously driven at a high rate of speed to get there. He hung around in the hospital's emergency ward just long enough to explain to the attending doctor what Malcolm Ridge's reason was for being there, saying only he was in some kind of shock after having witnessed a horrible tragedy and barely escaping with his life, so he said.

Wayne, however, wasn't totally convinced of Malcolm's mental condition, and maybe Malcolm was only pretending to be in shock. At first, Wayne had no doubts but to believe his story, seeing his bloody clothing and his lack of response when questioned, but during the ride over to the hospital, Malcolm seemed calm and cool, his normal self again. He was too composed for having just witnessed the murder of his two friends and barely escaping with his own life. Not only that, but Malcolm's story about what happened out at the Osborne farm had changed, only slightly, but it had changed nevertheless, and Wayne knew from experience that when a suspect, or a supposed witness in this case, changes their story most likely they are the guilty party.

Sure, seeing something as horrific as watching your friends being murdered by a crazy, axe-wielding person could possibly penetrate your fragile mind, causing confusion of the actual facts. Wayne, himself, had never been in that situation, not even close. So, he felt he shouldn't make a judgment on Malcolm's state of mind and to let the more experienced, like a psychiatrist, decide one's mental state, he thought as he drove toward the Osborne farm. But he also thought that any observations, no matter how insignificant they may seem at the time, were noteworthy and could make a total difference in finding the perpetrator. Wayne reminded himself to mention his concerns to the Sheriff when he saw him.

Ben Alden briefly informed Wayne they found two corpses inside the farmhouse. He then waited for Wayne to respond, to ask if one of the deceased was his relative, which he would have had no answer for. Wayne only took a deep breath and looked up toward the dark sky, and then turned to not show his remorseful expression.

"What's up with those two?" Wayne asked Ben a moment later when he spied the couple sitting in the backseat of Ben Alden's cruiser, smoking cigarettes. It didn't take him long to remember where he had seen them, the scene at the store was going to be almost impossible to erase from his memory.

"They said they were at the store when that Ridge kid came in, and they were curious about this place," Ben said, nodding toward the farmhouse. From between the spaces in the boarded windows, Wayne could see faint shafts of light flickering.

"Did Roger say he wanted me to go inside?" Wayne asked, hoping the answer was no, but at the same time, he wanted to confirm what he already knew, that one of the deceased was his cousin, Peter Finch.

"He only mentioned to tell you what was going on. The coroner will be here soon. Maybe you should go inside with him when he does."

"Did you get a good look at them?"

"I'm afraid I did. It was the most grotesque thing I have ever seen. At first, I couldn't figure out what I was looking at because the bodies were hacked up so much. It just looked like a pile of clothing, and then I saw blood and flesh and realized I was looking at two dead bodies. It was hideous. They must have suffered tremendously."

Wayne stared at his co-worker, wondering if he knew one of the mutilated bodies he was describing in horrible detail was his flesh and blood. He was thinking about telling Ben he had a good idea that one of the bodies was his cousin, Peter, when a familiar screeching sound broke his train of thought.

Off in the distance, they could hear the chilling sounds of the ambulance's siren, and before long, the headlights bounced up and down through the dark, tree-lined Osborne Road. Not far behind the ambulance was the coroner's dark colored station wagon. Both vehicles pulled around the cruisers and drove on the tall grass alongside the porch.

A moment later, one of the state troopers arrived and stood next to Ben Alden. The other trooper positioned his cruiser at the end of the Osborne Road, as requested. Trooper, Bud Fogg, was full of questions, eager to hear what was going on inside. Ben was more than glad to oblige, filling him in with exaggerated details and the Sheriff's reactions to the crime but omitting his own embarrassing moment.

Wayne told the ambulance crew to hold firm until he talked with the Sheriff. He then led the coroner inside the farmhouse, holding his breath all the way up the steps with dreaded anticipation, knowing what had happened inside was going to be bad, really bad. What started out to be an uneventful night was now a full-blown nightmare.

Having completed their initial search of the farmhouse, including a quick walkthrough down in the dreaded basement, Roger and Phil were waiting in the kitchen for the coroner, Doctor Mitchell Diehl, to arrive. It wasn't the doctor's first visit to the Osborne farm. He had been to the farmhouse almost as many times as Sheriff Lefebvre. The first time was twenty-two years earlier, when the Osborne family had been murdered. The Osborne murders were the most horrific case he had ever been associated with, and he had said, at the time, it would be his last.

Now, as he ascended the steps and followed Wayne through the door, the aging doctor was about to see his second, if not worst, most horrific case.

"Seems to never go away, does it, Mitch?" Roger said, shaking the doctor's hand like old friends at a reunion.

"The only times we see each other is at this godforsaken place, and nothing against you, Roger, but it's too many times for me. Like I said the first time we met here, I was going to retire after that one. Of course, I was too young then, but I'm beyond retirement age now, and before I left the house tonight, my wife reminded me of it. I'm absolutely sure I'm retiring after this one."

"I don't blame you one bit."

"How about you? You must be ready for retirement."

"End of the year, I'm all done. I've decided not to run for re-election, and my wife agrees with me. I think it's about time to let someone younger take over," Roger confirmed thinking Wayne would make a good sheriff and hoped he'd give it thought to run in the next election.

Doctor Diehl nodded his head in their agreement about retirement. "Good for you. By the way, Wayne, here," the doctor said, nodding at Wayne, who was in a conversation with Phil, "and your other deputy outside briefed me on what to expect. They said there were two fatalities, two young men from Denton."

"I can't confirm their identities, that's your job, but most likely, the two victims are Luke Townsend and Peter Finch. The Finch kid is Wayne's relative," Roger said, and then regretfully added, "Sorry, Wayne."

Wayne nodded. "When the time comes, I want to be the one to tell my aunt and uncle. It will be better to hear it from family. What do you want me to do now?"

The Sheriff thought for a moment, not wanting Wayne to get too involved with the case, but he knew he'd want to do as much as he could to help find the perpetrator, or by the looks of the crime scene, it was most likely more than one perpetrator.

"We're going to need to go over the whole house and do a complete investigation this time around." Roger was referring to the Osborne case, where they didn't do a thorough job. This time he wanted to get all the evidence. "I don't want to miss anything that might pertain to this investigation. I'm going to need your full cooperation. Do you think you'll be okay to handle this?"

"I'm with you, Roger. I won't let you down," Wayne confirmed.

"That's what I thought you'd say. Someday you'll make a good sheriff," Roger complimented. He then aimed his Maglite toward the doorway leading to the crime scene. "After Phil and I give Mitch a tour of the crime scene and help him set up his equipment, I'll get together with the both of you outside," Roger added, and then patted Wayne on his shoulder and nodded to him to wait outside, thinking it best he not to view the crime scene at this time.

Later, when Roger came outside, he found his two deputies chatting with the trooper, Bud Fogg, and the ambulance crew, who were waiting around to see if they were still needed. It had been a slow night for emergencies, and since there was another ambulance idling back at the hospital, ready to jump into action if needed, the paramedics weren't in an urgent need to return to the hospital, but it was nearing the end of their shift, and they had already worked the required twelve hours.

Roger could sense their uneasiness by the way they kicked at the ground and glanced at their watches. Roger looked at his own watch, hitting the button to illuminate the face, noting the time to be nearing midnight. It was later than he thought, and he wondered if he should call in the State Police investigators now and start the full investigation or leave one of his deputies to guard the place and start at first light, which this time of the year would be roughly in six hours. Thinking about it, it definitely made more sense to do a thorough search of both the inside and outside of the farmhouse in daylight than trying to find vital evidence with flashlights and maybe contaminating the evidence as well.

Without much debate, Roger decided to wait till daybreak and told Ben to get the crime scene tape out to cordon off the area around the house. He then informed his rookie deputy he'd have to stay put and guard the farmhouse until morning. He'd have the trooper who was stationed at the main entrance continue his surveillance.

"What about them two?" Ben Alden nodded toward his cruiser.

With all that was going on, Roger had completely forgotten about them. Phil had informed him about finding the teenagers hiding in the barn when he first entered the kitchen, but it hadn't entirely registered, and then the thought of them vanished when they began searching the farmhouse.

The teenagers may or may not have had anything to do with what happened inside the farmhouse, Roger thought, considering they were at the convenience store at the time Malcolm Ridge arrived. But he didn't want to leave any stone unturned, not this time anyway.

"Give them a ride home. I want to leave their vehicle where it is. Tell them we'll be in touch sometime tomorrow. Wayne and Phil will start putting the crime scene tape up around the perimeter. I'll see you when you get back. Oh," he suddenly remembered, "and pick up whatever you think you might need, food and water, et cetera. But I don't think you'll be here longer than a few hours. The sun still comes up early this time of year."

"Still need us around?" One of the ambulance crew boldly asked. He was more anxious than the other paramedic to get off work – he wanted to hit the last call at the Rustic Barn on the outskirts of Denton, formally the Barn Tavern. It was Saturday night, a lot of young ladies would be there, and being single, he was eager to flirt with one or two and brag about his job and how exciting it could be. Basically, brag about the interesting night he had at work.

"No, I guess not. We'll help Mitch load the bodies into his vehicle after he's done his preliminaries. You guys can go. We won't need you any longer tonight, I hope," Roger sighed.

As Ben Alden disappeared down the Osborne Road with the ambulance and the state trooper close behind, Roger suddenly remembered he had asked Ben to get the crime scene tape out of his trunk. He hoped Wayne had a roll of the yellow tape in his cruiser because he knew he didn't have any in his trunk.

"By the looks of the crime scene, that Ridge kid was lucky to get out of there alive. It must have been quite traumatic for him. No wonder he was traumatized," Roger said, as he watched Wayne unlock the trunk of his cruiser to retrieve the tape. "It's hard for me to believe there was only one person involved. Most likely, there were probably two, and while they were killing the Townsend kid and your nephew, Ridge took the opportunity to escape."

"My cousin," Wayne corrected, trying to remember what he looked like. He'd seen Peter Finch regularly, hanging around the Denton pool hall, but he was having a hard time visualizing his facial features. Peter was not at all considered handsome, his rutted face, along with his nose, was long and thin, and his dark hair was stringy, always looking unwashed. Wayne always referred to Peter as a rag of a kid, the runt of the clan, being the smallest. In the future, he'd remember him hanging around the pool hall, smiling and enjoying his brief, wasted life.

"What's that?"

"Peter was my cousin, not my nephew. Seems odd to say was."

"I can't wait to hear what that Ridge kid has to say about all this. Did you get anything else out of him on the ride to the hospital, or was he still in a state of shock?"

Wayne didn't answer. He was trying to find the roll of yellow tape and remember what Malcolm Ridge had told him on the drive to the hospital. After he found the tape at the bottom of a plastic supply box, he held it in his open hand, blankly staring at it.

Roger could see the confused look on his face, like he was unsure what to do with the tape. "Something wrong, Wayne?"

"Nothing, really. It was just something that occurred to me when you asked if I talked with Ridge. I don't think it means anything, really. It was just an observation."

"Indulge me. Anything, no matter how trifle it may sound, could be important."

"Well, when I arrived at the store, I found him curled up on the floor, all scared and bloodied, almost completely out of it. The store owner and the other two witnesses…the ones Ben just carted off in his cruiser, said he seemed calm when he first entered the store, and then he began to get hysterical saying something about his friends had died."

"Yeah, I can see why, having witnessed this shit."

"Right, but what was odd was on the way to the hospital, he seemed as calm as a cucumber. He started talking about some job he might be getting, some kind of a construction job. I asked him about what had happened up here, and he calmly said he believed the old man, Zeke Osborne, was the one who attacked him and his friends with an axe. Talking like it was nothing at all."

"He could have been in a state of shock. And it could be one of the four or five phases a shock victim goes through, like denial and grief and so on. I wouldn't worry about it…he'll get the help he needs at the hospital. They'll have some nut doctors examine him."

"I understand that, but that's not what he told me the first time when I asked. His story changed. He said the person who attacked them was holding some kind of a large stick with a horse head on the end of it. Not an axe."

"He must have been mistaken. By the looks of the bodies in there," Roger said, pointing toward the farmhouse, "they were definitely bludgeoned to death with some kind of an axe. There's no way in hell a stick could have done that much damage."

"Roger, Malcolm Ridge at first told me he was the one holding the axe."

Sheriff Roger Lefebvre stared expressionlessly at his deputy and then looked toward the farmhouse. In the dark, he could just barely make out the coroner, Doctor Mitchell Diehl, coming down the porch steps, waving a flashlight to get his attention. Roger knew he couldn't wait till morning; he had a suspect on the loose at the hospital.

CHAPTER TWENTY

Sunday Morning
August 12, 1989

Sheriff Roger Lefebvre slammed the door to his office shut with a thundering bang, rattling the pictures of prior sheriffs and plaques of achievements on the wall outside his door and the nerves of his longtime dispatcher, Helen. Dejectedly, he walked over to his desk and tossed the folder he had been holding tight in his hand on top of the cluttered desk, adding to the pile. He then stood bewildered in front of the window, running his fingers through his thinning hair, and looked across the street where he could see the District Attorney bend to lock the front door to his office and then casually drive off in his shiny new Cadillac Deville as though it was just another day in the peaceful town of Denton.

Heading home, no doubt, Roger assumed, since it was Sunday morning – a day he spent with family. Roger, on the other hand, had no particular day off. Being a sheriff meant being on the job for twenty-four hours a day, every day of the week.

"What does he care about? Surely not justice," Roger mumbled to himself. "He has all he wants, money and a young wife."

Roger had just come from a brief meeting with District Attorney Neal Russo and was not the least bit happy with what the District Attorney told him. Roger wanted to arrest Malcolm Ridge for the murder of Luke Townsend and Peter Finch in the worst way because he was dead certain Malcolm Ridge committed the murders, but the District Attorney argued that they didn't have enough evidence to get a conviction, let alone indict him for the murders.

Roger thought he had all the evidence he needed in the folder he carried into the DA's office to lock Malcolm Ridge up for life. He was even acting giddy when he entered the office, waving the folder in front of him before tossing it on the DA's desk. He then uninvitingly sat down on the dark-brown leather couch, which was pushed up against the wall underneath a colorful print of Denton's autumn foliage taken from the Overlook, the best spot to view the colors of the turning season.

"So, what do we have here?" Neal knowingly asked as he opened the folder. Roger called earlier that morning to arrange a meeting to review the evidence they collected against Malcolm Ridge. With the DA's approval, he'd arrest Malcolm Ridge for the murders of Luke Townsend and Peter Finch – lock him up in the County Jail over in Hancock until the trial date.

"That's all the evidence we need to lock him up for life... right there in that folder you're holding. We've got his bloody fingerprints all over the murder weapon, the blood-covered axe lying right next to the bodies. You just say the word, Neal, and I'll drive right over to the hospital and read him his rights. Lock his ass up where he belongs."

"Hold on, Roger, not so fast. There's nothing more I'd like better than to have an open and shut case, so let's make sure we have enough evidence first. What's the suspect's name again?"

"It's all right there, his name is Malcolm Ridge, and he's a local boy. You've probably seen him around town. He hangs out at the pool hall right next door to your office with his two buddies, the ones he hacked up with a fucking axe," Roger said, then added with a hearty laugh. "Ha, some friend he turned out to be."

Neal Russo shook his head. He hadn't seen the person in question and continued to concentrate on the material in the typed-up form, outlining the evidence the Sheriff and his crime team had collected.

"Not too tall, average built, I guess for a twenty-year-old, shaggy head of hair. You must have seen him hanging out at the pool hall."

"Can't say if I had, I've never been in the pool hall, myself."

"Well, anyway, the kid's a piece of work. Get a load of this. He says Zeke Osborne killed his friends. You remember Osborne, don't you? He's the one who slaughtered his whole family about twenty years ago. Cut his children's heads right off with an axe and stuffed them on wooden poles to make them look like those toy wooden ponies kids play with. He then took the same bloody axe to his wife and hung her headless body in the barn. It was the top story in all the New England newspapers for weeks."

"Yeah, I remember Osborne. How could I forget? How could anybody forget, especially you, for that matter?" Neal answered with a quick glance to catch Roger's eye and then refocused on the evidence. "I was about the same age as that bartender Osborne killed at the Rustic Barn. It used to be called something else, as I recall."

"The Barn Tavern," the Sheriff quickly answered. The name will be forever imprinted in his brain.

"Yeah, that's it, the Barn Tavern." Neal agreed, something he seldom did. Being an attorney, Neal Russo was always disagreeing with someone. Neal was in his early thirties when he first set up his law practice in Denton, only a few years before Zeke Osborne went on his killing rampage. Neal's appearance hadn't changed much over the years, still looking handsome and well-trimmed in his custom-made suits. *Lean and mean*, he liked to consider himself, and that's the impression most people thought when they were introduced to him. For a man in his fifties, he looked like he kept to a regular workout schedule at the local fitness club, but he never belonged to one. He kept fit by playing golf and tennis in the summer months and tennis indoors at the Racket Center club during the cold winter months.

"So, Neal, how's it look?" Roger sat up higher on the couch, leaning as if to rise and receive his 'Do Praise' for a job well done.

But he wasn't prepared for the DA's unexpected response.

"Is this all you've got on him?" Neal asked, as he placed the form back in the folder labeled 'Malcolm Ridge Case.'

"And those gruesome photos of the crime scene, in there." He nodded toward the folder. "What else do you need? We've got his fingerprints on the murder weapon. I think that's plenty enough to put him away with that alone," Roger hastily added. He was anxious to book Malcolm and lock him up so he couldn't do any more harm, even though he had one of his deputies guarding the door to his hospital room.

"I don't think that's a good idea right now, with what little evidence we've got. Besides, what would his motive be for killing his friends?"

"Maybe they knew something he did that was illegal and were going to squeal on him. I don't know...." Roger said, shaking his head and then leaned back against the couch and stared at the ceiling, trying to come up with a reason for someone like Ridge to hack his friends to death.

"Look, Roger, I know you think Ridge killed his friends, and most likely he did, but until we come up with more concrete evidence, is there anything else you can hold him on? Any pending misdemeanor charges or probation issues that may have been filed away?"

Roger thought for a moment but came up empty. "I'm afraid not unless we book him for trespassing, but I really can't lock him up for that. It's only a fine. What's wrong with the evidence we've got now?"

The District Attorney knew the trial would be one of those 'once in a lifetime' trials, which would be the highlight of his so far lack-lustrous career, but if he were to lose the case, his career would be tarnished, so he didn't want to go to trial without enough evidence to convict Malcolm Ridge. He wanted no doubt in the jurors' minds when the twelve, law abiding, citizens went into deliberation. All he wanted to hear was the lead juror say 'Guilty' to all counts.

"I'm sorry, Roger, but I don't want to go to trial with what little evidence we have on Ridge. You're going to need to dig up more... a lot more."

"What about the bloody axe with his fingerprints all over it? Isn't that enough evidence? And his bloody footprints are all over the farmhouse, and we even have the shoes and clothes he wore with their blood on them. What more do we need?"

"Roger, didn't you tell me on the phone this morning that Ridge told your deputy he was holding the axe when some crazy man attacked him and his friends?"

"Yeah, that was one version. What of it?" Roger defensively asked.

"Malcolm Ridge will testify he was there, and he held the axe during the attack but then dropped it and ran for his life. If he had any kind of lawyer, he'd eat us for lunch. If I prosecute this case, I don't want to lose. You're going to have to get me more evidence. Go back to the farmhouse and see what else you can come up with. Or better yet, find me an eyewitness."

"You need witnesses? We have the two potheads who were in the store when Malcolm Ridge came in, and we have the store owner, himself, to testify Malcolm was covered in blood and acting crazy."

"Whatever they say will only back up the defense's case that some crazy man attacked him. That's why he was hysterical."

Roger grabbed the folder, curling it tight in his hand, and disappointedly nodded toward District Attorney Neal Russo. "Okay, I'll try to come up with something we can hold him on until we can find more evidence, but I still don't see why we don't already have enough evidence."

"Maybe he didn't do it. Did you ever consider that?"

"No...because the kid's crazy," Roger said on his way out the door.

* * *

Roger Lefebvre sat at his desk for nearly forty-five minutes, racking his brain, trying to come up with something he could use to hold Malcolm Ridge until he could find enough evidence to convince the District Attorney that Ridge was guilty. Then the thought hit him – the kid was crazy.

On the night Malcolm Ridge was brought to the Hancock General Hospital, the hospital's young resident psychiatrist examined Malcolm to see if he was mentally stable and determined he was stable. His prognosis was Malcolm Ridge was not conscience of what was actually going on. "Sure, he was conscience," the doctor explained when he was asked to clarify, "but there are many layers of consciousness that are going on in the brain at the same time, and what you think you're seeing could be a blend of what is actually happening and what you think is happening, so the patient doesn't get the real picture. It's called fragmental awareness."

When informed, Roger was surprised at the doctor's prognosis, thinking Malcolm Ridge had to have been mentally unstable, having hacked his friends to death. Also, the way he acted after his lack of remorse at the death of his friends. But he didn't give it a second thought because, at the time, he hoped Malcolm would be declared sane so he could stand trial for the murder of his friends. Now, Roger was thinking about having a second opinion to see if Malcolm Ridge was slightly unstable. That way, if he were found slightly unstable, he'd have a reason to hold him for further evaluation until he could find enough evidence to convict him. And, if he happened to be found mentally unstable, which a defense attorney would probably most likely use as a defense anyway, Malcolm Ridge would still be locked up for a long time, maybe even forever. The bottom line was to get Ridge off the street and locked up.

Roger called District Attorney Neal Russo at his home to get his approval and then immediately went to work to locate another psychiatrist to examine Malcolm Ridge. Within an hour's time, Roger found that person and told the doctor to meet him at the Hancock General Hospital at a time that was convenient to her, hopefully, that afternoon.

CHAPTER TWENTY-ONE

Sunday Afternoon
August 12, 1989

Wearing a white blouse under an opened light-gray suit jacket and matching light-gray slacks, a middle-aged woman gently closed the door behind her and walked over to the uniformed officer guarding the room she exited. With a gentle smile and unwavering voice, she asked the officer if he heard any unusual sounds or voices coming from within the room. After the officer shook his head that it had been relatively quiet during the three hours he had been on duty, she thanked him, then lightly walked down to the end of the corridor and entered a small conference room. The room she entered was usually reserved for doctors when explaining a patient's condition to concerned family members.

Inside, she found two men sitting at a long rectangular table causally chatting to one another but immediately stopped and stood with respect as she settled into a comfortable cushioned chair. One of the men was Sheriff Roger Lefebvre, a man she had previously had the privilege of meeting when Roger gave her a brief overview of the situation and introduced her to Malcolm Ridge. The man on the other side of the table from the Sheriff was not familiar to her, but she knew from her conversation with the Sheriff he was District Attorney Neal Russo.

Doctor Carol Fleming had been a psychiatrist at Heaven's

Institution (the county's mental institution) for more than thirty-five years, and since she was in the waning years of her life, she was contemplating retirement sooner than later. When she agreed to examine Malcolm Ridge, she decided he would be her last case. Her plans for retirement were to move south and enjoy the rest of her years in the comfort of warm breezes, like most 'well to do' northerners.

"Good afternoon, Doctor Fleming. It's nice to see you again," Roger complimented and then added, "This is the District Attorney, Neal Russo. He's very interested in your evaluation of Malcolm Ridge."

"Nice to meet you, Doctor," Neal Russo said, extending his hand.

"And you as well, Mr. Russo," Doctor Fleming said, taking the District Attorney's hand.

"You can call me Neal. All my professional friends do."

"Do you have any non-professional friends, Mr. Russo?" Doctor Fleming asked, which the District Attorney took as an insult, thinking this meeting was quickly getting off on the wrong foot. He didn't want to come across as an egotistic person and didn't think he had, but obviously, with her retort, the Doctor had.

To correct the misconstrued meaning, Neal smiled while trying to find his soft side, which was buried deep in the back portion of his brain and seldom came to light and then added. "I do, many, as a matter of fact, and I also allow them to call me by my given name."

Doctor Fleming smiled back. "I'm sure you do. Being an elected official, you need all the local support you can get. My apologies if you took my comment as being offensive. I was only trying to soften what can be a sticky meeting. I guess I wouldn't make a good comedian. You can call me by my given name, Carol, if you prefer, Neal."

"Okay, Carol, it is. And no need to apologize. I wasn't offended one bit."

"Well, now that we settled that and we're all acquainted,

can we get started?" Roger politely interrupted. He was eager to hear Doctor Fleming's diagnosis.

Doctor Fleming flipped open her briefcase and pulled out a leather-bound three-ring notebook, placing it on the table in front of her. She then carefully adjusted her eyewear, which had been hanging loosely around her wrinkled neck by a thin gold chain, an appreciation gift given for her many years of service at the hospital. After a moment's pause to peruse the notes she had taken examining Malcolm Ridge, Carol looked up at the men in front of her and softly cleared her throat to begin.

"Well, gentlemen, as you know, I have been asked by Sheriff Lefebvre here to examine Malcolm Ridge to see if he had any mental deficiencies that would cause further harm to anyone else or even to himself. In other words, is Malcolm Ridge a danger to society?" Doctor Fleming started out, lacing her hands in front of her.

"That's why we're all here," District Attorney Russo said, sounding a little impatient. It was Sunday, and he was planning on having a barbeque in the backyard by the swimming pool with friends, who he assumed were already at his house being entertained by his lovely young wife. Neal had met Stephanie, his second wife, in a bar where she worked as a waitress. She was twenty years younger than Neal, but age didn't matter when prestige and money were involved, so they started dating soon after. Within five months, they were married in a simple ceremony and spent the next month honeymooning in Key West. After eight years of marriage, they both felt they were still on their honeymoon, Neal enjoying the pleasures of being with a much younger woman and Stephanie spending his money.

"When I asked him what he remembered of the night his friends were murdered, Mr. Ridge told me he couldn't remember anything about the night, only waking up in the backseat of Deputy...." Doctor Fleming paused to peruse her notes for the correct name, then continued, "Deputy Wayne Leon James's police vehicle wondering what was going on. I then asked him what the last thing he remembered before waking up in the police vehicle."

She then paused again and looked across the table at both men. "This is the interesting part. It's where you can tell if a person is telling the truth or is being deceitful. I could see his eyes narrow in deep thought, and his brows rise. He was trying very hard to remember. After a moment, Mr. Ridge then said he remembered playing pool and drinking beers at the Denton Pool Hall with his buddies sometime around six or seven o'clock Saturday evening, and then the three of them decided to take a drive out to the Osborne farmhouse for entertainment, see what it was like inside. The rest of the night, he said, was just a blur. He said he absolutely couldn't remember anything after they got to the farmhouse, not even being in the store when the deputy arrived."

"Well, that's not what he told me when I questioned him late last night. He had a lot more to say. Ridge told me he saw Zeke Osborne attack and kill his two friends, a man who disappeared over twenty years ago. Twenty-two years to be exact. Ridge then ran out of the house and didn't stop running until he got to the Groveville General Store. And that's precisely what three other witnesses told me, that he came in the store shouting that a madman attacked his friends, and they were all dead," the Sheriff attested with a cold hard stare. Like the DA, he didn't like the way the meeting was starting out either and wanted the doctor to know Malcolm Ridge could be just covering his butt by saying he couldn't remember anything because he knew he was guilty. To him, pausing in deep thought suggested he was lying.

"That may be what happened and what he told you, Sheriff, but I believed him when he said he couldn't remember most of the night. What he told you was what he had heard from your deputy. Mr. Ridge told me your deputy filled him in on the way to the hospital, telling him what happened at the store and what Malcolm was told he had said happened at the farmhouse. At the time, Malcolm had no reason to doubt him, so he may have only reiterated to you what the deputy had told him."

"How would my deputy know what happened in there if

Malcolm Ridge didn't tell him? Tell me that, Doctor?"

Doctor Fleming was starting to have a second opinion about Sheriff Lefebvre. When she first met him, Roger seemed very pleasant. Now, he seemed agitated.

"He probably did tell your deputy when your deputy found him lying semiconscious on the floor, but what I'm trying to explain to you, Sheriff is he doesn't remember anything after entering the farmhouse, not even going into the store. Anything he may have said would have been an incoherent response."

Roger frowned and looked over at the District Attorney, wondering how she could so easily believe Malcolm Ridge in that he couldn't remember anything of the night. With his years in law enforcement, he knew the first words out of a suspect's mouth were most likely a lie in an attempt to protect themselves.

"Is there anything else you uncovered about Ridge in your examination that might convince you he's insane? Even if he's only slightly insane, mind you, so we can have reason to hold him for a couple of months to reevaluate his mental condition," the District Attorney asked.

"I know what you're asking me, Mr. Russo, but I can only give you my professional recommendation. Now, please let me continue."

"Proceed," the District Attorney gestured with his hand.

"I asked him to give me an overview of his upbringing and what his life was like the last couple of years. He told me he was an orphan and had been adopted at age four. Although he couldn't confirm the exact age, he thought he could have been younger. His adoptive parents were nice folks but strict, so he quit school and moved out of the house at age seventeen. He said he had no idea who his birth parents were.

"In his last couple of years, he told me he was staying in the basement of a friend's house and working at odd jobs. Nothing exciting and nothing that paid a hell of a lot of money, as he put it," She emphasized it was Malcolm's words and not a phrase she would use to describe a low-paying job.

"Seemed like a pretty normal upbringing to me, gentlemen,

for someone without a biological family," Doctor Fleming concluded.

"So, what you're saying, Carol, is that Malcolm Ridge is a normal person. That is if someone who murdered his friends in cold blood can be called a normal person," District Attorney Russo assumed.

"Yes, Mr. Russo, your assumption sounds accurate, except, on the night of the crime, Malcolm could have had some kind of a mental breakdown."

"What are you getting at, Doctor?" the District Attorney asked. His forehead wrinkled with confusion – was she or wasn't she telling him Malcolm Ridge was a sane person.

Doctor Fleming folded her tiny hands over her notebook and smiled at the two men across the table from her. "I'm just saying seeing something as horrific as watching your friends being murdered could cause anyone to have some kind of mental breakdown. He told me he had frightening nightmares last night. They were only brief flashes, images like a fragmented movie clip, where a man wielding an axe was attacking him, hacking away at him like he was a log being chopped up for firewood. He woke up screaming, and the nurse had to come into his room and give him a sedative.

"My prognosis, gentlemen, is that if he did witness the horrific attack, then he could have had what I call a mental storm. It's when a person is suddenly traumatized by something so frightening that they go into a state of shock, and their memory of the event is completely wiped out, and it only resurfaces in dreams. This could go on for several months, even years, without therapy. And even then, he may never recover."

"So, are you saying that Malcolm Ridge is mentally unstable to understand what he had done? The bottom line, Carol, is he insane? Do you recommend we hold him?" the District Attorney asked.

"Not quite, Mr. Russo," Doctor Fleming answered, using the District Attorney's sir name, not wanting to be on friendly terms with a man she was beginning to detest. "From my preliminary findings, Mr. Ridge is not considered insane by no means. However, over time, if he goes untreated, he could become unstable because of the nightmares, and who knows what will happen to his mind. My recommendation is for him to volunteer to be treated at Heaven's Institution for an undetermined period of time. At the State's expense, of course, since I don't believe he has the resources to pay."

"Volunteer! He won't volunteer! As soon as I release him, he'll be off and running, and we'll probably never see him again," Roger stated, slapping the palm of his hand on the table.

"I think you need to calm down, Sheriff. Just to let you know, Mr. Ridge also told me, you," Doctor Fleming said, looking across the table at Sheriff Lefebvre, his face beginning to redden, "told him he was brought to the hospital for general observations and that he would be released the following morning. Being past noon and having to have to go through another screening, Mr. Ridge asked me when he was allowed to leave. I told him I had no knowledge of his required admittance in the hospital and he'd have to bring up his inquiries with the authorities. So, since you have not arrested him for anything, you might want to work fast and try to persuade him to check into our facility. We work wonders up there, and who knows, I may be able to bring back his memory."

Doctor Fleming closed her notebook and placed it back in her briefcase, and then slowly rose from her chair. "Well, gentlemen, I have nothing further to discuss at this time. The next move is up to you. Hopefully, for your sake, as well as Mr. Ridge's, you can persuade him to volunteer himself to our care. Good luck, gentlemen. It's been interesting meeting you both, to say the least."

After Doctor Fleming closed the door behind her, Roger brushed his fingers through his graying hair and then looked over at the District Attorney. "Let's say I read him his rights right now and lock him up."

The District Attorney shook his head and rose from his seat. "Like I told you before, Roger, go get me some incriminating evidence like an eyewitness. I'm going home. I have hungry guests waiting for me. My wife can only entertain them for so long before they start growling for something more to eat than just appetizers. I love my wife, but she can't cook a thing on the grill. The steaks are always overcooked, and the chicken is raw in the middle. Roger, don't let this get you down. Things will work out. You take care and call me later in the week if you have something new for me."

Sheriff Lefebvre watched the District Attorney pack up his leather briefcase and exit the room, leaving him alone with his thoughts. He was reluctant to release Malcolm Ridge, but he had no choice, so after the meeting with the District Attorney and Doctor Carol Fleming and the brief moment to reflect on what had just transpired, Roger left the room and pulled his deputy off guard duty and informed the hospital Malcolm Ridge was free to go.

CHAPTER TWENTY-TWO

Monday Morning
August 13, 1989

After he released Malcolm Ridge from the hospital, the first thing Sheriff Roger Lefebvre did the following morning was to re-interview both the two teenagers who were in the Groveville General Store the night of the murders and the store owner to find out if Malcolm may have said something incriminating. In his state of shock, maybe Malcolm happened to have mentioned he might have killed his friends. That would be as good as admitting to the crime, Roger figured. According to the District Attorney, Roger needed witnesses, and so far, they were the only known witnesses, along with one other potential witness, on his short list of witnesses.

Roger drove to Hancock and found the two teenagers hanging out by the pool in Alfred Molino's parents' backyard. Kerri was wearing a candy-striped bikini looking good and tanned. The Sheriff thought Mole was a lucky kid, being an odd match, but he figured money talks.

The teenagers told the Sheriff they saw a man in the highlights of the Volkswagen walking across the bridge on the old County Road, and when they were almost upon him, he lunged out at the vehicle like he was trying to commit suicide. They figured he was on an acid trip.

"If it weren't for Mole's good driving skills, we would have run him right over," Kerri Barr insisted and then added, "Later, when we saw Malcolm Ridge come into the store, we realized he was the same person we passed on the bridge. And when we saw he was covered in blood, I thought maybe he had almost succeeded in his quest to commit suicide, that he had jumped in front of another vehicle."

All this information they had already told Sheriff Lefebvre when they were first interviewed the previous day, the day after the murders took place. Other than that, the teenagers couldn't remember much of anything else, not even any conversation they may have had, which the Sheriff figured was because of the marijuana they had been smoking. He crossed them off the list and drove to the next name on the list.

The store owner could only confirm what Kerri Barr and Alfred Molino had already stated and that Malcolm Ridge was hysterical. And if you asked for his opinion, which he gave without being asked, Ridge was guilty as sin and should be hanged immediately and save the taxpayer's money. Roger crossed his name off as well, leaving only one name left.

Albert Deluca was on the list because Deluca may be Malcolm Ridge's only friend he had left. Roger hoped maybe Malcolm stopped over after leaving the hospital and confided in his friend or, if Malcolm hadn't, maybe Deluca had some other information he could use against him.

Roger had a pretty good idea where to find Deluca, so he told his deputy, Wayne Leon James, to take a walk over to the Denton Pool Hall, which was directly across the street from the sheriff's office, and pick him up for routine questioning. When the deputy entered the pool hall, he immediately spotted Deluca playing a game of pool by himself.

"Who's winning?" Wayne sarcastically asked.

Al Deluca looked up from his shot and noticed the deputy standing directly over the pocket he was aiming at, and without answering, fired off his shot, hitting the target dead center.

"Nice shot, practicing up for your next victim?"

"You could say that. You want to give it a try, Deputy?

Five bucks a game."

"Deluca, you know gambling is not allowed in this state."

"Okay, we'll play for beers. You are allowed to drink beer, aren't you? I'll even rack 'em up," Deluca said and pulled the ball rack off the hook from under the table.

"Maybe another time. I'm on official business."

"Yeah, what about?" Deluca asked, wondering if the official business had something to do with him.

"I need you to come with me back to the sheriff's office. The Sheriff wants to have a few words with you."

"With me? What does he want me for?" Deluca couldn't imagine what the Sheriff would want to talk to him about. Although the town was buzzing about the murders up at the Osborne farm, and the victims just happened to be his friends.

"You'll see when you get there."

Al Deluca grabbed his cap he had flung on the long counter running along the wall behind him and followed Wayne out the door and across the street to the sheriff's office. He felt slightly nervous the whole way, wondering if they suspected he had something to do with the murders. He was with all three of them in the pool hall that Saturday night and had contemplated on going with them when they mentioned taking a ride out to the Osborne farm. At the last minute, he decided against it because he remembered he was meeting his sister, Carmine, and a female friend of hers out at the Rustic Barn. Carmine had told him her friend was cute and had asked to meet her brother. They didn't hit it off, and at the time, he thought it was a wasted Saturday night, but after hearing what happened to his friends, he was glad his sister had invited him – even though he never thanked her for saving his life, something he could never do.

Once inside the two-storied brick building, Deluca was ushered into the sheriff's office and told to take a seat in front of the cluttered desk.

"Thanks, Wayne, don't go too far. I may need you later," Sheriff Lefebvre told his deputy, a remark made to slightly intimidate Al Deluca, but Deluca didn't need any more intimidation. He was already nervous sitting in front of the big man around town.

"I'll be right out here. Just let me know when you need me," Wayne said, and then closed the door hard behind him.

"Good afternoon... it's Al, right?" Roger asked as he stretched his meaty hand amiably out over the desk.

Al Deluca took his friendly gesture and lightly shook the hand, which felt strong enough that if the Sheriff wanted, he could have broken every bone in his hand even though Deluca's hand was of equal size. "Yes, it's really Albert, but most just call me Deluca."

"Okay, Deluca, it is." Roger smiled warmly to set his interviewee at ease, a way of getting honest answers. "Did my deputy explain to you why I had you brought in here?"

"Nope, he only said you wanted to speak to me about something."

"That's right, I do. Now what can you tell me about Malcolm Ridge? I heard you are good friends with him."

Deluca nodded. "Kind of. We play pool together. Other than that, we really never hung out."

Deluca was trying to be evasive, not wanting the Sheriff to think they were best friends, which they weren't, but the Sheriff didn't know that. The word around town was that Malcolm Ridge was a person of interest in the murders of Luke Townsend and Peter Finch, and he didn't want to be associated with him.

"When was the last time you saw him?"

Deluca hesitated a moment, taking a shallow breath. "Huh, let me think. I think I saw him last Saturday afternoon."

"You're not sure. You think you saw him?" Roger stared hard and could see Deluca looking a little nervous; sweat was starting to form on his forehead, and his eyes were losing focus, staring away.

"No, I'm pretty sure it was Saturday afternoon."

"Where was that exactly?"

"At the pool hall, across the street."

"Did you talk to him? Did he happen to mention where he

was going that night?"

Deluca cleared his throat. "Yeah, I guess. He said something about going out to the Osborne farmhouse with Luke and Peter."

"What time was that, exactly?"

"I'm not sure, probably around five-ish...something like that."

Sheriff Lefebvre leaned his upper body over his desk and folded his hands in front of him. "Just to let you know, I talked with Harve Bench," Roger had previously talked with Harve, the owner of the pool hall, that morning when he saw him standing outside sweeping the front steps and asked him if he had seen Malcolm Ridge the night of the murders. "He told me the four of you were still playing pool around seven o'clock. Do you want to change your timeline, Deluca?"

A drop of sweat dripped from Deluca's forehead onto his shirt. He knew he had nothing to do with the murders, but he wasn't sure the Sheriff did. "Yeah, well, maybe it was closer to seven. I didn't realize what time it was. I didn't see them after that."

"Harve also told me the four of you left together."

"Yeah, but I didn't go with them," Deluca mumbled.

"Do you know why they wanted to go out there? It seems like an unlikely place to spend a Saturday night, especially for young men. I would think they'd be out hitting the local bars for horny women."

"I have no idea why they went."

"Look, Deluca, I didn't bring you over here because I believe you were involved. I brought you here to find out if you knew any reason why Ridge would want to harm his friends. So, relax. Now, do you think Malcolm Ridge had some grudge against his friends? Did he seem agitated when you saw him last?" Roger asked, then leaned back in his chair to wait for the answer.

"No, not at all. He seemed normal to me."

"What about the other two, Townsend and Finch? Did they seem normal to you?"

"Well, yeah, they seemed normal. So, do you think Mal killed them?"

Roger smiled. "Deluca, don't get too relaxed. I'm still the one asking the questions."

"Just wondering. Word around town says he did, or at least he's your only suspect. Can I go now?"

"Hold on a second. Can you think of anything different about Ridge over the last couple of weeks? Like, did his demeanor change any? Has he been argumentative? Any fights? That sort of stuff."

Al Deluca paused to reflect on the times he had seen Malcolm in the past couple of weeks, but nothing unusual came to him. "No, I can't say if I noticed any difference."

"What about drugs? Did he do a lot of drugs?"

Al Deluca didn't know how to answer the question honestly. He knew Malcolm smoked marijuana, having often shared a joint (or two) with him, but to him, smoking a joint was not like being on drugs, and that's what he figured the Sheriff was asking him, so he answered 'No.'

"Well, that's hard to swallow. I thought every kid over the age of thirteen these days smoked pot at least once-in-awhile. But maybe you're the exception, and you had no idea if your friends did drugs or not."

Deluca shook his head that he didn't know and didn't care.

"Okay then, I think that's about it. Will you let me know if you think of anything else...and especially if you see Ridge again?" Roger said, then stood with his hand out for Deluca to shake.

As Al Deluca rose, he hesitated before completing the handshake and looked beyond the Sheriff, out the window, where the traffic slowly passed by.

"What is it? You think of something else you want to tell me?" Roger asked, wondering why the blank stare.

"Well, I wasn't quite honest with you, Sheriff, about the last time I had seen Malcolm. The reason I didn't mention it was because I thought I might be implicated in something."

"No, not at all. Malcolm Ridge is free to roam the streets as he pleases. When did you see him last?"

"Late, last night. He came over to my apartment looking for a place to stay. He asked me if he could sleep on my couch for a couple of nights. I told him no. I have two other roommates, and there was no way they were going to let him stay with us… not now after what he's been accused of."

"Did he say anything else?"

"Nope, I don't think so. Except…I felt bad not letting him stay there because I knew his options were limited since he didn't have family, so I asked him where he planned on going. What he told me sounded strange, and I really thought he was kidding, but he said he guessed he'd have to go stay in the Osborne farmhouse. There was no place else to go. Can you imagine that, the Osborne farmhouse of all places! I just shook my head and watched him walk down the street toward Groveville."

"That is unbelievable," Roger mumbled, but he didn't want to dismiss this new information. He had the road to the Osborne farm closed off the previous day with a lock and chain, which ran across the road, but that wouldn't keep anyone out from walking around it. It would be just like Malcolm Ridge to go back to the crime scene. Look over the evidence; blood splattered on the walls and across the floor. Malcolm Ridge was a sick young man, and going there proved it.

"How was he planning on getting there? He doesn't own a vehicle that I'm aware of. Did you happen to give him a ride, and you're not telling me?"

"Hell no, I didn't want anything to do with him. Besides, my car's not running good, it keeps overheating. I imagine he must have hitchhiked, always someone heading that way late at night from the Rustic Barn."

"So, he sounded pretty serious to you? You think he really did head out there?" Roger asked just as Deluca turned to leave.

"Maybe, I'm not sure," Deluca paused, then added, "Another thing I was thinking about after he left last night was something he said a few months ago, the day those two kids went missing up there."

"What was that?" Roger was starting to put two and two together even before Deluca told him."

"I was in the pool hall with Luke and Peter that Saturday, and he drove up in Luke's Charger. I asked Luke why he lent Mal his vehicle, and he said Mal had to run an errand over in Groveville. Mal came in looking a little rattled, his hair was tousled, and it looked like he had some blood on his shirt. I asked him what's up, you look a mess, and he just shrugged. I then asked him about the blood. He looked down at his shirt and tried to rub it off, but of course, it didn't."

"Where did he say the blood came from?" Roger was anxious to know.

"I can't quite remember what it was, but he said he had to pick up something, and he must have cut his hand and wiped it on his shirt. It wasn't a whole hell of a lot of blood, but you could tell it was blood."

"Did he show you the cut on his hand?"

"Nope, I didn't ask. But we played pool together, and I don't recall noticing a band-aid or anything."

"You sure it was the Saturday the kids went missing?"

"Yeah, I'm sure. Deputy James came in a couple of hours later and asked us if we wanted to go help out with finding them. I remember Mal saying no at first, something about he'd already been out there that morning. I thought he meant to Groveville, but he could have meant to the Osborne farmhouse. After what happened this past weekend, it got me to thinking he may have had something to do with those kids. But don't quote me on it."

CHAPTER TWENTY-THREE

Saturday Morning
May 12, 1989

Amanda Prescott took one last look at the open barn door and then reluctantly wheeled her red bicycle around, slowly pedaling back down the driveway while constantly fighting the urge to turn back around to explore the barn, with or without Kyle. Amanda had always been uncontrollably curious about the unknown mysteries her whole life, thirteen years worth, and she knew her future lay somewhere in the research field, and the urge to explore the barn was pulling at her backside, willing her inside.

Unhurriedly, she slowly came to a stop next to Kyle Bryant, her neighbor and best friend, since the day they met when Kyle's family moved into the house across the street eight years ago. "Okay, let's go. Where's this pond you're taking me fishing to?"

"Amanda, you left your pole back there," Kyle said, staring at his brother's fishing rod, which he borrowed without permission, laying on the ground near the old, dilapidated barn.

The last time Kyle borrowed something from his brother without asking for permission, he lost it, and his brother never let him forget about it, waving the broken gold chain in front of his face whenever Kyle asked to borrow something. *'Remember what used to be hanging on the end of this chain?'* He'd answer with a rhetorical question, teasing his younger brother. Kyle had borrowed Jimmy's pocket watch, an antique watch his grandfather, on his mother's side of the family, had given him for a present on his thirteenth birthday, a similar gift Kyle hoped to receive on his thirteenth birthday, which was only five days away. Kyle took the pocket watch with him down to Miller's Creek so he'd know what time it was to return home for lunch, but when he pulled the watch from his tight front pocket by the gold chain, the clasp holding the watch broke, and the watch accidentally dropped in the creek. Little Kyle anxiously extended his short arm as far as he could reach into the murky creek, touched but could not grasp hold of the precious watch with his tiny fingers, and then hopelessly sat at the edge of the creek, wondering what he was going to tell his big brother.

"Don't get a huffy. It's just a fishing pole. I'll go back and get it. I said I'd go fishing with you, didn't I?"

"I'm not getting a huffy, it's Jimmy's pole, and I know he'll brain me if something happens to it."

"I'll be right back," Amanda said. She then started to pedal her bicycle back up the driveway but stopped only halfway up and placed her feet firmly on the ground. It was a beautiful May morning, the sun was shining bright, and the sunlight angled its way through the open barn door, beckoning her to enter. Seeing what she presumed to be the guiding light was just too overpowering for Amanda to pass up. It was an invitation to explore the unknown, and Amanda relished the unknown. Even though she could speculate what may be inside the barn, like common things found in every barn in New England, there was always the off chance of surprise.

Amanda knew by looking at the farmhouse, seeing its dilapidated condition and boarded windows and doors, it was vacant, and she also knew it was from the stories she heard about the farmhouse being vacant for many years, longer than her lifetime of thirteen years. So, in her mind, there was nothing to worry about. Whoever the farmer was who murdered his whole family was long gone, and she wasn't going to let some exaggerated story scare her from exploring the place.

Not on her birthday, anyway.

She recalled her mother telling her the night before, as she trotted up the stairs to bed, she could do whatever she wanted on her birthday, meaning whatever Amanda wanted to do with her mother, which was never enforced as her mother sat home while Amanda was enjoying her birthday with a friend.

Amanda had no fear whatsoever about not knowing what lay beyond, and that was one reason why her mother, Janelle Prescott, kept a close eye on her only child. Lately, however, Amanda had been arguing with her mother about letting her wander off on her own without a watchful eye. Begrudgingly, her mother finally consented. Amanda was becoming a young woman, maturing at a rapid pace, and Janelle Prescott knew she had to untie the invisible rope around Amanda's waist, or she'd resent her forever for being so restrictive.

Kyle's mother, Candi Bryant, on the other hand, never worried much about Kyle when he ventured out of her sight because, for years, he had spent his adventurous time with his older brother, Jimmy, and by now, was well aware of pending dangers. The boys first began exploring the small, wooded area behind the family's house together. It was a sparse section of woods that ended abruptly at the edge of County Road and only held their interest for a short time. Later, they expanded their exploration to the other side of the County Road, where the forest grew thicker with tall gnarly pines mixed with hardwood oaks and maples and small patches of poplar trees. There, under the poplar trees, they'd sit for a spell in the tall soft grass listening and seeing nature surrounding them. Below, where it sloped toward the west, they found Miller's Creek. Some days they'd walked the creek for miles on both sides, unaware of the time. Only their hungry stomachs saved them from coming home late for supper.

Amanda turned back toward Kyle and watched as he held his fishing rod high above his right shoulder, slightly swinging the rod out in front of him to practice his casting form. Even though Amanda was only five days older than Kyle, seeing him now, she suddenly realized she was much older in maturity and knew their days as playmates were nearing an end. Her mother had told her, hinting as much, but it wasn't until she watched Kyle's innocent mannerisms that she realized what her mother was trying to tell her.

"Kyle?" she said compassionately.

Kyle stopped swinging his fishing rod and looked up toward Amanda. "What, are you going to get it? We don't have all day," Kyle said in a bossy tone. He was thinking even if she liked fishing, he would go alone the next time. After all, in his mind, fishing was a man's sport.

"It's my birthday, I should be able to do as I please on my birthday, and I want to explore that barn," she said, pointing her finger up the long driveway.

"No, Amanda, you said you wanted to go fishing," Kyle said, frowning, knowing it was probably too late to talk her out of it because lately, Amanda had been doing what she wanted whenever they spent time together, like the previous Saturday when she insisted they ride their bicycles across town to visit a female classmate. Kyle spent most of the afternoon brooding in silence, listening to the painful girl-talk while Pammy giddily unveiled every item in her bedroom. After three boring hours of torture, Kyle finally persuaded Amanda it was time to go and vowed, on the bicycle ride home, to never go back to Pammy's house again for as long as he lived.

"We can go fishing after if you still want to. Come on, follow me. It will be fun," Amanda urged and, without waiting for a response, pushed off with her legs and started pedaling up the driveway.

Kyle hesitated a moment, thinking of leaving his fishing rod at the foot of the driveway, but quickly decided against it. He then began to follow her, pumping his shorter legs harder to catch up. When he reached the wooden ramp, Amanda had already disappeared inside the cave-like barn.

"Amanda, wait for me," he called out, hoping she was right inside and not off hiding on him. Amanda often liked to tease Kyle, running ahead and hiding and then scaring him when he approached.

"Don't worry, I'm right here," she answered.

Kyle walked his bicycle up the short wooden ramp and disappeared into the darkness of the barn. Inside, he spotted Amanda standing next to her bicycle in the middle of the spacious barn looking up at the loft. His eyes hadn't adjusted to the change of light, and he couldn't see what was up there. But his sense of smell detected an unfamiliar odor of dust and musty old hay.

"See anything up there?" he inquisitively asked. A bit of excitement rose from the pit of his stomach just standing there.

"I can see hay. That's about all. Want to go check it out?"

"No, I'm not going up there."

"I wonder where the stairs are?" Amanda asked as she inquisitively walked slowly under the loft. She then abruptly turned left and headed toward the far side of the barn, looking for a stairway that led to the loft.

On that side of the barn, Amanda noticed a long wooden bench and what looked like a backboard of rusty tools hanging by hooks behind it. Further beyond, she could see a row of cow stalls built into the wall and a matching row opposite. She then walked over to inspect them to see what was inside the stalls. To her disappointment, the stalls were mainly empty. Only patches of hay brushed along the bottom edges and what looked like small, pellet size piles of dried grayish feces. Beyond the stalls, in the back of the barn, Amanda spied what she was looking for, a wooden ladder built into the wall.

"Over here, Kyle, there's a ladder we can climb."

Amanda walked over to the ladder and started to climb up to the loft. Before disappearing through the four-foot square hole, cut into the floor of the loft, she glanced back to see if Kyle was behind her and saw he was still anchored to the floor in the center of the barn.

"Are you coming?"

"I guess. What's up there?"

"I don't know what's up here…that's why we're going to check it out, dummy."

Kyle hesitated and kept his ground. He liked exploring even more than Amanda, but the idea of being in the same building where dead bodies were found scared him.

"Well, don't just stand there. Come on, it's easy," she coaxed him.

Kyle watched Amanda disappear through the hole and waited for her to appear again over the loft's edge.

A moment later, he saw her peering down at him, smiling. "Coming up? It's pretty easy."

Kyle looked out the barn door, wanting to leave, but instead followed in Amanda's invisible footsteps to the back of the barn and slowly climbed up the ladder. He wanted to show her he wasn't scared, but he was somewhat.

"Pretty cool up here, huh?" Amanda said to Kyle when he poked his head through the opening.

Once Kyle crawled out of the hole and was standing on the floor of the loft, he felt safer and walked up close to the edge, where Amanda was sitting with her feet dangling over the edge.

"What do you think?" she proudly asked.

"I guess it's okay. There are a lot of spider webs, though. Look at that gigantic one over there in the corner. I'm not going anywhere near that."

"I think it's pretty fascinating."

"You do? Girls aren't supposed to like spiders."

"Oh, I don't like spiders. I think they're gross. And they bite. They really do. My mother told me she knew someone who had been bitten on her upper thigh while she was sleeping in her bed by a great big black spider and almost died. She was in the hospital for three days."

"Really!"

"Yes, it's the truth. I swear to God."

"I believe you. It just sounds gross. So why do you like spider webs?"

"Oh, I just think spider webs are kind of cool looking, like that one. That one is the coolest one I've ever seen."

After taking another look, Kyle also thought it looked

pretty cool but didn't tell Amanda.

"Nice view from here. If you bend your head down and look out the door, you can see halfway down the road. Look over there. That's the cemetery we were just looking at," Amanda said, pointing out the barn door.

"Where? I don't see it?"

"You can't see it from standing. You have to get down low. Here, sit down next to me," Amanda said, gently tapping the edge of the loft.

Kyle cautiously glanced over the edge, looking straight down. It looked higher from where he stood than from standing below. Gingerly, he sat and inched his way toward the edge, next to Amanda, and looked out the barn door. From his view, he could only see as far as the end of the driveway.

"Where? I still don't see the cemetery?" he disappointedly asked.

"Right there. You have to duck your head down real low like this," Amanda said, leaning her head close to the loft floor and looking out the open doorway."

He followed her finger out past the driveway and beyond the golden, sunlit field, where thinly leaf poplar trees lined the edge of the woods. There, he could see where she was pointing but could barely make out the area where the cemetery was supposedly located.

"Yeah, I think so. I can see where we were through the trees, but I can't see the gravestones."

"They're hard to see, but that's the cemetery. The sunlight is shining on it, right over there where it's lighter."

"I see something else…." Kyle said, squinting.

"What… trees?" Amanda laughed.

"No, I think it's a car coming up the road. I can see the dust."

Amanda set her sight out toward the road and saw a trail of dirt and dust billowing from a fast-moving vehicle driving up the graveled road. In an instant, a red Charger emerged from the woods and continued at the same fast speed until it came to an abrupt stop at the end of the driveway. The car then slowly turned into the driveway and stopped. A moment later, the driver killed the engine.

"I hope whoever is in there doesn't come in here," Amanda whispered.

"I told you we shouldn't have come in here," Kyle said, sounding scared.

"Shhhh, we don't want them to hear us."

"I wasn't talking loud," Kyle whispered.

"Yes, you were. Can you see who's in the car?"

Kyle looked and could see the driver's dark outline through the windshield. "No, I can't see who it is, but it only looks like one person."

Suddenly, the driver's door opened, causing Amanda and Kyle to brace against one another as they anxiously waited to see who was about to emerge, but no one exited the vehicle. All they could see was a person's head leaning out the door and the retching sound the person made, grinding up a slimy wad of mucus and spitting it to the ground.

Kyle glanced down at the floor beneath him and spotted the bicycles. They looked smaller, like the bicycle he learned to ride on, the one that had training wheels. "The bikes. We'd better hide the bikes in case he comes in here."

"Oh, that's right, he'll see the bikes and know we're in here. You're going to have to climb down the ladder and hide the bikes behind one of the stalls."

"Me, why me?" Kyle griped.

"Because you can do it quicker than I can. I'll keep an eye out for him and let you know if he's coming. So, go now before he comes up here."

"What do I do then? I don't want to be down there alone."

"Climb back up the ladder. We'll hide behind the bales of hay over there." Amanda nodded toward the broken bales of hay on the other side of the loft.

Kyle climbed down the ladder while Amanda watched the occupant in the vehicle. She could see the person lean back against the seat and then noticed a faint flicker of light appear.

After Kyle hurriedly hid the bicycles behind a cow stall, he scampered back up the ladder and sat down next to Amanda, this time less fearful of the height.

"What's he doing now?"

"Nothing, he's just sitting there." Amanda could see smoke coming from within the vehicle. "I think he's smoking a cigarette."

They sat in silence for the next few minutes, watching puffs of smoke drift out the open door, wondering what the person was going to do next – hoping he would leave and not venture into the barn. Soon, the person behind the wheel closed the door and started the vehicle up with a loud roar, which startled the youngsters. They then cautiously watched the red vehicle back out of the driveway and drive down the road at the same rate of speed it had driven up. It then disappeared beyond the cemetery, leaving behind a cloud of dust.

"Whew, he's gone," Amanda said, patting Kyle on his narrow bony shoulder. "You can breathe now."

"I know. Can we go now? I don't like it in here."

Amanda glanced around the loft before answering to see if there was anything interesting to look at. Seeing only broken bales of hay and discarded wooden crates, she quickly assessed there was nothing of interest to see in the loft and led Kyle back down the ladder. Once they were back on the ground floor, Amanda felt she hadn't had her fill of exploration and began to snoop around the spacious barn. There were plenty of interesting objects to look at, that she had no idea what they were used for. She knew they must have had something to do with farming, but she had no idea for what use. One item she found hanging on a hook near a stall was a long rubber hose with several suction cups on one end, which she thought was quite amusing and shoved it in front of Kyle's face.

"I wonder what this thing was used for?" she asked, teasing her bored and still slightly nervous friend.

"I don't know what it is, and I don't care to know. I think

we should leave before someone else comes."

"I believe this was probably used to milk the cows, don't you think?" Amanda said, ignoring Kyle's concerns.

Kyle took a better look at the object being waved in front of him, grabbing it to stop her from wiggling the odd contraption in his face. "I don't know. I guess it could be."

Amanda dropped her end of the rubber hose and moved toward the side of the barn, where she spotted a narrow door. She slowly pulled on the brass handle, creaking the door open. Inside, she could barely make out anything in the darkness.

"I wonder what's in here?" she said, taking a step inside.

"No, Amanda, don't go in there. It probably leads to the house. The farmer could be in there."

Amanda stuck her head back out the door. "Nobody lives here. The place is condemned."

"How can you be sure you've never been up here before?"

"It doesn't matter if I've ever been here before. You can tell just by looking at this old place that nobody lives here. Come on, there's nothing to be scared of."

Kyle was not planning on following Amanda inside, but he walked up to the door anyway to take a curiosity peek. From outside the door, he could see Amanda's dark, outlined silhouette standing a few feet inside the dark room, but beyond her, the room was in total darkness, except for a weak, narrow shaft of light at the far end.

"Hey, what's this?" Amanda asked, touching, but not picking up, a small glass container on the shelf in front of her.

"What is it?" Kyle curiously asked.

"I don't know, I can't see too good in here, but there's a lot of neat stuff on these shelves. Come check it out?"

Before he made the crucial mistake of walking inside, Kyle heard the loud engine roar from the Dodge Charger driving back up the driveway.

"He's back!" Kyle yelled.

Both Amanda and Kyle raced over to the small window next to the barn door and anxiously watched as the driver killed the engine. Slowly the man creaked the driver's door open and flicked a cigarette butt out on the grass. He then bent his body and stepped out of the vehicle. The person who stepped out into their view was tall and lanky, with a tangled mess of shaggy curls on a narrow head. The frightening-looking man then started to walk over toward the open barn door but stopped before he reached the barn. He then glanced around for a moment as though he was checking to see if anyone was watching him, and then bent and picked up the fishing rod Amanda left on the ground.

Jimmy's fishing pole! Kyle almost mouthed out loud. The man was going to take the fishing rod, and there was nothing he could do about it. He was too frightened to confront the man to tell him the fishing rod belonged to his brother.

Amanda was holding her breath, hoping the man would just leave, take the fishing rod with him if he'd only leave. Kyle could buy a new one for his brother. And if he insisted, had a huffy over it, she'd give him some of her birthday money her mother had given her to pay for it. *Besides, how much did one of those cheap, skinny-looking things cost anyhow?* She wondered.

The man was still holding the fishing rod when he started walking toward the barn. They could hear his heavy boots clomping up the wooden ramp leading into the barn. There was no time to run and hide, so Amanda and Kyle held their breath and hid where they were, in plain sight, huddled beneath the window.

CHAPTER TWENTY-FOUR

Sunday Night
August 12, 1989

It was pitch black when I neared the entrance to the cemetery as the waxing moon once again disappeared behind a cloud. The moon had been in and out of clouds, and at times I could hardly see where I was going, stumbling in ruts and coming close to walking into the ditch that ran along both sides of the half-mile long, graveled Osborne Road. Only when the moon reappeared could I see the road in front of me, the rises and dips, and the slightly familiar curves. The last curve, where the cemetery rested a few yards from the edge of the road, was most familiar. When I approached the cemetery, the near full moon coincidentally reappeared, illuminating the gravestones. Seeing them like that, seeing the light flicker across the stones like ghosts dancing on their trifle plot of ground at midnight, I thought of the family who was buried there and how gruesome their deaths must have been.

How could they dance? Their deaths were horrible. They should have been weeping for each other – cursing the awful man who wronged them, ending their lives too soon.

The children were horrified, watching their father chop their mother's head off with a bloody axe, the head rolling at their feet, her eyes still helplessly wide open. And then, watching the man who toiled on the farm day after day to put food on the table and tuck them in their cozy beds at night with kisses upon their foreheads for love, chop their siblings' heads off, one by one, until it was their turn to die. Or did they watch? No one would ever know.

Beyond the cemetery, past the open fields, I could barely see the farmhouse. Only the outline was visible to the human eye, the haunting outline of the death house. The barn, where I was heading for the open door, rose higher than the main house and stretched long toward the open field.

In hindsight, I should have turned and walked away, found some other place to shelter, but I felt a strange, overpowering force drawing me inside the dreadful house, pulling me against my will. Or maybe I wanted to go there, and the overpowering force was within me.

I hitched a ride to Groveville, being picked up by a stranger who had no idea who I was and what I was accused of doing. Then after being dropped by the side of the road next to the convenience store, the same store I had my mental breakdown, I walked several miles to the Osborne farmhouse all along, thinking it was an ill-planned idea. My reasoning, however, was simple – I had no place else to go. My two friends were dead, so they told me, and my only other friend, my pal, Al Deluca, wanted nothing to do with me. Who could blame him? Surely, not after having been told I was the number one suspect in the murder of my friends.

A couple of days in the farmhouse was better than a couple of days camped out in the woods where bugs grew nasty this time of year. From what I remembered about the farmhouse, being in the house previously on a few occasions by myself for curiosity purposes, there were beds in the upstairs bedrooms, many to choose from. There, I could make plans on where to go next, where to hide from what I knew was about to come down on me. I figured the farmhouse would be the last place they'd look for me when they finally got around to accusing me of the crime I did not commit and came searching for me. In a day or two, I'd be gone anyway. Far away from Groveville and the neighboring town of Denton.

According to Sheriff Roger Lefebvre, the evidence they had was stacked up against me, and after hearing the evidence myself, he almost had me convinced I had committed the murders.

'We have the bloody axe with your fingerprints all over it. We found it lying right next to the mutilated bodies. The bodies of your two buddies.' He said with his face no more than three inches from my nose, spitting the words as he yelled them at me. He was so close I could see his yellow coffee-stained teeth and smell the distasting aroma of coffee reeking from his mouth.

I tried to tell him I thought I was carrying the axe around for protection, but I wasn't exactly sure because the night was mostly just a blur of fragmented images. *'What were you protecting yourself against?'* He asked me. I had no answer for him. I should have said it was dark and scary.

When the Sheriff came back into my hospital room late Sunday afternoon, I thought he was coming in to arrest me, but instead, he asked me again, for the umpteenth time, what happened inside the farmhouse. From my raised position in my bed, I could see beyond the window the sun was setting, and I imagined it was the same fiery sunset I had seen the night before when we drove toward the farmhouse – fiery orange reflections bouncing off the broken windowpanes looking as though the farmhouse was on fire. I wished it were on fire. I guess everyone wished it were burning to the ground.

"Sheriff, I remember smelling the stench of his cold breath on my face and his rotting flesh reeking of death. That's how close he was to me. That's how close he came to killing me. And that's why I swung the axe. And when he kept coming closer, I swung again and again. And then I turned and ran and kept running until I was far away from that horrible place." That's what I told him for the umpteenth time. Then after a long pause to catch my breath, I added. "I swear that's the truth, Sheriff. That part, I remember for sure. You've got to believe me; I didn't kill my friends."

The Sheriff shook his head at my wild story, not believing

a word I told him. Most likely, he thought it was fabricated because I couldn't remember anything before when he first asked me. But, being alone in the hospital bed all day, I had time to think. I tried to remember, step-by-step, of what happened when I first entered the farmhouse, and with the woman doctor's help, I slowly began to remember bits and pieces of what happened, and then I put it all together.

I was standing alone in the barn, wondering if I should continue to follow my friends inside the house or wait outside for them. I saw myself looking around in the kitchen and then walking into the dark living room. The frightening pony heads coming down on me. The horrible screams. I saw myself running for my life.

I was almost certain the Sheriff was going to arrest me right then and there. Put me in handcuffs and yank me off to jail in my hospital gown, but to my complete surprise, he told me I was free to go. There was a hitch, however. He informed me I was not to leave town because I was still considered a suspect in the deaths of Luke Townsend and Peter Finch.

At first, I was relieved, not wanting to spend another night in the hospital, or in jail for that matter, but suddenly I realized I was homeless. I had been staying at the Finch's house, a room in the basement Peter's parents fixed up for me. I made friends with Peter when we were both spending some time at a juvenile detention facility over in Hancock. I told Peter I had been adopted and wasn't getting along with my adoptive parents, and when I got out, I wasn't going back there. Peter told me his parents were really cool and would let me stay there when I got out. That was six years ago, and I'd been living there ever since. Then, with Peter dead, I had no place to go. I couldn't even go back there for a change of clothes. The only thing I owned was the recycled clothes the hospital gave me. Probably donated by some poor soul down in the morgue.

After having been given a ride back to Denton from the hospital in the Sheriff's personal cruiser, I optimistically walked the two miles from the sheriff's office over to Deluca's apartment, which he shared with two other guys I hardly knew, in an off chance he might let me stay on his couch awhile until I found other accommodations. I knew we hadn't been real close friends, but Deluca didn't seem the type to leave a guy stranded, and basically, he was my last hope.

The apartment he lived in was a two-family duplex located out by the railroad tracks on the west side of town, close to Groveville. The other side of Deluca's half of the duplex lived a single mother with her three snort-nose children, all under the age of five. An odd setup, if you asked me, three party types on one side, snort-nose kids on the other.

I had only been over there once before, the time Deluca needed a ride in town to pick up a radiator hose for his clunker. Luke Townsend asked me along for the ride, and then after, we were going to shoot a couple of games of pool and drink a few beers. When we got there, I noticed a couple of young kids playing near Deluca's porch steps and Deluca in the driveway leaning against his car. I can't remember what model of car he owned, but I was pretty sure it was a Ford, some small two-door thing. Better than nothing, I suppose, seeing I didn't own a vehicle myself.

After Deluca jumped in the back seat of the Charger, I asked him what's with the kiddies, and he mumbled something like one of his roommates was screwing their mother.

"So, I suppose when they're in the sack together, you get stuck babysitting the kids," I said jokingly.

"No, wise guy, they never come over to our house. Mickey usually goes over there after he gets out of work."

"So, what are the kids doing on your side of the yard?" I asked Deluca as Luke backed his prized Dodge Charger out of the driveway and headed toward the auto parts store.

"I don't know. I guess the kids think they have privileges since their mother is screwing Mickey."

"What's the mother like?" I asked, picturing an overweight broad with red hair rolled up in curlers and wearing an ugly pea-green housecoat.

"She's okay, not bad for a woman with three kids. You probably know her. Her name's Evelyn, Evelyn Myers."

"Nope, name doesn't ring a bell. How about you, Luke?"

"Yeah, I think I do know her. Wasn't she the one married to that asshole Bobby Myers?"

"That's the one," Deluca answered.

I tried to remember all the assholes I knew with the name Bobby. There was Bobby Fitzgerald, an older, chubby bald guy who sometimes hung out at the pool hall and drank draft beers until he could hardly walk home. He didn't seem like a bad guy, but he was still an asshole by the way he stared at me as though he was wondering if I was the guy screwing his wife. And there was Bobby Helms, another guy I didn't care for. But other than those two, no other Bobby came to mind.

"What does he look like?" I asked to no one in particular.

"Tall guy, I guess," Deluca said from the back seat. "He works down at the box factory. I'm not sure where he hangs out, but I've seen him at the liquor store recently. He's a real asshole, though. The creep left Evelyn last year with those three rug-rats and doesn't pay his child support on time, according to her."

"Nope, still don't remember him."

"Hey, Deluca?" Luke asked, looking in the rearview mirror. "Ain't she the sister of that girl who got murdered down at Miller's Creek a few years ago.

"Yeah, that's her. We were just talking about it the other night. It happened about seven years ago, and Evelyn is still pretty shook-up about it. She told us they never did find out who did it."

Hearing them talk about the girl who had been murdered, I could picture her face that covered the front page of the local newspaper the day after they found her supposedly nude body partially submerged in murky Miller's Creek. She was twelve years old at the time. Only twelve.

From what I read in the newspaper, the girl had walked to the neighborhood store with her older sister for sodas, which was only a couple of blocks from their house. On their way back from the store, Evelyn got into a car driven by a male friend of hers to go for a ride, and her younger sister had to walk home alone, but unfortunately, she never arrived. A month later, they found her body in Miller's Creek. She had been stripped to her bare skin and left to rot as though she was no more than a carcass of a dead animal. Some guy probably lured her into his vehicle, raped and tortured her to death, then dumped her nude body off the bridge.

"What about you, Mal? Remember when that happened?" Luke asked.

How could I not? I just nodded my head in remembrance.

* * *

When I knocked on Deluca's apartment door, I was glad he was the one who answered. Instead of inviting me in, however, he stepped out on the porch and quickly closed the door behind him. Deluca stood awkwardly, shifting from one foot to the other, making me feel uncomfortable. He didn't seem like the same person I knew from the pool hall. In the pool hall, where I usually saw him, Deluca seemed cool and collected, king of the pool hall, always winning. Watching him then, I could see his other side, his weaker side. I wished I had seen this side of him before and wouldn't have been so intimidated and maybe have won a few more games of pool against him.

"What's up?" he asked me, sounding like I was intruding.

I told him I was hoping he could let me stay on his couch for a couple of days. I could see the answer on his face the second I asked. His expression was blank, and then he turned toward the door and nodded inside.

"Hey man, if it were up to me, you know I'd let you stay, but I've got two roommates."

"Are they home? Can you ask them?"

"Espo's here," Deluca was referring to his other roommate, Andy Esposito, someone I have never met. "And Mickey's next door."

"Well, can you ask Espo, see what he says?"

"No, I already know they won't let you. They've been talking about you all day, about how the cops think you did it."

"I didn't do it! You don't think I could have killed them, do you, Deluca?" I was getting mad, already being convicted before being indicted. The whole town probably came to the same conclusion. It was my word against everyone else's belief.

"Who me? No way."

I stood looking at him on the dark porch steps wondering if he believed me. I then told him my side of the story about the crazy man who attacked us, leaving most of the night vague.

"So, Al, can't you let me in for just a while, at least until I figure out where I'm going to go?"

"No, Mal, I'm sorry, but these guys don't like you."

I looked hard in Deluca's face and could see the sorrow in his narrow eyes, which opened wider than I had seen them before but not wide enough for me to tell what color they were. I suddenly felt sorrier for him than I did for myself, having no place to go, and then it hit me – a place where I could go and be alone, away from accusing eyes.

I started walking down the steps when Deluca sympathetically asked where I was planning to go. I think his conscience was bothering him. If it were anyone else, I would have told him to shove it – it was none of his damn business – Deluca, however, was my only friend in the world.

"Back to the scene of the crime."

"You're going back to the Osborne place? What about the man who attacked you? Aren't you afraid he's still there?" Deluca asked with concern, then his expression changed, wondering if I had lied about the man.

"He's probably long gone with the police crawling all over the place," I explained to put his thought process in the right perspective.

Deluca weakly shook his head. I knew he wasn't buying it, but I didn't care because I did, and that was what counted. I also felt I had to go there because I had this strong feeling like something powerful was luring me out there. I asked him for a ride so I wouldn't have to walk the seven or eight miles, but as usual, Deluca's car was broken down. Dejectedly, I waved my hand and disappeared into the night.

CHAPTER TWENTY-FIVE

After Midnight
August 13, 1989

After the ride to Groveville and the long dark hike to the farmhouse, I finally found myself standing in the center of the creepy living room. I know, a stupid place to be after what I had been through, but there I was smack in the middle of evil.

It was extremely dark inside the farmhouse, and I didn't have a flashlight or any other means like a handy lighter or match to navigate my way as I crept along the creepy floorboards toward the stairway leading to the second floor. As I walked through the room, I felt a strange presence, like I was being watched by someone, but I just assumed it was because of the murders that had happened the previous night. Their spirits, or something like that, were drifting around the living room, looking for a way out.

Once I reached the top of the stairs, I stepped into the first bedroom on my right and inched my way toward the bed. I touched the coarse blanket that was covering the queen size bed and pulled it down, and then settled in with my clothes still on. It was well past midnight, and I was totally exhausted, physically and mentally. It wasn't just the repeated questions the Sheriff continued to ask me that taxed my brain mentally; it was mostly the pestering questions the female psychiatrist kept asking.

I was already a nervous wreck thinking about the night before and wondering what was to come of me. She wanted to know everything about my past life. What my childhood was like, did I have any friends growing up, did I like my adopted parents (which I told her I hated them), and what I had been doing recently. I told her everything, to my best recollection, and didn't elaborate on any significant event except the things I hated most about my adopted parents. So, when I hit the bed, I quickly fell into a deep sound sleep.

My dreams came in flashes, images I couldn't recall when I awoke, except the one about Kristen Vale. In the dream about her, we were lying in a bed with the covers pulled over our heads. Under the blanket, I saw her small soft hand slowly reaching toward my face. The white palm of her hand I could see clearly as though the hand was real, physically in bed with me. The deep lifelines running across the palm suggesting a long, fruitful life. I could even smell the freshness when she gently touched my face. I buried my face in her hand and moved closer to her. Kristen then turned to her backside and wiggled into me. Her voice was soft and sweet when she told me she wanted me to wrap my arms around her and hold her tight.

I could see the whiteness of her body glowing under the dark covers and smell her youthfulness – the sweet, enticing aroma girls give off. With one arm beneath her, holding her tight, I moved my other hand over her shoulder and inched it toward her smooth belly. As I rubbed her small stomach, she hummed with delight and pushed my hand lower down to where she wanted me to touch her. I could feel my chest pumping against her back and my warm breath breathing over her neck and face. Turning toward me, I could see her eyes were wide open, the blue was like the waters of the Caribbean, and her lips pressed warm against my own. I felt like I was in heaven. And suddenly, it was over, disappeared as though it were only a dream. Then I realized it was only a dream. It felt so real. I could still smell her sweetness and feel her warm moist flesh on my hands.

I wanted Kristen to come back to me. I had never been that intimate with her before. When we dated, it was for only a brief time, two weeks at most, maybe three if I count the day she asked me to meet her outside of where she worked. Right there where her coworkers could see us from inside the window. There, out on the sidewalk in front of the Denton Beauty Parlor, she told me point blank that she was dating someone else and to not call her anymore. I remember the look on her stern face, eyes the color of a raging sea, not the blue of the Caribbean, a look to let me know she was serious. I loved her and told her so many times. It was my only defense to save our relationship. It failed, but I still held out a minuscule of hope. As I turned and walked away, I could imagine her yelling back to me, telling me she was sorry and didn't mean it. But she never did until she came to me in that dream.

And I wanted her back, even if it were only a dream.

I tried to go back to sleep and conjure her image up again, but all I could visualize was a dim impression of her face, which continued to fade away the longer I tried to hold her in my mind. And the noises pounding in my head didn't help my concentration any.

The harder I tried to concentrate, the louder the noises pounded in my head. They became so loud and annoying I had to sit up in my bed and clasp my hands over my ears to keep them out. That's when I realized the noises weren't imaginary noises in my head but real voices coming from somewhere beyond the bedroom door. The voices were muffled, coming through the closed door, and I couldn't understand what was being said or even if there was more than one person doing the talking. But as I carefully crawled out of bed and slowly inched my way over to the door, placing my ear against the thin wood, I believed the voices sounded childlike, and they were whispering right outside my door.

I suddenly realized I was not alone. This was not good.

I immediately thought of the two youngsters who had gone missing three months before. Maybe the murderous old farmer, Zeke Osborne, had kidnapped them, hiding them in some unknown hiding place, a secret room or underground chamber that was behind a wall in the basement. Maybe in the attic above where I stood hunched. Who else could they be?

My first impulse was to rush open the door and tell the youngsters not to be afraid. I would protect them from that evil man and take them home to their parents. I would be a hero. I would be exonerated of the wrongful accusations of murdering my friends.

Realizing this as a possibility, I slipped my hand over the doorknob and slowly began to twist the knob, then stopped before it clicked open. I had to think for a minute. I knew I was wide awake and not dreaming like I had dreamed about Kristen because you can tell when you're awake, all your senses are working. I could feel the wood pressing against my ear and smell the stale air that had not escaped the room in years, and my mouth was dry from the lack of fluids and the rush of adrenaline. I could taste the dryness. But it just seemed too preposterous to believe those children, or any child for that matter, were on the other side of that door.

Before making the mistake of opening the door to some unknown person, I started to think about who else could be beyond that door. After all, the voices I heard were muffled. They could have been whispers from an adult. It could have been the voice of Zeke Osborne himself, the insane man talking to himself.

I pressed my ear harder against the door to concentrate on the voice, but I heard nothing, no sounds at all. After a few moments of not hearing anything, I slowly opened the door, twisting the doorknob until I felt the latch release, then cautiously inched it open just enough to stick my head out. Gripping the door handle with one hand and the other clutched firmly on the frame, I peeked out into the hallway.

The hallway was in complete darkness. I couldn't even see the door across the hall from me, only a few feet away. It was impossible to tell if anyone was standing down the hall. I held my breath and listened, but I could only hear my heart beating fast against my chest. You don't know how scared I was at that moment. Even though, at first, I assumed it was children's voices I heard, I then truly suspected the voices were those from an adult, and the person was hiding down the hall in the dark, waiting. Zeke Osborne was waiting for me to come out.

In a low dry voice, I attempted to call out, 'Who's there,' but the words were weak and came out like a whisper so low I could barely hear myself say the words. Daringly, I stared down the hall. It was as black as black could possibly be. Nothing existed beyond. Even my words dissolved into the blackness. There was nothing down that hallway. No children, no Zeke Osborne. Nothing! The voices I heard were nonexistent, something I conjured up in my fragile mind.

There was nobody there. I was alone. I walked back into the bedroom and closed the door tight, wishing there was a latch to lock evil out. Once I was back in the bed, I pulled the covers over my head and closed my eyes in a vain attempt to sleep the horrors away. After a while, I finally fell asleep.

In the morning, when the sun rose above the treetops, waking me from my slumber, I tiredly pulled myself up and sat on the edge of the bed, rubbing my tired, sleepy eyes. I sat there for a while thinking about the dreams that kept me from a good night's sleep, especially the dream that brought Kristen back into my life. There was no reason for me to have been dreaming about her. It had been almost a year since I last saw her. She was laughing with friends inside a diner I happened to pass by. When I noticed her, I briefly stopped outside the window, hoping she would notice and motion me inside, but she didn't. I was disappointed but let the notion of our reconciliation drift away in the breeze that tousled my hair, and I jogged across the street to the pool hall.

After I shook the thought of her away to focus on my immediate situation, I noticed a green footlocker pushed up against a wall near the door. I flipped the top open and saw the locker contained toy pony heads, five in all, and of different colors. I picked up one of the heads and noticed the wooden pole had been sawed off. There were other items in the footlocker, mostly small toys, and after I emptied the footlocker out, tossing the pony heads and the other toys on the floor and shoving them under the bed so nobody would notice them. I then dragged the awkward footlocker down the stairs and into the kitchen.

My intention was to haul the footlocker out to the road and use it as a prop to hitch a ride. Seeing the footlocker, some guy with a truck might take kindly and offer me a ride. But after giving the ridiculous plan a second thought, I rejected the idea and just left the footlocker where I put it, in the kitchen next to the old wooden icebox.

For the rest of the morning, I just roamed around the empty farmhouse, familiarizing myself with the place, the lay of the property, so to speak. I toured the farmhouse from top to bottom, hitting the basement last, which I found very interesting with all sorts of crap, mostly junk, I assumed. I then walked around the outside, staying close to the house but far enough away to get a good outside view of the farmhouse. From what I gathered, how it looked in daylight being alone and not being influenced by others, the place didn't seem as horrible as everyone made it out to be. In fact, the farm seemed quite peaceful, very serene and full of nature. It definitely was a different lifestyle, but one I could see myself living.

Out beyond the house, I noticed several deer gently walking through the fields, stopping here and there to sample the vegetation, whatever was left of the old crops, and occasionally perking their ears when something spooked them, like me when I tried to get closer. Crows and larger birds, hawks, flying overhead, circling in a swirl of wind, enjoying their flight of freedom.

Later, when I got bored of roaming, I rested on the porch step and just looked around. I watched the smaller birds, sparrows and finches, fly in and out of the barn through the small opening where the boards had rotted off. I watched the clouds form odd shapes, large dragons, prehistoric birds, clown faces and oval spaceships coming in over the horizon. I watched the sun rise high in the sky and then later begin its descent as the day moved on.

A dragonfly harmlessly landed on my shirt. At first, I hadn't noticed he was enjoying lunch, feasting on a tiny insect, and I wondered how long he was going to stay. As I curiously watched, I noticed the insect kicking his legs and flapping tiny wings. Slowly the little insect disappeared deeper inside the dragonfly's mouth until only the back pair of legs was visible, still kicking, trying to escape. It was too late for me to intervene and save the little bugger from a horrible death, but I couldn't watch its demise any longer and shooed the dragonfly away.

After the dragonfly disappeared into the blue, I looked at my shirt where he had been feasting and noticed a tiny black wing. I brushed the tiny wing from my shirt with sad feelings, how short its life had been. Was it one day or two, or just a few hours?

While I was thinking about that nonesuch, I heard a rumbling sound coming from somewhere down the Osborne Road and looked with a bit of anxiety. Down the road, nearing the cemetery, I could see a cloud of dust coming at a high rate of speed, and when I recognized it was a sheriff's vehicle, I quickly scrambled off the porch and ran into the barn.

Suddenly my instincts told me not to stay in the barn, as it would be the first place they'd look. I quickly made the decision to hide away from the farmhouse and made my way unnoticed out across the open field, where the deer had feasted only an hour or so before. I then hid in a small thicket of scrub brush to watch the action.

After kneeling for several minutes, staring at the backside of the farmhouse, my knees began to ache, so I decided to sit down on the tall grass and wait them out. From my view, I could see the wide-open fields of sun-dried alfalfa and pictured how the scenery would look with tall green cornstalks sprouting out of the ground against the sky-blue background instead of the golden-brown alfalfa. Inside my gut, somewhere, I felt I could have been a farmer, grown all the food I needed to survive and raised cattle for milk and meat. I even thought of raising a family with lots of children. I thought of Kristen again, how real she had felt to me in my dream. I knew that very moment as I sat there contemplating what I wanted to do with my life – if it was still possible for me to have one.

The first thing I was going to do was go back to Denton and clear this mess I was in with Sheriff Lefebvre. He seemed to me like a man who would believe in me and that I was only an innocent bystander. I would tell him about the noises I heard last night, noises that were made by the man who killed my friends, the man who also murdered his whole family. I would tell him again it was Zeke Osborne who had done it, and he was still somewhere in the farmhouse.

I quickly made a beeline straight for the barn, zigzagging around patches of wild prickly brush, and ducked around the back corner, out of sight. I figured it would be a good place to watch them without being seen, see what they were up to, and see if maybe the Sheriff himself was there. But there was no 'them,' and there was no Sheriff either. There was only Deputy Wayne Leon James, and he was standing next to his cruiser talking to someone on the police radio.

While he was talking, I could see he was looking at the farmhouse, mainly looking at the porch that led to the kitchen, but occasionally he would glance up and point at a second-floor bedroom like he was explaining something to the person on the other end of the radio. The same bedroom I had been sleeping in the night before.

This didn't look good. I knew he had gone inside and most likely found something by the way he was pointing and all. Deputy James was always looking to get credit for something; bagging me for breaking and entering would top his list of achievements, I'm sure.

I could have turned myself in, told the deputy I wanted to talk with the Sheriff to clear my name, tell him it was Zeke Osborne who had killed my friends. But Deputy James could have had a different version of what had transpired out at the farmhouse and that I hadn't turned myself in, and it was he who had single-handedly apprehended me, so he could get rewarded. The Sheriff would definitely go with his word against mine, thinking I was only trying to save my butt.

Not wanting Deputy James to get the collar, I headed back toward the tree line at a slow pace, crouching low to the ground at first as not to be seen, then quickly ran through the tall alfalfa and around the prickly stuff until I reached the cover of the woods. This time I found myself nearer the cemetery than before and decided to hide behind one of the gravestones and watch the ongoings until I could figure out what to do next. The only idea I came up with, however, was to get to the main road and hitch a ride back to Denton. There, I would walk into the sheriff's office on my own accord. It sounded like a good idea, but that's not what happened. Unfortunately for me, I stayed and watched longer than I should have, causing the window of time to close.

As I continued my surveillance, watching Deputy James pace the driveway looking at the house, looking down the road, and a couple of times just looking out across the field with me, wondering if he could see me staring back at him, I heard the sirens, and then all Hell broke out.

CHAPTER TWENTY-SIX

Monday Afternoon
August 13, 1989

After interviewing Al Deluca about what he knew of Malcolm Ridge and where he might be staying, Sheriff Roger Lefebvre somberly sat at his desk and gazed out his office window, searching his cluttered mind for any valid reason to believe the man who had just left his office was telling the truth. After all, Deluca was supposedly Ridge's friend, so why would Deluca try to implicate him? Saying Ridge may have been to the Osborne farm the morning the kids went missing, mentioning the blood on his shirt.

The answer had to be Deluca wasn't his friend and wanted to see justice prevail, like every other decent citizen. There were a lot of decent folks in the world, and even though Deluca didn't look like the sort of person that gave a rats-ass about justice, Roger knew you shouldn't judge a person by appearance alone.

"Unless," Roger thought out loud, "Deluca was trying to lead the focus away from himself?" But the more he thought about the possibility of Deluca being involved with the disappearance of Amanda Prescott and Kyle Bryant, he realized Deluca would only be implicating himself for even bringing the subject up in the first place.

No, Deluca had to have been telling him the truth about Malcolm Ridge being in the vicinity of the Osborne farm on the morning the children went missing. He also had to have been telling the truth about the bloodstain on Ridge's shirt.

'But how large was the bloodstain?' Roger winced, his thick forehead creased with aging wrinkles. *'For Deluca to have noticed it, the bloodstain had to have been quite large. At least large enough to not think it was only a stain of some other kind, like ink.*

"Why didn't I ask him how large it was?" Roger closed his fist and pounded the top of his desk, cursing his weak interrogation techniques. He'd have to be more thorough when he questioned Deluca again, or Malcolm Ridge, for that matter. But all that would have to wait, for now, he had to get Ridge brought into the office, and then he could question him all he wanted.

"What's up?" Deputy Wayne Leon James asked his boss after lightly rapping on the opened door and then entered the room without a response. Wayne stood slouched, with his thumbs tucked in his gun belt, staring at the back of Roger's balding head, waiting for him to turn from the window and acknowledge him.

Roger was still staring out the window, thinking about Malcolm Ridge, wondering if the young man was responsible for the missing children and, if he was, why did he miss the clues? He remembered the first day they searched the Osborne farm for the missing children, seeing the three hooligans drive up in the fire-engine red Charger and then lazily leaning up against it – two of them dead now.

'Had the three of them been involved, or just the one?' He wondered. *'Had Ridge killed his two friends to keep them quiet?'*

There were so many unanswered questions, but at the end of the day, after Ridge was brought in, Roger knew he'd get all the questions he was formulating in his mind answered.

Wayne cleared his throat with a quick grunt, stirring Roger back from his calculating thoughts.

"I saw Deluca bolt out of here a few minutes ago, heading back toward the pool hall. How did it go with him? Get any good information?" Wayne asked with interest and then moved over to the chair previously occupied by Deluca and sat, hoping for some good news. It had been a long weekend for everyone in the department, and Wayne was hoping something good was coming out of the long hours they had put in. He glanced at Roger's drawn face and tired eyes, waiting anxiously, like he often did, for his boss to answer his inquiry.

"Just that Ridge stopped by Deluca's apartment looking for a place to stay, and Deluca told him he couldn't. I was hoping he knew more about Ridge, but I guess they weren't the best of friends," Roger disappointedly said.

"Probably a good thing for him. Who knows, he could have been another victim."

"Yeah, you're probably right."

"Did you get anything else out of him? Did Ridge happen to have confided with Deluca about killing his friends?"

Roger shook his head. He wished it were that easy.

"No, not about them. But he did mention something pretty interesting about the day those two young kids went missing. He told me Ridge borrowed Luke Townsend's vehicle and had blood on his shirt when he showed up later at the pool hall. Ridge told him he must have cut his hand or something and wiped it on his shirt."

"Sounds fishy to me that Deluca would bring that up. Just remembering it now," Wayne said, trying to remember himself if he had seen blood on Ridge's shirt, but he couldn't.

"Yeah, it sounded fishy to me at first, but why would he lie about that? Then again, it could only be just a coincidence. But never-the-less, I'm going to follow it up."

"Is there anything I can do to help out?"

"Yes, as a matter of fact, there is. Deluca also mentioned Ridge told him last night he was heading up to the Osborne farm. Said he didn't have any other place to go."

"The Osborne farm? Is he crazy?" Wayne questioned with a bit of skepticism.

"That goes without saying." Roger and everyone in the department thought Malcolm Ridge to be crazy. The only ones who didn't were the two psychiatrists who examined him.

"I still can't believe he'd want to go back up to that place. You can still probably smell them...smell the blood and all," Wayne said, thinking about the mutilated body of his cousin, Peter and Luke Townsend.

"Well, he might not have, but I think we should go under the presumption that he's there at the farmhouse. If he is, I want you to bring him in. I'd go with you, but I've got something I have to do at the other end of town, so I'm going to be sending you out there alone." Roger wanted to take a look inside the trunk of Luke Townsend's Dodge Charger to see if maybe there were any signs of the children having been stuffed inside. He mainly wanted to see if there were any bloodstains. The children weren't found at the farmhouse, but their bicycles were, so Roger knew they had to have been moved, and by vehicle seemed to be the logical explanation. If that was blood on Ridge's shirt, and it matched the children's blood type, it would be the key evidence they were looking for, the nail in his coffin.

"Yeah, that's okay with me, Roger. I'm on it," Wayne answered, then stood to leave.

"Wayne, if he's there, I want you to arrest him for trespassing and also for leaving town when I specifically told him not to. Don't mention anything about those missing kids."

"What if he's not there? Want me to stake the place out?"

"No, but take a good look around to make sure he's not hiding and look for any signs he may have been there recently. From what Deluca told me, Ridge didn't have any baggage with him, so look for things that are out of place, like a water glass on the kitchen table or maybe food wrappers."

"I'll keep an open mind and do a thorough search."

Roger followed his deputy out into the lobby, passing the staring inquisitive eyes of Helen, and continued through the glass door out into the midday sunshine, the sun at its peak. Out on the steps, he gave Wayne an encouraging smile, tapping him lightly on his shoulder, and then watched him pull his cruiser away from the curb. It was a one-man job, and Wayne was his best deputy to do the job professionally. His other deputies were good at their job and could have performed the job professionally as well and not made any mistakes in apprehending Malcolm Ridge, and he would have still felt comfortable sending another, but Wayne was his best.

Roger knew immediately when Wayne interviewed for the job in the department that he'd have no regrets in hiring him. He sat firm, spine straight against the back of the chair with his shoulders squared, and most importantly, kept good eye contact with every question Roger asked. His answers were adequate and enhanced with thoughts of his own. He knew what he was talking about and not just regurgitating what he had learned in the academy. Though he was thin built, he seemed athletic, and Roger presumed he could handle himself when trouble aroused. After the interview was over, Roger told Wayne he'd let him know in a day or two as he had other candidates to interview, but Roger called him that very afternoon to let him know he was Madison County's newest deputy.

After watching Wayne's vehicle disappear in the direction of the Osborne farm, Roger squeezed in behind the wheel of his own cruiser – the one with his name stenciled on the door, the one that said he was responsible for the county's citizens and his troops. Once he was comfortably settled in the seat, which took a couple of ass-wiggling moves to smooth the creases in his pants, Roger stretched his neck over his shoulder, feeling the tension, and glanced down the street to make sure there wasn't any traffic behind him. Seeing none, Roger quickly peeled out, driving off toward the fenced car lot where the Dodge Charger had been impounded.

There was nobody assigned to guard the lot, as there was never a need for security with the high wire fence. Roger used the key on his key chain and unlocked the gate, pushing it wide. He then drove his cruiser through the opening and headed straight for Luke Townsend's previous prize possession. There were only a few vehicles parked inside, and all, except the red Charger that was parked behind the others in the rear of the small lot, had been abandoned in fields or logging roads.

The first thing Roger did when he pulled up alongside the vehicle was open the trunk. He had previously looked inside, before it was impounded to the lot, for anything that could implicate Ridge on the murders of his friends. Now he was looking for different evidence, evidence for a different murder.

CHAPTER TWENTY-SEVEN

Monday Afternoon
August 13, 1989

The entrance to the Osborne Road was chained off with a sturdy heavy-duty chain attached to a high-priced security bolt lock. There were also two newly printed signs posted at the foot of the road, one on each side for maximum effect, replacing the old, less effective one nailed to a tree that nobody seemed to pay attention to. The new signs basically told any potential trespassers to stay away, with an added note on the bottom of the poster board signs stating violators would be severely punished, per Madison County Sheriff Department.

The chain, however, only prevented vehicles from entering. Anyone on foot could just as easily walk around or even simply hop over the sagging chain. When Deputy Wayne Leon James arrived, he used the key he was given to unlock the bolt lock. He then dragged the heavy chain to one side of the graveled road and drove in, leaving a trail of dust and bits of gravel in his wake.

Wayne hadn't really expected to see Malcolm Ridge inside or even anywhere near the farmhouse. To him, it just wasn't a place he could phantom anyone would want to be near, let alone spend a dark night there. But his boss, Sheriff Roger Lefebvre, sounded concerned when he gave him the order that Ridge was possibly there, so here he was driving back up to the farmhouse, a place that gave him the shivers just to think about it. At least it was daytime, he reassured himself.

He drove slowly past the cemetery, unconsciously glancing at the gravestones, and continued at the same slow pace toward the farmhouse, looking on both sides of the road. When he neared the farmhouse, he came to a sudden stop before pulling into the driveway to get a wider view of the perimeter around the farmhouse. The farm seemed vacant of all life to him. Only a few black crows could be seen flying high above the old, dilapidated farmhouse itself and continued their flight over the fields out behind the house. As he watched the crows flap their wings with ease and slowly evaporate into the distant blue sky above the tree line, he thought he glimpsed the shadow of a person disappear into a thicket of scrub brush.

Thinking it could have been a person, and possibly the person of interest, Wayne cautiously climbed out of his cruiser and walked around to the trunk, pulling out a pair of binoculars. Standing as still as he could to keep his arms from moving, Wayne adjusted the lens and focused in on the tree line. He then slowly moved his line of sight in the direction of the thick scrub brush. After staring at the same general area for a good minute, he determined it must have only been an animal he had seen. He then set the binoculars back in the case and closed the trunk.

Wayne stooped his lanky body back inside the cruiser and radio-in to the sheriff's office and informed Helen he was at the Osborne farmhouse, and so far, there was no sign of Malcolm Ridge, or much of anything else for that matter. The place was dead quiet. He then told Helen he was going to check out the barn and then take a quick peek inside the house itself to see if there were any signs of an intruder. Before he could sign off, Helen told him the Sheriff had just gotten back from the car lot and wanted to have a word with him.

"Roger that," he told Helen and then waited for his boss before driving up the driveway.

A moment later, Roger's husky voice came over the mike.

"Wayne, you out at the Osborne place?" Roger asked, not using the correct radio etiquette.

"Ten-four, over."

"Good. Before you go inside the farmhouse, I want you to take a look around the perimeter to see if he's outside somewhere. Then I want you to go in the house by way of the barn. If he's in there, I don't want him sneaking out through the barn. If you find him, just tell him I need to ask him a couple more vital questions that may help clear him. I don't want to scare him any. Over."

"I did a quick perimeter search with my binoculars, but if you want, I can do a walk-around to make sure. Is there anything else? Over."

"No, don't bother with doing a walk-around. I don't think that's necessary. Just keep an eye out for him or anything that looks suspicious, though you may not find anything. For all we know, it may just be a wild goose chase. Radio in as soon as you've finished. Over."

"Okay, I'll check the front, some of those thick bushes I see over there, and then a quick look out behind the barn. Hey, Roger, Helen mentioned you were at the car lot. Anything I should know about? Over."

"No, I was just investigating a hunch I had, but it didn't pan out. Over."

"The Townsend vehicle? Is that the vehicle? Over."

"Yeah, I was hoping to find some evidence those missing kids may have been stuffed inside the trunk and then driven off to a different location, but I didn't notice anything unusual. No visible signs of blood that I could see. I'll ask the State Police to send their forensic team over to do a thorough search. We'll know for sure then if they were inside the vehicle. If they were, we've got him. Over."

"Roger, that. Ten-four and out."

After Wayne hung up the mike, he instinctively reached over the console and fished his Maglite out of the glove compartment, thinking it may come in handy as another weapon and for searching the rooms where windows were still boarded. He then slowly drove up the driveway, passed the yellow crime tape that stretched from a large maple tree at the end of the driveway to the side porch, and parked in front of the side porch, wanting his vehicle to be near as possible to the door in case Malcolm was inside. Seeing the vehicle may deter him from exiting the door and trying his escape by way of the barn where Wayne would be coming in.

It wasn't until Wayne was a few yards away from the barn that he noticed the yellow crime tape was lying on the ground where it once stretched across the front of the barn. He also realized the door was partially open, just enough for a person to side inside. It was the first indication Malcolm had been there unless the wind had blown the tape loose and the door inauspiciously left open.

Wayne skipped checking behind the barn to put his focus on the inside. He could look out back later. As he cautiously walked inside, he turned his Maglite on and held it firm in his hand. If he had to use the heavy flashlight for self-defense, he wanted a tight grip on the handle. It wasn't the first time he had been inside the Osborne barn alone, but even a hundred times wouldn't have been enough to calm his nerves, and as soon as he entered, he immediately felt the nervousness rising from the pit of his stomach.

Wayne flashed the beam of light along the far wall and up in the loft area. There wasn't much to see in the loft from his angle, so he moved a few steps back for a deeper view.

"Hello, is there anyone up there? Malcolm, are you there?" he said in a dry, raspy voice. "Malcolm, you know there's no trespassing on this property, so if you're up there, speak up now, or I'll have to arrest you. I know you don't want that to happen."

Wayne waited a moment, and, when satisfied Malcolm was not up in the loft or hidden elsewhere in the barn, he then moved toward the door that led into the main house. With each step he made, Wayne could hear the creaking of aged wood below his weight break the eerie silence that engulfed the creepy barn. When he pulled open the door to the dark pantry, the rusty hinges creaked even louder than the weak floorboards had.

"I'm not going to like this," he said aloud, then followed

the beam of light from his Maglite down the narrow pantry and into the kitchen.

Wayne hadn't been in the kitchen during daylight since they had searched for the missing children back in May. On that day, the door to the kitchen and the two windows on each side of the door had been boarded over with wooden planks blocking out the daylight, leaving only the small window over the sink as the only source of light. Since then, the wooden planks had been removed, and Wayne was happy to realize he no longer needed the use of his Maglite and gladly flicked it off, but he needed to turn the flashlight back on when he entered the semi-dark living room, which still had the windows boarded over and only minimal light protruded through the spaces between the boards.

As he stood there shining the light in different areas, Wayne could easily see by the amount of blood splattered across the walls and even on the ceiling how traumatic it must have been for the two deceased, one being his own kin. Even though it had been two days ago since the senseless slaughter, the bloodstains on the walls seemed to drip like molasses. On the floor beneath him, Wayne could see splatters of blood everywhere, with a larger pool concentrated in the center of the room where the bodies had laid. Wayne deliberately sidestepped around the pools of blood so as not to get any blood on the soles of his shoes, but with so much blood covering the floor, he couldn't avoid all the sticky splatters and noticed he was leaving his bloody footprints in his wake.

On his way up the stairs to reach the second-floor bedrooms, Wayne shined the light on the steps and noticed other faint bloody footprints on each step. At first, he wondered if the footprints were Malcolm Ridge's, then disappointedly realized they could have come from Sheriff Roger and Phil Hardy when they ascended the stairs and probably a half a dozen other investigators who had walked all over the place looking for other evidence. Nevertheless, whether some of the prints were Malcolm Ridge's or not, he kept the thought of the footprints in his mind and followed the blood trail into the bedroom on the right side of the hall.

The bedroom was well illuminated from the two large windows overlooking the driveway side. The bright sunlight shining through the windows seemed to stretch soundlessly across the floor toward his feet, looking like tall glass doors, entryways to unknown rooms. Wayne flicked off the Maglite and placed it in the loop on his gun belt.

At first glance, the bedroom looked the same as he remembered the previous time he had been in there, uncluttered with only a couple of bureaus and a queen size bed with an uncomfortable-looking chair next to a window. Simple living, he assumed, and thought of his cluttered bedroom; clothes lying wrinkled on the floor and on the back of a chair even though he had a clothes basket next to his closet, an unused treadmill pushed up folded against a wall, his one bureau with odds and ends piled on top, and his unmade bed with the blankets in disarray.

On top of one of the bureaus, Wayne noticed the photo of Zeke and Elaine Osborne was laid upside down. He thought back to when he last touched the photo, when he was in the room with the Sheriff, and remembered placing it back the way he had found it, facing out.

But maybe he was wrong. It was months ago and a stressful time. He could have unconsciously laid it down, not wanting to look at it.

Just to make sure someone else hadn't laid the framed photo upside down, Wayne did a thorough search making sure nobody was hiding in the room. He walked over to the closet and quickly twisted the brass knob, and pulled the door open. His nervous system took a sudden jump, and he automatically placed his hand on his gun when the door creaked open. What he first thought was a person standing inside the narrow closet was only a woman's orange-tan hat on top of the shelf and a plain-colored worn-looking dress hanging from a wire clothes hanger. On the floor, he noticed a pair of woman's tan slippers. Other than those items, the closet was empty. There was no male clothing at all.

Wayne released a deep sigh and pushed the door closed. He then turned to leave the room, but before closing the bedroom door and going to check the other rooms for Malcolm Ridge, Wayne suddenly realized the bed was unmade, like his, which only meant someone had slept in it. The last time he had been in the room, the bed was neatly made up, bed sheets tucked in the corners, and the blanket turned down.

Wayne walked up to the bed and picked at the covers, peeking under them, and then dropped them in a heap. He then knelt on one knee and ducked his head under the bed to see if Malcolm Ridge was hiding under there. It would be just like Ridge, or any kid on the run, to be hiding in the most obvious of hiding places, but instead of finding Ridge sprawled on the dusty floor, Wayne only found several insignificant objects underneath.

Inquisitively he reached in and pulled one of the objects out and slowly turned it around in his hand, concentrating on the facial feature. Staring at the black eyes and the long-spouted nose, and the smiling toothy mouth, Wayne instantly knew what he was looking at and where he had last seen one. In his hand, he held a child's toy wooden pony head, a similar toy pony head he had seen inside the footlocker, sawed-off from its wooden pole at the neck.

Still kneeling, Wayne excitingly turned around, expecting to see the green footlocker pushed against the wall behind the door, but it wasn't there. He then rose to his feet and quickly fled the room to check the other bedrooms to see if the footlocker had been moved to one of those rooms but found the rooms to be the same as before, with only beds and bureaus.

In the last bedroom, he stood silently, feeling slightly disappointed. He then pulled off his official tan cap and brushed his hand through his short brown hair, wondering where the footlocker could have disappeared to and, more importantly, who would have wanted it moved. What would be their motive? The only logical explanation he could come up with was that someone other than those doing the investigation had moved it, like Malcolm Ridge.

Wayne awkwardly walked down the narrow hallway, wondering if his assumptions that Ridge must have spent the night there but fled sometime during the morning, before he had arrived, were feasible. Wayne was feeling more than just slightly disappointed now at not finding Malcolm Ridge in the house, but, at the same time, he felt confident he had done a thorough search, so all that was left for him to do was to radio into the office and tell Roger what he had uncovered, which was only that Ridge may have been there. He didn't want to elaborate on his assumptions that Ridge had definitely been there if it weren't true.

After walking through the living room, stepping on sticky pools of blood without concern other than exiting the house as quickly as he could, Wayne suddenly froze when he spied the green footlocker sitting on the floor next to the antique wooden icebox. He was now positive someone had spent the night there, and the person was most likely the man he was looking for – Malcolm Ridge.

Inside the footlocker, he noticed splatters of blood on the sides and larger areas of blood covering the bottom. Other than the blood, the footlocker was empty. Wayne bent over and touched the blood to see if it was sticky, a sign that the blood was fresh, but the blood had dried. He then stood, keeping his gaze and thoughts inside the footlocker, wondering what possibly could have caused all those blood stains. He thought of all the items that had been inside, the toy wooden pony heads and the other insignificant, smaller toys that were too far underneath the bed to identify what they were. The pony heads, however, he remembered their significance. The sordid details he had been told numerous times by Deputy Phil Hardy of how the Osborne children had been found. Their stoic faces blindly peering out the windows and their bloodied heads stuffed on top of wooden poles that were meant for the toy pony heads, not innocent young children's heads.

Wayne braced himself against the icebox, placing his hand on the top for support. He was feeling nauseous thinking about the possibility that the blood inside the footlocker could have been the missing children's blood, Amanda and Kyle. He tried to shake the horrible images of them being stuffed inside, but he couldn't. The footlocker was just the right size for two youngsters' bodies. Or was it large enough to fit both bodies? Maybe one, he thought, but definitely not two bodies, unless they were hideously chopped up like his cousin, Peter, and Luke Townsend.

Wayne was about to go outside when he noticed a faint bloodied palm print on the icebox handle and several drops of blood on the floor below it. At first, he thought the blood was probably from the other night's massacre, and the icebox had been searched. But then a horrible thought crossed his mind, and he knew if he opened the icebox, he'd find something horrific, something he didn't want to see but knew he had to look – it was his job, what he had signed up for five years ago. He had looked inside the icebox before, when they were searching for Amanda Prescott and Kyle Bryant, and found it empty.

This time he knew it would be different.

As he slowly pulled the brass handle to open the door, he told himself he had seen worse, but as the door swung open, Deputy Wayne Leon James nearly screamed when he saw the headless, decomposed boy's body squished inside, holding, in his tiny hands, a wooden pole with a girl's grotesque head mounted on the end.

CHAPTER TWENTY-EIGHT

Monday Afternoon
August 13, 1989

Malcolm Ridge sat motionless on an orange wooden bench, the same brilliant color of the setting sun outside the holding cell he had been locked in three hours earlier, but from his windowless cell, he could only visualize the gorgeous sunset outside. He had only been told he was under arrest for trespassing and he was being locked up for his own protection, which he assumed was a common comment to ease the nerves. But, after being locked up in solitude for what seemed like more hours than it actually was, he had an awful feeling he was in much more serious trouble than a trespassing charge, and he was being detained as a suspect in the deaths of his two friends, and the 'protection' comment was meant for protection from the victim's relatives who were out to get him.

When told why he was being arrested, Malcolm asked the Sheriff if he was only being arrested for trespassing, why did he threaten to shoot him. The Sheriff had seen Malcolm Ridge running down the Osborne Road, and when Ridge hightailed it in the other direction, the Sheriff abruptly stopped his vehicle and shouted to Ridge to stop, or he'd shoot.

"I wanted to make sure you stopped, and most importantly, I wasn't sure if you were armed. Police work is a very dangerous profession, son, and you have to expect the unexpected," Sheriff

Roger Lefebvre said as he pulled his cruiser into his marked parking spot in front of the sheriff's office.

Malcolm Ridge was still handcuffed when he was led into the sheriff's office and re-cuffed to a chair, and told to remain silent while Roger retrieved the keys to the holding cells. Helen watched as Malcolm glanced around the office, taking in the framed photographs of the men who had previously been elected to the position of sheriff. Most of them looked old with plump faces, like the current sheriff, he thought. Others had thin, drawn faces, and all wore the same serious expression.

Malcolm saw the same serious expression on Sheriff Lefebvre's face when the man returned with a large ring of keys; his unwavering eyes meant business. The Sheriff then led him down a long, green-tiled corridor in silence and shoved him inside one of the tiny holding cells.

"How long am I going to be detained in here, Sheriff? What's the penalty for trespassing anyhow?"

"Trespassing in itself is only a misdemeanor punishable by only a fine, but in your case, I'm afraid we have other, more serious violations that you could be charged with."

"Like what? I didn't do anything."

"Leaving town when I specifically told you not to, for one. I'm not sure how long I can hold you or even if I'm going to charge you. So, for now, I'm locking you up for your own protection. You just sit tight, and I'll be back," Roger told him in a stern voice as he locked the door behind him.

Malcolm held onto the bars with both hands and watched the Sheriff walk back down the corridor. The heavy soles on his black shoes clicking hollowly against the shiny green-tiled floor left an empty hole in his stomach. He was alone and knew nobody would come to his rescue. He had been arrested before as a juvenile, and his adopted parents angrily came to retrieve him, but he knew this time they'd have nothing to do with him, nor would anyone else. He was on his own now, and all he could do was sit and wait for justice to prevail, to be released on his own accord.

So, Malcolm dejectedly sat in silence on the uncomfortable bench and waited for the Sheriff's return, which was a lot longer than he had expected. It wasn't until after seven that evening before the Sheriff returned with a notepad in one hand and the jingling key ring in his other – three and a half hours after he had been arrested.

At first, he thought he was being released, and the notepad was a form for him to sign, but he was soon to find out the notepad was intended for his interrogation. More questions he had no answers for.

* * *

Before questioning Malcolm Ridge about his involvement in the murders of Amanda Prescott and Kyle Bryant, and new questions pertaining to the deaths of his two friends, Roger Lefebvre went back to his office. Once there, he pulled out the files on every unsolved murder committed over the last ten years and came up with three, counting the multiple murders (or disappearances since the youngsters were never found and only speculated that they had been murdered) as one.

The oldest unsolved murder in the county's records occurred back in June of 1982, seven years earlier. It was the murder of a twelve-year-old girl and the first murder committed in Madison County since the Osborne murders unless you counted the accidental hunting deaths, which at least one occurred annually during hunting season – a sad statistic that was the highest among all the other counties in the state.

After looking at the young girl's picture in the file folder, her sixth-grade graduation photo given to him by the girl's mother when she went missing, the unsolved case came flooding back to him as he thought it only just happened a short while ago. He could still see the mother's disheveled appearance when she came storming into his office, insisting her little girl had not run away and something bad must have happened to her.

It was the first day of the school's summer vacation, and Vicki Pendexter had just graduated from elementary school and was looking forward to attending junior high in the fall. For her summer vacation, besides having fun, she was taking a foreign language class to better prepare herself for the upcoming school year. She decided on studying French since it was a language her grandmother, on her mother's side of the family, spoke, and she thought it would be nice to have a conversation with her grandmother, speaking her native language. Unfortunately, Vicki never had the chance to attend the class.

The day she went missing started out pleasantly warm, with morning temperatures in the mid-seventies and reaching well into the eighties by noon. It was a perfect summer day, and Vicki and her sister, Evelyn, who was seventeen at the time, decided to walk the three blocks to the neighborhood variety store to purchase sodas. Evelyn told her mother when she returned two hours later without her sister, she went on a car ride with a friend from school, and Vicki declined to go with them, insisting on walking home alone.

Worried, her mother immediately called the sheriff's office and told Helen Pinkham her daughter had not returned home from the store and should have been home hours ago. Helen told the distraught mother they usually don't take a missing person report unless the person had been missing for at least twenty-four hours, but since the girl was only twelve and had never run away before, she'd take the information and pass it along to the Sheriff. Helen then promised her the Sheriff would either call on her himself or, most likely, send one of his deputies over, but she wasn't sure how long it would be. There was also the possibility he wouldn't do anything until the following day, given the underlying policy on missing persons.

In the meantime, Helen told the mother to call all her daughter's friends to see if she had gone over to one of their houses. Mrs. Pendexter started to cry on the phone as she told Helen that Vicki didn't have many friends and other than her older sister, Vicki only played with her next-door neighbor, whom she had already called and was told she hadn't seen her all day.

As soon as Roger Lefebvre returned from an errand,

an errand that was personal in nature, Helen handed him the information about Vicki Pendexter, which she had jotted down on notepaper – not an official missing person's form. Roger took a quick look at the information and nodded to Helen. If it had been a rather busy day, he would have told Helen to set it aside until the next morning, but the only thing pressing at the moment was filing a report on a vehicle break-in that occurred overnight.

While he sat in his office, considering whether to take a ride out to Mrs. Pendexter's house or wait until the next day to contact her, the disheveled mother came bursting into his office unannounced (just like Mrs. Prescott and Mrs. Bryant will when their precious ones disappear).

Sadly, seven days later, Sheriff Roger Lefebvre officially called off the search for twelve-year-old Vicki Pendexter. They had found no clues whatsoever to her whereabouts or who could have abducted her. It seemed she had simply vanished into thin air. Some folks blamed it on aliens, abducted and whizzed the missing girl clear across the galaxy to another planet. Mrs. Pendexter was flabbergasted when she heard the idiotic assumption.

Two weeks later, on the fourth of July – a day to celebrate with the whole country – a local boy named Josh Miller, whose family owned the farm adjacent to the Osborne farm, had gone fishing in the creek that ran behind their farmhouse and uncovered a horrible scene. Josh walked along the creek about a mile down from the family farm toward Old County Road to a spot where he liked to fish. The creek was the deepest just before the bridge, and he liked to sit on an old log that washed up along the bank. After fishing for a few hours, with only catching a couple of small hornpouts, which he immediately tossed back in the creek, Josh decided to head home for lunch. Before he did, he noticed what he thought was a store mannequin partially submerged in the water and tangled in the old tree's branches. After investigating, poking the end of his fishing rod at the mannequin, he realized it was a real person and ran home yelling and screaming there was a dead body in the river.

Roger never forgot the frightened expression on Josh Miller's face when he interviewed the fourteen-year-old. His large dark eyes seemed to bulge from his head when he described seeing the body. Mrs. Pendexter had the same frightening expression – only hers aged her twenty years. Roger swore her face grew wrinkles right in front of him when he told her the devastating news.

Roger Lefebvre tossed the cold case file on his desk and rolled his red-rimmed eyes toward his closed office door. He thought best when his door was closed, with no one to walk by and notice his agitated stirring or his soft emotional side whenever he thought of young, innocent victims of crime. His own daughter being one of them, though she was a victim of cancer – the crime of Mother Nature.

"Where was Ridge living back in 1982?" Roger mumbled and stared blankly at his cluttered desk, searching for an answer.

He grabbed the notepad next to his phone and quickly scribbled the question down in handwriting only he could decipher, noting that it was question number one. After a moment of staring at the question, trying to come up with a second one to ask Ridge, he pushed the notepad aside and grabbed up the file to go over it again. He wanted to make sure he covered all the key elements of the case.

After methodically reviewing the file a second time, he couldn't find anything new to accuse Ridge of the girl's murder. Roger then started to wonder how old Ridge was at the time, back in 1982, so he could either rule him out or still consider him a viable suspect. Roger quickly estimated Ridge to be about twenty-three or twenty-four now, which would have made him about seventeen back then, the same age as the victim's sister at the time – maybe known to her.

He then realized he had two more questions. One being his current age, and the other question, did he know the victim's sister? Finding the answers to those could be the key. If he were the same age as the sister, they could have been acquaintances and had met Vicki previously. This would have made it easier for him to lure her away. He may even have owned a vehicle back then.

Question number four – own a vehicle or have access to one.

Suddenly the page was filling up with questions, and Roger hadn't even begun to peruse the other two cold case files on unsolved murders. He pushed the Pendexter file aside and grabbed the next file lying on his desk, which was the unsolved murder of Whitney Gorman, the young real-estate agent who was found hanging nude in the Osborne barn. That murder happened two years after the Pendexter murder, and Roger knew Ridge was definitely living in Denton at that time. He had been in and out of trouble back then, mostly drunk and disorderly charges with a couple of break-ins to his credit, his dead friends being accomplices.

Roger remembered the Gorman case well and how traumatizing it was for him and his whole staff to not find the monster that had brutally murdered the young woman. There were no clues left at the scene for them to go on, which ultimately ended with not finding a suspect. Now, Roger was feeling confident they had one. All he had to do was place Malcolm Ridge at the scene of the crime or in the vicinity and pressure him to confess. If he did confess, he'd get Ridge to confess to the others, telling him he wouldn't be punished any harsher and maybe even get a lighter sentence for admitting to the crimes. A lie that just might work.

After realizing what he had locked up in his cell, Roger leaned back in his chair and threw his arms up in the air, stretching them in a sign of victory like finally crossing the finish line of a marathon. Then, after the brief celebration, he started to think of the possibility he could be wrong about Ridge and had the wrong person locked up. Maybe Malcolm was just in the wrong place at the wrong time? But after briefly entertaining the notion, Roger shook his head at the absurdity of it. Of course, he had the right person locked up. Who else could have done it. Malcolm Ridge was the only other person at the farmhouse when his friends were murdered, and he was placed at the farmhouse, or at least in Groveville, at the time Amanda Prescott and Kyle Bryant went missing. All he had to do now was to find out where Ridge was when Whitney Gorman and Vicki Pendexter were murdered and get him to confess.

'*Six murders, he'd be locked up for the rest of his sorry-ass life.*' Roger thought, which brought a smile to his face.

Roger reviewed his questions to ask Ridge one more time and then, when he was sure he had all his ducks in a row, pushed himself up from his desk and headed for Malcolm Ridge's cell. He tried to focus on his expression, not his emotions and imagined something pleasant to give Malcolm Ridge a fatherly impression, but all he could imagine was the hideous crimes Ridge had committed and walked into his holding cell with a contemptuous smile.

CHAPTER TWENTY-NINE

Monday Evening
August 13, 1989

Malcolm Ridge rested his weary head on top of the cheap polyester pillow and blindly stared up at the unseen ceiling trying to make light of his dire situation. All he could think about were the relentless questions Sheriff Roger Lefebvre had asked him and what his answers meant in determining if he was innocent or guilty of the crimes he knew he was innocent of. Malcolm had responded to the Sheriff's inquiries, at least the ones he could answer, to the best of his knowledge, but the Sheriff's cold glaring stare, his unwavering blue-gray eyes boring into Malcolm's own sad, dark eyes, told him differently and that the Sheriff didn't believe the answers he had given him.

Before leaving Malcolm alone in his isolation, the Sheriff told Malcolm the District Attorney would be stopping by in the morning to have a talk with him, and it would be in his best interest to tell the truth and not give the man any bullshit answers like he had just given him. He then snapped two of the three hallway's light switches off, leaving the hallway in semi-darkness, and closed the heavy metal door behind him with an echoing thud.

Malcolm had never met the District Attorney before, although he had seen Neal Russo in passing and thought of him as a man to avoid. He figured the man was one of those educated rich types who had gone to an ivy league college and had played one of those sports he never had the displeasure of watching or understanding, like polo. Now, as he lay on the uncomfortable bench with only a thin gray blanket to cover over him, a blanket along with the pillow given to him by one of the deputies during the interrogation, Malcolm knew when the morning came, he'd most likely have to answer the same grueling questions over again, and even other questions the Sheriff had not considered asking.

How should he answer the questions? Tell the District Attorney the same answers he told the Sheriff? And if he did, would he not believe him as the Sheriff hadn't, or should he just tell him what they wanted to hear? And what was that, that he was guilty of murdering his friends and all those other people he had only vaguely remembered hearing about?

Malcolm desperately wanted to sleep and not think about the trouble he was in, but sleep did not come easily, for his mind wandered from what he was being accused of and what would become of him if they found him guilty of those crimes, crimes he did not commit. He knew the punishment would be severe. Murder was a capital offense no matter what state it was committed in, and in some states, the accused could be sentenced to death.

Closing his eyes, Malcolm pictured himself dressed in a dark suit he did not own, standing before the judge. A lawyer, his court-appointed lawyer, young and untested, standing at his side telling him not to worry, the only evidence against him was circumstantial, and no jury in their right mind would convict him. And Malcolm knew that was all they had against him; how could it be anything else but circumstantial – he didn't do it.

Malcolm told himself the truth would come out in the end, and life would return to normal. Normal, that is, without his friends, they would never return. Yes, he reassured himself, this living nightmare would soon be over, and when it was over, he would improve himself, set goals, like going back to school and getting his high school diploma, and even, maybe, go to college. Not like before when his life was pathless, when he first came to Denton, and that was the way he wanted it. His only goal then was to have fun. Anything else would only get in the way of what he considered a perfect life. He was living in his best friend's parent's basement, free of paying room and board, and any money he received from the odd jobs he did went right into his pocket to spend as he pleased, mostly at the pool hall where he spent the most of his wasted time, with Luke and Peter.

Even though he did not remember seeing his friends' dying bodies on the living room floor when he fled for his life, he could still visualize the horrible images of their mutilated bodies sprawled on the floor. He could see arms and legs twisted at unimaginable angles, wiggling like a puppeteer was controlling their movements, and the grotesque faceless heads with empty eye sockets and large gaping toothless mouths trying to speak, pleading for help.

Malcolm shook the horrible image away from his mind and buried his head in the pillow, his arms over the back of his head. Soon, without realizing it, he fell into a deep sleep where fragmented dreams floated through his subconsciousness. One dream after another until they turned into more than just dreams, dreams that turned into nightmares. Horrible nightmares like the one he was living.

He dreamed he was strapped to an uncomfortable steel bed, a black mask covering his face. Somebody with large, callused hands was holding his arm down while another person was trying to stick a thick needle in his vein. He could feel the needle jabbing his skin and desperately wanted to pull his arm free, but the callused hands held tight, and the harder he tried to wiggle free, the grip tightened. Beyond the small room, he could hear muffled voices and then a roar of laughter when the needle finally hit the spot. He could feel the cold poisonous solution crawl up his arm. It felt like a slimy snake slithering through his veins.

Before the poison reached his heart, his body lifted off the bed and floated out the door, escaping death. He next found himself slowly floating above a long winding graveled road with his arms stretched out straight as an arrow, pointing the way. His body twisted with the contour of the road and rose higher when necessary. Toward the end of the road, his head turned sharply to the right, where he could see an old cemetery with gravestones that seemed to sprout out of the earth – gravestones that grew taller and thinner in the light of the day.

Beyond the cemetery and past a field of tall grass, golden against an ominous background, he could see a farmhouse. Its crooked frame and attached barn looked menacing against the darkening sky but aligned with the ugly leafless trees that surrounded the old, dilapidated farmhouse like skeletons from another world, a dead world. Branches from the trees swiftly grew skyward, stretching over the porch and crawled up toward the roof like fingers without flesh.

As his body slowly floated toward the house, Malcolm could see faces in each of the windows, familiar faces – all too familiar faces. Smiling faces that seemed to imply he would be the next victim. Suddenly a window on the second floor blew open, and glass floated aimlessly to the ground like feathers. A strange-looking man appeared in the frame of the window. The man's face was ugly, creased with aging wrinkles and one horrid eyeball glazed over like it had been diseased. His fat fingers dripped with blood, beaconing him to enter.

In the darkness of the jail cell, his eyes fluttered from the horrible nightmare. Grinding his teeth, he attempted to steer away from the horrible sight of the farmhouse, but the bony branches surrounding it reached out and grabbed a hold of his legs, pulling him into a dark abyss. His body began to spiral downward, twirling into the unknown darkness at a high rate of speed.

Suddenly he found himself standing in the barn, high up in the hayloft, looking down at the open barn door. A bright white light was streaming in through the opening, like a gateway for escaping the horrible nightmare he was in. He felt all he had to do was walk through the opening, and he'd be free, but first, he had to find a way to climb down from the loft. He knew there was a set of stairs to climb down, he had climbed down them numerous times, in other dreams, in other times, but in this dream, he could not turn around and look for the stairs.

Without considering the consequences, he jumped from the loft. Even though it seemed a long way down, he landed softly on his feet and then awkwardly shuffled his feet toward the light. He felt anxious to reach the white light, but his body was moving very slowly, and it seemed to be taking him forever. Just when he was about to walk into the light, he felt someone, or something evil, staring at his backside, causing him to deliberately crank his head around. When he did, he noticed a woman hanging from a beam beneath the loft floor. Her staring dark eyes were large against her frail bluish-white face, which seemed to burn like laser beams into his flesh. Her toothless mouth gaped open with flies crawling on the dangling tongue and blue thin lips. He wanted to run, but his legs refused to cooperate. The rope tied around the woman's neck started to swing faster and faster, closer and closer, until she was able to reach out with her long bony fingers and touch his face, scratching his cheek with her long-pointed fingernails.

"You're next," she said with a toothless smile. He could see blood dripping dark red from her fingers onto the floor, where the blood had formed a large pool.

A jolting surge of pain pounded hard against his brain, and after the impact was over, he found himself far beyond the farmhouse, walking down a narrow path with thorny bushes and twisting branches hanging erratically from ugly trees. As he continued to walk and brush away the last of the branches, he came to a small pond covered with lilies, lots of white lilies floating in the stagnant, greenish colored water. There, amongst the lilies, he noticed something very strange floating on top of the water. What he saw were the bodies of two young children.

Malcolm tried to turn around and run back up the path, but instead, a strange, powerful urge came over him to plunge headfirst into the pond. He stripped off all his clothing, tossing them aimlessly on the ground, and walked nude to the edge of the pond. Then, instead of diving into the pond as he had been urged, he began to wade in. After only a couple of steps into the cold, murky water, he found himself sinking and struggling to stay afloat. He reached out and touched one of the bodies for support, like reaching for a life preserver. The body felt slimy, and he quickly pulled his hand away and noticed his hand was covered with a slimy green substance.

Just as he was about to swim away, the two bodies came alive and grabbed him, four arms pulling him under the now turbulent, slimy-green water. He struggled to free himself from their grasp by swinging his arms and legs violently. But no matter how hard he struggled, he couldn't break away from their tight hold. They kept clawing and clawing at him, cutting deep into his flesh. He began to run out of breath and felt himself drowning, choking profusely on the water he had swallowed. He kicked his feet and swung his arms violently again and again, tossing his blanket off and onto the cold cement jail cell floor.

It was morning when Malcolm awoke. The blanket that barely kept him warm lay crumpled on the floor, his clothes drenched in sweat, and the horrible nightmares were still fresh on his mind. When he finally washed the nightmares away by sitting up on the bench and rubbing the sleepiness from his eyes, he suddenly realized where he was, and the horror of his reality slowly began to sink in.

All the hallway lights were back on, so Malcolm assumed it had to be morning, and the Sheriff most likely had come in to check on his well-being, to make sure he was still alive, and finding him asleep, decided to leave him be. He wished he had a window to look out to make sure it was indeed morning and have some sense of what time in the morning it was, but there were no windows, and now all he could do was wait for the Sheriff's return.

So there in the enclosed cell, Malcolm nervously sat alone on the hard-wooden bench staring at the gray cement walls closing in on him like claustrophobia and waited. After a while, his impatience grew, and he could not stand the solitude any longer. Awkwardly he stood, his lanky body slightly bent at the waist, his curly hair disheveled and clumped in a mass on one side, the side he slept on, and began to pace the eight-by-ten cell. He counted the steps from the gray wall to the locked cell door. Five short strides. Each time he reached the iron door, he grabbed hold of the bars with both hands and attempted to shake it open, but the clattering only reaffirmed his captivity.

He could smell the sweaty odor reeking from his body. He hadn't remembered when he last showered and wondered if they ever allowed prisoners, which he felt he was, to take showers. If it were someone else's reeking odor, he would have been offended, but since it was his own, he paid it no mind and continued his methodical pacing. Soon he heard the heavy door at the end of the hallway open and heavy footsteps clicking across the green-tiled floor. They were the same sounds he had heard the night before when the Sheriff had left. So, he was confident the person walking down the hallway was the man himself.

Sheriff Roger Lefebvre unlocked the cell door and, with authority, swung it wide on its hinges. He had a satisfying smile across his broad face, which contradicted his puffy, tired eyes, giving Malcolm an uneasy feeling of what to expect and causing him to sweat more than he already was. He was hoping to be informed the whole thing was a mistake and they had found the person responsible for the murder of his friends, but the minute he saw the look on the Sheriff's face, he knew that wasn't going to happen.

"Did you have a restful night's sleep, I hope, Mr. Ridge? There's someone waiting in my office who wants to speak to you," Roger said and grabbed Malcolm by his arm and led him out of the cell and down the hallway. His grip was tight, and Malcolm could feel the strength in the Sheriff's meaty hand on his thin arm. He wondered if his arm would bruise, picturing four purple fingertips on his bicep and a fat thumbprint on the underside of his arm.

Roger continued to grip Malcolm's arm tightly and didn't

release his hold until he sat him down on the lone visitor's chair in his office, where Neal Russo stood by the open window, impatiently waiting.

"This is District Attorney Russo," Roger nodded toward the tall, well-dressed man, his graying hair trimmed short and neatly combed, leaving not one hair out of place. "He's here to ask you some questions about the murders of Luke Townsend and Peter Finch. And it would be in your best interest to answer him honestly."

Malcolm looked up at the Distinct Attorney and then glanced at the Sheriff's cluttered desk and the vacant chair behind it, hoping at least one of the two authority figures would occupy the chair. He felt intimidated with the district attorney towering over him and the Sheriff standing directly behind him, wondering what they were planning on doing to him. He had seen plenty of movies where the cops would threaten the person they were interrogating with bodily harm, and he didn't want to be one of those. But they were always two regular cops, not elected officials.

"Mr. Ridge," the District Attorney slyly began and, without looking at the nervous young man he was addressing, moved over to the vacant chair behind the cluttered desk, pulling it out to make room for his tall, lean frame.

Malcolm nodded and watched the District Attorney settle into the Sheriff's brown-leather chair, moving it back and forth until he seemed comfortable, and then waited for what seemed like forever before the first question was asked. While he waited for the District Attorney to begin his questioning, Malcolm told himself to remain calm, but that was like telling his body not to sweat on a humid day after running from a guard dog and climbing over a chain link fence, all the while holding a half-filled five-gallon gas can, which he had done that very summer. Luke and Peter were to detain the dog while Malcolm climbed the fence behind Spencer's junkyard, but not knowing much about guard dogs, the German Shepard turned out to be much smarter than they had given him credit for. Malcolm only managed to fill half the gas can when he heard his friends telling him to run. He just barely made it over the fence in the nick of time.

Neal Russo looked firmly at his suspect, who was squirming uncomfortably before him, moving his clasped hands from one knee to the other. His dark eyes moved quickly about the room searching for an ally, but all the men in the room were against him. It was a tactic the District Attorney often used when he confronted a viable suspect. Make the person anxiously wait for the inevitable question, which basically asked if the person was guilty of the crime they were being accused of committing. But first, the District Attorney would always, and very slowly and precisely, go over all the evidence he had against the person, and Malcolm Ridge's introduction to District Attorney Neal Russo, was no exception.

Mr. Russo, who had patronizingly insisted on Malcolm Ridge calling him by his surname, cleared some of the debris away from the Sheriff's desk and then deliberately pulled out a bright orange folder from his briefcase and dropped it on the desk. He then slowly opened the folder and pulled out the paperwork, including the grotesque photographs of the crime scene.

"I have here a whole list of evidence pertaining to the deaths of Luke Townsend and Peter Finch, former friends of yours, I am told, and all the evidence (and let me tell you, there is quite a substantial amount, I'm sad to say) is all against you," the District Attorney said, emphasizing the last part.

After a long pause to peruse some of the highlighted evidence the Sheriff had marked with a yellow highlighter, the District Attorney continued to go over what they had found at the scene and the testimonies from the eyewitnesses, Albert Molino and Kerri Barr, the two teenagers from the Groveville General Store. Although District Attorney Russo knew those testimonies didn't amount to a hill of beans when it came to trial time, he knew it would come in handy during the interrogation.

"It's all against you, Malcolm, I'm afraid," the District Attorney told him, almost sounding apologetic, but, again, this was his tactic to be kind, to presume the role of a friend and father figure. "But it isn't as bad as it may seem. I'm here to help you make this as easy as possible. To get through this whole mess you're in without any further complications. Of course...." The District Attorney again paused, picking up another document from the folder to let the friendliness sink in before bringing up the other cold murder cases they planned on accusing Malcolm of.

Malcolm had been silent during the DA's practiced speech and tried to comprehend what the District Attorney was trying to convey. He knew he was fingering him for the murders of his friends. With all the evidence he spit out at him, evidence he knew made him look guilty, but none of it could prove his guilt because he knew he was innocent. But why was he trying to tell him it wasn't all that bad? Killing someone had to be the worst crime any human being could commit. He was hoping now, maybe, the District Attorney was worried they didn't have enough evidence and maybe there would be some kind of a plea bargain, one that would keep him from having to go to prison. But that hopeless thought was short-lived when the District Attorney added more troubling news.

Neil Russo tossed the document he had been looking at over an uneven pile of folders and loose papers stacked on the Sheriff's desk and watched it land on the floor in front of Malcolm's feet. Malcolm looked down at the twisted, stapled pages but didn't bend to retrieve them. For all he knew, the document could have been a prepared confession he wanted Malcolm to sign, and just touching it would be an admission of his guilt.

"Do you know what that is, Mr. Ridge?" Distinct Attorney Russo asked, with his wide dark eyes aimed at the floor, but proceeded without waiting for an answer. "Those are unsolved murders. There are four of them, and they all happened in the last seven years, and all took place at, or near, the Osborne farmhouse. The most recent is the two darling little children that went missing last May and were found mutilated yesterday afternoon inside an old icebox in the kitchen of the Osborne farmhouse.

And you, Malcolm Ridge, were the last person in there, and we have an eyewitness that places you at the farmhouse on the very day they went missing," he angrily shouted, causing Roger, who was leaning up against the door barring anyone from entering, to almost laugh out loud at the DA's defiant acting but only smiled.

"I didn't do it," was all Malcolm could say.

Neil Russo rose to his tall stature and paused to face the window. He knew Ridge was guilty, but he also knew he didn't have enough evidence to accuse him of those cold case crimes. The only crime he may have enough evidence on was the murders of Luke Townsend and Peter Finch unless they could find his fingerprints in the icebox or on the footlocker, and from what he had been told, the investigators may have found prints on the footlocker, so he went with the assumption they were Malcolm Ridge's prints.

The District Attorney abruptly turned on his heels and glanced over at the Sheriff. "Roger, did we identify those fingerprints yet, the ones we found on the footlocker?"

"Not yet, but it shouldn't be too long before we do. We sent them over to the lab in Hancock to be analyzed," Roger stated with authority.

"Before you go to all that trouble, I'll tell you right now, those fingerprints probably are mine. I dragged the footlocker down to the kitchen yesterday morning from the upstairs bedroom. What's the footlocker got to do with anything?" Malcolm frowned, tossing his hands up in gesture.

"So, you admit to having knowledge of the footlocker?"

"Yeah, I just told you. What of it?"

"Well, Mr. Ridge, it just so happens the children's bodies had been stored in the footlocker before being removed and stuffed in the icebox, parts of them anyway. We haven't been able to locate the rest of the bodies. Hopefully, with your help, we'll be able to retrieve all their body parts. It would be the decent thing to do, for the parents' sake," The District Attorney somberly informed him, hoping Malcolm would feel remorseful and give up the whereabouts of the missing body parts.

"I don't know anything about that. You've got the wrong person. Why are you accusing me of their murders, anyhow? That happened months ago, and I wasn't even anywhere near the place. Ask Deputy James. He saw me at the pool hall. I even help search for them," Malcolm nervously answered, trying to persuade them he was telling them the truth.

"That may be true, but we know you were there that morning at the farmhouse when the kids went missing. We have a witness who will testify you were there. When the house was searched two days ago, last Sunday morning, their bodies weren't in the icebox. They were still hidden someplace else. And you went back Sunday night. We suspected you went back to hide the bodies in a location that had already been searched. Hence the icebox."

"That's not true, Mr. Russo. I didn't do it. I'm telling you the truth."

"I don't believe you. You're lying. We both know you're lying. You're lying right through your eyeballs."

"No, I'm not."

"Well, if you didn't, whom do you suppose did?"

Malcolm gazed down at his feet. He was almost positive he knew who the person was, and it was the same person who had attacked him and his friends.

"It was you, Malcolm, so admit it. This will go a lot easier for you if you just admit you were the one who murdered those two innocent children," the District Attorney said and then leaned over the desk, staring into Malcolm's nervous eyes, waiting for Malcolm to admit it. He didn't have to wait long for the answer.

"Last night, while I was in one of the upstairs rooms, I heard voices outside my door. There was someone else in the house. Probably the same person who killed Luke and Peter, and most likely the same person who killed those kids," Malcolm said sternly, hoping he sounded confident.

"Bullshit, that's ridiculous. I suppose you're going to say next it was Zeke Osborne who came back from the dead," Roger answered in an angry tone.

Malcolm looked over his shoulder and noticed the Sheriff lurking over him like a giant ready to pounce. He was twice as big as Malcolm and very intimidating.

"I don't know who, but I believe it was the same person who attacked me Saturday night. He's probably still out there someplace, hidden."

"We searched the house from the basement to the attic, the barn and outside. You were the only one ever there," Roger added.

Malcolm said his peace. There was nothing else he could add, so he just sat there staring at his feet and listened as the District Attorney took his turn.

"From all the evidence we have uncovered, I'll tell you exactly what you did. After you murdered the children, you must have hidden their bodies someplace where we couldn't find them. Then sometime later, after the house was searched, you removed them from the hiding place and, for some unknown reason, stored them in the footlocker. That's how the blood got there. Then, Sunday night, you moved them from the footlocker and hideously arranged their little bodies inside the icebox. That's what you did!" Neil Russo defiantly told him only a few inches from his face. He could smell Malcolm's body odor and wondered when the last time he had bathed. A quick guess told him it had to have been at least two or three days ago.

"I'm telling you, there weren't any bodies in the footlocker when I moved it downstairs. Don't you think I would have known? All it contained were toys, which I removed and threw them under the bed."

"Well, if that's the case, tell me. When you emptied the footlocker out, didn't you see the blood inside?" The District Attorney knew the blood was dry and had to have been in there for some time.

Malcolm paused to recollect the image of the footlocker and what it looked like on the inside. "Uh, uh, I didn't recall seeing any blood. But it was early in the morning and kind of dark in the bedroom."

"Mr. Ridge, if you had looked inside like you said you did, you would have seen the blood. There was so much blood you couldn't have missed it."

Roger Lefebvre slowly moved over toward the DA. He wanted to look into the eyes of Malcolm Ridge to see if he was lying. Roger was confident he could tell when a person was lying or not.

"I'm being honest. I didn't see any blood. I'm not saying there wasn't any. It's just that I didn't see any." Malcolm looked up at the faces of the two men staring down at him. He was sure they didn't believe him. "I'm telling you the truth. I didn't have anything to do with those missing kids. Just because I was there doesn't mean I did it. I didn't do it, plain and simple. If that's all you got on me, my prints on the footlocker, I don't see how you can pin this on me.

The District Attorney shook his head and looked over at Roger. "You want to tell him, or do you want me to?"

"I'll tell him!" Roger harshly growled, then bent at the knees to retrieve the document on the floor next to Malcolm. "It's not just the children murders we're accusing you of. Besides being the prime suspect in the murders of Amanda Prescott and Kyle Bryant on May 12 of this year, you, Mr. Ridge, are also the prime suspect in the murders of Luke Townsend and Peter Finch on August 11 of this year. You are also being considered the prime suspect in the murder of Whitney Gorman, who was found hanging from a beam in the Osborne barn back in May of 1984, almost two years to the day after Vicki Pendexter's mutilated body was found in Miller's creek. A crime we are also considering charging you with," Roger paused a moment to let the accusations sink in before he continued.

"Mr. Ridge, you are the most despicable human being I have ever met. You're a lowlife maggot, the scum of the earth." After finishing his tyrant rage, Roger tossed the document on his desk, adding to the clutter.

"Look, Malcolm, you are in a lot of trouble and could spend the rest of your life in prison. If you confess to all these murders and tell me everything you know about them, I'll see what I can do to get you off on a lighter sentence. Maybe you'll get less than twenty years and only have to serve half the time. You'll still be a young man when you get out. Start a new life for yourself. In the meantime, we'll get you something delicious to eat and let you take a shower. So, what do you say, Malcolm? You ready to tell us all about it? I promise I'll be easy on you," Neal Russo told him as he gently rubbed his new friend's narrow shoulders in an attempt to ease the young man's tension.

"I want a lawyer."

PART TWO

CHAPTER THIRTY

Heaven's Institute
Saturday Morning
May 20, 2011

As the sun ate away at the morning fog, the sunlight slowly filtered through the partially open blinds in the spacious patient lounge on the east side of Heaven's Institution, where the daily group meeting was in progress, giving Carl Neumeyer a slight fit of anxiety. His fingers moved in random clicks across his lap as he sat impatiently, waiting his turn to speak. Doctor Jennifer Greaves took note and waited to see how long it would take Carl to interrupt the man who had the floor, a loud, obnoxious man who was discussing his discomfort of having to sleep next to a man who snores as loud as a pig grunts.

"How do you expect me to get a good night's sleep, which you say is vitally important in my recovery, when I have to be subjected to this man's disgusting…and I repeat disgusting, rude behavior. What do you say to that, Doctor Greaves?" The fat face man angrily demanded to know.

"Well, Steven, first of all, Mr. Mackie's sleeping disorder has no bearing on his behavior, and by you bringing this up, you are the one being rude. There are others in the same room as you, and none of them are complaining about Mr. Mackie's snoring. I would suggest if you are uncomfortable sleeping next to Mr. Mackie, you should bring the issue up with Nurse Morrison to see if you can swap beds with someone else, but you'll still be in the same room, and Mr. Mackie will still be snoring. Or, if you like, I can make out a prescription for sleeping pills."

"Pills, you want me to take more pills? I think I already take enough pills. Don't you agree, Doctor?"

"Doctor Greaves, can we move on? I've got something I need to discuss," Carl Neumeyer blurted out.

"Carl, I can see you are fidgeting to speak, but you'll have to wait your turn. Mr. Thomas has the floor at the moment... unless he has finished," Doctor Greaves said while writing a comment in her notebook.

"I told you my name is not Carl. It's Albert."

"Right, you are, Albert. You have the right to be called whatever name suits you. Steven, would you like to continue?"

Steven Thomas glared his dull gray eyes hard at Carl Neumeyer, he didn't like the man much, and neither did most of the other six men seated in the room, and the same could be said of Steven Thomas. Of the eight who attended the daily meetings, Thomas and Neumeyer were the two most disliked. The others were more passively content to listen to the doctor and hope for good news, but as the hour wore on, so would their patience, and they would become anxious to go back to their dull routines, which varied for each individual. Some played checkers or cards, others only stared out the windows at their future or past – it didn't matter which, they were both the same.

"Steven! Would you like to continue?"

Steven turned his attention away from Carl and looked directly into Doctor Greaves' soft blue eyes, eyes that had softened after years of searching the disturbed minds. "No. Not now after I was rudely interrupted."

"Well then, I guess you may have the floor, Mr. Neumeyer. What would you like to discuss with the group this morning?"

Carl looked around the room, taking in all the staring eyes. He then looked out the window, making sure the sun was still shining.

"Go on, old man. The Doctor said you had the floor,"

Steven Thomas grumbled.

"Okay, Steven, let Mr. Neumeyer speak."

"Thank you, Doctor Greaves." Carl turned to face the doctor. "I would like to discuss my theory on the fourth dimension."

"The fourth dimension?" Steven smirked, causing the whole group to break out in laughter.

"Please, gentlemen, let Carl...I mean Albert talk. You'll all have your turn, if not today, then tomorrow. Please continue, Albert."

"Thank you, Doctor Greaves. As I was saying, I'd like to talk about my theory on the fourth dimension. The fourth dimension is something you can't actually see because your brain can't comprehend it. But believe me, it's there. Now let me try to give you an example you might be able to understand."

"Doctor Greaves, do we have to sit here and listen to this bull?" Steven shouted.

"Yeah, do we have to listen to this bull?" Richard Craven seconded the request. Richard was a quiet person and never volunteered to speak, only to regurgitate what someone else had already uttered.

"Hush, let Carl continue." The doctor gestured with her finger over her lips.

"It's Albert, Doctor, but thank you." Carl nodded toward the doctor. "If you permit me, I'd like to borrow that notebook you're holding, Malcolm, to demonstrate an example of the fourth dimension."

Malcolm looked down at the blue Mead notebook he held on his lap. He brought the notebook to every Group Meeting but never actually wrote in it. Reluctantly he passed the notebook over to Carl. "Here, Albert, I want it back."

"Thanks for correctly remembering my name, Malcolm."

Malcolm nodded his acknowledgement, but he was more concerned with getting his blank notebook back than being praised.

"All right, see this notebook?" Carl held it up in the air for a moment, and then opened the notebook to a blank page and set it on his lap. He then seemed confused as he turned a few more blank pages. "What's this, Malcolm? Why do you hold on to this notebook like it's a precious gem when there's nothing in it but blank pages?"

"Give it back to me. I want my notebook back," Malcolm demanded.

"In do time Mal, in do time. Don't worry about a thing. I won't ruin your precious treasure. Fact is, this is just what I wanted, blank pages."

"What are you planning to do with my notebook?" Malcolm nervously asked in a lower tone, his hands knotted, hoping to get the notebook back in the same condition.

"Be patient. You'll see. I'm not going to do anything to it," Carl answered, then paused a moment to see if he still held his audience's attention, which he did as all eyes were on him.

"See, it's just a blank white page, nothing on it," he continued. "Now I'll need someone to stand over by the window and hold up an object, like a pencil."

Carl looked around the room for someone to raise a volunteered hand, but all seven held their hands clasped on their laps. He then noticed Malcolm's pencil sticking out from behind his ear. "Malcolm, could you stand over there by the window and pull open the blinds to let more light into the room? And then I'll want you to hold your pencil up to the light."

"Me? Why me?"

"Because you seem to be the only one who has a pencil, Malcolm, that's why," Carl answered the inquiry, but Malcolm relented and looked over at Doctor Greaves, who was writing something down in her notebook.

Carl followed Malcolm's gaze and noticed the doctor was using a pen to do the writing. "I want to use a pencil for the prop, not a pen, Malcolm. I'm not asking you to do something I wouldn't do myself, but I can't demonstrate my theory by myself. So, are you going to volunteer or what?"

"Okay, okay, I'll do it. Where do you want me to stand?"

"Just go over to the window and pull the blinds up, and then hold the pencil up in the light."

"Don't get so pushy about it."

"Thank you, Malcolm."

Malcolm walked over to the window, which was directly behind Carl, and carefully pulled the cord to raise the blind, letting an abundant amount of light into the room. Standing in the sunlight, his shadow covered Carl.

"Now Malcolm, I want you to stand to one side of the window and hold the pencil up in the light. Can you do that?"

Malcolm stood back as he was told and held the pencil up in the light. Carl moved the notebook slightly so the pencil's shadow was created on the blank page.

"See this shadow? It was instantly created by the pencil Malcolm is holding up."

"I can't see it from here?" Steven Thomas interrupted.

"Richard can see it. Right, Richard, you can see the pencil's shadow on the page?" Carl asked Richard Craven, who was sitting in the chair next to him.

Richard lifted his head toward the notebook and saw a long thin dark shadow on the blank page. "Yup, I see it. Right there, plain as the nose on my face."

"Some beak you've got there, Richard," Steven commented on Richard's Roman shaped nose. "But I still can't see the darn shadow."

"Well, if you can't take Richard's word for it, then you'll just have to imagine you can see it," Carl told him, then continued. "What happened in that nanosecond it took to create the shadow? Something happened in the space between the pencil and the notebook that your eyes could not see. And that, my friends, is the fourth dimension."

"What kind of crap is that? It's the light shining on the pencil that caused the shadow, you dummy," Steven cried out in anger.

"Look retard, it was just one example that I thought your brain might be able to understand, but I guess your little pea brain is not capable of comprehending anything that simple."

"You're the retard…Carl," Steven snorted with a wide grin.

Everyone laughed at the remark except Doctor Greaves, who continued to write in her notebook.

"Who are you calling a retard?" Carl retorted.

"You, you retard," Steven snapped back.

"All right, all right, now calm down. Now, you both know we don't call anyone names in here. And we never ever use that word. Do you understand me? Malcolm, you can go back and take your seat," Doctor Greaves said defiantly.

"But doctor, I haven't finished," Carl protested.

"That's enough for today, Mr. Neumeyer. Let's have someone else speak who hasn't spoken yet. We've only got a few more minutes left," Doctor Greaves said as she looked at her watch.

Hearing no one speak up, Doctor Greaves glanced around the room to see if someone had raised their hand, but from past experience, doubted very much anyone would; the ones who usually volunteered had already spoken. But just when she was about to adjourn the meeting for the day, she noticed the meek-looking man sitting at the end of the semi-circle, the balding man with thin-wired spectacles and who was barely visible, shyly inching his hand up off his lap.

"Yes, Mr. Harris, do you have something you'd like to contribute to the group today?"

Wendell Harris glanced around the room at the eyes that were upon him. He was afraid to speak, thinking everyone would laugh at him.

"Wendell, go ahead. We're all anxiously waiting to hear what you have to say," Doctor Greaves encouraged.

"Yeah, Wendell, we're sitting on the edge of our seats," Steven smirked.

Doctor Greaves gave Steven a harsh glare to remain silent.

Wendell looked down at the floor and spoke to his white slippers that were tapping against the green-tiled floor. "Well, I was just wondering what happens to your dreams after you die."

This brought out a roaring laugh from his fellow patients.

"Please, gentlemen, please. You all had your turn. Now let's let Mr. Harris finish what he has to say. Go on, Wendell."

"That's all I had to say, Doctor Greaves. I only wanted to know what happens to my dreams after I die."

"I'll tell you what happens," Steven blurted out, "you're dead. There are no more dreams. They died with you."

Malcolm held up his hand to speak. "No, no, that's not it at all."

"Okay, Mal, enlighten us," Steven sat back with his arms folded over his chest and a satisfied grin across his fat face.

"What happens," Malcolm said, addressing Wendell Harris, "you are now living your dreams. You are no longer seeing reality. You are only seeing what you want to see."

"You really think so, Malcolm?" Wendell said ecstatically.

"That's what I believe. You never really die. You just keep on dreaming."

"You're a retard!" Steven laughed.

"All right, Steven, you know what I said about using that word."

Steven nodded.

"Okay, gentlemen, I think we'll end this session for today. I believe Nurse Morrison is ready to distribute your morning medication," Doctor Jennifer Greaves said, looking over toward the nurse's station. "I'll see you all tomorrow morning at the same time."

* * *

After the meeting adjourned, Malcolm Ridge immediately walked over to the window and gazed out at the sunny day. He had been institutionalized in the mental hospital for nearly twenty-two years now, and he held no hope of being released in the near future, or anytime for that matter. The crimes he had been convicted of were too hideous for anyone to believe he could ever be rehabilitated. And, if he were someday declared sane and released back into society, the general public would be outraged. Malcolm knew he was a sane person and always had been. The only reason why he was placed in Heaven's Institution was because his lawyer had convinced him to plead guilty by reason of insanity, that way, he would be institutionalized in a mental hospital instead of having to spend the rest of his life locked up in a prison where he would have been repeatedly beaten and raped by other inmates, and, most likely, because of the nature of his crimes, killed – unmercifully stabbed with a dull, crudely made, shank.

Now, he realized, as he looked out over the driveway that wound its way between the leafy red maples and the spacious green lawns (which seemed to stretch forever on both sides of the long driveway) and ended abruptly at the wrought-iron gate, this is where he'll be until the day he dies. And the way he felt about his boring life in the institution, he hoped his death would come soon.

Malcolm knew his life at the institution was meaningless, and nobody would care if he died or lived except the relatives of those he was convicted of murdering. They would rejoice in his death and prayed he went to Hell. But they would be wrong, or more likely, wasting their precious prayers on where he would be spending his eternity because God already knew he hadn't committed those hideous crimes.

"Mal," Carl Neumeyer said, tapping Malcolm on his narrow shoulder. Carl had remained in his chair after the others had departed, thinking and writing in Malcolm's blank notebook ideas he had about the fourth dimension, a subject he had been interested in his entire life – fifty-five years worth. After he scribbled three pages of illegible worthless notes – ripping the pages out and then folding them in his pant pocket – he closed the notebook, and, before heading to the nurse's station for his morning medication, he noticed Malcolm at the window, quietly staring at another world.

Malcolm turned around and gazed into Carl's light-blue eyes, wondering what he wanted from him. Carl Neumeyer never sought anything from anybody that Malcolm was aware of, and if he were doing so now, it would be a first.

"Yes, Albert?"

"I like you, Mal. You're the only one who knows my name and the only one who understands my theories."

Malcolm didn't have the same mutual feeling about liking Carl as Carl had for him and would have burst out in laughter, but he was very interested in Carl's theories on the fourth dimension and wanted to learn more about the subject, so he held back his hilarity for a later time.

"Thanks, Albert, that's nice of you to say so."

"I wanted to give the notebook back to you and thank you for being my assistant," Carl said, handing the notebook to Malcolm. "I took the liberty of a few pages, which I had used to jot down some ideas I had thought of before I forgot them. The mind's rather full of information after all the years of scientific study, so it's quite easy to forget if I don't write them down at once," Carl added, tapping his hairless noggin.

Malcolm looked at him quizzically, wondering what he meant by taking the liberty of a few pages. After a moment, it finally dawned on him what he meant, and he quickly flipped the notebook open. He could see the strips of torn paper stuck in the ring binder. Malcolm felt a sudden rage building knowing his precious notebook was ruined.

"Carl, you idiot, you ruined my notebook," Malcolm shouted and then dropped the notebook to the floor.

"Sorry, Malcolm, it's only a friggin notebook. I'll get you a new one," Carl angrily responded. He wanted to say more, do more, like spit in his face, but he could see Malcolm's chest heave and the terror in his dark eyes, so he let it rest at that.

"I've had that notebook for a long time, Carl. Now look at it. It's ruined. Why did you tear those pages out?"

"Like I said, I didn't want to forget the new example I had thought of to use as a demonstration when we talk about the fourth dimension in tomorrow's meeting. It's very important that everyone understands. I didn't mean anything by it. Like I

said, I'm sorry if it inconvenienced you." Carl could see Malcolm
was starting to soften. His angry expression now seemed to show
a side of concern.

"More stuff about the fourth dimension?" Malcolm
excitedly asked as he looked down at his notebook, thinking it
finally had some worth to it. After all this time, holding an empty
notebook, wondering what its purpose was.

"Yeah, the notes are right here," Carl said, pulling the
notebook paper out of his pant pocket for proof.

Malcolm looked at the creased pages, happy to see the
penciled notes scribbled on them. He then bent down and retrieved
his notebook, and flipped it open. He stared for a moment at the
torn shreds of paper in the binder and pulled one out, dangling it
between his thumb and index finger like an expensive necklace.
"That's okay, Albert. As long as it had a useful purpose, I suppose.
Here, would you like to have the notebook? I can ask for a new
one." Malcolm held out the notebook with a friendly smile.

Carl tentatively took the notebook from Malcolm,
wondering why the sudden change in attitude. He started to
turn and walk off toward the nurse's station, where he could
see Nurse Morrison sitting in her high, uncomfortable looking,
chair rechecking the names of those who had already taken their
medication and searching for those who had not. Occasionally
she would look up and glance over at Carl and Malcolm. She said
nothing, but she looked impatient.

"Carl, I thought what you said about the fourth dimension
was very interesting stuff."

Carl glared at Malcolm and pointed a fat finger at his
chest. "It's Albert, not Carl. I thought you, of all people, would
remember that."

"Sorry, Albert. I was wondering if you had a moment to
discuss it with me in more detail?"

"Sure, Mal buddy, what do you want to know?" Carl had
as quickly forgotten about the little incident as Malcolm seemed
to have forgotten.

"I was interested in understanding the fourth dimension

some more to see if it had anything to do with what happened to me."

"Yeah, I forgot...what was that again? Wasn't it about some old man's ghost in a haunted farmhouse?" Carl laughed.

"Something like that, but it wasn't actually a ghost. You see, the old man was there. It was just too dark to see him very clearly."

"Yeah, what does the fourth dimension have to do with it, then?"

"I'm not sure, but what if the old man wasn't physically there. I mean, like, maybe he couldn't be seen because he was caught in the fourth dimension." Malcolm seemed confused as he tried to explain.

"But you just said you saw the old man."

"I did, but it was for only a second when I lit the match. He was there, and then I dropped the match and started swinging the axe I had been holding. I could have sworn I hit him with it, but the Sheriff said I hit my friends with the axe. I didn't even see them in there. I only saw the old man. The psychologist, who examined me, tried to explain to me what I really saw, but I know what I saw."

Carl rubbed his chin, like he was pulling on a beard that was no longer there, and then looked up at the ceiling as though he were looking for an answer. After a long pause, he motioned Malcolm to take a seat.

"Let's see if I can explain it in a different way by using the example I had just written down on these pieces of paper." Carl again pulled out the folded notes from his pocket; the creased pages were beginning to wrinkle. He then pulled out his reading glasses from his shirt pocket and hooked them behind his large ears. "It's almost the same as the example I had used previously today but a little easier to understand."

Carl took a moment to peruse his scribbling while Malcolm anxiously looked on. When Carl was finished, he removed his eyewear and placed them back in his shirt pocket, then proceeded to explain, hoping it wasn't going to be too complicated for

Malcolm to understand.

"Okay, here's basically what it is. Let's say the object that was creating the shadow on the page is a fly and not a pencil and is roughly seven feet away from the page. Now it would take the fly at least a second or two to fly over to the page. But the shadow only took a nanosecond to materialize, much faster than the fly could fly there. If you could see what was between the fly and the page, just before the shadow image is created, that is the fourth dimension. But your eyes can't see it. It's faster than a blink of an eye. Much faster, it happens in a microsecond, even in a nanosecond. Now, in your case, it may just be possible that you saw a glimpse of the fourth dimension."

"Do you think that's what happened to me, that the man I saw was actually in the fourth dimension?" Malcolm hopefully asked.

"I'm not sure. I wasn't there. What did the doctor say was the cause, again?"

"The psychologist that examined me said that layers of consciousness caused the confusion, and in the dark, what I thought I was seeing was not what I actually saw."

Carl thought it over for a minute, then explained what he thought could have happened that night in the living room of the farmhouse. "Yes, there are many layers of consciousness, and in a state of fear, your mind starts imagining things. When you lit the match that night, your brain was trying to comprehend all the layers of consciousness at the same time, along with things you were probably imagining. Somewhere, mind you, when the match was lit, that nanosecond right after it was lit, you could have seen something hidden in the fourth dimension."

"You think so? You think I could have seen something in the fourth dimension?"

"There is only one way to find out that I can think of."

"What's that?"

"You'll need a camera that can take fast images, a camera that can automatically take a series of pictures in a microsecond - some expensive digital camera. You set the camera up in the room where the incident happened and set it on autopilot. Know what I mean?"

"I think so."

"Or, now that I think about it, you could use one of those camcorders. I believe that would be more efficient to pick up an image than a still camera."

Malcolm scratched his head and gave Carl an unsure look.

"Now, Mal, the first thing you're going to have to do is find some way of escaping out of this place. However, that might not be easy to do."

"Thanks, Albert. You're a pretty intelligent guy. What did you say you did for a job when you were on the outside?"

Carl frowned at the question and then, after a brief moment wondering if he should make up a lie, answered honestly. "I was a janitor at a high school."

"A janitor?"

"Yeah, a janitor. But my father was a great scientist," he lied.

"That's good to know."

* * *

Later that night, Malcolm Ridge quietly sat in a chair by the same window in the patient lounge he had been looking out earlier, thinking how idiotic it was to believe a patient at Heaven's Institute could have the knowledge of a genius. Especially someone who thought he was Albert Einstein.

"Fourth dimension, my eye," Malcolm mumbled aloud. He then turned to see if anyone was staring at him. He had felt someone was watching, but when he turned, he saw no one. All his fellow patients were in the recreation room watching a television show or either playing checkers or cards at the round card tables set up in the same room away from the television. Malcolm was alone in the patient lounge, just him and his imagination.

"They never found old man Osborne because he was hiding someplace in the farmhouse, someplace where nobody would ever find him," Malcolm said, pointing out the window into the darkness. "But I know he was hiding in the attic. No one searched the attic. I'm sure that's where he hid. He's probably still roaming the farmhouse waiting for his next victim. It's the only logical answer. Everyone here wants me to believe I did it," he said, the last sentence a little too loud and again glanced over his shoulder to see if anyone was standing in the room.

I need to find out what really happened. He thought to himself. And then, after staring at his glaring reflection in the dark window, he added in a whisper, "I need to know the real answer and prove to everyone that I'm not insane. But I'll never find out in the boundaries of this establishment they call Heaven's Institution, definitely not confined to the space between these four walls, which I've been staring at for the last twenty-two years," Malcolm said, waving his arms around.

Malcolm stood and leaned his face into the window, looking deep into the dark night. He placed the palms of his hands against the glass, pressing the unbreakable glass hard. He could almost see the farmhouse through the darkness as though he were standing in the Osborne driveway in daylight. The old, dilapidated house and barn with the broken clapboards and windows, the dying diseased elms that stretched their bony fingers across the metal roof, scratching and clawing. The sounds that the branches made when they scratched at the roof almost caused him to scream in pain. He wanted to jump out of his mind, out of the nightmare he was living in. He couldn't stand it any longer, and he yelled at the window that he had to get out of this horrible place. He yelled in his mind so loud he could feel the hairs on his head rise. And then, thinking he had yelled out loud, he placed his hand over his mouth, knowing someone was quietly standing behind him.

It's Nurse Morrison. I know it's her – she always sneaks up behind me. I hope she didn't hear me talking out loud. I've got to stop doing that. She's no doubt come to administer my nightly meds. She looks calm, but inside her, I can see the meanness, hear it crawl around in her stomach like an angry tapeworm. As soon as she opens her mouth, I can see its ugly head with those protruding fangs. Sometimes I pretend to take the pills and spit them out when she leaves. I got caught a couple of times. I don't think I'll take the meds this time, either. I don't want the drugs to interfere with what's the truth and what they want me to believe happened.

"Hi Malcolm, it's time to take your medicine."

I can't wait till I get out of this horrible place.

"Thank you, Nurse Morrison. What time is the laundry truck coming tomorrow? I'm out of clean duds."

"Oh, don't worry about that, but I do believe the laundryman arrives around ten o'clock every Monday and Thursday morning, so you'll have to wear those same clothes one more day."

"Thanks for the information, Nurse Morrison. Did I ever tell you how helpful you are?"

CHAPTER THIRTY-ONE

Early Monday Morning
May 22, 2011

Monday morning, it rained. The hard, cold spring rain came down in buckets, making it miserable for anyone to be outside without wearing the proper weather gear. Carl Neumeyer disappointedly knew there would be no proper clothing given to him which would allow him to venture outside in the recreation area after the daily meeting, and even if there were raincoats, and such, to keep the cold and rain off him, they would never permit him, or any other patient, outside on such a miserable day. But worse than not being allowed to go outside, Carl knew he would not be able to demonstrate his new example for them to easier understand the complicated fundamentals of the fourth dimension.

His new example, as did the one he had demonstrated on Saturday and the brief explanation he had told Malcolm Ridge about, required plenty of sunlight. Artificial light would not be efficient enough, or even appropriate, for such an elaborate demonstration as natural light would to prove to Steven Thomas and all the other skeptics that there was indeed a fourth dimension. He would now have to wait at least one more day to prove his theory and have the redemption he sought.

As Carl Neumeyer stood in the window watching it rain, he could see a delivery truck moving slowly along the driveway toward the gated entrance. He noticed the truck's taillights were on and the occasional flash of red when the driver tapped the brakes as he came closer to the guardhouse. Carl knew the routine, from watching other vehicles leave the premises, that a guard would exit the small wooden shack and peer inside a car's passenger side window and, on occasion, have the driver open the trunk for a quick peek inside, and then, if all were fine, he'd give a friendly smile and a wave of his hand and the driver would be off, to where Carl had no idea but knew it would be a better place than where he was spending his miserable life. If the vehicle happened to be a truck, like the one he was watching now, the guard would always insist the driver open the back doors so he could do a thorough inspection.

Behind him, Carl could hear the scrapping of metal chairs against the green-tiled floor as the patients, in matching white garb, settled into their respective chairs, always sitting in the same positions, and the patients mumbling complaints about trifling issues. He had not bothered to turn away from the window and join the others just yet. He wanted to first watch the guard search the rear of the truck that was now pulling up in front of the guardhouse. The red taillights blinked several times, indicating the truck was coming to a stop, and then turned solid red for a moment before the driver put the transmission in the park position and took his foot off the brake pedal.

Before the guard came out to inspect the truck, Carl heard Doctor Jennifer Greaves call to him that the meeting was about to begin and to take his seat with the others. He didn't want to miss what was sure to happen next at the guardhouse and pretended not to hear her. From his view, he could see the narrow space between the truck and the small wooden shack and impatiently waited for the guard to appear, but the young guard stationed at the entrance to Heaven's Institution was ill-prepared for the inclement weather and remained in the guardhouse, and all Carl could see was the guard's arm and a wave of his hand. And then, to his disappointment, the red brake lights blinked on and just as quickly off as the truck slowly drove through the wrought-iron gate, disappearing into the hard rain.

"Carl, will you please take your seat over here so we can start the meeting," Doctor Greaves insisted.

Carl turned toward the group, noticing the glaring faces staring at him. He then deliberately walked the long way around the row of chairs to reach his, which was on the opposite end of the eight chairs that were evenly spaced in a semicircle. Without hesitating, he then deliberately sat in a chair that was usually occupied by Malcolm Ridge.

"You're in the wrong chair, Carl," Steven Thomas blurted out. Steven had his arms folded across his chest and had the look of a mean dog across his face. His droopy ears seemed larger than normal with his newly shaved head. It was a look he had hoped would intimidate others. He had practiced his hostile stare in the bathroom mirror for a good fifteen minutes that morning. When he was satisfied, he had the look down to perfection. He pumped his fist and gave the mirror one last hard glare.

Carl Neumeyer, however, was not in the least intimidated and did not move or even return a look; he only sat there in Malcolm's regular chair and flashed a smile at Doctor Greaves. It was a smile that said he knew something no one else knew, and he was rejoicing at the fact.

"Does anyone know where Malcolm is this morning?" Doctor Greaves asked no one in particular. And when no one answered, she directed her question to Carl, who seemed, from the expression on his face, to have some knowledge of Malcolm's whereabouts.

"Why would you think I know where he is, Doctor? I'm not his keeper," Carl sarcastically answered.

"Well, Mr. Neumeyer, by the look on your face, I can tell you're gloating about something. And seeing Mr. Ridge is not with us, I'm guessing you know of his whereabouts."

Carl could see all the heads turned to face him, which only made him gloat even more. "I'm gloating? I hadn't realized."

"Yes, you are. Now, please tell me where Malcolm is. This is very important, we all have a responsibility for the safety of others, and we need to find out where Mr. Ridge is immediately. So, Carl, could you please tell me where he is?"

"My name is not Carl. It's Albert," Carl said, with a defiant poise, crossing his arms over his chest.

Doctor Greaves waited a moment for Carl to give her an answer to her inquiry, and when she noticed his stern mouth slightly curve into a smile, she got agitated and began to threaten him with punishment if he didn't answer immediately. A threat of isolation usually worked, but Carl was not giving in to it and stubbornly sat firm, waiting for the Doctor to address him correctly.

"Okay, Mr. Neumeyer, have it your way. Johnson, can you go take a look around to see where Mr. Ridge is, he seems to be on his own schedule this morning?" Doctor Greaves loudly asked the attendant in charge in a tone that was more a demand than a question.

Marvin Johnson, a stout man in his mid-fifties who had been working as an attendant in the same ward for nearly twenty years, was standing nearby talking with Nurse Morrison about the rain and setting up some indoor activities for the patients. On good days the patients spent two hours in the enclosed outdoor recreation area where there were basketball hoops, swings and picnic tables for board games to enjoy, but on rainy days the staff had to come up with some other recreational ideas to keep the patients actively entertained.

When he heard the Doctor's request, Marvin quickly stepped into action and went looking for Malcolm Ridge. It was his responsibility to make sure the patients were safe from any harm and remained in the confined areas. The patients in this ward were less restricted than the ones in other wards, so they were allowed in more unsupervised areas, but even the unsupervised areas, like the bathrooms and the cafeteria, were enclosed in a locked environment.

The first place Marvin searched was the bedroom Malcolm shared with several other patients. It was one of the most logical places he could be, Marvin figured, as sometimes a patient remained in their bed, which was fine as long as they knew of the patient's whereabouts. Marvin wasn't sure which bed was Malcolm's, but it didn't matter much because the bedroom was empty. All the beds had been made up, sheets tucked under the mattresses and pillows, wrapped in white cases, fluffed up ready for the sleepy heads to plop down on them.

The next places he searched were the bathrooms. There were three on the second floor. Two of the bathrooms were for the male and female staff members. The third bathroom was a much larger bathroom for the patients, which had a row of toilet stalls and several basins, with a shower area in the rear. Marvin hadn't bothered to search the women's bathroom and only quickly stuck his head inside the men's. He did, however, do a thorough search of the patient's bathroom, checking each toilet stall and peeking in the shower area. Satisfied no one was there, he then headed down the corridor and checked the cafeteria to see if Malcolm may have wandered in there for a cup of coffee, something Marvin had seen him drink alone numerous times before. But the cafeteria was almost completely empty. The few customers that were in there were either having a late breakfast – considering the late morning hour – or sipping mugs of coffee, chatting with another or alone reading a magazine or paperback novel.

Outside the cafeteria door, Marvin scratched his head, wondering where Malcolm Ridge could have disappeared. There weren't too many places he had access to, as most of the building was off-limits to patients, and the doors to those areas were locked. The only way he could have gone through those locked doors would have been to steal a key or follow an authorized person out the door.

Worried he hadn't found Malcolm, Marvin raced back to the patient lounge, where he found Doctor Greaves scribbling notes in her notebook while the patients impatiently squirmed in their chairs, waiting and watching for news of Malcolm's whereabouts. Marvin cleared his throat to get the Doctor's attention, and when she looked up from her note taking, he disappointedly informed the doctor of his findings or lack thereof. Doctor Greaves immediately called security to inform them one of their patients was missing. She then hastily adjourned the daily meeting and had Marvin bring Carl Neumeyer into her office for a chat. She was determined to get to the bottom of this mystery and knew Carl held the key to unlocking it.

For several minutes all Doctor Greaves did was stare at Carl Neumeyer and scribble in her notebook, waiting. It was a psychological tactic to coerce the patient into revealing what they were holding back. Carl sat with his head down, staring at the floor or his white slippers. Doctor Greaves did not know which, but at this point, she could care less. She only wrote in her notebook things pertaining to Carl's stubbornness.

After a while, she put her ballpoint pen down and closed her notebook with a loud slap. Carl took notice and glanced up. He could see the hard glare in her blue eyes and knew she was mad, and he was in trouble. But he couldn't understand why he was in trouble. He had done nothing wrong. It was Malcolm Ridge who should be the one sitting there, not him.

"This has gone on long enough. I need to know where Malcolm Ridge is, and I need to know now. If he's hiding somewhere, I want you to tell me. This isn't a game, Carl. He could be in serious trouble, and so could you if you continue to refuse to tell me where he's at."

Carl hesitated, wanting to think it over before telling her what he knew, which wasn't a whole lot, only speculation. He had heard Malcolm mention an idea he had on how to escape from the institution, but at the time thought the plan was foolish and improbable. But when Malcolm failed to show up early for the daily meeting, which he always did, and then when he saw the delivery truck being waved through without being searched, he knew Malcolm Ridge's escape plan had worked to perfection, and he was somewhere on the outside, heading toward the farmhouse he often talked about.

But still, he wasn't entirely sure. For all he knew, Malcolm could still be somewhere in the building. He never actually saw him leave, only speculated. If he told the Doctor what he speculated had happened to Malcolm, that Malcolm had high-tailed it out of there, flown the coop like a carrier pigeon – only he'd never return like the pigeons would – would the Doctor accuse him of deliberately holding back the information and punish him, suspend him from the outdoor recreation area for a week, or maybe even longer? No, he couldn't let that happen.

"Carl, I'm waiting! Your stubbornness has gone on long enough, and I'm demanding that you tell me this very second."

Then he had an idea, a new theory on what had happened to Malcolm. He was now almost positively sure Malcolm was in the delivery truck when he had seen the truck exit through the main gate, but he hadn't seen Malcolm, and no one had, because he was in the back of the truck. It was like a photograph of a house. Looking at the picture, you could plainly see the exterior of the house but not the interior. So, if there were someone on the inside of the house, you couldn't see the person when looking at the picture, but they would actually be in the picture. And according to Carl's new theory, that is exactly what happened to Malcolm.

"Mr. Neumeyer, I'm still waiting! And you are not leaving this office until you tell me what you know. And the longer you wait, the harsher the consequences will be."

Carl looked squarely into the Doctor's glaring eyes, his smile stretched wide across his flushed face.

"Well?"

"Doctor Greaves, I know what happened to Malcolm Ridge. He's in the fourth dimension."

CHAPTER THIRTY-TWO

Tuesday Morning
May 23, 2011

Sheriff Wayne Leon James dropped the one-page report he had been reading on his cluttered desk and apprehensively reached for his coffee mug, twirling the remaining lukewarm contents, and then repulsively swilled it down. He liked his coffee hot, steaming hot. He thought it wasteful if he didn't finish it, and, like every other morning, with his busy schedule of trying to keep up with the increasing demands for policing in a booming population and a dwindling staff because of budget cuts, he finished his only mug of coffee for the day in disgust.

Wayne had read the report twice. The first time he hastily perused the contents reading only the important details and skipping the nonessential data such as names and dates of the incident. With all the work he had piled in front of him, he only wanted to concentrate on the sections in the report that stated its priority level and if the matter pertained to his department. A lot of reports that came into his office, mostly via email, were for informational purposes only, as other law enforcement agencies, like the police department or State Police, were handling them. This report, however, required his immediate attention, so he made sure he was very thorough the second time he read it, paying special attention to the names and dates, data he hadn't read the first time.

At first, after reading the report for a second time, Wayne still hadn't comprehended the magnitude of the situation, it had been over twenty years since he had last heard of the name on the report, and then, as if a light switch had been turned on, everything he feared came flooding back in one giant wave of emotion. His skin began to crawl with goose bumps, and the fine blond hairs on his arms reacted with electricity, rising straight up like grass reacts to sunlight, only there was no sunlight shining on him today. Yesterday's torrential rains had continued into the night and only began to slowly diminish the next morning, and it was still drizzling when Wayne glanced out his office window, out toward Groveville and the old Osborne farmhouse that should have been burned down years ago. But, because of the poor bureaucracy of a small town where no one seemed to have control over who did what, the farmhouse was left in limbo, or a better way of putting it, left to the ghost who was said to be roaming the farmhouse and wielding a bloody axe.

Wayne laughed thinking about Malcolm Ridge's ridiculous accusations that it was the old man, Zeke Osborne, who had hacked up his two friends, one being Wayne's own flesh and blood, and Malcolm would have been a victim himself if he hadn't escaped the crazy man with the giant axe. He was like a ghost, materializing out of thin air, he told Roger, who was the sheriff at the time. Malcolm was also adamant that if the Sheriff didn't go after Zeke Osborne, there would be more victims, and the blood would be on his hands. 'You'll see,' Malcolm said before he was driven off to the institution, 'there'll be more gruesome murders in that horrible place, and then you'll know it wasn't me who had killed them. It was that monster, Zeke Osborne, the whole time.'

That was the last time Wayne had heard anything of Malcolm Ridge, and since he had been sent away, the Osborne farmhouse had been relatively quiet, so Wayne, and everyone else who had been involved with the horrific case, were confident they had convicted the right person. Everyone that was still alive, that is.

Deputy Phil Hardy had died a few years later, having

finally retired for good, but unfortunately for him, Phil could not find anything worthwhile to occupy his time and spent his idle time drinking beers and watching game shows on television. His wife, Maureen, having given up trying to persuade him off the couch and into a more active retirement, watched his dwindling body wither away. After returning from a three-day trip to visit her ailing sister, Maureen found Phil's desiccated body on the couch with a beer bottle in one hand and the remote in his other.

Helen Pinkham had also passed away. Helen died doing what she said she was born to do, and that was to control law and order. After thirty years of sitting behind the desk in the sheriff's office, dispatching the law enforcers to help and control the safety of the citizens of Madison County, Helen died with her hand holding the radio's microphone. Her last words had gurgled out of her mouth.

And Deputy Ben Alden was gone, although not dead and buried in a cemetery like Phil and Helen. Ben had decided to change careers and joined the Denton fire department, saying the worse he'd see being a fireman would be burned victims, not mutilated corpses like the bodies of Luke Townsend and Peter Finch. He never got over the sight of them as Wayne had when he discovered Whitney Gorman's gruesome body hanging in the barn.

Wayne hadn't seen his old boss, Sheriff Roger Lefebvre, in close to five years, even though he still lived close by with his wife. For years Roger had stopped in the office to see how his successor was making out, the man he had groomed to take over the responsibilities of being a sheriff. One day Roger had just stopped coming into the office, and with the work piling up, Wayne never got around to checking up on his old boss.

Now he had a new troop of people working for him, and none of them were familiar with the Ridge case. He was the only one in the department with firsthand knowledge of the case.

Later, there was a soft rap on Wayne's closed office door, causing him to stir from his thoughts of the past. Having a good idea who it was, even though he had never previously met the person, Wayne rose from his chair and answered the knock with a friendly greeting inviting the expected woman in instead of yelling his customary 'enter.' The woman had called not more than an hour earlier requesting a meeting to discuss the urgent report, and now she was standing before him.

After inviting her to sit, Wayne took his own chair and looked across his cluttered desk at the attractive woman who was sitting opposite him. To him, she was somewhere close to forty or maybe a year or two older, but at his age of fifty-three and close to retirement, he wasn't sure. In time, he was informed she was forty-five. The woman was dressed conservatively but not exactly in the attire he had expected for a psychiatrist. The doctor was wearing an indigo sports jacket over a clover-colored blouse with a tight, light gray knee-length skirt. He had expected to see the doctor wearing the typical matching pantsuit most female doctors wore. But times change. It was no longer the nineties. They had been riding the new century for six years now; even his uniform had somewhat changed, the same color but different fit and comfort.

"What makes you think he'll come back here? It was twenty-two years ago, and he doesn't have family here. He was a transient, so to speak, staying in the basement of a friend's house, a friend he killed, along with his only other friend. He has no reason to come back to this town, Doctor."

Doctor Jennifer Greaves sat still with her legs crossed at the knees, revealing a good amount of leg, and her hands folded over a black, diary-size notebook she had resting in her lap. Before contradicting Wayne's assessment, Doctor Greaves took a moment to adjust her thoughts. After placing her notebook down on the desk in front of her and brushing a few strains of her light-tinted hair behind an ear, Doctor Greaves smiled at the man sitting across the desk from her.

"Oh, on the contrary, Sheriff James, I believe he does have a reason to come back, a very good reason. You see, after all, this is Malcolm Ridge's hometown. Well, Denton and Groveville."

"Doctor, the kid was adopted. They lived in a different

town, several miles from here, over in Hancock," Wayne said, lifting his eyes from her well-formed tanned legs, not thinking about her comment that Denton and Groveville were Malcolm's hometown and not just Denton. "His adopted parents have since passed away, and even if they hadn't, they wouldn't have had anything to do with him anyhow. He was a troubled kid, in and out of reform school. And they never even went to his trial. He has nobody here or over in Hancock."

"All that may be true, Sheriff James, Malcolm Ridge was adopted and sent away to a reform school, once, that I understand. But that doesn't matter. It's not relative to this case. There's more to his story, much more."

"I'm well aware of what he did, Doctor. I've seen his destruction and witnessed it firsthand," Wayne stated, shaking his head in memory. The horror Malcolm Ridge had caused would never be erased from his memory for as long as he lived.

"Yes, of course you are. But let me try to fill in the blanks for a more complete picture of his real life. After you hear what I have to say, I'm sure you'll understand the situation we are in with him being on the outside."

"Proceed," Wayne gestured with his hand and leaned back in his chair.

"Thank you, Sheriff. Let me start by telling you about his childhood. In the spring of 1970, John and Phyllis Ridge adopted Malcolm at the age of four, which is considered to be too old for adoption and harder to nurture as their own. Most children are adopted at a much younger age, but Malcolm was the exception to the rule."

Doctor Greaves paused before continuing to finish what she had to say until she was sure the Sheriff's attention was concentrating on her words and not on her legs, as she had noticed his eyes bouncing repeatedly as she talked. She had thought to wear her gray slacks but at the last minute changed her mind as the weather promised warm sunshine in the afternoon.

"The Ridge's did their best to raise Malcolm, but having no child-raising experience, Malcolm quickly became a handful.

By age ten," the Doctor said, looking down at her notebook, "Malcolm had been expelled from grammar school four times. Twice for stealing classmates' lunch money by bullying them, and once, get this, once for breaking into school on a weekend with an axe, smashing the window in the door.

The last time he had been expelled from school was for urinating on a girl during recess. He told the teacher the girl asked to see his pee-pee, so he pulled it out and urinated on her. He was ten years old at the time, and the girl was only seven.

"Five years later, when he was fifteen," she continued, "he was caught breaking into a neighbor's house and stealing the woman's underwear. He was subsequently sent away to a reform school for two years. When he was released to his adoptive parents, the situation at home had gotten worse, so he moved out and quit school. He was only seventeen at the time with no job and no money."

Doctor Greaves paused to push back a lock of her light-brown hair that had fallen across her forehead. She could see the Sheriff anxiously staring, waiting for her to continue, which she assumed meant he was following along.

"I'm not sure what he did during those years," she said, continuing, "only that he stayed with friends and occasionally worked at odd jobs. That's what he told me anyhow during our weekly one-on-one sessions at Heaven's Institution. But I'm sure you are well aware of what happened back in the summer of 1989, Sheriff."

Not thinking it being rude, Wayne turned around in his comfortable, black-leathered, swivel chair and stared out the window, looking toward Groveville, remembering the horrible night when Malcolm Ridge brutally murdered Luke Townsend and Peter Finch, and the day he discovered the decomposed bodies of Amanda Prescott and Kyle Bryant in the icebox. He could still see Amanda's gruesome head stuffed on the end of a wooden pole and Kyle's bloodied, mutilated body.

"How could I ever forget," Wayne answered as he continued to stare out the window at the unforgettable past. "I think that summer will forever be imprinted in my brain."

"I suppose you are right about that. I can not imagine something so horrific could ever be totally wiped clean," Doctor Greaves symphonized. Then after a short pause to give the Sheriff a moment to regain his presence of mind, she continued with her notes on Malcolm Ridge. "And I also see, according to my notes, that he was found guilty of murdering a real estate agent five years prior. The woman was found hanging in a barn, the same farmhouse where they found four other bodies – the Osborne farmhouse. Is that correct?"

When Wayne did not answer immediately, Jennifer Greaves took that as a yes and continued to state her reasons to believe Malcolm Ridge was heading their way, or he was already there.

"And not to mention the little girl, Vicki Pendexter, who was also found brutally murdered in a creek, which coincidently flowed in close proximity to the Osborne farmhouse. Is that correct, Sheriff?"

Wayne swiveled his chair back around to face her. "That one I'd have to disagree with you on, Doctor. A year after Ridge was committed to your institution, we uncovered evidence on that cold murder case and eventually caught the person who had committed the crime. It was the same kid who had found the girl in the creek. His name was Josh Miller. He was fourteen at the time and was coming from the same store Vicki and her sister had gone to buy sodas. When he saw Vicki's sister jump into a vehicle and drive off, Josh Miller went up to Vicki and struck up a conversation. They had known each other by sight but hadn't actually talked. Josh had told us he convinced her to take a walk down to Miller's Creek, where he had left his fishing pole and was going to let her fish. His intentions were true, and he let her fish, but he also had other intentions. You see, he liked Vicki. He liked her a lot and said he had been fantasizing about her in his dreams. He said things just got out of hand. All he wanted to do was kiss her, nothing sexual. Josh insisted he had no intentions of raping her, although that doesn't explain why she was found partially nude. He said he stopped grabbing her the minute she started screaming and told her to calm down and that he meant no harm. When Vicki stood to leave, she told him she was going to tell her mother on him. That's when he stabbed her with his fishing knife a few times. He said he just went crazy because he knew if she told, he'd be in a whole lot of trouble. When he realized she was dead, that he had killed her, he dumped her body in the creek and ran home."

"That's interesting to know. I'm glad you finally caught the right person. Anyway, besides that case, you still believe he's responsible for the other crimes I mentioned, don't you?"

"Absolutely, there's no doubt about it. Ridge confessed to those crimes. He never did confess to the Pendexter murder, but at the time, we were almost positive he was the person who had killed the Pendexter girl since there was no evidence to pin it on someone else. But that's still not a good reason for him to return to this town. He'd be stupid to come back here; it's the first place he'd expect us to search for him. Besides, he'd stick out like a sore thumb, everybody here knows everybody, and he'd be spotted in a minute."

"That may be true for someone with a normal thinking process, but let me remind you, Sheriff, Malcolm is not a normal person. There is a reason why he was institutionalized and not sent to a prison. And there is one more reason why I believe he's heading this way. Before he was adopted by the Ridge's and had his name changed, his last name was Osborne, Malcolm Osborne."

Wayne's forehead creased, trying to put two and two together, wondering if what the doctor was trying to imply was that Malcolm Ridge was somehow related to Zeke Osborne.

"What are you saying? Malcolm is kin to the Osborne family?"

"What I'm saying, Sheriff, and this is a true fact, is that Malcolm is Zeke Osborne's son. He was the little boy who was found alive in the farmhouse's basement back in January of 1967. And he believes his father is responsible for all those murders, not him. And that Zeke Osborne is still alive and living up at the farmhouse in Groveville. So, you see, Sheriff James, I believe Malcolm Ridge has come home to prove his innocence."

"I wonder why we never found out about him being Osborne's kid? It wasn't even brought up at trial."

"Probably sealed records. We, of course, had permission."

"Well, if that's true, about him being Osborne's kid and he knows, then that puts a whole new light on the situation. I'll get someone out there ASAP," Wayne said, then reached for his phone to get one of his on-duty deputies out to search the farmhouse.

"Wait, Sheriff, I want to go out there myself, with you or one of your deputies. I think I can get him to come peacefully without anyone getting harmed, especially Malcolm. I've been close to him for the last fifteen years…he trusts me."

Reluctantly Wayne agreed and placed the receiver back in the cradle. "Okay, you might be right. You can go with me," he said, deciding to handle the situation himself since he was the only one in his department familiar with the Malcolm Ridge case.

"By the way, Sheriff, I'm curious to know what happened to the boy who murdered the Pendexter girl? Committing a horrendous crime at such an early age, I would have thought he would have been sent up to Heaven's Institution unless it was before my time, and he had since been released."

"Funny you ask, I was just notified a couple of weeks ago that Josh Miller had been released from the State Penitentiary. I've been meaning to go up to the family farm and pay him a visit, but I've been a little busy this year with all the cutbacks."

* * *

On the drive over to the Osborne farmhouse, the rain had suddenly stopped falling, and Doctor Jennifer Greaves noticed a patch of blue in the sky. Seeing the sky beginning to open reminded her of the weather report and how their prediction was finally going to be correct for once in calling for sunny skies. The clearing weather also reminded her of her decision to wear the skirt instead of the light gray slacks, she almost chose and consciously pulled at her skirt, which did not go unnoticed.

After a quick glimpse, which gave the Sheriff an embarrassing rise, Wayne focused on the road ahead and the reason the gorgeous Doctor was with him in the vehicle. He then slowed his cruiser down when he neared their destination and took the right turn onto the Osborne graveled road with a feeling of apprehension. It had been several years since he had last driven up the road, and he wasn't anxious to do it again any time soon. He had hoped, like his predecessor, the next time would be to see the farmhouse burning to the ground.

"At one time, there was a locked chain across the road to keep the kids out, but it didn't do any good. They still found a way of getting in. Every once in a while, usually in the spring when the kids get restless from the long winter months of being indoors, we get a call from the Millers about kids partying out here, and I have to send a deputy out to check on it. There hasn't been any this year that I'm aware of, but that's not saying there hasn't been any."

"Who owns the property now?" Doctor Greaves asked.

"The town of Groveville, they've owned it since old man Zeke Osborne murdered his whole family, except Malcolm, as I'm just finding out thanks to you."

"Why don't they put it on the market and try to sell it? The property must be worth a lot of money with the prices of land these days."

"Beats the hell out of me. I know they tried selling it years back. That's when the real-estate woman was murdered. She had come up here to take some photos of the place, and our dear friend, Malcolm Ridge, hung her up in the barn for her effort. I was the unfortunate person to have found her. Found her swinging right up there." Wayne nodded toward the barn as they drove past the cemetery, reaching the uncultivated alfalfa fields.

"It must have been very traumatic for you."

"Yes, it was. And in some ways still is, I guess. To me, this place is like Hell. Seems every time I come up here, there's another mutilated body to investigate."

With a strong sense of growing anticipation, Jennifer Greaves quietly stared at the old, dilapidated farmhouse. She had heard, on the drive over, what to expect, and seeing it for the first time, she wasn't disappointed. In fact, the place looked in worse shape than what had been described to her. Wayne mentioned the broken windows and damaged doors, the weathered clapboard and the barn that seemed to sway in a light breeze as though it could collapse at any moment. But he failed to mention the ugly leafless trees surrounding the house like giant bony skeletons and the overgrowth of weeds and bushes that reached halfway up the first-floor windows.

"Not sure if you should go inside. From what I've heard, the place is a total disaster. There are broken beer bottles and trash lying on the floors from all the parties the kids had in there," Wayne stated as he pulled his cruiser into the driveway.

"Sheriff, don't worry about me. I have an idea of what to expect. Believe it or not, I used to be a teenager once and have attended my share of wild parties. I'll be careful where I step."

"Okay, be my guest. I just wanted to warn you first," Wayne said as he opened his door and slid his tall frame out. Before going inside the farmhouse, he stretched his arms to relax his nerves and then led the Doctor up the porch steps and into the house.

Inside was just as Wayne had surmised; the downstairs – kitchen and living room – was littered with beer bottles and cans and other trash. The couch was legless and sat low on the living room floor. The two chairs that had once shared the room with the couch were no longer there, and Wayne suspected they probably were burned in the fireplace as well as the seven wooden kitchen chairs that once surrounded the Kitchen table, which were also missing.

"Looks like they burned most of the furniture. I wish they had burnt the whole damn house down. I would have pinned a medal on them if they had," Wayne said, looking around the living room.

"What's over there?" Doctor Greaves asked, pointing toward the front hallway.

"That's the front parlor. It leads upstairs to where the bedrooms are."

"After you," the Doctor said, gesturing with her hand.

Wayne led the way up the stairs, picturing in his mind what the bedrooms looked like the last time he had seen them and wondered, after seeing the trashed downstairs, what condition they'd be in now.

In the first bedroom they entered, he noticed the queen-sized bed was completely busted up. The bedsprings and wooden frame were in a heap against the far wall, and the mattress, which was intentionally placed in the middle of the floor, was covered with bloodstains. The stains could have come from a past murder, he thought at first, but with the blood concentrated mostly in the center of the mattress, Wayne suspected the cause more likely came from teenagers having sex at the wrong time of the month.

The other bedrooms were in the same disarray as the first bedroom had been, so they didn't spend too much time looking around, just a quick look to see if Malcolm was hiding up there. And to their disappointment, he wasn't.

Back downstairs in the kitchen, Wayne asked the Doctor if she was satisfied that Malcolm Ridge was not there and if she wanted to head back to Denton. She indicated they hadn't searched the barn and asked if the door in the kitchen led out to it.

Wayne hesitated in answering, not really wanting to go in there. "That's not a good idea. By the looks of the barn, I'm thinking it could collapse at any moment. One side of the barn, the backside, had already collapsed. I wouldn't want you to get hurt on the account of Ridge; he's already responsible for five deaths. I'd hate to see another one added to his infamous list. Let's go outside and get some fresh air. The smell in here is getting to me."

Outside, Doctor Greaves stood facing the open barn door, wanting to have a look inside. She had an anxious feeling Malcolm was hiding there, watching and waiting for them to leave.

Wayne stood by his vehicle with his hand on the doorframe, watching her hesitation. "Ready, Doctor?"

Doctor Greaves slowly turned to face him and, after a brief pause, said, "Let's have a quick peek inside there. I have this uneasy feeling he's in there."

"Wait. Like I said, I don't think that's a good idea. Just look at the rickety thing. It's ready to collapse at any moment."

"Just the same. I'd feel better if we took a look inside. I promise, if he's not in there, you can take me back to town," the Doctor reluctantly told him. She was confident Malcolm was at the farmhouse or on his way, so she wasn't going to give up her quest so readily.

"Okay, if you insist, but let me go in first," Wayne reluctantly said and made his way past her.

Wayne held his hand against the barn doorframe and poked his head inside for a look. The only difference from the last time he had seen the inside of the barn, besides the large holes in the roof and collapsed back portion, was the trash littered across the pine floor. It seemed the parties were not exclusive to the main house itself and had extended to the barn as well.

"You really want to go in there?" Wayne asked, looking down at the determined woman.

"Yes, why not? Move aside," the Doctor lightly pushed an elbow against the Sheriff's side, walking past him.

She stood in the middle of the barn and glanced around in the semidarkness for any sign of Malcolm Ridge. Behind her, Doctor Greaves could hear an empty beer can rattle across the floor, scattering several small barn swallows out through the open holes in the roof, causing her to look up from where the birds had come from.

"Sorry about that," Wayne said about unintentionally kicking the beer can. "I guess they had been partying in here as well."

"What's up there?" She pointed.

"The hayloft," Wayne sarcastically answered.

"I know that. I was wondering what that object is, over there, near that beam in the far corner."

Wayne squinted his eyes for a better look and noticed what she was pointing at, but even though he could see it, he had no idea what he was looking at. "I'm not sure. It wasn't there the last time I was in here. It looks like a statue figure or something."

They both waited to see if the figure would start to move, but it remained motionless.

"I think it would be wise to check it out, don't you? How do we get up there?"

Wayne nodded over toward the back wall. "There's a built-in ladder over there. I'll go check it out. No need for you to go up there."

"I'm going...you don't have to worry about me. I'll be fine."

"I meant what you're wearing," Wayne said, looking down at her skirt, thinking about her long slender legs.

This day, and the light-gray skirt, he figured he'd remember for a long time. It wasn't often he was in accompany of a beautiful woman. His wife had been beautiful when they first married and still was if he had taken notice, but they became complacent, each in their respected careers, and stopped trying to appeal to one another. She, the former Kristen Vale, who just happened to have been Malcolm Ridge's only girlfriend, soon got bored with their marriage without romance and had met another at work. Wayne's ex-wife was the last woman he had been romantically involved with, which, in his long absence without a female companion, felt like years ago, even though she had only taken flight in the spring of last year.

"What I'm wearing is no concern of yours, Sheriff. Even though I'm flattered that you noticed. But if you can't contain yourself, I'll let you go up first."

Wayne's face was flustered, but even though Doctor Greaves couldn't see the color in his face change in the diminished light, she knew he was embarrassed by his awkwardness.

"Sorry, I didn't mean anything by it," he said, trying to

cover up his inappropriate thoughts. "Follow me right over here."

Doctor Greaves followed the Sheriff toward the back of the barn, the part that was still standing, and watched him climb the wooden ladder and disappear through the small opening above him. Wayne then poked his head back through the opening and courteously extended his hand to help guide the Doctor through. She grabbed his hand and used her other hand to push herself through the opening, placing her knee on the loft floor and pushed herself to a standing position. After brushing the dust and hay off her knee, she quickly looked toward the beam where she had seen the statue figure.

"Wow, what is that? I hope it isn't what I think it is?" She wondered out loud and watched as Wayne slowly made his way over to the unknown figure. When she had first noticed it from below, she instantly thought it may have been a person standing there, hoping it was Malcolm Ridge, but the longer she looked at it, she felt whoever, or whatever, the figure was, it wasn't going to move on its own and never would.

Wayne was only hoping it wasn't another corpse hanging from a beam and cautiously moved closer to it. The closer he got to it, he could see the figure was hanging with its back toward him, and he nervously reached his hand out to touch its shoulder and felt the soft touch of straw. Relieved it wasn't another body, he started to laugh.

"It's only a scarecrow some asshole hung up here. A silly prank, I suppose, to cause some juveniles to freak out." He then pulled the scarecrow down from where it had been strung up with old, tattered rope on the beam and carefully tossed it in Doctor Greaves' direction for her to verify.

"It sure looked real to me," she said, looking at the straw dummy.

"Yeah, I guess it had me thinking too. My heart was in my throat when I reached out to touch the damn thing. Well, I guess there's nobody here," Wayne said, looking around the loft to make sure. "I think we should get out of this place and head back to town, as you promised."

Outside, Wayne opened the passenger door for the Doctor, placing a soft hand on her back, helping her in. He then walked around and climbed in the driver's side.

"Some place, huh?" Wayne asked before starting the vehicle. He was hoping it would be his final glimpse of the place.

"Sure is. I don't like the thought of coming back out here tomorrow much, but I suppose we'll have to keep coming until Malcolm is caught."

"If he's not here now, I don't believe he's coming. When did you say he escaped?" Wayne asked, looking at her soft blue eyes, staring a bit longer than was appropriate.

"Yesterday morning, around ten. He somehow got into the back of a laundry truck and hid inside a dirty clothes bin."

"How did he manage that?"

"Not sure. I was hoping to find out when we caught him so we can change the way we handle security at the institution. Maybe you could give us some input seeing it's in your field of expertise." Doctor Greaves smiled.

"Well, it's not exactly my field of expertise. I'm better at catching criminals than trying to keep them from escaping. But I'm sure we'll find him before long. He can't stay hidden forever."

"I hope you're right, Sheriff. He doesn't belong on the outside. Not that I think he'll do harm. I'm more concerned for his safety."

Wayne looked at her skeptically, knowing what Malcolm was capable of, but let the comment slide. "Okay, let's see and try figuring this out. If he escaped yesterday morning, that means he's been gone for over twenty-four hours. That gave him plenty of time to get here, even if he walked. It's what, twenty-five miles from here?"

"About that. But it rained hard last night, and he was only wearing his issued grab and a light blue jacket he stole from one of the attendants. So, he could have found a dry place to spend the night and keep warm."

Wayne nodded his head, knowing the Doctor was probably right and that Malcolm Ridge could have hunkered down somewhere and may still be planning on coming. He was disappointed at the thought of coming back tomorrow with all the work piling up, but he tried to look at the bright side and that Jennifer Greaves would be accompanying him at least one more day. And she may even be planning on staying in town for the night, which means she may want some company to share dinner with. Women were always attracted to men in uniforms, and his being the sheriff should be more of an attraction.

"You plan on staying somewhere in town tonight, Doctor?" He still hadn't gotten around to asking the Doctor if she minded him calling her by her given name. If she accepted a dinner invitation, it would then be in his right, he supposed, to call her Jennifer.

"No, my girlfriend is expecting me home tonight. She has something planned to celebrate our first anniversary together."

Wayne swallowed his pride like a gentleman and started backing out of the driveway. "She's a lucky woman, Doctor Greaves."

CHAPTER THIRTY-THREE

Osborne Farm
Early Tuesday Evening
May 23, 2011

Josh Miller slowly walked out of the barn with his head angled down at his feet and headed toward the house, and even though his eyes were watching his slow stride amble across the dirt driveway, his thoughts were on the strange man he had dropped off an hour ago at the foot of the graveled road that led to the ominous Osborne farmhouse. The man had said nothing about why he wanted to be dropped off at such an unusual location, only that he wanted to be let out there, thanking him for the ride. Josh pulled his green Ford truck over to the side of the road, anchoring the wheels in the soft sandy shoulder as required by law. He then waited for the man to exit his vehicle before heading down the road to his own destination, which was less than a quarter mile away. Down the road, a piece on the same side as the Osborne farm. From the rearview mirror, Josh watched the empty-handed man wave at his truck and then saw him abruptly turn to face the Osborne Road. The man was still standing in the same tall pose when Josh rounded the corner and headed for his family's farm.

Josh had picked the stranger up on the road just outside of Hancock, a town ten miles away, and offered the man a ride. His clothes smelled damp of wet hay, an odor he was familiar with, and he wondered if he was a farmer. When he asked his destination, the man told him he wanted to go to Groveville, which wasn't an unusual request since the road he had picked the man up on was once the main road to Groveville and its larger neighbor, Denton. A new road had been constructed through the woods and over confiscated farmland to create a faster road for a faster life, getting to your destination quicker. Josh and most of the locals enjoyed a slower pace choosing the old County Road.

Josh had asked the man if he had family there and wondered if maybe he knew the family since Groveville had a small population, most being around for generations. But the man said no, there was no family and no one he knew either. And when Josh pressed on about his quest for going to a town that offered no employment, or even a place a stranger could stay, he fell silent and only stared out the window at the dwindling daylight. No more was said between the two. Each had his own thoughts; Josh wondered what a stranger with no family or friends, and an introverted disposition, would want with his hometown if his intentions were good or evil. But he couldn't come up with any rational answers to explain, only not to dwell on it and ruin his good mood. Josh was coming home from Hancock, where he had landed a job at the hospital as a custodian. It was his first job since being released from prison, and he wanted to make the best of what life he had left and to forget about the past. If the man he had picked up was coincidently here about him, about revenge for what he had done that had put him in prison, he did not know, but the thought was always with him if someone, someday unexpectedly, paid him a visit one cold dark night and requested his life – a life for a life. He would not be angry with the person and would not fight to stop him. He only hoped God had forgiven him as his parents had.

But the stranger said nothing about who he was or his purpose for wanting to be dropped at the foot of the Osborne Road, and Josh offered nothing about himself, and the stranger had asked for nothing, only a ride to Groveville. A ride he was happy to oblige even when the man seemed unpleasant. Josh had only just gotten his license himself and knew how difficult it was to bum a ride from a stranger and the pleasure of having been offered one.

The sky behind the Miller's farmhouse was lit aglow, one of the most brilliant sunsets Josh had the pleasure of ever witnessing, and he rushed inside the house to share the fiery sunset with his aging parents. Josh's parents slowly descended the steps and obediently walked out into the driveway to where they could see the glowing phenomenon. They had seen plenty of brilliant sunsets in their lifetime and were not overly excited about this one being any different from the others, but their son had been locked away from seeing even one of the simplest occurrences Mother Nature offered, and they wanted to share in his delight.

"I have never seen a sunset that magnificent. Look how bright it is. It looks almost like the whole forest is on fire," Josh said in awe.

His parents said nothing at first, only shared in their son's enjoyment and watched the fiery flames licking about the tree line. And then they saw the smoke rising above the trees, which at first, they had only presumed to be clouds, but the rising black plumes changed their thinking.

On the other side of the woods from the Millers, Malcolm Ridge stood silently out on the porch staring out across the alfalfa fields toward the town of Groveville. Behind him, the sky was aglow, and the night was slow to arrive. It had been a long two days, and he was tired and hungry. He knew he would have plenty of sleep soon and cared nothing about his hunger; food was the furthest thing from his mind, he had another, more important, agenda to deal with, and he knew it was only a matter of time before his feat would be accomplished.

He had completed the first step in his plan with relative ease, escaping from Heaven's Institution conveniently hidden in the back of a delivery truck. And even though he hadn't known the truck's destination and cared less, for he knew his. When the truck pulled over for its next scheduled stop, Malcolm slid out the back unnoticed and casually strolled down the street in the rain like he was a local resident, even though he had no idea which town he was in.

Having no money to purchase rain gear, Malcolm looked for a place to hide out until the rain subsided. He found a barn outside of town and an old woolen blanket inside to cover himself with. His clothes, the dirtied white grab he had worn for the previous three days and Marvin Johnson's dark-blue cotton jacket he had stolen from a locker inside the Staff's male bathroom, held no protection from the intense rain. Although he shivered, the blanket felt good around his cold, wet body, and he soon fell asleep. Several hours later, late in the afternoon, he awoke and took another look outside. The rain was pouring down hard, so Malcolm decided to spend the night in the dry barn.

The morning did not bring much relief from the weather as it was still raining, although the rain had subsided somewhat. Malcolm decided he'd take a chance before they came looking for him and began hitching a ride. The first person to offer him a ride was an older gentleman driving a small compact vehicle. It was red, like Luke Townsend's red Dodge Charger. When he first spied the vehicle slowing to a stop, he thought of Luke and his enthusiastic smiling face, the smile that led them to exciting adventures, but unfortunately, those adventures traveled the illegal road of life. But then again, those troubles always seemed to end with happy results, lucky results, except for the last adventure they went on.

But the vehicle that stopped to give Malcolm a ride was not the same fiery red color Luke had his car painted. The color of this vehicle was a flat red, dulled by the hot summer sun. Malcolm squeezed into the front seat, realizing it lacked the legroom of the Charger, causing him to bunch his knees up. All though it was confining, he didn't complain.

The man asked where he was going, and Malcolm told him he was heading for the town of Groveville. The man had no idea where Groveville was but said he could give him a ride as far as the next town, which was called Lincoln. Malcolm asked the man which direction was Lincoln, and when told it was south, Malcolm knew he was heading in the right direction.

"Do you know the town of Hancock?" Malcolm asked, thinking Hancock was a much larger town than Groveville, and the man may have heard of it.

The man looked at him and nodded. "Yes. Is that where you are going, Son?"

"Yes. It's near Groveville."

"Well, I'll tell ya, you're still going to have a good twenty-five miles to go when I drop you off in Lincoln. If I were going that far, I'd give you a ride. But unfortunately, I'm not."

Malcolm nodded his understanding and stared straight ahead, keeping his eyes on the rain falling and the wipers swishing across the windshield. Soon, before he had a chance to enjoy the ride and relax his mind on what he was doing, the man pulled over to the side of the road and let him out. Malcolm thanked the kind gentleman and stuck his thumb out for another ride. He slowly walked along the shoulder, kicking littered cans and discarded bottles down the ditch that ran alongside the road where the signs informed him he was on the right road to Hancock.

By early afternoon the rain had stopped, and the sun shined bright and warm, but no one offered him a ride. He felt uncomfortable walking as his clothes were soaked to his tender skin, and his wet cotton pants rubbed uncomfortably at the thighs, causing them to chafe, but the discomfort did not deter him from continuing his quest. His disheveled appearance didn't help in his effort to obtain a ride either. He assumed people might mistake him for a bum, and he was resigned to the fact that he may have to walk the whole way to Hancock. It wasn't until late afternoon when he was finally offered a ride. A salesman named Ray Dodd, driving to Hancock, felt sorry for Malcolm, reminding him of the days when he hitched rides that were far and few. After a quiet ride, Ray Dodd dropped Malcolm off near the old County Road and wished him luck.

His next ride came sooner than he had expected. A green Ford truck came to a stop beside him, and the driver opened the door with a smile and then asked where he was headed. It was always the same greeting when offered a ride. They exchanged introductions, first names only, and drove the first few miles in silence. It was a short ride lasting only fifteen minutes, and the few questions that were asked were answered in one word and always no. There was nothing to say about his purpose for going to Groveville. It was none of the man's business. Malcolm thanked the man with a friendly wave when he was dropped off and then watched the truck disappear around a bend.

Malcolm Ridge was finally home. After twenty-two years and two days of travel, Malcolm was standing at the foot of his family's long half-mile graveled road. He deliberately walked the road at a slow pace wanting to enjoy every step of the way. He paused briefly at the family's small cemetery, visiting each of the gravestones and kneeling longer at his mother's. After kissing the headstone, he then walked through the uncultivated alfalfa fields, pulling a few stalks with his hands and smelling the fresh wheat aroma.

The farmhouse looked different to him now, still old and dilapidated as when he had last seen the place, but now, it looked smaller and less intimidating. Maybe because he knew he was no longer afraid. The farmhouse and the ghost of his father could no longer hurt him. He was in charge now, and it was his destination to do what he had to do.

When Malcolm arrived, he took a tour of the inside and immediately felt disgusted with its condition. When he had last seen the farmhouse, it was in decent order, nothing broken and nothing out of place. Even the beds were made up for the night. The beds now weren't even suitable to sleep on.

Out in the barn, he found what he was looking for. Underneath his father's workbench were the two five-gallon gas containers he had seen previously, stored there since before 1967, most likely by his father for the purpose of refilling the tractor and lawn mower and what else he needed to fire up.

Malcolm spread one gas can around the barn soaking the floor and the large pile of hay he had piled high in the middle of the barn. And with the remaining gas can, he emptied the floor throughout the downstairs, knowing the upstairs would be engulfed in flames in no time, considering the dryness of the wooden farmhouse.

Standing inside the barn, Malcolm said his goodbyes to a house he loathed and then tossed a match onto the pile of hay and watched it quickly burst into flames. One match was all he needed to accomplish his feat. Through the smoke, he thought he saw a ghostly image of an old man. The eyes were not hollow like he had expected ghost eyes to be, but still, there was something odd about them. When the flames grew higher and hotter, and the smoke turned to a grayish blue, the ghostly image disappeared behind the flames.

As he stood on the porch, he thought of all the horrible deaths Zeke Osborne had committed. He pictured all those horrible acts in his mind, the graphic details of how they each died, the axe coming down hard, ending their young lives. He especially thought of the deaths of Amanda and Kyle, the two young children who never got to live their dreams. Amanda, too frightened to scream, watched as the horrifying old man decapitated her friend Kyle. She then watched as he slowly walked over to her and watched as he swung the axe high over his head and the slow motion of the axe head coming down upon her. And her dreams appeared, the dreams she had always dreamed. Malcolm pictured all the victims' deaths that way, too frightened to scream, and then, there were only dreams. They dreamed their dreams and kept on dreaming until there were no more dreams, just a flash of white light and then darkness. Beyond the darkness was unimaginable, but he knew he'd find out.

Malcolm stared across the open field toward the long, winding, graveled road that led past his family's cemetery. He could not see the cemetery, or even the road, for night had fallen, but he imagined he could. He imagined the gravestones he had visited only an hour earlier, seeing his amongst them. The words etched upon his gravestone told whoever wished to read it that Malcolm was only guilty of having been born to a father who was a monster.

Off in the distance, he could hear sirens, eerie haunting sounds to some but to him they were sounds of accomplishments. Lights flickered in the woods as the vehicles moved along the graveled road with great speed. When the vehicles reached the cemetery at the edge of the field, Malcolm turned and walked into the burning farmhouse, shutting the door behind him.

EPILOGUE

Retirement Home
Saturday Afternoon
September 30, 2011

The yellow taxicab moved quickly along the long narrow dirt driveway kicking up bits of gravel and dust, and then skidded to a stop in front of the Sunset Valley Rest Home, which was located just outside the Hancock town line in a quiet country setting. The quaint rest home was modestly painted white, including the trim work, and attractively enhanced with a wide veranda that stretched the length of the home on the front side, facing east for the early morning sun. A nice place to spend your final days, relatives must have surmised when they dropped their elder family member off unless you arrived by other means like the aged gentleman in the yellow taxicab.

The young female cab driver exited the vehicle and then energetically hopped around to the other side and helped her fare out of the backseat, and at the same time, retrieved the man's lone suitcase that had been placed in the backseat next to him. She then politely led the old man up the many steps to where he was met by Mrs. Vivian Truman, the owner of the rest home.

Mrs. Truman gently patted her grayish-blonde wig, making sure it sat firmly in place and smiled at the man with an offering hand. After the brief handshake, which felt weak even in her small hand, she turned and thanked the cab driver for safely delivering her fare. The cab driver returned a friendly smile and then trotted back down the steps and hopped inside her taxicab. As the cab drove away in what seemed like the same rapid speed as it had arrived, Mrs. Truman's gently grabbed the man's frail arm and slowly escorted him toward the front entryway.

Mrs. Truman's contemptuous eighteen-year-old grandson, who was standing on the porch next to her, picked up the man's suitcase and brought it inside the rest home, holding the door open for his grandmother and the new arrival. The grandson impatiently watched as it seemed to take the old man forever to cross the threshold.

The rest home was beautifully decorated with antique furnishings to make the residents feel at home. Beyond the lobby, where the residents picked up their mail and other necessities they needed from the seemingly unenthusiastic woman seated on a high stool behind the counter, was a spacious parlor, specifically situated on the south side of the home for its sunny exposure. In the parlor were several comfortable floral cushion chairs and a matching couch with side tables on each end. Inadequate lighting for reading was never a concern in the parlor room for the aging residents. Besides the bright overhead fluorescent lights, reading lamps were positioned next to each of the chairs and on both sides of the couch.

At this time of day, nearing the end of lunch, most of the residents were still finishing their meals and, if not still seated at the dining tables spooning the last of their soft, low-calorie desserts into their mouths, were either resting up in their rooms or walking off the food in the spacious outdoor lawns, so the parlor room was nearly vacant, only one person occupied the room.

"Cory, bring the nice gentleman's belongings up to his room and then put them away for him like a good young man."

Cory Truman looked at the slouched man as he shuffled his feet along the carpeted entryway, slowly making his way inside, thinking the old-timer already had one foot in the grave and wouldn't be around for long. Cory had expected the new arrival to be somewhat younger looking, or at least have a little more oomph in his step, having been told the man was in his mid-seventies. Most of the residents at the rest home were of similar age, in their seventies and eighties, and from his observations of the other residents, this man seemed to be much older.

"No problem, Grams. How long do you think he'll be with us? Maybe I should just leave the suitcase out," he sarcastically answered his grandmother and then giggled at his own remark as he walked up the stairs thinking he'll never get that old. He was planning to remain young looking his entire life like all teenagers dreamed but sadly found out differently when their day of being old and frail came, that is if they lived that long.

Mrs. Truman shook the remark off as being more ignorant and not so much as trying to be rude and slowly walked her newest resident into the parlor and set him down in a chair nearest to the window so he could bathe in plenty of sunlight, keeping his frail body warm. She then graciously settled into the chair opposite to his and crossed her legs at the knees.

"Now, Mr. Lefebvre, you just settle yourself comfortably in that chair and let the sunshine warm you until my grandson, Cory, finishes setting up your room nice for you. I have your information form right here, and I would like to go over a few things with you if you don't mind."

The man nodded, but he wasn't sure what he was agreeing to. For the past several years, his mind had been slipping away from him, and now he only recalled fragments of memorable events that occurred years ago, recalling things that had happened in the recent hours, or even minutes, escaped him.

"Let's see, it says your first name is Roger. Would it be all right if I call you Roger…Mr. Lefebvre?"

Again, he nodded. This time he knew what he was agreeing to. He liked his given name; it had a sense of comfort to it when called.

"You can call me, Vivian if you like. Okay, Roger?"

Roger attempted a friendly smile, but the weak attempt didn't make much difference to his impassive expression.

"It says here you are a retired sheriff. How exciting your career must have been apprehending the bad guys and keeping the peace! Well, you don't have to worry about any bad guys here. This place is about as peaceful as you can get," she said with a proud smile.

"Do you remember how long ago you retired?"

Roger paused, trying to recall the years he worked as a sheriff. It seemed a lifetime ago, and it was, as far as he was concerned. The life he led as a sheriff had all sorts of daily emotions, from proud and happy serving the fine people of Madison County to being resentful on the days he failed them. They were the best years and also the worst years of his event-filled life. His life now had no emotions, and his expressionless face showed it.

"It's okay if you don't remember. I know the years can fly by. It seems like only yesterday I opened the Sunset Valley Rest Home, and I have a hard time myself trying to remember when exactly that was." She looked beyond Roger's blank stare and gazed out the window remembering the day she greeted her first residents, ones that have long since passed away.

"Now, where was I? Oh, yes, it also reads here you were born in May of 1937, which makes you seventy-four years old. My, my, you are still a young man, plenty of years ahead of you."

Roger looked at the kind lady telling him about himself. He knew some of what she was telling him, like he had been a sheriff once – it was hard to forget those days, especially the ones that haunted his dreams at night. His age and her telling him he was still a young man were confusing. He surely didn't feel young.

"Now, before we bring you up to your room, I want to give you an introduction as to who your neighbors are going to be. Okay, Roger?"

Roger nodded his agreement, but he knew it would be a waste of time because he'd never remember their names.

"There is a very nice lady who has the room just at the head of the stairs on the second floor and conveniently next to the elevator. And, wouldn't you know it, she just happens to be sitting right over there in the chair against the wall," she said, smiling at the woman who was sitting quietly pursuing a children's book, Sleeping Beauty, one of her favorites.

"Hi, Janelle. How are you feeling today?" Mrs. Truman smiled then nodded when the woman lifted her head and attempted to return an acknowledging gesture, a weak rise of her thin lips.

Roger politely looked at the woman. It was difficult to tell her exact age because of the heavy makeup she had applied to make herself look and feel younger. Her lips were as red as overripe cherries matching the rouge on her cheeks. Her grayed-blue eyes and brows had a thick layer of black liner, and her face dripped sad like a clown even when she attempted the smile when she was acknowledged.

"Your room is one door down from hers, on the same side," she said, continuing, now focusing her attention on Roger. "The lady's name is Janelle Prescott. She has been with us for a very long time, for twenty-two years now. She is our longest surviving resident here, you know."

And then, in a low whisper, she added. "Something terrible had happened to her, and she had a nervous breakdown because of it. Janelle is much better now, but she still tends to stay in her room a lot, not wanting to socialize. I'm surprised to see her down here. All she seems to want to do is listen to her music and read books, mostly children's books. I have no idea why, but she likes them anyway."

Roger frowned, trying to recall the name. He had heard the name Janelle Prescott before, he was almost positive, but he couldn't bring the person to mind just then. Looking at her didn't help either. Maybe it will come to him later, he thought.

"And then there is an older gentleman residing in the room directly across the hall from yours who just moved in here four months ago. He may look a little odd at first – he has this lazy eye thing going on," she said, pointing to her own eye. "It's glazed over, if you know what I mean, with a whitish haze. A cataract, I believe they call it. His other eye is quite normal, though, and he's the kindest man I have ever met, always smiling like he knows something wonderful no one else knows. Almost as though he has knowledge of the afterlife, where people go after they die."

Roger looked at Mrs. Truman, wondering why she was rubbing her eye. At first, he thought she was wiping a tear away, but her eyes were dry.

"Oh, here he is now. He's right over there, just coming in from his daily walk. Zeke, could you please come over here and meet your new neighbor."

A stocky bald man with one eye partially closed, and a wide grin across his cheeky face slowly walked into the parlor room and over to where Mrs. Vivian Truman was sitting in a chair, waving her delicate hand.

"Here he is, Roger," Mrs. Truman said proudly, "this is the nice man I was telling you about. Roger, I'd like you to meet Zeke Osborne."

ABOUT THE AUTHOR

Geordie Gilman is the author of three novels, including *Ice Lake* and *Mister Zero,* and *Wooden Ponies*. He has a degree in computer technology. Besides working in the computer field, he has had a variety of other interesting jobs and met many strange characters, which have greatly inspired his writing. His passion is writing horror and science fiction stories. He lives in southern Maine.

www.ingramcontent.com/pod-product-compliance
Lightning Source LLC
Chambersburg PA
CBHW022028260626
47156CB00017B/458